# PHASES

## ELIZABETH MOON

PHASES: The Revised & Expanded Lunar Activity

Copyright © 1997 by Elizabeth Moon

"Bargains" copyright © 1986, first published in *Sword & Sorceress III*. "ABCs in Zero G" copyright © 1986, "A Delicate Adjustment," copyright © 1987, "Too Wet to Plow" copyright © 1988, "Gut Feelings" copyright © 1988, "The Generic Rejuvenation of Milo Ardry" copyright © 1988, all first published in *Analog* magazine. "New World Symphony" copyright © 1988, first published in *The Magazine of Fantasy & Science Fiction*. "Just Another Day at the Weather Service" copyright © 1988, first published in *Analog* magazine. "Politics" copyright © 1990, first published in *The Far Star Wars: The War Years*. "In Suspect Terrain" copyright © 1991, first published in *The War Years II: The Siege of Arista*. "The Happy Frog" copyright © 1989, first published in *The Magazine of Fantasy & Science Fiction*. "Horse of Her Dreams" copyright © 1995, first published in *Sisters in Fantasy*. "Knight of Other Days" copyright © 1995, first published in *Tales of the Knights Templar*. "Aura" copyright © 1995, first published in *The Magazine of Fantasy & Science Fiction*. "Those Who Walk in Darkness" copyright © 1990, first appeared in *Lunar Activity*.

A Baen Books Original

Baen Publishing Enterprises
P.O. Box 1403
Riverdale, NY 10471

ISBN: 0-671-87855-7

Cover art by Vincent di Fate

First printing, December 1997

Distributed by Simon & Schuster
1230 Avenue of the Americas
New York, NY 10020

Typeset by Windhaven Press, Auburn, NH
Printed in the United States of America

# CONSTANT IN ALL HER PHASES

# BAEN BOOKS by ELIZABETH MOON

*Sheepfarmer's Daughter*
*Divided Allegiance*
*Oath of Gold*
*The Deed of Paksenarrion*
*Surrender None*
*Liar's Oath*
*The Legacy of Gird*

*Hunting Party*
*Sporting Chance*
*Winning Colors*
*Once a Hero*

*Remnant Population*

*Sassinak*
with Anne McCaffrey
*Generation Warriors*
with Anne McCaffrey

# CONTENTS

Introduction .......................................................................... 1

Bargains ................................................................................ 3

ABCs in Zero G .................................................................... 9

A Delicate Adjustment ...................................................... 45

Too Wet to Plow ................................................................ 99

Gut Feelings ...................................................................... 125

The Generic Rejuvenation of Milo Ardry ................. 171

New World Symphony ..................................................... 183

Just Another Day at the Weather Service ................. 217

Politics ................................................................................ 221

In Suspect Terrain ............................................................ 249

The Happy Frog ................................................................ 279

Horse of Her Dreams ..................................................... 293

Knight of Other Days ..................................................... 311

Aura .................................................................................... 335

Those Who Walk in Darkness ...................................... 347

# INTRODUCTION

This collection includes stories originally published from 1986 to 1995. About half are held over from *Lunar Activities*, and the rest are from various other sources. The earliest, "Bargains," was my first fiction sale. I wrote it, and a group of related stories, after finishing the *Deed of Paksenarrion*. "Those Who Walk in Darkness," from the same period, closes the collection. The latest, "Knight of Other Days," was written for *Tales of the Knights Templar*.

Why does a novelist write short fiction? Sometimes it simply pops out unbidden. Milo Ardry and his feathers . . . the Weather Service and its balloons . . . the venerable granddaddy of all bullfrogs and his pond . . . all popped into my head in one piece. Sometimes a long project (such as the story of Paks) leaves story-debris loose in the mind like shavings around a carpenter's workbench . . . and some of these demand to be written. Some stories are assembled from found objects of imagination, picked up over the years and stored (very messily) in the mind's cellar and attic . . . discovered while rummaging around for novel-fragments. Occasionally someone says, "Can you write a story about . . . ?" and names something that starts resonating with other story-debris.

At least that's why I write short fiction . . . because it's there, and I can, and someone nudges me.

*In the spring of 1985, approaching my fortieth birthday, I set out to show my mother (and others) that age and motherhood had not diminished my ability to ride. (Not sit on a moving horse: ride.) A newspaper ad for a bay gelding sent me out to look at a wonderful bargain, that perfect horse of the imagination. He looked as good as the ad had indicated, just what I'd always wanted (and cheap, too.) Tacked him up, rode him up and down the farm lane. Since it was too muddy to ride in a plowed field, I turned him into a brushy downhill slope . . . and a few minutes later was knocked cold when I messed up an emergency dismount. Woke up to my mother saying "Do you know who I am yet, dear?" (This really ruins the illusion that you're a strong, independent, capable grownup by forty . . . )*

*This otherwise unfortunate day ended up inspiring my first fiction sale, an article in* The Western Horseman, *a poem, and the realization that mothers of young disabled children should not buy horses whose previous riders were fourteen-year-olds in love with speed. (Remembering how I rode when I was fourteen . . . ) The other factor in the equation was the fifth rejection letter from Marion Zimmer Bradley, commenting that she had room for only 1500 humorous words in the anthology. "Bargains" sweated down from 2300 words to 1500, one word at a time.*

# BARGAINS

The horsetrader waved his helper aside and turned to Rahel. "Lady, you can see for yourself this horse would pass for Marrakai—but you, because anyone can see you know horses—I'll tell you the truth of it. His sire was Marrakai; his dam was a Valchai-Marrakai cross."

Rahel said nothing, staring at the horse she'd always dreamed of. A compact bay, not too heavy, short-backed with a long underline. Hard black hooves danced lightly on the cobbles. Wide dark eyes stared at her. Alert ears, a good shoulder, withers to hold a saddle in combat or on mountain trails. The trader took the lead, brought him forward, backed him. Straight motion, a powerful solid hock, spring in the pasterns. Rahel swallowed.

"How much?"

"Well, for you—you see, lady, this horse is special." Generations of horsebreeding ancestors clamored in her head. Rahel ignored them. "He needs a rider, I'll say that for him."

"What about training?"

The trader shrugged. "He's had his ground work—carries a saddle—I've taken him on the road from here to Cestin Var. But he needs a rider, a real rider, lady—like you are."

"How much, then?"

"For you—you were made for this horse, lady—for you, only eighty—"

The price was low; Marrakai halfbreds went for more than a hundred.

"Here—try him." Before she could answer, he'd scooped the saddle off her hip, and thrown it on the bay horse's back. The horse stood quietly. Rahel watched, eyes narrowed, as he tightened the foregirth and started to unbuckle the war harness.

"Fasten it."

He stared at her. "But lady, in the market you don't need—"

"I don't need a horse that blows up when you put a crupper under his tail. Fasten it." The man shrugged and bent to the task. The horse accepted the crupper and reargirth. She held out the bridle slung over her shoulder before the trader reached for it, and watched as the horse took the bit quietly. Then the trader held the rein and beckoned.

"Now try, Lady Rahel. The only horse in this market fit

for your pleasure. In fighting, you might want to use a different bit—a curb—"

"How'd you know my name?" she asked, turning the stirrup to mount.

"Everyone knows of the lady—and her friend." He managed to bow without loosing his hold on the rein. Rahel swung up, checked her stirrups, and nodded. The horse stood, alert yet motionless. She nudged; the horse stepped forward. Around the square, into the ring at the center. She thought of having that springy stride under her on all her travels and suppressed a grin. Hooves pounded behind her; she legged the horse aside as a loose horse ran by. Her horse—she already thought that—had not spooked.

Eighty natas. Pir would be stunned. This was exactly the horse she'd been looking for.

Pir was waiting at the west gate, a delicate veiled figure standing beside her white mule. She didn't recognize Rahel until the bay horse stopped; then she stared.

"Rahel! That horse—you're broke—"

Rahel grinned down. "I'm not that bad a bargainer, partner. I had enough left to fill my bags with something to eat—so as soon as you're ready—"

"I'm ready." Pir mounted, swinging her veils over the mule's rump with practiced ease.

"I thought you were going to buy some replacement—"

"Hush. I did." Pir nudged the mule, and it stepped forward. Rahel rode after her, frowning. Once clear of the gates, she came up beside her.

"You said it might take all day—"

"But it didn't. I, too, found a bargain." Pir looked around, then pulled a slender black wand a little way out of her sleeve. "See? Fireballs."

"Really?" Rahel stared. "How about that healing spell?"

"Better—I got two copies of clearhead, and a ring of horsecatching." Pir looked smug, and turned to look at the scenery. Their way led up a narrowing valley, into the Westmounts. Traffic had thinned by the time they came to the branch trail to Horngard. Rahel looked back, seeing dust from a caravan they'd passed just outside Pliuni, and a couple of foot travelers headed east. She reined the bay horse onto the Horngard trail, and loosened her sword.

"How did you buy all that, Pir? Are you sure the stuff's real?"

"Oh, yes—I'm as good a bargainer as any horse-trader's daughter."

"Horse-*breeder's* daughter," corrected Rahel.

The trail wound upward along a mountain flank. The bay horse stepped out easily, and Rahel relaxed. Soon they were out of sight of the main road. Rahel heard a marmot whistle—then another. The bay horse slowed and stopped. Rahel closed her legs.

"Come on," she said firmly.

The horse shook itself like a wet dog. Pir snickered, and Rahel turned to glare at her as she nudged the horse again and shortened her reins. The horse took a few more mincing steps, and Rahel smiled.

Then the bay horse dropped out from under her and bolted straight down the mountain into the worst looking brush Rahel had seen since she left home. She heard Pir's cry behind her; she could not look. She had both feet braced, but the horse ignored her pull on the reins. *Might* need a different bit, she thought angrily, yanking one rein to pull the bay horse's head around. He kept running, half-sideways. They crashed through one thorn-bush. He jumped the next crooked, landing with a jolt that threw Rahel forward, and pounded on. She looked ahead. More thorn, lots of it, and thorn trees with low limbs. The horse paid no attention to voice or rein. Rahel ducked sideways; thorns scraped her leather jerkin and raked her arm from elbow to shoulder.

The horse burst through a wall of thorn into a space as large as two caravan wagons side by side. Ahead was a dropoff steeper than the other, great boulders tumbling down to a dry wash. Cursing, Rahel kicked free of the stirrups and swung down, rolling clear of the clattering hooves. The horse veered, running along the edge of the bluff and turning uphill. She clambered up, checked her sword, and peered back into the thorn. It would be a miserable climb back to the Horngard trail.

She had made only half that distance when she heard the voices. Pir's, angry and defiant. Others, heavy and amused. She drew her sword and crept closer. Two men held the white mule. Another held her bay horse. Two more had Pir backed against a thorn tree: Pir pointed the black wand at them.

"Fireballs," Pir was saying. "I will fry you like fishsticks if you don't tie my mule and that horse and go."

The men laughed again. Pir flipped her other hand free of her veils and began to gesture; Rahel ducked. Then she stared. Out the end of the black rod came an orange glowing sphere that rolled sluggishly through the air until one of the men stepped aside; it turned a darker orange and vanished. Pir muttered furiously, swinging her hand, and another ball of orange light appeared, this one slightly brighter and moving faster. One of the men stepped back, but the sphere touched his chest and popped like a soap bubble. He broke into nervous laughter, and came forward with his fellow.

Rahel stormed out of the thorn, sword high, and slammed into the man holding her horse; she was not surprised to recognize the trader's helper. The bay horse snorted and clattered away. Next came the men with the mule. One of them had whirled to meet her charge; she dodged, and vaulted the mule to thrust her sword into the other's neck. The first man cut behind the mule. At Rahel's command the white mule planted both hind feet on his chest and tossed him backward into the thorn.

When she looked, a sickly green cloud veiled the far side of the opening. Someone was choking; Rahel shook her head and turned back to the three she'd fought. One was dead, the trader's helper was unconscious with a flap of scalp hanging loose, and the third groaned pitiably from his bed of thorns. She heard footsteps and looked back. Pir stepped carefully over the rough ground, holding her veils clear of the thorns, and carrying a plump purse.

"Some bargain horse," she said cheerfully.

"Some bargain fireballs," said Rahel. "Do you have anything that works?"

"This." Pir took out the horsecatching ring and thumbed it. In a moment the bay horse reappeared, wide-eyed, and came forward until Rahel could catch the trailing rein. They mounted and rode back up the hill; once again the bay horse moved steadily. Some time later they stopped to count the rest of their loot: all the gold they'd paid in Pliuni, and more.

"How did you know the horsecatching ring would work?" asked Rahel, tucking away the whistle that had signalled the bay horse.

"Oh, that. I don't take chances with important things. You said you'd heard they were using a good horse for this trick, worth spending something on. I paid Guild prices for that ring." Pir resettled her veils. "Our bargain came first, partner."

*"Bargains" had not yet sold when I sent "ABCs in Zero G" to* Analog. *This story had come into my head one cold clear night on the way back from the regional trauma center. The brilliant stars, the cold air, the two A.M. emptiness of the country roads, all suggested "What if we did this in space? What would we need? How would it work?" Stanley Schmidt wanted some revision on "ABCs . . . ", and as usual his suggestions greatly improved the story . . . but the exciting thing to me was having two stories bought back-to-back as it were. One fantasy, one science fiction. I didn't quit my nonfiction writing (not yet . . . ) but hope surged.*

# ABCs IN ZERO G

When the alarm rang, I rolled off my bunk. Only I didn't. I rolled into the Velcro-fastened safety webbing that reminded me, as my stomach did, that my bunk was in Sector Yellow, Station One, rather than Colorado. I fought my way out of the webbing and managed to fumble across the wedgi to the airlock where our unit was docked. Fairley was at the station console.

" . . . Code Three at Sector Blue. Clear at 1325." He flipped up the microphone wand and turned to me. "Get any sleep?"

"Enough." I hadn't, though. I wrenched at the airlock controls. Fairley was rummaging in the lockers for our gear. He followed me into the lock, and we helped each other into EVA gear while the lock checked to be sure that our unit hadn't vacuumed on us. Then we crawled into the modified cargo raft that was the Station equivalent of the Advanced Life Support module housed in your local fire station. Flashing lights and all.

9

It's not quite the same, of course. Instead of an oblong box with a bench on one side and a gurney on the other, its cross-section is pentagonal. The front compartment closes off with a narrow airlock, and two locks service the back: one large enough to take a full-size construction worker, in space suit, with a medic at his side. The whole inside is lined in Velcro instead of shiny vinyl, so that our working shoes will hold in zero and low gravity. Because EVA suits have powerpacks built into the back, the gurney is in two pieces.

The Zero itself carries only the equipment needed for EVA work; every sector and ring stores trauma and emergency gear inside as well. So we have no backboard (useless with someone in a space suit), and the few splints we need are racked on the overhead. But the paramedic on your local unit would catch on quickly; it's not that different. Our protocols are much the same. ABCs first: airway, breathing, circulation . . . simple. Only up here, nothing is quite that simple, not even ABC.

It was Fairley's turn to "pilot," and I watched as he flipped the radio wand and spoke.

"Sector Yellow Zero, Station Central."

"Go ahead, Yellow Zero."

"Route to Code Three, Sector Blue."

"Link computer band 47."

"Linked 47."

"Disconnect when ready."

"Disconnect." Fairley's sole contribution, if all went well, was this single button push; we'd been told that only the Traffic Computer could manage traffic within the work radius. The computer picked our route, and controlled the thrust of our engines. We were pushed first one way, then the other by the computer's "priority route" thrust changes. Zeros, like ambulances on Earth, are fuel wasters.

"Wonder where Blue Zero is?" I asked, as we started off.

"They had a possible coronary in the cafeteria. The guy was hooked up to the monitor already." Fairley sighed. I felt the same way. Inside the Station, we had a chance to do our job. Outside . . .

"Station Central to Yellow Zero."

"Go ahead, Central."

"Stand by for graplons." That last shove must have been relative deceleration; now the working crews near the accident site would shoot magnetic-tipped lines to snare us where we were needed.

"We're ready." I struggled out of my couch and back to the working compartment. Code Three was a major injury involving the trunk; we'd had five since they started using the Zeros. All had died. None of us were happy about that.

I had already locked my helmet on, and checked my suit radio; now I cycled out through the medic-lock, careful to clip my safety line to the rings. Outside made no visual sense at all. I'd learned to ignore it on a run; it took too long to become oriented. We had plenty of time off-duty for sightseeing. From a side rack I pulled a jointed aluminum frame, descended from the old scoop stretcher. With it, we could transport a victim in whatever posture he was found. Nothing else could be done until we had the victim in the Zero. That was one of our problems.

"Pat, they're coming in on red graplon." That was Fairley, back in the Zero setting up equipment. Red graplon was, by convention, the starboard one. I pussyfooted carefully around the Zero's belly, trailing the stretcher. I saw them almost at once: two suited figures towing a third along the graplon.

"Shift super Varrib to Zero medic."

"Medic here," I replied. "What's the problem?" I began to move slowly along the graplon, trailing my safety line. I was pleased to see that they slowed down. Early on, we'd lost one patient entirely when the construction crews moved too fast and launched him across the whole ring.

"Crush injury; his powerpack's damaged too. Vitals look bad."

"What hit him?"

"The second supply packet on our shift. We think it was the conduit."

By then we were only a few feet apart. I could see the damaged section of the powerpack; the cooling fins on one side were twisted almost off. I adjusted the aluminum frame stretcher to the victim's suited shape, and looked at the vital signs readout on his helmet. Vitals were bad indeed: fast pulse at 130, blood pressure well below normal at 90/40, and his arterial oxygen, or pO2 was only 76.

"Try to get him back in time," said the second worker, whose helmet was marked Deans.

"We'll do our best," I said, a bit crisper than I meant because our best hadn't been so good lately. I was already moving the victim toward our Zero.

"Want any help?"

"No thanks. It's hard to compensate for the extra movement."

"OK. See you later."

Fairley helped me cycle the victim through the patient airlock. By the time we hauled him into the compartment, we had his helmet off. I had flicked on the recorder, and now started my report as we worked.

"Respirations spontaneous, but rapid and labored; the face appears slightly cyanotic. The patient is unresponsive."

"This stupid suit!" Fairly snarled. "It's worse than football pads. And these so-called joints—!"

I was too busy to help him. The VS monitor showed a pulse now at 145, BP 80/40, and pO$_2$ 70; downhill in all directions. "We need to assist respirations; I think he's got a pneumothorax. He sure isn't getting enough oxygen, even with the prongs. Can't you get his head back at all?" We knew from bitter experience that intubation worked much better than mask-assisted respiration—nobody could keep a mask in place with unpredictable accelerations.

"No. The powerpack must've bent the neck coupling. It won't go."

I picked up the Garfield tube set. "I'll have to try it this way, then."

"Go ahead. I'm not getting anywhere here."

The man's mouth gaped slightly. I shoved in a bite block and used the sponge forceps to pull his tongue forward and to the side. On the clear side I slid in the guide channel of the Garfield, a curved green plastic device that fit into his mouth and made intubations possible even when you couldn't position the head properly. The old way, you had to have direct vision of the trachea with a laryngoscope, but not any more. The Garfield had channels to guide a remote visual and the necessary tubes into the right place.

I clipped the magnifier eyepiece to my headset and threaded the fibreoptic scope into its groove. Beneath it I threaded the two tubes—one for the trachea, one for the esophagus—into their respective channels. I needed five hands: one for the suction tip, one for the forceps controlling the tongue, one for the lightsource fiberscope, and one each for the tubes. Fairley gave up his attack on the suit and took over suction and forceps. That left me only one hand short—not bad at all. But I had to hurry. Not only the man's condition compelled that, but our protocol gave us only four minutes on scene after loading the patient before the traffic computer moved us.

"Suction now," I told Fairley. The red blot obstructing my view cleared and I advanced the lightsource. With the man's neck forward and his jaw slack, the airway was not visible. "Try hoisting the jaw." That helped a little. "Pull his tongue" A blood-streaked pink wall heaved up, leaving a dark crease that might be the opening I was looking for. "More," I said.

"I'm nearly pulling his tongue out now," warned Fairley.

"OK. I can see . . ." On one end of the crease a widening cleft showed; I slid the lightsource toward it. The cleft opened and flattened as the victim exhaled noisily. Blood obscured my view. "Irrigation and suction, deep," I told Fairley. I could see again, and moved the lightsource further. There— at the back—a pink cleft now full of blood-stained fluid—was the esophagus. I hoped. Emergency care specialists are still fighting over the best use—if any—of the esophageal obturator, which closes off the passage to the stomach, but our medical director had a good reason for insisting that the esophagus be plugged first. When someone vomits in a zero-G ambulance, it's a worse mess than Earthside.

I advanced the esophageal obturator and it slid easily into the cleft. Now I had to find the tracheal opening, ventral to the esophagus. At the victim's next breath, I saw for an instant the white V of the vocal cords, almost drowned in blood. I pushed the endotracheal tube forward. Even with the guide channel, I had trouble forcing the tube around the sharp bend of the flexed neck. At last I had it lined up, and slipped it through the larynx. "Got it!" I inflated the cuff.

"Here's the tape." Fairley handed me a strip of tape and I wound it around the tube and onto the man's face to keep the tube from slipping out of place. While I taped, he hooked the oxygen to the endotracheal tube and set the meters.

And then the Zero lurched sharply to the left. My hand, still on the tape, ripped it off the man's face with such force that the ET tube came out.

I don't know what we said during the next few seconds—it's on tape somewhere, but I'm not really interested—but I do know what we did. We tried desperately to keep an oxygen mask on the victim's face while the Zero jerked us from side to side. We watched the VS monitors as the signs went downhill . . . listened to the gurgle of blood in his airway . . . tried to suction, and nearly impaled him on the suction tubing as the Zero shot off in another unpredictable direction. It was hopeless to try to intubate. It was hopeless to try to start an IV. It was hopeless, start to finish, and when the deathly efficient Traffic Computer docked us at last, the man was dead. Malcolm Berenson, technician, electronic, second class. Father of two, we found out later, with another on the way.

I came out of the ER, after the resuscitation had failed, in the blackest mood I'd been in since NASA first announced it didn't want female astronauts, back when I was in grade school and didn't know girls were supposed to be second class. Fairley, a step behind me, radiated grimness. It didn't help a bit when we met the man's work crew on their way to find out how he was. We were all very polite about it, but that didn't bring Berenson back . . . nor had we.

Our shift was over, and Fairley and I went back to the off-duty quarters area without speaking. Paula Arnold and Jeff Sevier (Blue Zero, shift three), and Ginny Buchanan were in the common room, glooming over coffee. I went to the machine and dialed myself a lemonade. Fairley slumped into one of the seats in front of the computer display screen.

"How'd it happen?" asked Paula. That was brave of her; I wouldn't have spoken to me yet.

"That stinking Traffic Computer, of course." Fairley answered before I could. "Pat had just gotten a tube down . . . and it wasn't easy . . . and the computer jerked us around before we could get it tied down."

"Guy'd been crushed by a conduit load," I added. "Powerpack bent all to hell, neck ring bent, maybe, and Fairley couldn't get an IV past that all-too protective suit. He had a pneumothorax (we'd found that out in the ER) and heaven only knows what else."

Jeff, Blue Zero's senior crew, drained his coffee and stood. "Sorry you had to take one in our sector. Especially one like that—"

"It's OK, Jeff—"

"No, dammit, it's not. I mean, sure you take up the slack for us and we do for you and that's all squeaky clean. But it's not OK that we've been up here for five months and haven't saved a single EVA major trauma."

"That femur fracture?"

"You know what I mean. And we lost the guy with the broken ankle—a broken ankle of all things—because his suit failed and we couldn't patch in an air supply."

"We might as well hang it up where the Zeros are concerned." said Paula. "Inside we do as well as Earthside, but out there, which is where we're needed most, we can't do tiddly squat."

Sector Green's crew, coming off duty, paused in the doorway.

"Another bummer?" asked Juan.

"Yeah," I said. "All the usual trimmings."

"Tough," he said. "By the way, Pat, you've got mail in the bin." I nodded, but didn't move. I wasn't in the mood for mail from anyone.

"I think we ought to go tell 'em." Ginny stretched as she spoke. "If we don't, they'll come storming in griping about how we're costing 'em a bundle and not producing."

"They try that and I'll give them what they won't forget." Juan's partner Ivan stomped over to the drink machine as if it were a NASA rep. Ivan is Irish, not Russian (his mother had a sense of humor, he says), but big enough that we nicknamed him Bear.

As if in answer, the comunit chimed for our attention. "All off-duty Zero crews please assemble in Blue 345. All off-duty Zero crews please assemble in Blue 345, immediately. On-duty Zero crews switch your comunits to Internal, Channel 7 please. Agenda item for assembly is unacceptable losses in EVA operations."

"Those . . . those utter . . ." Paula's voice trailed away in disgust.

"Bastards," said Jeff.

"Camel droppings," offered Juan.

I was already headed back to Sector Blue, angry enough to be quiet. Soon we were all together, ducking down to Two Ring, and around to Blue, then back out and right along the ring to the big conference room. We were joined along the way by Jill and Bob Delgracio (Blue Zero, shift two), and Jess Hightower, Ginny's partner (Red Zero, shift two) who drew an expressive finger across his neck and pointed to the room ahead. Already in the room were Jim Hackett, our acting director, Dr. Mossler, our medical director, another physician, two huskies in construction workers' coveralls, and a bunch of people in the spaceworker's version of a gray flannel suit. And standing against one wall, wary as steers in a stockyard, were the rest of our fellow paramedics. When we came in, everyone drifted to seats, all of the Zero crews clumped together and the others somewhat separated. Jim Hackett stayed on his feet and glanced around for attention.

"You all know, I suppose, why this meeting has been called," he began. The physicians and construction men nodded crisply. I don't think any of the paramedics moved a muscle. "Although the EMS program we developed has worked well inside the station, it is not up to expectation outside, and we feel that after six months some improvement should have been seen. It's not just today's . . . uh . . . problem . . ." he looked at me and I glared back. He looked away. "Now we all know you people have tried, but you don't seem to be getting anywhere. We think it's time to turn elsewhere for suggestions . . ."

"Suggestions!" That was Ginny erupting. "And what are you going to do with suggestions? File 'em where you filed ours? You can't shift blame on us; you haven't listened to anything we've said, and when was the last time you rode a unit, Hackett?" I couldn't have said it better.

"There's just no way we can do effective EMS up here, as it is." Fairley broke in, sounding as disgusted as I felt. "The whole point is quick response, evaluation, and being able to stabilize ABCs. But we can't get to the airway, the suits frustrate any attempt at assisted ventilations, and we can't do anything about circulation until we can expose some skin. Which takes too long."

"And you keep saying 'We can't modify suits, we can't modify traffic control, we can't do this or that' but you want us to work miracles," added Ginny.

"You can take your miracles," muttered Jeff.

"There's got to be some answer," said one of the flannel suits. "Surely you people—so experienced—can devise new techniques . . ."

"And when we do you'll tell us it's too expensive! We have devised new techniques, and they get shot down. I'm sick of it." I was so angry I was shaking all over. "Next time you can go out and try to intubate somebody blowing blood in your face, and try to do it when you can't manipulate the neck or get to a superficial vein. Then when you get it done, the dumb computer shoves the unit off somewhere without warning, and you lose the connection and the guy dies before you can get the tube back in."

"The tube should have been secured," snapped the other physician, not Mossler. Just like a doctor; they can always find something wrong with whatever you've done. "And even if it came out, you could use a bag-mask."

"I was securing the tube when the unit moved," I snapped back. "And I've held tubes and taped tubes on the roughest riding ambulances on the worst road in the Rockies. But that miserable computer—"

"Garbage in, garbage out," snarled the programming chief, a tall skinny blonde named Pillaffson. "Don't blame the computer. You asked for a fast transfer; it's on the record."

"Fast transfer, yes. Goddam Brahma bull ride, no." That was Jess, our oldest and wiliest paramedic. "You think you're so smart at designing rides; you just try to work on an injury while you're being thrown all over the unit."

"The workers don't complain."

"They're not trying to do precision work on transfer, either. They're strapped in. Besides, how often are they routed fast?"

"It's the same thing here that they had on Earth when EMS first started," said Paula. "Trying to get the people who make the protocols out in the units to see what it's like out there."

We had obviously thrown the others off balance, and we could practically see their prepared speeches being dumped. Mossler looked concerned and thoughtful—a doctor's best defense, I thought sourly. The other doctor looked mad, his lips a thin line.

"OK," said another flannel-suiter. "What can we do?"

"Go home," muttered someone on the comlink between the duty crews and the conference.

"Quit," muttered someone else.

"Just one constructive change?" pleaded the rep.

"A suit we can get into from the outside," I said. "Give us back our direct access to vital signs and the ABCs."

"But Godalmighty, Pat, do you realize how expensive it'd be to redesign all those suits?"

"Look, right now you're paying for an expensive EMS that's not doing you any good. Inside the station, yes. We've saved quite a few there. But outside, everything you've spent on us is wasted. We've lost every single bad trauma since we've been here, and only three of them would have been lost on Earth. Everything you put into the Zeros, our EVA gear—all of it—is wasted. Either give up the idea of EMS outside the station, or realize that this approach won't work."

"Well, we'll start looking at it—"

"Changes in suit design will have to go through union contract negotiations," interrupted one of the construction men. His name tag read Construction Chief Blanchard. "We had to fight for those safety couplings, and now you want to get rid of 'em."

"No. Not get rid of them. I agree they probably save a lot of head injuries. But *modify* them so we can get to the patient's airway and some other vital areas."

The meeting broke into small clumps and clots of muttering, arguing, and handwaving. Pillaffson, the programming chief, edged through the clumps to bear down on Fairley and me.

"Look," he began. "We've got to have the Traffic Computer pilot your Zeros. We can't allow any slow-reaction-time humans to pilot inside the work ring. We found that out when we started construction up here. We'd have more wrecks than any EMS could take care of."

"Can't it at least tell us when it's going to fire, and which direction?"

"Not enough in advance to help you. It's making those decisions in real-time, relative to the movements of all other EVA traffic—not just vehicles, but individuals, tools, equipment—and trying not to interfere more than necessary with the schedule. The unpowered movements can't be deflected, either. Now is it really that bad?"

"Worse. I'll show you. Just a sec—" Fairley peered around the room and beckoned to several people. "Dr. Mossler, Chief Blanchard, why don't you let us show you what we're talking about. You, too, Mr. Pillaffson. We'll take a closed suit, simulating a victim—"

"Why not me, in my suit?" asked Blanchard. "I work out there every day."

"Great. Five will crowd the Zero, but we can patch the rest in on the com . . ."

"Or we can set up our own demonstrations," said Ginny. "We have three back-up Zeros."

✧            ✧            ✧

"We'll need to simulate a call location," said Fairley, when we were all crowded into the unit. I was "piloting" this time, and he was in the couch to my right. Behind us, in the working compartment, Mossler and Pillaffson clutched the grabbars, and Blanchard, in full suit, lay webbed to the litter.

"I can do that, with a vocal," said Pillaffson.

"Fine," said Fairley. "At least a half-sector away, please."

We couldn't hear his mutter to the computer, but we heard the computer up front: "Station Central to Baker Blue Zero." (Baker, because we were a backup unit.)

"Go ahead, Central."

"Code Three, Sector Yellow."

"Route."

"Link band 47."

"Linked."

"Disconnect when ready."

"Disconnect." I pushed the button. With a sharp shove "back" and "down" we were on our way. This time two direction changes slammed us from side to side. When we "stopped," strung in a web of graplons, I noticed that our passengers were hanging on with both arms.

"It is a bit rough back here," conceded the doctor. "Feels worse when you aren't strapped in."

"Now what?" asked Pillaffson.

"Now we pretend Chief Blanchard has a major torso trauma." Fairley wormed past the others to the litter. I followed, as Fairley pointed out the vital signs monitor on Blanchard's helmet. "If nothing has damaged this side of the helmet, or the connections inside, we get a readout of pulse, blood pressure, and arterial $pO_2$. His are fine, now, but the one we just lost had a pulse of 140, blood pressure 60/0, and $pO_2$ 40. Now for the suit." He reached down and began to undog Blanchard's helmet connection. The shock absorbing ability built into the suit made it a complicated process: dual seals and interlocks all around the neck. The faceplate could not be opened separately, as ours could, so we had no access until the entire helmet was off.

When we did manage to slide the helmet off, Blanchard's head and neck were held in neutral position by the high protective steel rings on the coupling. To extend his neck (and thus, in an unconscious patient, open the airway) we had to take off these rings. Theoretically, the rings were jointed and could be unfastened for easy opening. In practice, the workers inserted themselves into their suits from the belly, since the neck rings were easily large enough to push a head through. The rings were stiff from disuse, and hellish hard to undo.

"Here's the second problem," I said. "Once the helmet is off, we need to hook the VS sensors to our monitoring devices. The $pO_2$ sensor is no problem, but there's no good way to get blood pressure and cardiac function. We can't use our sensors because they're designed for a specific body part we can't get to. The best we can do is a Doppler pickup on the carotid pulse, and you see—" I demonstrated, "—what a lousy access we have to the carotid."

"You can palpate a pulse, I hope, Pat," said Mossler. I managed not to glare. Doctors! They've always suspected us of not knowing our work.

"Certainly, Dr. Mossler, but not while hanging an IV or doing an intubation. Constant monitoring by palpation means constant use of one hand. And it still doesn't give us blood pressure. Another thing—" I gestured to Fairley, who was removing one of Blanchard's suit gloves. "As you know, the availability of IV fluid therapy in the field made a dramatic difference in trauma management on Earth. It would here, too, if we could get to a useful vein. Chief Blanchard is not in shock, but notice that even so his hand veins aren't standing out. And we can't put on a tourniquet to engorge them, thanks to the suit. If we needed to pour in fluid replacement, we'd need to get to a larger vein . . . but look what the suit does at wrist and elbow." Fairley tapped the corrugated plastic joint. "This stuff is designed to be tough and impervious, and it sure is. We can't cut it."

"I see what you mean," said Mossler, peering past Fairley's hands. "Can't you open the suit torso, though? Could you do a sub-clavian stick, or a jugular?" I noticed Blanchard's face pale at that last word.

"That's a yes and no question, Doc," said Fairley. "That protective neck portion comes down so low that if you can't undo the neck rings you really can't do a subclavian. You can open the suit, but it's so stiff that you can't keep it far enough open to do much. Try it and see."

Mossler fumbled at the exterior fastenings of Blanchard's suit and pried it apart in the midline. Unlike the EVA suits of shuttle era, it was made in one piece to give extra protection to the torso, and support the extended EVA power-packs and sanitary arrangements that let construction workers spend a full shift outside. It snapped back together like a coin purse the instant Mossler tried to let go of one side to pick up an instrument. I managed not to snicker.

"Ouch!" he said, and jerked his other hand out. "Hmm. So you really can't attach the cardiac monitor easily."

"No. You can do it, but it takes two people. And defibrillation is out of the question."

"Wait a minute," said Blanchard. "I don't have this much trouble getting into this thing. Why is it so much worse when I'm inside?"

"It's one of the safety features," I said. "Think what you do before you get out of it. You release a valve that lets the fluid in the suit system back to its reservoir. Unless someone hits that release, the pressure of your body parts in the suit keeps the torso section rigid. And the release is carefully designed so that it can't be hit from outside."

"Oh . . . yeah . . . I do, don't I? I've gotten so used to this thing that I forgot."

"Very few people could describe what they do when they button a button," said Fairley. "That suit's like an old shirt to you." He worked his way back into the forward compartment.

I was setting up an IV line, reaching around the extra bodies, when Fairley added another bit of realism. I saw him reach for the controls, but didn't say a word. They needed to know what "without warning" meant. I made sure I had two feet firmly on the Velcro unit lining, but the others weren't so lucky.

Mossler had just turned to Pillaffson when the unit accelerated "up" and "back/left" strongly. Pillaffson tumbled against the wall opposite the litter, and for one awful second I thought he'd activated the patient airlock. Mossler, who happened to have both his feet attached, folded over and hit his head on the forward bulkhead. I managed to catch a grabbar with one flailing arm and stay put, but the IV setup slipped out of my other hand and slithered into the front with Fairley. Abruptly we were back in free-fall. After a few seconds the next thrust pushed us "forward" and "left," and the IV bag sailed through the cockpit opening, catching Mossler (who'd managed to stand up again and find a grabbar) in the midsection. The tubing was royally snarled—even Pillaffson had a loop around one foot. We were back in free-fall in a second or so, and Pillaffson got himself straightened out and attached to Velcro and webbing. Mossler peeled the IV bag off his middle and hitched it to the wall by its Velcro patch.

"Does this happen every time?" he asked.

"Sure does. That isn't all, either. Here—" I shifted cautiously around Mossler, ready for another acceleration, but none came before I reached the small seat at the head of the litter. After strapping in, I plucked an oxygen mask from its attachment on the wall, and put a hand on either side of Blanchard's head. "Now watch what happens when I try to keep the mask on."

This time two quick thrusts—right, then down/right—shoved us around. They could see how I'd had to use both hands, hard, to keep the mask more-or-less on Blanchard's face.

"I see what you mean about not having a hand free," said Mossler. "But couldn't you get all the necessary stuff hitched up before starting back to the ER?"

"No. Remember that work order we griped about when we first came up—about time-on-scene?"

Mossler shook his head. "I wasn't medical director then. Which one?"

Fairley spoke up from the front compartment. "Whoever it was—maybe Halberson—had a thing about paramedics not spending too long at the scene. Said he'd had trouble enough down-station with smart-alecs horsing around playing surgeon at a car wreck . . ." There was no mistaking Fairley's bitterness; his drawl carried a whiplash on the end of each word. "So he insisted on a time limit at the scene, no matter what. When that limit is up, the Traffic Computer takes us off, and that's it."

"But—" Mossler began, but I interrupted him.

"And in case you think it's long enough, Dr. Mossler, on this simulated run we had two minutes more than we're allowed before that first acceleration. It wouldn't be so bad if we could work while in transit, but as you've seen—"And just then another surge of acceleration caught us all unprepared. I lost the mask, and my other hand clipped Blanchard on the nose. Fairley swore as his hand hit the edge of the seat frame, and both our standing passengers let out a yelp. Then we heard the smug tone that meant we were docked at the ER lock, and a sharp warning blip that meant another Zero was coming in behind us.

"Now," I said, "we have two minutes to unload our patient before the next one docks." I was working as I spoke, and Fairley, coming through to help me, pushed our passengers on out the docking lock. Then we wrestled the litter with Blanchard still on it out of the narrow opening, and along the passage to the ER.

When we let Blanchard off the stretcher, and he'd peeled himself out of his suit, he leaned on the passage wall outside the ER, shaking his head.

"I had no idea what it was like in there," he said. "I can see that you can't do your work as it is—"

"Pat," interrupted Dr. Mossler. Blanchard glared. "I just thought of something. They've had those fingertip blood-pressure gauges for a decade now, on Earth. You can get the gloves off—why not use those?"

Fairley and I glanced at each other. Typical doctor again. Mossler's background was industrial medicine, not emergency or trauma. "Because," I began slowly, "if the blood pressure is low enough, say from a serious injury . . ." He caught on, quickly.

"Oh . . . yeah . . . sure. Peripheral shutdown. Not good enough. Damn."

"About these suits," said Blanchard, still intent. "Even if I get the union behind it, it'll take months—years, maybe—to redesign and make the things. They still have to protect us, you know."

"That's true—" I broke off as Paula and Jeff came out of the ER with two of the "gray flannel suit" administrators, both pale. Jeff jumped on our chief programmer immediately.

"Now you see what we mean, don't you?" he demanded. "We can't do anything with that stupid computer jerking the Zeros all over the place."

Pillaffson stiffened. "The computer is not stupid! Whatever problems you have are not the fault of the computer, nor, I might add, of its programs. They do exactly what they were designed to do, which is keep all traffic around the station in order. If it weren't for that 'stupid computer' as you call it, this station would have been battered to bits months ago. You aren't even a licensed shuttle pilot!" I could have slugged Jeff . . . we had just gotten Pillaffson convinced, I'd thought, and he had to make him mad.

Jeff opened his mouth, but once more Mossler interrupted. This time I was glad.

"Well, one thing that wouldn't be hard to change—and wouldn't affect the traffic computer's control, as I understand—is the time-on-scene delay. Surely it would be possible to let the paramedics initiate the return to ER just as they initiate undock in the first place, wouldn't it?"

Pillaffson was still fuming, but he did consider Mossler's question. There's this about doctors—you can't ignore them. "Yes," he said finally. "That could be changed, though a very long delay would always involve some drift, and in the end could require a powered adjustment."

"Could that adjustment give a warning?" asked Paula. "I don't mean a complete readout, just a warning bell or something."

"I suppose it could," said Pillaffson ungraciously. "If you really need it. But of course any changes at all in Station software must be approved by the Station director. And the EMS director and medical director would have to convince him that these changes are necessary."

Mossler grinned. "As far as the medical staff are concerned, I think a trip like the one I had would convince them." I was surprised; he actually seemed to be trying to help us.

The ER disgorged another of the teams into the already crowded passage, and we shifted toward a larger area, still talking. I didn't notice that Mossler was no longer with us until after all the crews had reassembled, and the arm-waving was intense again. Then Mossler appeared at my side with a big grin on his face (it occurred to me for the first time that he was actually a nice guy), and called for quiet.

As the talking and yelling quieted to muttering, and people turned to look at him, he spoke.

"I want to thank the Zero crews," he said, "for giving the rest of us a much clearer picture of their problems." He caught my eye, and smiled. From anyone else, it would have been a personal sort of smile. "We've made one change already. I got hold of Jim Hackett and the Station director, and the automatic limit to time-on-scene is gone. As of now, when you have stabilized your patient on scene, you'll have to contact the Traffic Computer again and initiate movement. You will hear a tone every three minutes the graplons are on, just as a reminder, and if the Computer has to shift you for some reason, you'll hear a double tone before that. It—"

"How'd you do that without my consent?" yelled Pillaffson. "Any change in the programming . . ."

"It's not exactly a change," insisted Mossler. "It's just putting the Zeros back in the same category as everything else . . . your duty programmer said all that was necessary was removing the delay limit."

"I still think it shouldn't have gone past me." Pillaffson scowled at us. "Seems to me you've all gotten excited about this, and ready to change everything, without taking the time to see what the changes will do."

I saw Jeff open his mouth again, but Paula grabbed his arm. He subsided. Mossler cocked his head. "I'm sorry,

Steve, if you thought we were bypassing you on purpose. I knew you'd been out there, and seen the problem, and you had agreed that removing the delay limit wouldn't affect the traffic computer's management much."

"Well, thanks for that. If you have any more bright ideas for my computers, I hope you'll see that they go through channels." Pillaffson turned on his heel and went out. For a moment everyone just stood there, watching, then the discussions began again.

The group broke up a few minutes later, with the administrator types still touchy about cost-analysis and estimate overruns. I saw Blanchard and Mossler deep in conversation in one corner, but I was too spent to eavesdrop. It was halfway through the next shift, and I wanted to sleep in peace and quiet for a few hours. I didn't remember my mail until I was already showered and ready to sleep, but padded back out to the terminal in the off-duty lounge. I called in, and they put my file on.

It was short and bad: a note and a news item. My old partner, Dave, had been injured while working a wreck. Paraplegia. I shivered, and thought of the four years we'd been together, working 24 hour shifts in an advanced life support unit that covered everything from cardiac arrests to newborn transport to mountain rescue. He would have been with me on the Station—should have been—but he'd fallen for a resident in pediatric surgery. I wondered if she was with him now. I tapped a few keys, asking for a printout, and turned the screen down. Tired as I was, it was going to be hard to sleep. And of course I couldn't do anything, not from the Station. I read the printout twice more before finally falling asleep.

On my next workshift, Mossler dropped by our station. "I've been talking to the other crews about this suit problem. Have you got any ideas?"

I looked at Fairley, who shook his head, and back at Mossler. "I'm not sure," I said. "When we first came up, I tried to figure out a way to hold the suit open. But that means extra equipment and something else to spring loose."

I didn't really care. I kept seeing Dave's face—and, to be honest, Dave's strong body. We weren't lovers, but you can't work that close and not know what someone looks like. Not our kind of work. I wished Mossler would go away. Doctors always messed things up. If it hadn't been for Sally, Dave would be up here—safe—not crippled in some rehab hospital. If I'd been his partner, he wouldn't have had to go back across the road for anything, either. That's what the clipping had said, that a friend had sent—his partner had forgotten something, and Dave had gone back . . . I shook myself into the present.

"Jeff Sevier had something," Fairley was saying. "Remember that drawing he carried around for the first couple of months, Pat? It looked sort of like a big salad server with a bar on it to hold the tongs apart."

"Yeah, but they said it wouldn't work." I went back to filling out the daily log. Something always happens to good ideas—and to good people, too.

"Who said—and why?" Mossler looked interested.

"I don't remember. Something about the tongs damaging the suit opening, or something like that." Fairley gave me a worried glance. I hadn't said anything about my mail, but I must have looked odd. I managed a smile.

"With every suit a custom model, they ought to realize that if the person in the suit dies, it won't matter if the opening is messed up."

"Think about it," Dr. Mossler said. "I'll talk to Jeff. And what about starting IVs?"

"I'd rather have an arm for blood pressure," I said. "If we knew blood pressure for sure . . ."

"IVs for me, though." Fairley drummed his fingers on the desk. "That elbow joint is the worst. We've got to get above the wrist." I was beginning to be interested in spite of myself.

"Maybe it could unscrew . . ." I twisted my hands, and then laughed. "That won't work."

Fairley sat up suddenly. "Wait. How's that stuff fastened on, anyhow?"

"Glue? It can't be just sewn in."

Fairley was throwing open the locker and dragging out his suit. "Confounded thing! You can't even *see* inside. Pat, get me a light."

I got the emergency flasher from its bracket and passed it over. "What are you looking for?"

"How it's fastened . . . I just saw something." He glared at Mossler and me when we didn't respond. "Don't you . . . ? You don't. What if Pat's right? What if it can just screw in, like a jar lid?"

Mossler's brow furrowed. "For one thing, it's not a screw—the corrugations are parallel."

"Yeah, they are now. Does that mean they have to be? A screw seal can be airtight all right—look at canning jars."

"Would screw corrugations have the flexibility?" I asked.

"Sure it would. Didn't you ever have a Slinky? You know, that spring toy that goes down stairs?" He was peering into the sleeve of his suit with the flasher. "Aha. Now why didn't I ever notice that?"

"What?"

"It's—kind of a ring, that's stitched in—gunk, too. Glue, I suppose, or fabric cement—"

"Who designed the suits in the first place?" I asked, trying to see past Fairley's ear without any luck.

"I don't know," said Mossler. "But I think we can find out who's making them now, and see about changes."

"We can do better than that," said Fairley firmly. "Pat, doesn't the Hobby Corner have a heat-setting—"

"It sure does," I broke in. "I'd forgotten Lillian and her models. I'll bet she could form us an elbow joint."

"Wait a minute. You mean make one up here?" Mossler looked worried. "Whose suit are you going to take apart?"

"Mine." We both said it, then exchanged glances.

"My suit," said Fairley. "I thought of it."

"I said screws first," I said. "My suit."

"Not you," said Mossler. "You're both active crew. What if . . ." He let it trail off, but we knew what he meant. What if it didn't hold?

"We can test it first." I had my suit out, too, then remembered. "But not until the end of the shift. Blast."

Fairley began to chuckle. "The thought of getting access to a real, honest-to-goodness arm—"

"If it works. If it was that simple, Fairley, somebody would have thought of it before." I went back to my paperwork, and my thoughts. At least it had been a distraction.

It wasn't that simple. Lillian, whose hobby was making models for the role-playing gamers, let us know that at once. She may be a mild-mannered paper-pusher during her workshifts, but in the crafts lab she's an expert—and knows it.

"I do molds," she said firmly. "Molds. Irregular molds. What you want is a cylinder with molded corrugations, in a spiral, that will screw into . . . what were you going to use for the other part? Plastic? Metal?"

"We hadn't thought—"

"I can tell. Do you know anything about screws at all? What pitch did you want?"

"Pitch?"

"God's blood, I have to start teaching beginning mechanics again." Lillian sighed. "Now look—" She was sketching on a yellow pad. "Let's take just the male screw." Someone snickered—I thought it was Ginny—and Lillian scowled. "None of that. It's the proper term. Now when you talk about screws, you have to specify the pitch, and the radius, and the handedness, and the threads per centimeter. That's for a cylindrical screw, which is what we have here. If you were talking about a conical screw, it would be trickier."

"Yeah, well . . ."

"But you're not. Good. But now you want it to screw into something— the female screw—and even those of you without any background should be able to see that this requires the same pitch and thread count, and just enough smaller radius that the screw will fit snugly and not bind."

"OK." I thought that made sense. "I can see that. But why can't we use a simple ring for the female part? I've seen caps that screwed on past a single ring."

"Yes. But I wouldn't want to bet my life on that, and you shouldn't. Those ring-held screws aren't for anything important. Even canning jars have two and a half or more threads to hold."

"Well, if canning jars are so common, what's hard about making male and female threads?"

Lillian looked disgusted. "Would you like to sculpt an IV bag? Or a hypodermic syringe? It's not hard at all with the right machinery, which we haven't got. I can make a terrific thief, and a passable dragon, but I cannot hand-carve matching male and female threads. Yes, it was done in the old days, but not by me, and I'm not risking your lives on it."

"Oh."

"And neither can you."

She didn't have to add that. I knew that already. I opened my mouth and shut it again, and looked at the others. They looked as blank as my mind. We shuffled out, as Lillian turned back to her latest work, a busty female with a double-headed axe. I never have understood that sort of thing. If you want an exciting life, work on an ambulance; don't play pretend games.

Having our best idea go bust didn't help my mood. I tried to think what to write Dave, and what I could do to help, and kept coming back to how stupid he was to hang around waiting for a pediatric surgeon to fall for him. Any paramedic knows that doctors don't have anything but an extra degree and a lot of pride—and the money, of course. I was still depressed and glooming over the latest issue of a magazine for water pollution control officers (and I never have known how that got into our common room), when Jill DelGracio bounced in. I don't know what it would take to depress Jill; she might even handle something like Dave's injury with the same perkiness. If she wasn't also a damn good ambulance jockey, I'd hate her.

"Guess what? Bob found a female screw."

"A what?" It took me a minute to figure out what she meant.

"He was talking to an electrician who has a friend who's working in the new construction, and he's found what he thinks will work." Bob appeared in the door behind her, grinning from ear to ear. He's almost as upbeat as Jill, but a little quieter about it.

"Look at this, Pat." I looked. It looked like a few coils of heavy cable with a plastic skin that kept the coils from separating very far. When I said so, he nodded. "Yes it is, sort of. That is, it's cable covered with heavy plastic: it's the computer connections for the docking bay out on Purple Four. It spirals out, but has the plastic to keep it from being stretched. And it just fits into a suit arm . . ."

"How do you know that?" I was wide awake now, and sitting up.

"Because I cut the elbow joint out of mine, and tried it." He looked smug and apprehensive together. He should have—our suits, we had been told, were worth more than a year's salary. "I can always live on Jill's money," he went on, grinning.

"Have you tried it?" I asked.

"In the airlock—partway. It hissed a little, but—"

"Hissed!"

"Well, yeah—now I need to figure a seal that will still unscrew."

"That's easy," said Fairley, who had overheard the last as he came in. "Just use the fat in your head."

Bob had his mouth open to bite back when Jill stopped him. "It might work after all. No, not that fat—but that thick sealant grease they use—"

We trooped back to Lillian in the hobby shop; she was painting howdahs on a lot of little elephants with a brush that looked like no more than three fine hairs. She gave Bob the look he deserved, then took his elbow joint apart and examined it.

"Yeah. OK. I see what you mean. I'll bet a double ring, sealed with that white gook would work. And maybe an elastic thingo between them, to be sure." Jill had called Mossler on intercom, and he arrived just as Lillian had it all back together. Mossler turned white then red when he realized what Bob had done, but recovered enough to supervise the next airlock test. The joint held without losing pressure, and unscrewed easily in the ER.

"Now all we have to do," said Mossler, "is convince the unions and the bureaucrats that someone crazy enough to design and test this has made a better joint than they did. You're going to have a rugged time convincing construction workers to trust a screw-on arm or leg." He hitched a hip onto the gurney in the trauma room, where we'd brought the suit after testing.

"I just thought of something else," said Jill. "Bob, you pulled your hand up into the arm while we were turning it, didn't you? An unconscious person couldn't—"

"No, but the gloves come off. You've got a point, though; we can't use this on legs until we can do something about the feet."

"The main thing is, we can get to a good vein, and get blood pressure. How's that can opener coming, Doc?"

Mossler frowned. "Jeff's idea was good, but when we tried it the thing kept falling over if anyone bumped it. You don't need something else to hold in place. I've been working on it—look at this." He rummaged in the bottom drawer of a cabinet, and pulled out something that looked like Jeff's original "salad-tongs" crossed with an equine speculum. When he demonstrated, on a construction suit they'd brought to the ER (I could see the scrubbed-off traces of a man's name, and realized this was one we'd lost), the device pried open the midline and held it—until Mossler touched it with one finger. Then it fell, as he'd said, and the suit snapped shut as the tongs flew off the table.

"I thought of adding locking nippers at the bottom," he said. "But that's something else to break, or fiddle with. Jeff thought of adding another leg to it, but you need all the access you can get. If you've got any ideas, tell me."

We stared at the thing for a few minutes. Then Fairley started chuckling, and the rest of us glared at him. He shook his head, and laughed harder.

"I don't get it," said Bob, a little testily.

"I was thinking of my grandmother. Smart old lady—the first woman to get an engineering degree from her university."

"So?"

"So her word of wisdom to the whole family was 'don't fight gravity'—if something has a strong tendency to go one way, make it do what you want while it's doing what *it* wants. Claims she got her degree by agreeing with her profs that women were indeed frivolous, flirtatious, and bound to quit when they got married. They were so charmed by her honesty in admitting that the only reason she wanted to take calculus was to meet intelligent men that they let her into the class. Now—what I see is something that wants to fall over. OK. Fix it so it holds the suit open while it's lying flat."

"But it—" Mossler stopped in midsentence and squinted. "By—you know, you're right, Fairley. It could work lying flat. In fact it'd work better lying flat." Right before our eyes he grabbed the thing off the floor and started beating it into a new shape. I'd never thought of doctors as having any skill with tools, other than scalpels. Mossler just wasn't like the doctors I'd known back home, the kind who chewed you out for every little thing without knowing damn-all about hauling someone out of a smashed car at 2 A.M. in the rain. If Dave was going to fall for a doctor, why couldn't it have been someone like Mossler? I wouldn't have minded that so much. Sally always looked at me as if I should be carrying her bag and opening doors for the princess.

Thinking of Sally reminded me that I had to write Dave. I had to. I glanced at the clock, and it gave me no help at all; I had plenty of time before my next work shift. Fairley followed me into the off-duty lounge, and cleared his throat.

"Uh—Pat?"

I looked at him, almost grateful for an interruption. I just hoped he wouldn't start up again; we'd settled our lack of passionate involvement in the first month on Station. "What?"

"You've been acting funny since the Berenson run. It still bothering you?"

I shook my head.

"Something is. You've been—the others have noticed too."

I thought of telling him where to go, but on the Station he couldn't. Silently I took the printout from my locker and handed it to him. He should know the name; I'd told him about Dave before. His face hardened.

"Tough," he said finally, handing me the printout without meeting my eyes. "That's bad."

"Yeah." Suddenly I wanted to cry, and I wanted a shoulder to cry on. But Fairley—for all the complex reasons the psychs still don't know—wouldn't do.

"From what you've said—he'll take this really hard."

"Anyone would," I said, and surprised myself with the venom in my voice.

"Yeah. Well—I'm sorry, Pat."

"It's not me," I said, still sharply. "And I can't—he's not—"

"He's going with that doctor, didn't you say?"

"Yeah." I took a long shaky breath. "I hope she's there." I hope she cares, I thought savagely to myself. I hope she knows what she's done.

"I'm sorry," Fairley said again. "For anyone—but a good paramedic—that's bad. Listen, the others—do you want me to tell them what's on your mind?"

I nodded. They had a right to know, and—being paramedics themselves—they'd care as much as anyone could without knowing Dave. Fairley left without saying any more, and I poked around on the terminal, writing and rewriting a flat little note that said nothing I really wanted to say. Words wouldn't say it anyway. I had just sent it on to the Communications Center when Mossler showed up.

I have reasons for my feelings about doctors. Any paramedic has seen enough to know what I mean, and the details don't matter. But Mossler didn't seem quite as bad as some others. He was a clear improvement over Halberson, our first medical director, the one who had insisted on the time-on-scene limit. He had listened to us, more than once. And I couldn't ignore the way he kept turning up and smiling at me. I may not like doctors, but I'm normal enough to like being smiled at by intelligent young men.

Now he gave me a friendly grin and settled into one of the lounge chairs. "We're making progress, Pat—any more good ideas?"

"No." I finished closing down my files in the terminal. "Not now."

"You're upset about something—should I come back later?"

"A friend of mine—" I told him, in one long bare sentence, about Dave's accident. He whistled.

"That's too bad. Had you known him long?"

"We were partners over four years." I looked away, expecting the usual question, but Mossler didn't ask that one.

"I'm surprised he didn't come up here with you," he said quietly. "He didn't want to look at the high frontier, huh?"

"It wasn't that." He waited, silently, and eventually I looked at him. He had that professional concerned look some doctors have, alert and listening. It's very effective, until you realize it has about the same depth of meaning as a video-star's wide eyes and open mouth. Right then it made me furious.

"He was in love," I said, biting off each word. "With a doctor—a pediatric surgeon in her last year of residency. *She* didn't want to take a year off to come up here. She didn't want Dave to come. Not that she's given him any promises. Says she's not sure. Says she wants to finish and get her career going."

"And you—?"

"I'm not in love with him." I gulped back that old rage and hurt, and went on. It was true now, whatever it had been a long time ago. "But—I could count on him. For all those years—" I told Mossler some of that. The time we worked a kid with a broken neck down a four hundred foot cliff, a kid who's walking today because we did it right. And my life and his had hung on both our skills. The way we worked wrecks, handled "family violence" the polite name for rapes and wife beatings and too many murders. He'd saved my life more than once, and I'd saved his, and we'd both had the good sense—I'd thought then—not to mess up a good working relationship with anything else.

"It goes sour," I went on. "I saw plenty of that. Crews that start sleeping together end up fighting, or breaking up. We didn't. We were there for each other, 24 hours every other day, and I would trust my life—" My voice failed then, thinking of Dave crippled. I turned away, stiffened as Mossler came up behind me and touched my hair. "Don't—" I managed to say, and he went away. Then I cried it out, or most of it. I know what the rehab people say. Things are better now, and people in wheelchairs have regular sports and all that. But not for Dave. As if he were there talking to me, I knew he wanted nothing but what he'd done. And you can't be a paramedic when you're paralyzed below the waist.

Before I heard back from Dave, the crews had three more EVA trauma calls. Two made it in good shape—because of the change in the Traffic Computer, according to the crew.

"We actually got the IV started and running, and thoroughly secured," said Harry Gold, Red Zero, shift one. "And I got the oxygen mask taped on, and the tubing under control, and we were settled when Max called the computer. Terrific. Nothing came loose. And I was thinking, if we had wider elastic on the masks, that would help." We promptly tried wider elastic on the masks, and it did.

The third, though, nearly halted the whole project. We all had a version of Mossler's "can-opener," and about a dozen of the construction supervisors had volunteered to let their suits be modified with Bob's new screw-on elbow section. We thought we were lucky when the victim turned out to have on a modified suit. We were wrong.

Fairley and I got the call, about midway through our shift. Everything went well until after he had the man hooked to the stretcher frame. Then I heard a muffled curse in my headset.

"What?"

"This—wait. This is a bad one, Pat. And it's Blanchard."

As soon as the patient lock cycled in, I could see for myself. It looked like something had hit the right shoulder; we learned later that he'd been caught between an arriving packet and the ring frame itself. The cargo packet hadn't decelerated enough, and he'd ducked, forgetting that no gravity helped him drop. Anyway, the new elbow joint had been flattened. We'd tried to flatten it before, and the springy coils had always regained their shape—but this time they hadn't.

His vitals were bad; it was clearly a severe crushing injury. We got his helmet off, and I worked on the joint of the other arm. For some reason it resisted unscrewing; I cussed and kept after it. Fairley got oxygen going on him, and reached for the can opener.

That's when he stopped breathing. Like an idiot, I kept clawing at the elbow joint, until Fairley said "Pat!" I looked up. He was glaring at me, mouth bloodstained from mouth-to-mouth, and I scrambled for the Garfield set. He grabbed it, and I took the suction catheter and sponge forceps.

Fairley's one of the best intubators I've ever seen—and he had the endotracheal tube in place in seconds. We connected the oxygen tubing and ventilator, and watched our man's chest begin to rise and fall. His face pinked up. Fairley checked his pulse (fast) and I picked up Mossler's tool to open the suit.

Inside was a mess. There's not supposed to be anything that sharp on the inside of a suit, so even if someone is crushed they won't be punctured as well. But he had several broken ribs, and something (broken rib or suit component) had lacerated his side; blood smeared everything in sight. We thought about putting in a chest tube, and decided he could make it to ER first. We punched in a priority transfer, and rode out the roughness, not happy at all.

Medical wasn't happy either. The collapsed elbow joint had crushed his arm. Even though the human arm flattens out, it's not that flat. Six hours of microvascular surgery later, they still weren't sure he'd keep the arm. And everyone was very sure they wouldn't keep the new suit joint.

Except, of all people, Supervisor Blanchard, when he finally woke up.

"It's not perfect," he said. "But I'm alive—and I was hurt worse than Berenson. I won't lose my arm; I'm too stubborn—" (and he was right about that, too.) "You go back and redesign this thing so it won't collapse, but it'll still unscrew. It's a damn good idea, and I'll fight for it."

"All right," said Mossler, looking at the rest of the medical staff, and us. "I'll help—from this end. But there's something else." And now he looked at us, and I knew he had noticed our error on the transcriptions of the run. "Fancy gadgets are all very well—and we need them—but the most important thing is now, and always was, the basics. The ABCs." He held up his hand and ticked them off on his fingers. "Airway, breathing, circulation. I don't want my paramedics to get so clever they play around with new toys and forget to notice if the patient's breathing."

He didn't have to look at me like that. I was already convinced. For once I had to agree with a doctor's criticism—and I couldn't claim Mossler didn't know what it was like. He did.

"Hey, doc," said Blanchard, already looking more like a crew chief than a patient. "You lay off them—they got me here alive."

"I want them to get everyone here alive," said Mossler. "Everyone we possibly can."

When the group broke up, Mossler beckoned for me to come into his office. I expected another chewing out, but that wasn't what he had in mind. He offered me a seat, and gave me an unprofessional look I couldn't figure out.

"You don't like doctors," he said flatly. Before I could think of an answer, he went on. "I don't exactly blame you. I've seen some real idiots, even in industrial medicine. Maybe particularly in industrial medicine. I knew a guy one time who insisted that all emergency gear be locked up so that the employees couldn't misuse it—had to threaten to call in OSHA to change his mind. And with your friend's problem—"

"I don't—"

"Just a minute," he said, and I glared at the interruption. "What I wanted to say was that I do respect your professional standing and knowledge. If I didn't when I got here, I do now. I want you to know that. You made a mistake today—so have I, plenty of times. But on top of that—" He looked around the room, and then back to me. "I wish you'd quit hating doctors quite so much . . . it makes it hard to ask you out."

"Out?" My jaw must have dropped. That idea was so old-fashioned—and on the Station, where there was no place to go, in that sense—that I almost laughed. He was grinning again.

"Yeah, well—we're not the oldest, or second-oldest profession, but we're old and stodgy enough. Thing is, you're smart, and I like talking to you, but I don't like the feeling that you hate the guts you won't admit I have."

"Oh—you have." I'd admit that much. "But I don't mess with doctors. It doesn't work."

"Look, I'm not declaring undying romantic whatevers. Just interest. I'd like to talk about things, and—" He paused. I waited. "Besides, have you heard what your friend down there has thought up?" He nodded toward the planet outside.

"Dave? What?"

Mossler leaned back. "In free fall, how much do you use your legs in your work?"

"Well—I don't." That was obvious. Nothing hit me for a long moment. Then, "You don't mean—Dave wants to come here? Onto the Station?"

He nodded. "You told me Dave had filed an application when you first did—before he fell for this girl." I nodded. "Well, he's reactivated it. They were about to squash it, automatically, but Timmy—that's Dr. Hargrave in medical clearance, he's an old friend of mine—told me about it. As a joke, I'm sorry to say." I could feel my face stiffen. "Yeah—I feel that way, too. I have a cousin who's a quadriplegic, a lawyer, and she can't get work. Finally started doing legal research at home with a computer and modem, and just doesn't tell clients about her injury. She's got a lightbeam device she uses. Anyway—"

I nodded, thinking hard. Dave hadn't written me yet, and I hadn't heard about his application.

"I don't know if I can make any difference," Mossler went on. "I had a few words with Timmy; he's willing to consider it, if everything else checks out. Maybe. I don't know how your friend—Dave—will work out if he gets here. With the job, or with you, either. But two things, Pat: I'm not here to cause you trouble, and I'm not helping your friend to get a line in with you. If he's good enough—and if he can manage the work—I'd like to see him up here. Low and zero-gravity environments should give a lot of people a chance they wouldn't get down there."

"But he couldn't—he's helpless—" Tears stung my eyes again, thinking of the Dave who had started me in rock work, the hard, muscled legs I'd followed up one cliff after another.

Mossler exploded as if I'd hit him. "He is not helpless! Dammit, Pat, you ought to have more sense than that! You were his partner; he's depending on you to back him—"

"But he can't move—"

"His legs. His legs—that's what he can't move. Helpless! I'd thought you knew more—! He's got everything he ever had except controlled movement from the waist down, and you just said you don't use your legs in zero G." He took a long breath, still glaring at me. "Pat, if you think he's help-less—if you treat him like he's helpless—he can't do it. He wants to try something that's never been done, and he's got to have someone—someone he trusts—who will trust him, believe in him. And that's you. If you're going to hold that surgeon, whatever-her-name-was, over his head—"

"No!" Now I was angry too. "It's not that—"

"Good. I don't know this man—you do. I've got to depend on your judgment of him, in part. You told me about your work together, and he sounded like exactly what we need to replace those who don't return. I know his exam scores, and all that, and he's got plenty of guts or he wouldn't be trying this. But it won't be easy, no matter how good, or how tough, or how determined he is. You haven't worked around rehab; I have. He has to have the respect of someone he trusts and knows—respect, not pity. If he comes up here, you're the only one he'll know. You can't duck it, Pat. If you insist on seeing him as ruined and crippled and helpless, then he'll be useless to us and himself."

I chewed that over. The back of my mind insisted that crippled is crippled, and all the fancy speeches in the world can't change that. Wheelchair races, wheelchair basketball, 'plegics swimming and doing gymnastics—that's all shiny paper and bright ribbon wrapping up the same hopeless package. A few people wheeling around in and out of office buildings doesn't make that much difference. My job, as a paramedic, was to prevent crippling complications to injuries. After that it was someone else's problem.

But now it was Dave's problem. We had never been lovers, no, but we had been partners. We had depended on each other. I had depended on him, when I applied to work on the Station, too. And he had stayed behind. I didn't like the anger that still flickered when I thought of that. Had it been a betrayal? Had I had a right to expect him to leave Sally and come here? More immediately, could I give him the support Mossler said he needed? I found myself shrugging mentally; I couldn't do anything else. If it had happened while we were still partners, I'd have done what I could, and the same applied.

"I'll try," I said, looking up. His face relaxed. "I—I know we spent a shift or so in rehab, when we were in training. I hated it. It seemed so—"

"Hopeless?" When I nodded, he went on. "Yeah, if you only see it for that short time, it does. But my cousin, Gina—I saw what she learned to do, and how she makes it. She needs help, but she can give help, too, with what she's got left. She's not the only one. If we can get people like that up here, give them a chance—"

"But what if it doesn't work?"

"What if anything doesn't work—we try something else. Good grief, Pat, you're the one who thought of making a spacesuit with a screw-on arm—and if that's not a crazy idea I don't know what is."

I found myself grinning. "I'm sure you'll think of something."

"And I'd still like to eat dinner with you sometime," he said.

"I'm not looking for—"

"A lover. Fine. But someone to eat with? Until he gets here?"

I had to laugh. "All right."

The new suits are made with an improved, screw-on elbow joint that's supposed to be immune to collapse. Up here we converted what we had in less than a month. It's amazing how many of those construction workers could do it themselves. Mossler and Jeff Sevier hold a joint patent on the "can-opener"; Mossler promised Fairley his first patent bonus check for his grandmother's wit. And our recent record on EVA trauma shows that we're doing almost as well, injury for injury, as downside services.

In two months I'll be on leave, downside, and talking to Dave. He's determined, and the rest of the gang up here agrees it's worth a try. It's the only place he might be able to work as a paramedic. He hasn't said a word about Sally in his notes, and I haven't asked.

Mossler? Well, he's a nice enough guy, but his real extra-curricular interest is pre-Baroque music. He used to sing with a choir in college, and so on and so on. We're good co-workers, as far as emergency medicine is concerned, but I don't care if I never hear another word about early church music. Or another tape, either.

*Mammalian cloning was not as advanced in 1985, when I wrote this story, as it is now. But the ethical issues are right where they always were, right in the middle of every parent's heart. When does biology become destiny? When does linked DNA become human? Who has a right to whose biology, for what purposes?*

*In the past decade, these issues have become matters of public debate . . . but they are always matters of private anguish.*

# A DELICATE ADJUSTMENT

When the phone rang, Dale fumbled around the bed-side table, finally grabbing the receiver just as it slipped off.

"Dale?" He grunted; the voice went on. "Cancel Tuesday."

"What!" He felt Paula stir beside him at that, and lowered his voice. "What do you mean, cancel! We can't, we—"

"Cancel. Trouble." The line clicked and blanked; he lay a moment, now wide awake, appalled. Paula rolled over, one elbow jarring his ribs. He wasn't sure if she was awake or not. Carefully, trying not to move anything but that arm, he slid the phone back onto the table.

"Dale?" Her voice was sleepy; he took the chance to slide back down into his place, and patted her gently.

"Wrong number," he lied. "It's OK; go back to sleep." She murmured something, rolled back onto her other side, and snored lightly. He felt himself sweating, wanted to lift the covers a moment, but he knew that would wake Paula completely. Cancel? Trouble? What could have happened?

45

Was it a trick, to take their money and give them nothing, no embryo, no (as he thought of it) child?

They had no recourse if that was it. Not as things were, not with the laws on embryo transplant that had been passed in the late '80s. It was so unfair—he forced himself to lie still for Paula's sake, but he was furious every time he thought about it. Embryo transplants limited to federally certified facilities, requirements for psychosocial study on all infertile couples seeking transplants, a fee (to recover "taxpayer's money" supposedly), and then, on top of that, the lottery—because there weren't enough embryos to go around. He remembered the two years of testing, probing, being visited, having their friends and co-workers questioned about them—and then the fee, based on their income tax to make it fair for all income levels, and then the lottery. They had had two chances. They had lost. Three years gone.

They would have adopted a child. But decreasing fertility and increasing abortion rates had virtually wiped out the supply of children in the States. And overseas babies, once a last chance, were no longer available—not since the United Nations adopted the Stearns-Gutierrez resolution in '93. Dale mouthed the words soundlessly: "Adoption of children from underdeveloped cultures into developed cultures is a form of genocide . . ." Better to let them starve at home, apparently. That wasn't what the United Nations resolution had meant, but that's what happened; the charities still used pictures of hungry children, crippled children, to gather money every year. Dale quit giving, but he knew Paula sent money when she could.

Surely it wasn't a trick. He knew some of the women who were pregnant now—pregnant with those government embryos. That was illegal—hell, everything was illegal—but they were pregnant. And Paula's cousin had had hers, a boy. Everything fine, everything normal. He never had understood why it was illegal anyway. If you could transfer an embryo from one woman to another, from a culture plate to a woman, why not use the ones at the Institute? He'd heard the debates on TV—that research embryos weren't normal, they'd been tampered with—that they weren't really human—that they might carry strange diseases—that the clones were an attempt by scientists to create a master race. But he'd seen Sue's baby, a red, wrinkled baby boy who seemed perfectly normal. Where did Congress get the right to regulate reproduction anyway? It wasn't in the Constitution. He lay awake fuming, stomach churning, until the alarm went. They wouldn't get away with this, whoever they were. He and Paula had paid for an embryo—a baby—and a baby they would get.

Marilyn Lewis folded her cold fingers around the plastic cup of coffee and waited for Jennicott, the acting director, to say something. He was shuffling a pile of papers—she could see a computer printout, and a couple of graphs, and something on yellow legal-pad paper. Ken Murry ambled into the room and took the seat beside her.

"Coffee any good?"

She shrugged. Murry grunted and settled back in his chair. She heard it groan in response, and air whistled out of the cushion. She felt, rather than saw, him lean toward her again.

"I think we've got a success in the chimaeras," he murmured. "Come by and take a look, why don't you?"

He knew what she thought of the chimaeras. "Success by whose standards?"

"Mine. Naturally. It's a three-two: classy little thing. Sixteen and going strong."

Despite her ethics, she was fascinated. "When will you sacrifice—?"

"Hush. I don't talk about that. We'll see how she grows."

"She?"

He waved one massive hand. "Historical term. She as in ships, spacecraft, and locomotives."

"Please, Dr. Murry." Jennicott looked and sounded pained. The rest of the senior staff were now around the table; neither Marilyn nor Murry had noticed. Murry waved his hand in a different gesture (Marilyn still wondered how much he had learned from his protohoms), and Jennicott flushed. "We have a matter of grave importance to discuss," he said. Marilyn bent her head to sip the coffee. They had had matters of grave importance twice a week since Tony Baker's heart attack and Jennicott's grasp of power. She was beginning to agree with Ken Murry about the gravity and importance of Jennicott's mind.

After a moment's silence, Jennicott went on.

"We have unacceptable levels of wastage in two units: Dr. Lewis's, and Dr. Praed's." He cleared his throat. "At Michigan, the wastage is never higher than 4.8; I did a literature search last night, and the average cited is in that range. Under ten percent, anyway."

Marilyn took another sip of coffee. She'd expected something like this. Praed was already speaking, his blurry voice rearranging intonations to suit his native tongue.

"Cited, my dear sir. Cited wastage. You cannot believe that these other laboratories cite every cell that goes out the drain, surely." The others nodded. They all knew about wastage figures: they had to be low enough to satisfy the grant committees, and the legislative committees behind those. Some things simply didn't count; no one counted them, or published them, or did anything but squirt water down the pipes afterward. Jennicott looked even more pained.

"That is not the point, Dr. Praed. The point is that if you were to publish now, your published wastage would be much higher. Much. And in my opinion, the Institute is open to severe criticism from—well—several parties, Congress among them. They want to know—they would want to know, that is—where these embryos are going."

"Just a minute, Alan." Murry's drawl cut into the formalities. "What do you mean by want to know where? Have you told them of the wastage?"

"Dr. Murry—"

"Just Ken, Alan; let's not be press-conferencey at this hour of the morning. What, precisely, does Congress—or one of these other hypothetical parties—know about unpublished data from the Institute?"

"That's not for me to say. And I was not speaking of your unit—"

"Bull! We aren't cut off from each other by steel walls. Yet. If someone's blabbing to Congress—and I assume that means Cernak's committee—about our research, when we haven't even published, then they'll be blabbing about mine next. Now, dammit, answer my question." Murry, angry, dominated the table: even sitting down his size was impressive.

Jennicott seemed to freeze in place. "Dr. Murry—Ken, if you'd rather—it is certainly my responsibility to see that all the requirements for full disclosure are met. If that means preparing the committee that oversees our research for the possibility of embarrassment before that embarrassment becomes public knowledge—"

"Then you'll peach like a good 'un. Alan, you're a pimp."

"Stoolie," muttered someone across the table.

"No, pimp and stoolie. Possibility of embarrassment! Poppycock in the original sense. As if you weren't about to precipitate the embarrassment—as if the committe itself wouldn't go straight to the press." Murry sat back again, with another complaint from his chair, and rumbled to himself.

"Nonetheless," said Jennicott loudly over the scurry of whispers. "Nonetheless, I want to know why such excessive wastage has occurred, and where the embryo tissue is." A sudden total silence. Marilyn stared at the table top, and felt the eyes resting on her head. "And I want to know now. Dr. Lewis?"

She looked up the table and met Jennicott's accusing gaze. "I assume, Dr. Jennicott, that the tissue is somewhere in the city sewage system. Have you a reason to think it might be elsewhere?"

"I have no record of its being dumped."

"That's not surprising, since you have only the weekly summaries. On the—"

"No." He shook his head, interrupting. "I have the daily worksheets from your lab as well."

She raised her eyebrows, angry herself, now. "May I ask how? Or will that prejudice me in the minds of your . . . associates?"

"As acting director, I feel it my responsibility to ensure that accurate records are kept. I am not one of those who takes the name and lets the work slip by. Besides, after the Simmons debacle—"

"Very well. Then you should have seen the notations, for each shift, of the serial numbers of the discarded tissue."

"I did. That's how I know too many were discarded." He looked around the table. "You are not aware, perhaps, that a new monitoring system was installed in the Institute drainage this past summer. Briefly, it monitors the protein load in the effluent, and—"

Guffaws around the table. "Protein load? There goes the lab picnic!" That was Ginger Harkness. "I'll never wash dishes in the lab sink again."

"You aren't supposed to—" began Jennicott sharply. Murry interrupted.

"So now the snoops are monitoring our sewage, are they? What do they think we're doing, sneaking embryos home to sell for adoption?"

In the silence that followed, by the look on Jennicott's face, they knew that was exactly what had been thought.

"I wish it had occurred to me," said Ginger into the blankness. "Hell, that would finance a whole new electron—"

"Ginger, no!" Marilyn found herself shaking. "How horrible! That would be—"

"Profitable, though." Praed looked thoughtful. "I see. So many wanting children, and the waiting so long. Yes. And the cost to the thief very low, because of the grants, needing only to take the embryo and transport."

"You see now," said Jennicott, "how serious this is."

"But surely you don't think it's actually happened! A few missing bits of tissue—perhaps something else—" Marilyn realized that she was floundering, saw it in other eyes than Jennicott's. She stopped. When she had her breath back together, she said simply, "I don't believe it. I don't know what model you're using for protein analysis—something's wrong somewhere. But that anyone in my lab would make off with embryos—no."

"Or mine," said Praed quickly, emboldened. "It is not reasonable. How could they be transported and still be viable? The special cases are large and obvious—these cannot walk out the doors."

"You said yourself, Doctor, that the cost would be low—"

"Yes, yes, I did. The money cost, I meant, because of stealing the embryo, but what about transport?"

"You yourself move them from lab to lab."

"Yes, but Alan—" Marilyn shut her eyes a moment; she had almost ordered him to think, something Ken Murry said he couldn't do. "Alan, to transport one even down the hall takes a tank, a rolling cart, and a bunch of wires. No one could simply walk out the front door with something that size without the guard noticing."

"So I hope. I have instituted reviews of external security procautions as well. Dr. Lewis, here is the model of protein analysis of the effluent; it was approved by Dr. Baker before his untimely illness—"

"Tony approved this?"

"Dr. Baker was apprised of the need for some form of reliable accounting." Marilyn wondered if he ever talked like a human. She was beginning to doubt it. "Experts in the field have gone over it, but I want you to see if you can find sufficient error to explain the missing tissue." He passed across a stapled sheaf of paper. "Dr. Praed will want to see it too." Before she could ask why Praed had not been furnished his own copy, Jennicott explained. "Please don't make copies of this—it is quite confidential, as you must realize."

"Yes—all right." She was already immersed in the first paragraphs.

"You'll find it includes a plot of sampling locations; you will find that it can be quite specific about location."

Marilyn looked up. "Oh? What would happen if someone used a different drain than usual?"

"The excess would be noted in another drain, and in the overall totals."

"And just how many grams of protein do you think a few embryos provide?"

"It's all in there, Dr. Lewis. Please read it first. If you have any questions you may confer with me."

Marilyn looked back at the page angrily. Confer, indeed. Jennicott was always conferring, or apprising, or briefing— he never just talked to anyone. She put her finger on an equation as if thinking about it. The symbols seemed to writhe under her gaze.

"Dr. Lewis—" Jennicott again. Marilyn looked up. "We still have matters to discuss. He paused, as if waiting for her to apologize for inattention, but after a long moment went on. "I want you and Dr. Praed to review all personnel files, with particular attention to staff who are free to work here when you are absent. You know your staff better than I, I'm sure; you can find out who needs money, or has recently come into money, or has unsavory connections. By Friday I should think you would have progress to report." He looked at the others. "I need not tell you all how serious this situation is. Nothing must come to the attention of the press—"

"Unless it comes from you or Congress," growled Murry. Jennicott put on a pained look.

"Please, Dr. Murry. And the rest of you must be particularly careful in your own work. Other than human embryos have economic value." With that, he swept his papers into a pile and unfolded himself like a carpenter's rule. When the others did not move, he sharpened his tone. "The meeting is over. I'm sure you all have work to do." He stood stiffly by the door until they had all filed out.

Marilyn headed for the elevator, still seething. She heard the others' footsteps, but no one said anything. Ginger Harkness reached the elevator first, and thumbed the button. The light came on at 10. Marilyn watched as it went on up to 11 before starting back down.

"Embryos," murmured Ginger. "Look out, Ken, or your fancy chimaeras—or is it chimaerae?—will be popping out all over."

"Shut up, Ginger." Ken seemed more abstracted than annoyed; usually he defended his research with more vigor than that.

"What I'd like to shut up," she went on, "is Jennicott—and his fancy sewage monitors."

"Why, Ginger? Been dumping old lovers down the drain?"

Ginger laughed. "Not me. I sell them in the meat market."

"Ginger!" Despite herself, Marilyn couldn't let that pass. Even knowing what Ginger was like. Sometimes she went too far.

"I'm not serious, love." The elevator arrived, and the door rolled back into its slot. Ginger moved to a back corner and leaned on it, waiting to speak until Marilyn, Murry, Praed, and Dick Stovall had entered and keyed in their floors. "It's just—if they can tell from our drains that a few grams of tissue didn't pass through there—it makes me nervous. Suppose that new rationing bill goes through—are they going to monitor all the toilets to find out who's getting black-market beef?"

"Oh, surely not!" Dick Stovall looked shocked. "That's barbaric. Besides, it'd cost too much."

"Dick, barbarians don't have computers and protein sensors. If they don't do it, it'll be because it costs too much, and that's a hell of a protection for my liberty."

"Because it won't cost too much in a few years," murmured Ken Murry.

Ginger flashed him a glance. "Exactly. Besides, how do we know their information is real?"

"I don't—" The door opened on five. Dick Stovall got out. "Good luck," he said. The door closed again. Ken Murry shifted his weight and the elevator car swayed.

"Ken, don't fidgit." Marilyn put her hand on the wall. The door opened on six. He put his big hand on the opening to hold the door, and looked at her.

"You really should come see my pet."

"I really should get to the lab. You know how I—"

"Yeah, but just for the sheer intellect of it. Who else can I brag to? I won't let you stay too long; we're starting another cycle today anyway."

"All right." Marilyn smiled at Praed and Ginger. "See you later. Good luck."

Walking down the hall to Ken's main lab, she was aware, as always of how different labs could smell while still smelling like labs. In the anteroom, she scrubbed and gowned, pulling paper booties over her shoes, gloves over her hands. The room was small; she felt crowded by Ken's size. He reached over her shoulder to open the next door. This set off an alarm, and a light over the inner door. Through a thick pane of glass, Marilyn could see one of his assistants coming to let them in.

"Dr. Murry—staff meeting over?" Marilyn had not been in Ken's lab for months; she didn't know the masked face before her.

"At last. Jo, this is Dr. Lewis from upstairs. She's come to see 458."

The cheeks widened on either side of the mask. "Hi, Dr. Lewis. I'm Jo Cassidy. I took your embryology course in the summer of '92."

Marilyn had never been good at remembering old students, and summer students were a lost cause. She smiled behind her own mask. "I haven't seen you around here—"

"No, I just came this fall. And Dr. Murry keeps me busy—"

"When she's not talking a streak. Come on, Jo—Dr. Lewis has things to do. I dragged her in here with a logging chain, to see our triplet. How's it going?"

"So far, so good. Night crew had to increase the $O_2$. But as it's going, it'll be transplantable by tomorrow." Jo led them toward a tank similar to ones Marilyn had in her own lab. Marilyn glanced around. Several other gowned and masked figures worked at the tables and counters. She assumed they were doing the same sorts of things here that her own students and assistants did.

"Now—look at that." Ken tapped his finger on the front of the tank. Marilyn peered through. Instead of the standard 51mm culture plates in which her own cultures grew, Ken had designed rectangular trays to hold the medium and the cultures. Set into the side of the holding tank was the barrel of a microscope. After a dubious glance at the tiny

smudges of material on the tray, Marilyn put her eye to
the microscope and looked more closely.

"Double chimaeras," Ken boomed over her head, "have
been known since the early '80s. Goat/sheep, that sort of
thing. Curiousities, really, though the protohom line—"

"I know," said Marilyn, twirling the fine-focus. A lump
of cells came sharp, wavered."

"Well, then, what I've got is a triple, here. And more
than that, what I hope I've got is a selective triple."

"I thought the whole idea of a chimaera—"

"No. No, and double no. Think of a mule." He plunged
into his ideas with such enthusiasm that Marilyn almost
agreed that chimaeras were worth the trouble. Finally she
tore herself away, and went on upstairs.

Marilyn shuffled the files on her desk. If the samplings
were right, who would be doing this? She herself was a
prime suspect, but she knew she hadn't. Who else? She
looked at the computer printout of the drain samplings
again. They were arranged in four hour segments, roughly
corresponding to the three shifts. The protein load was
higher on day shift. That was natural. More work went on
in the lab, more things went down the drain. She called
up a week's worth of daily logs on her computer, and looked.
It didn't seem to be as different as that—

An hour's fiddling with the computer, and she had a
group of graphs that showed exactly where the discrepancy
was. And, she was sure, Jennicott had already done this:
he probably wanted to see if she would or could. From mid-
second to mid-third shift, someone had reported wastage
which didn't show up in the drain. If the sensors and
computer were right.

She decided to test that first. Pulling on her gown,
shoecovers, cap, mask, and gloves in the anteroom, she
thought about it. The sensors could be wrong, though the
theory seemed sound. They could be missing tissue because
of sampling error. Maybe they weren't sensitive enough.
Maybe the computer had missed signals from the sensors.
Or it had a glitch in its programming. Or maybe someone

was feeding in false data, like the college students who had changed election results in Iowa last Presidential election. Or maybe—she frowned at the thought—maybe someone in her lab was stealing human embryos. Even selling them.

Dr. Padhari, her senior research assistant, bustled up as she entered the lab itself. "Dr. Lewis—we're behind schedule—"

"I know, I know. Dr. Jennicott had a long talk today."

"So. He does not know the importance of time in research?"

"His time," said Marilyn shortly. "Now—what's up?" Padhari plunged into a quick review of the previous night's work, and the transfers scheduled for that morning. He nodded sharply when Marilyn glanced at the clock. "You see? We can't possibly finish that by noon, and we must if we—"

"All right. Here's what we'll do. We'll transfer the ones, chill the twos—we can do them an hour or so later that way, and try that new cell-stasis technique you told me about on the threes."

"But Doctor—the loss. I am not sure what the wastage will be, but it will be high."

"That's OK. If it's high we will have plenty of embryos to examine for the reason." Marilyn knew she was about to waste thousands of dollars of tissue, but she was in a bad enough mood not to care. If they could spend whatever that fancy protein sampler cost to watch her drains for wastage, she could by God give them wastage to watch. Four hours later, she smiled grimly under her mask, as the last of the wastage swirled down the pipes. She had asked the main computer to dump current figures to her desk; by the time she got to her office, she should have the data to show whether the system worked. Padhari, who had had to weigh every discard, was puzzled but compliant.

Jeri Kinsey, arriving for the second shift, heard about the morning's delay from Padhari. She had already seen the pile of numerical printouts on Dr. Lewis's desk, and she made the connection at once. She felt the prickle of sweat coming out on her neck, but went on with her work silently, listening to Padhari's musical voice. When he turned away, she glanced up, looking for Rickie. He shrugged at her, and she realized that he hadn't caught on.

"Kinsey." Dr. Lewis had come in; her gray eyes seemed even cooler than usual.

"Yes, doctor?"

"We have a problem."

Kinsey felt her stomach clench again, but hoped her face didn't show it. "Dr. Padhari said something about a delay—and you had to dump the threes?"

"Most of them. We tried that cell-stasis thing he'd talked of, but it didn't work. But that's not it. We have some problems with wastage the past few weeks."

"Oh?" Kinsey set down the rack of culture plates she had held, and began marking them. "What kind of problem—I know we lost that rack of twos last week, but I told you then—"

"Not that." Dr. Lewis's voice lowered. "You probably don't know that the Institute installed a protein load monitor in the drains last summer."

Kinsey felt her mind freeze, exactly like the description of a mental weapon in a science fiction story. Then it clicked back into action. "No—I didn't. Did you?" That was slightly cheeky, but then Kinsey knew her reputation. And she was willing to bet that Lewis didn't know, wouldn't have known even if there'd been a memo out on it.

"My point is that the system works—it's accurate—and we have too many instances of reported wastage when no protein went down the pipes."

"Oh."

"Some on your shift, and some on third. And I want to know where that tissue went."

Kinsey knew better than to argue facts. If Lewis said the system was accurate, the system was accurate. And if she had connected the missing tissue with stolen embryos, then the only thing to do was make sure her own neck stayed clear of the noose.

"I don't know." That was always a safe beginning. She

kept her voice low, a little puzzled. "I flushed some of it down myself—those twos last week. But you know we don't have a way to identify who dumps each precise embryo, doctor. We never thought we needed it—" And it was safe, she hoped, to identify herself that way with the powers, with law and order and all the rest of that nonsense. She saw that Lewis took it that way, relaxed just a bit, and nodded, as if to a colleague.

"Then you're not selling our embryos on the black market?" asked Lewis.

"Holy God," said Kinsey, letting her jaw drop. Dr. Lewis smiled, then.

"I take it that means no. Good. I can't think of anything slimier—"

I can, thought Kinsey. Washing them away, just little bits of protein load for the sensors to find—but I won't argue now. But Lewis was moving away, and Kinsey turned back to her work, beginning to shake with the reaction of discovery. So close—she had not known of the sensors—should have suspected. She could imagine what Roy was going to say, and Chris. And the ones who were pregnant now. At least the Harrises had theirs. And her sister. She spared a glance at her professor's back, now bent over a bench on the far side of the lab. If she could only fool Lewis a few more days: but Lewis was notoriously hard to fool. Others had tried; she remembered the Norwegian exchange scientist, who had tried to smuggle in a European reporter. But why, Kinsey wondered, carefully marking the last plate and putting the marker neatly in its place, hadn't the boss warned them? Surely *he* must have known about the protein sensors.

At break, she and Rickie headed for the basement snack bar as usual.

"What's got the doc all upset?" asked Rickie. Wide blue eyes stared at her; Kinsey didn't trust that wide-eyed look for a moment.

"She didn't tell you?"

"Not her. Asked me about how many dumps I'd made this week—I can't remember. I put it on the sheet, just like you said, Kinsey."

"Good. Sounds like the paperpushers in Admin are fussed about something. She wants all the records initialed, and that kind of thing." Rickie swore his usual stale oaths, and tossed his curly hair back.

"Does she think we're goofing off? Me with my thesis coming up, and—"

"I don't think so." Kinsey fed coins into the sandwich machine and punched for her selection. The machine groaned and hummed, finally clicking the door release. She pulled out a meagre stale-looking ham on rye and turned to the microwave. "I think," she went on, "that they jumped on her, and she's just passing it on."

"Yeah, but what about?" Suddenly he leaned his pointed chin on her shoulder and breathed into her ear. "Not about—you know—is it?"

"What?" Kinsey had no need to feign annoyance. "You breathe in my ear again, and I'll clout you. I don't know what about, Rickie. As far as I'm concerned, I've kept my records straight, and I assume you've kept your records straight, and this is just that idiot in Admin making sure we know he's in charge." Rickie stared at her, his mouth loose for a moment. He looked around at the barren little room, scarred from years of neglect, and started to speak, but Kinsey held up her hand. "And if your records aren't clear, Rickie, don't tell me. I don't even want to know. I've told you often enough—"

"Dammit, Kinsey—" His eyes had widened farther, as if he'd caught her intent; she shook her head, scowling.

"Listen, Rickie," she said, biting off each word. "As far as I know, the boss has her hair up about something—I think Admin—and there's no reason. No reason at all. My hands are clean, and your hands are clean—and if they aren't, you can damn well confess to her. I'm not a grant holder, and I don't want to be."

"Okay." He had his own choice now, an orange and the same kind of canned pudding he ate every night. Kinsey shuddered at the thought, but he ate it steadily. "I just asked, is all. Usually the doc is a sweetie, but—"

"Lewis?" Even after the months of working with Rickie,

he could startle her, and calling Lewis a sweetie certainly qualified.

"Sure. Great little lady. Now don't get yourself steamed, Kinsey: I know she's a great scientist, and all that. That's why I'm here, after all; that's why I took her courses. But she's a sweetie, too. Nice face, and figure, and I'll bet she—"

"Is kind to dumb animals," said Kinsey, to stop that in its tracks. "Like first year graduate students, especially male ones." As she had hoped, Rickie turned bright red and shut up, finishing his horrible little meal quickly. When he was gone, she bought herself a carton of milk and sat down again to think. Rickie could make trouble—real trouble—but his neck was even farther toward the noose than her own, and if he wasn't smart enough to see it, she wouldn't worry about him. At least they had planned no transfers for that night— none in fact for a week—and maybe that one could be cancelled. The real worry was who knew what, at what level. If Admin had started bugging Lewis, then someone in Admin suspected. Who? Kinsey thought it over. In the five years she'd worked in Lewis's lab, she had met most of Admin at one time or another. She had better, she decided, find the boss as soon as possible before the leaks let too much out.

Marilyn Lewis took a short nap near the middle of second shift; she was determined to confront her third shift crew the same night, before the second shift could warn them. In her uneasy sleep, dreams of research and old vacations warred for dominance: she found herself climbing a challenging pitch of crumbly granite with a chimaera and two embryos on her rope. Dr. Padhari and Kinsey—unlikely partners at best—were singing a German song she'd heard in Switzerland, while swinging wildly, suspended from a peculiar apparatus of steel rods.

She woke with a snort when her phone buzzed, and shook her head as she stumbled to the desk. Line four— the internal line she and Ken used most often. She picked up the receiver, ready to growl, but it wasn't Ken.

"Marilyn? Ginger. Listen, I need to have a chat with you. Can you spare a few minutes?"

"What about—I'm trying to do that stuff for Jennicott."

"Important. Come on down to my lab, will you?"

"Dammit, Ginger—" She cut that off short, and took a deep breath. Something in Ginger's voice came through, and suddenly she was wide awake. "Are you OK? Are you alone?" She wasn't even sure why she'd asked that.

"In a manner of speaking. Bring a notebook, Marilyn." And the line went dead in her ear. Bring a notebook. What did that mean? Marilyn hunted around in the pile of computer printouts for her favorite red notebook and a pen. She had two hours before anyone from third shift showed up. With a yawn, she pulled on her gown and mask, and stuck her head in the lab to tell Kinsey where she was going.

To her surprise, Kinsey was alone in the lab, and responded to Marilyn's questions without at first seeming to understand their importance.

"Rickie? He said he had a gut bug—it's no wonder, the way he eats. Honestly, Dr. Lewis, even when I was a freshman I didn't try to live on vending machine fruit and pudding."

"Yes, but when did he leave?"

Kinsey turned to look at the lab clock. "I didn't know it was this late—it's taken longer than I thought to do these transfers. I'm not sure. We'd come back from break, and I was—let me think—probably about a quarter of the way through."

"Hmm. Well, I'm going down to Dr. Harkness's lab for a bit. If anyone comes in from third shift, please don't tell them about the missing tissue—I want to ask them myself."

"I understand, Dr. Lewis. I doubt any of them will be here for another couple of hours. Stacy comes in early sometimes, but not this early."

"I didn't expect anyone—just if. I doubt I'll be gone long."

Marilyn glanced in the offices she passed on the way to the elevator. Dark, empty, most of them locked: the secretarial and statistical staff for Embryology Division. A bank of pay phones along one side of the hall; two water coolers, one low enough for wheelchair occupants. The hall branched; elevators to the right, halfway down another hall.

Ahead was a short hall ending in double lab doors, with "Human Cell Systems Research Team: K. I. Praed, Principal Investigator" on the plaque. Through the frosted glass panel she could see light, but no details.

She went on to the elevators; one was only a floor below, and came up at once. In the night silence, the groaning engine and cables were loud; the elevator itself smelled of cleaning solution. Marilyn thumbed the control, then leaned against the wall as the floor sagged under her. When the elevator door slid open, Ginger was waiting, leaning on the wall, with her lower lip stuck out.

"You're missing a research assistant," she said bluntly.

"Rickie?" asked Marilyn, with a sensation of sudden doom.

"Male, blue-eyed, dark-haired, young. Nametag says R. J. Dunkett, Lab 813-A, Human Embryo Tissue, Class-J, Dr. M. Lewis, supervisor." Ginger's usually laughing eyes were cold as gray stone.

"Rickie." Marilyn took a deep breath. "What happened? Is he hurt?"

"You could say that." Ginger moved, and Marilyn followed automatically. But Ginger merely shifted a few feet to one side, and gestured at one of the other elevators, now held in place by a door locked to open. Inside, sprawled against the far corner, Rickie lay in a stinking heap, a pool of vomit drying around him. Marilyn gagged. Behind her Ginger's voice went on; Marilyn felt each word like a hailstone striking cold and hard.

"That's what I found when I called the elevator to go home. He was already dead, but still warm. So I called you—it took you a while to answer, Marilyn—"

"I was asleep." She had never seen anyone dead like that; never seen anyone dead, close-up, but that one cadaver in gross anatomy, that made her decide to go into research instead of clinical.

"In your office?" Ginger's disbelief woke her anger; she welcomed that warmth after the cold shock.

"Yes, in my office. Dammit, Ginger, what are you saying? D'you think I killed him, or what? You know what

Jennicott threw at me—I've been working all day to find out if that damned sensor system works—and it does. And then I tackled my second shift staff, and was waiting for my third shift to come in, and took a nap."

"You said you were working—"

"I had been, and then I slept, and I didn't want to come down here for a friendly chat, if that's all you had in mind." Marilyn hated herself for the shaking in her voice. Ginger's eyes had warmed a fraction, but not into trust.

"I notice you assume he's been killed."

"I—damn, I did. I don't know. It's unlikely—unless—"

"Unless you are having embryos stolen, and he's part of it—or found out. What do you know about him?"

"Look, Ginger, shouldn't we call Security?"

"We will. But I want to know a few things first. Are you selling embryos? Was he selling embryos? And am I likely to be killed for finding him?"

Marilyn took a long shaky breath. "No, I'm not selling embryos—but that protein sensor works—I tested it today myself—and I do have recorded wastage that never showed up. So either someone is selling embryos, or stealing them without selling them, or flushing them down the staff toilets for some reason. I don't know if Rickie was involved. He's only been here one semester. Kinsey knows him better than I do."

Ginger scowled. "If I thought you were—but I don't. You don't think that way, that I can see. Never had to—"

"Ginger—" Marilyn thought of the little she knew of Ginger's background: an inner-city welfare childhood, a chance meeting with a friend of her mother's probation officer, who had gotten her into a summer science program, scholarships and work-study, and a PhD years later than most.

"No, I'm not criticizing. You were lucky. Dammit, Marilyn, I like you; I'd hate to see you in something like that, peddling babies. But something's going on . . ." She glanced at Rickie's body again. "If that's natural death, I'm a blue-eyed blonde Swede. I saw enough of that on the street. So—you don't sell embryos, and you didn't kill him, and you don't know who's selling your tissue or who did— is that your story?"

"That's the truth," said Marilyn steadily.

"Truth or not, don't change a story once you've started," said Ginger. She flashed a quick startling grin. "Them as don't ask don't get lied to; you'd best watch yourself, Dr. Lewis."

"But—"

"Now we call Security. And you'd better stay here; they don't like it if people leave the scene." At Marilyn's puzzled stare, she elaborated. "Security is cops; cops is always cops— that's street, but true. You leave a murder scene, they'll wonder why."

By morning, Marilyn Lewis felt she'd been awake a week, not just one night. She had endured the disbelief of Security ("You mean you're a doctor, and you can't even tell what killed him?"), the pettish annoyance of Jennicott, who dithered in a crisis exactly as she'd expected, the clumsy attempt of Ken Murry to "protect" her from the strain, Ginger's apparent contempt ("What'd you expect? Kid gloves from the iron hands specialists?"), and the nervous backbiting of other staff who seemed to think she'd arranged Rickie's murder just to cause them trouble. Kinsey, on being told, had turned white and dropped a tray of culture plates (luckily empty); Marilyn told her sharply to go lie down somewhere. She left, and returned only just before shift change, quiet as usual. Third shift was so obviously excited by events that Marilyn didn't bother to try springing the wastage problem on them; she knew she could tell nothing from their reactions. That whole shift was wasted anyway. First shift's loss of tissue meant that third had little to do, and Marilyn spent most of her time with Security or staff.

Padhari arrived fifteen minutes before first shift, as usual, and smiled when he saw her in her office. "Ah—today we can make up for yesterday, eh?"

"Not quite. Come on in." In a few brief sentences, Marilyn outlined what had happened, both Rickie's death and the missing embryo tissue. He shook his head.

"I don't know, Dr. Lewis. This hunger for babies—it's normal, of course, but—from our unit?"

"The tissue's missing. If it wasn't used for transfer, then what?"

"I see. You've checked the monitor efficiency—yes, of course, you would. When we dumped yesterday, you were checking—" Padhari was sharp enough, but he had no desire to be a principal investigator. So he'd often explained: he had no liking for "the politicals." "It cannot be this shift. Too many people around—anyone would notice the transfer chambers in the halls or elevators—or even a visitor."

"Visitor?" said Marilyn idly.

"Yes—well—of course the easiest way to take an embryo out is inside a woman." Marilyn stared at him, and kicked herself for not having thought of that. She knew it; had known it for years, but it had become background information, rarely called on since she did no transfer work herself. No clumsy transport chambers, no need for the oxygen tanks, the filters, the temperature regulators, not even the simpler but still conspicuous nitrogen tank for frozen embryos—just slip the embryo into a waiting uterus.

With that thought came another. It didn't even require a visitor. Serial transfers weren't done in humans—but not because they couldn't be done. Large animal embryos were routinely transported in utero—serially transferred from one to another—even other species—until the final surrogate.

"It could be," Padhari went on in his musical voice, his eyes carefully averted, "that no visitor would be needed . . ."

"I just realized that," said Marilyn.

"It would take skill," he went on. "Someone to do the transfer—it would be difficult to do on oneself . . ."

They stared at each other, appalled. "Second or third shift," said Marilyn slowly. "Either a woman comes in—and I agree that's less likely—or a woman from the Institute—and probably from this lab—carries the embryo herself."

"Kinsey?" asked Padhari, then shook his head. "That one lives quietly, needs nothing, has no lovers."

"You know her that well?"

He shrugged. "She is always on time; we have talked a

little, of my family, of my home. She has no envy—a rare thing, Dr. Lewis. It would require the need of someone she loved, if she loves anyone."

"Then Ellison or Peters on third shift," said Marilyn. Her heart sank. She liked all her staff: Kinsey for that cool efficiency, Ellison for her cheerfulness in the midst of the night, Peters for a luminous intensity, a total immersion in research. Which? And why? She could imagine Ellison needing money; she'd seen Ellison's locker bulging with clothes, a new coat every winter, bright patterned sweaters, colorful scarves. Peters was a half-time student, working this job and another: she needed money. But she had seemed so interested, so committed to the research. Marilyn shook her head, clearing it.

"We don't know yet, but we will," she said to Padhari. "Meanwhile, we need to salvage what we can, or we'll lose six months work. If we start today, we can be ready to repeat yesterday's work by Tuesday. If you'll set it up, while I deal with this . . ."

"Of course, Dr. Lewis," he said. "I shall be glad to do that." He gave a jerky little bow, and disappeared toward the lab. Marilyn thought for a moment of calling Tony Baker at home. Surely he should know—surely Jennicott had told him. She wavered, and finally put the phone back down. If he didn't know, it wouldn't help his recovery to hear it. And she needed every spare moment to prepare for that afternoon's conference, the quarterly grant review which always sneaked up on her blind side.

To her surprise, Ken Murry chose a seat across the aisle from her in the small presentation room. She smiled at him; his lips quirked but he looked away. No one sat near her as the room filled. She felt almost guilty, as if she had done whatever they suspected. When Ginger Harkness came in, as Jennicott was moving to the podium, and sat down only one seat away, Marilyn felt the shock. Ginger piled a stack of micrograph cartons in the chair between them, and topped it with two clipboards and a spiral-bound book. She leaned over the pile and whispered, "Now I have something to show—just wait." She winked at Marilyn, who felt her tension ease a notch.

Jennicott coughed, the social cough of a busy man, and Marilyn startled. Ginger leaned back in her seat, obviously unconcerned. The meeting opened with the Virology Division reports. Marilyn drew spirals in her red notebook, pretending to take an interest. Dick Stovall had another 100,000 base sequences of H-131, and a preliminary draft of the paper going to Nature concerning the protein superstructure it coded for. The doctors Armand (Phyllis and Joseph) had to admit that their computer simulation had bombed, but argued quite well for continued funding of the project: conversion of language might get it done. Someone she didn't recognize showed a lot of slides covered with illegible labels.

From Virology to Embryology the reports went in the usual way: research going well, going slowly, stymied; papers in progress, submitted, just out; cost overruns, projections, surpluses (only one of these). Ginger carried the entire pile of micrographs to the podium, and explained (or so Marilyn assumed) how her computer graphics program interfaced with the different imaging technologies to reveal molecular structure. Some of it Marilyn recognized, but some was so far from her own field of interest that she could make nothing of the what she saw. The front row—Congressional aides, Institute administration experts, two science reporters for major publications—took copious notes, even though the official reporter would provide a transcript of proceedings. Then Ken Murry got up, and loomed over the podium to give his report.

Marilyn hardly listened. She knew as much about Ken's research as she wanted to, and it had nothing to do with hers. But as the room achieved the silence of shock, she tuned in again.

"—in short," Ken was saying, "as I've mentioned before, I strongly believe that chimaeras are a better model for this type of research than human embryos. Now that it's possible to provide specific tissue types in the desired genetic mosaic—"

Marilyn stiffened. She couldn't believe it. He had taken advantage of her problems to fight that old battle.

"—less emotional turmoil," he said. "Public resistance to human embryo research continues, and the existence of embryos unavailable for transplant fuels resentment among infertile couples. As well, those who fear a eugenic take-over consider the existence of thousands—no, hundreds of thousands—of cloned embryos as proof that scientists—we, that is—are trying to eliminate so-called normal humans with 'test-tube monsters.' It's precisely this public turmoil which the use of chimaeras can prevent. No one considers even the protohoms human—"

"Just a minute!" Marilyn's anger overcame her manners. "You—"

"Please, Dr. Lewis." Jennicott had turned quickly to silence her. "This is Dr. Murry's presentation."

"Yes, but it—" She shook her head, furious, and settled back, seething. Ken gave her a long steady look before continuing. She had heard the argument before. She and Ken had fought it out for the past ten years or so—he wanting more money for chimaeras, his personal fascination. She had been able to show more results more quickly, working from pure human tissues, truly human embryos— biologically human, she thought quickly. Not human in the sense of persons, of course. But obviously an embryo of completely human genome would provide more and better data about human development, human genetics. And he didn't know even now if he had a stable triplet, a selective triplet.

He argued from the protohoms, as she'd known he would. Not true chimaeras, the protohoms were—had been named—illegal. All had been killed. But she had to admit that the research on tropical diseases, based on the proto-hom models, had been extremely valuable. She suspected that he was trying to reintroduce them, create them by making a protohom chimaera, so to speak, instead of true hybridization. The legal definition of human genetic material was just vague enough—she thought she knew how he could get away with it. But she hadn't asked, not wanting to know.

"I am requesting a reconsideration of grant allocations," he finished up, not looking at Marilyn. "In view of the present situation in Embryology, I feel that the sooner we change to a chimaera model, the better." He nodded and returned to his seat, still not looking at Marilyn.

When Jennicott called her, after Praed had blundered through an incoherent report, she was still angry. But Ginger's warm smile steadied her. As Ken had avoided her eyes, she avoided his.

"First," she said crisply, "I want to give a brief report of progress." She had prepared duplicates for the front row, and this went quickly: a successful insertion for thalessemia resistance, a new line of clone high-survivors that nearly doubled embryo quantity, and a paper accepted by *Human Embryonic Culture Techniques*. "As for internal matters," she went on then, "I was informed by Dr. Jennicott that these would not come under discussion this afternoon. However, Dr. Murry's request for grant reallocation makes some mention mandatory.

"While it is true that the existence of substantial human embryonic tissue is tempting to opponents of human research, the value of such material for research clearly outweighs the problems involved. Even a stable, tissue-specific human/nonhuman chimaera—which I assume is Dr. Murry's preferred model—cannot provide the range of response which a 100% biological human embryo can. As you know, much of my research involves interactions between tissues: control mechanisms that may span several organ systems, for instance. We now have an economical, reproducible biological model for this research: the cloned, biologically human, embryo. Before chimaera research could be beneficial to humans, it would have to be used on a human model. It is much less expensive, and much quicker, to do such research on human embryos in the first place."

"But how do you control the embryos?" asked one of the front row. Marilyn recognized a Congressional aide.

"With ID numbers, and records. The protocols were set up originally by NIH, and are in both the grant proposals and the initial publications."

"But if someone—I mean—" he said, with a fast look at Jennicott, who was making shushing motions, "—if someone wanted to steal—"

"I don't know if you're aware," said Marilyn slowly, "that all embryos are required to be biologically inactivated at the end of an experiment?"

"You mean killed?"

She allowed herself to smile. "More than that; they're research material, as you know, and it's illegal to implant a research embryo, even if one were available. In order to make certain that it couldn't happen, certain genes are altered—in the course of research—so that—"

"Oh, I see." He settled back in his chair, taking the hook. "Even if someone stole an embryo, it wouldn't survive to term. Is that what you're saying?"

More or less, thought Marilyn, and simply smiled.

She tried to get away before anyone spoke to her, but Ken moved quickly to the door, and caught her arm.

"Listen, Marilyn, I had to—you know what I've always said—"

"And you know what I've always said. Dammit, Ken, it's a dirty trick to play—using this to change grant allocations!"

He shrugged. "Name of the game. You've had it fat for years; I've got to try. These chimaeras are worth it; they—"

"I don't care." She pulled loose from him, and strode quickly to the elevators.

Kinsey arrived on time for second shift, as always. The boss had been unavailable; after Rickie's death, she'd almost expected that. Was it murder? Had someone else figured it out? She signed in, and hung her coat in her locker. There'd be plenty of work to do without Rickie. While Padhari explained what he'd set up, she took notes, as usual.

"Can you work alone, Miss Kinsey?" he asked. "Will it bother you, the lab being empty?"

She shook her head. "Where's Dr. Lewis?"

"The quarterly grant committee meeting. She said she would go home from there, after last night."

"I see."

Padhari looked at her, she thought with sympathy. "I think, Miss Kinsey, that you should not be here alone. Have they said to you that they think Mr. Dunkett's death was intended?"

"No one's said anything, Dr. Padhari. Intended—you mean suicide, or—"

"Murder. They have not said suicide. But you must not stay alone. Dr. Lewis mentioned the wastage problem?"

"Yes."

"Yes, well—it is for your own protection, Miss Kinsey. When no one else is here—it is not that we doubt your word, you see, but you should have someone else in the lab."

"Well—" She tried to think. All she could think of was the couple on Tuesday. She looked up as the door opened and Dr. Lewis came in.

"Ah—Dr. Padhari, you're still here. Good. That so-and-so—"

"Please?"

"Ken Murry. Used this as an excuse to argue switching to a chimaera model. Kinsey, I'll be here until about midshift, and I'll be getting you some help. We've set up a full work schedule to try to make up for yesterday's losses."

"I saw that."

"Yes, well—have you worked with any of the other students—other than Rickie, I mean?"

"Stacy—Stacy Peters, she's come in early sometimes. On first shift—not really. I know some of them, but—"

"I'll call Peters, and see if she can come early—she could leave midshift on third, and if someone came in early to be with Ellison—"

"I can do that easily, Dr. Lewis," said Padhari. "I think we should have staff, or someone senior like Kinsey, here around the clock."

"You're right. Damn, I wish Lee wasn't in Europe." Their colleague, Lee Dunstan, was attending the Common Market biomedical research conference and wouldn't be back for another week.

"When will we be making the big section transfers, Dr. Lewis?" asked Kinsey.

"Hmm? Oh, Tuesday. If all goes well, and it had better."

Dale could not call the contact until nearly midnight. No answer the first time. On the second call, a voice he hardly recognized.

"Yeah?"

"It's Dale. Listen, I need to know—"

"Dammit, it's cancelled. He told you—the boss said—"

"You can't do this." He knew as he said it that they could. "We paid—"

"That's not—" He heard a couple of odd sounds on the phone, and then the voice returned. "I can't talk now. It's not a trick; we've had problems. It's not safe now. We'll call you. But not Tuesday; it's cancelled."

"No! I want—" But he was talking to an empty line. He slammed the receiver into the cradle and went back to the den where Paula was curled up, knitting. He stood watching a moment, and almost wished he could drop dead at her feet rather than tell her. She looked up and he saw her face stiffen at the sight of his.

"Dale? What is it?"

"Problems." He came over and took the hand she held out. Her other hand went to her belly, protecting what had never been there.

"The—the baby?"

He nodded. "Paula, they said—"

"They want more money."

"No. They said some kind of trouble. They said—"

"Not Tuesday?"

"No." He watched. No tears yet, just a quiver across her face. He wanted to smash something, throw things: she sat too quietly.

"Not Tuesday. Maybe not ever." Her voice was soft, softer than usual.

He wanted to kill them, the bastards, the ones who had stolen his children—he thought of the doctors' reports. Low sperm count, low motility—and when he asked why, they shrugged and showed him all the things that could do it. The lawns sprayed with one chemical, the orchards with another. Something for the shade trees in the park, something in the water, in chemistry labs (but more likely, they said, the year he spent on his uncle's farm, when his folks were killed).

"I want a baby," she said. He thought of her, of the other reports. Was it the day-care worker, or the seventh-grade gym teacher? Who had given her the infection that scarred her tubes? She looked at him, and now the tears came. "I want *my* baby," she said, crying softly, trying not to upset him. "Just a baby—my baby—just what my mother and grandmother had, all the way back to the beginning." He held her, fighting his own tears, wanting his own babies too. At least she could pretend, could feel that what grew in her was hers. He had no chance at all.

"You'll have a baby, love," he murmured, soothing her. "I promise. It will be OK. I promise."

"I want names," said Jennicott, lips folded primly. "I want names and backgrounds." Marilyn Lewis and Dr. Praed sat each in a red-cushioned chair across Jennicott's wide walnut desk. Not his, actually; it was Tony's desk, and a family heirloom: real walnut, actual wood. Marilyn wondered if he'd found the secret drawer yet, the one Tony had kept chocolates in. She wasn't going to tell him.

"I have names," said Praed. He handed across a list. "I assume, Dr. Jennicott, that you have gone through the same computer analysis that I did: mismatches occurred on second or third shift. Nonetheless I have included first shift personnel because these sometimes substitute." Jennicott looked over the list slowly, running his finger down the pages. He looked up abruptly.

"Dr. Lewis?"

"Here." Marilyn slipped her list across the desk. He glanced at it and then back at her.

"Any further word on that poor young man?"

"From Security? No—they'd tell you first anyway."

"Perhaps. Not suicide, they told me."

"He certainly had no reason to." Marilyn took a breath. "My time analysis showed much the same as Dr. Praed's—whatever happened happened on the fourth and fifth sampling intervals, on the dates listed. That corresponds to mid-second through mid-third shift, on days when we would normally have a high wastage anyway."

"Any suspects?"

"I am not a detective," said Dr. Praed sharply. Marilyn glanced at him. "I am not a political person, and I have nothing to do with this—this ferreting out of any so-called suspect. I have only employed people in my lab that I trust, that I know do good work. If it is true someone is doing this criminal thing, then it is for the professionals, the police detectives to find out."

"But if we could avoid involving the police—" suggested Jennicott. Praed became even stiffer, if possible.

"Even in this country there are worse than police, Dr. Jennicott. To avoid the police, you would use—what? Private, unskilled detectives? Suspicion among colleagues? You saw what happened to Dr. Lewis in the grant meeting—and, Doctor, had I not already been seated where I could not readily change my place, I would not have left you so—" He gave Marilyn a look that heartened her, though she could not have said why.

"He's right," she said quickly. "Murder—that's police business, not ours. And this must be tied in. Tony would say that, if—"

"But Dr. Baker is not here." Jennicott's deprecating smile looked sour. "It is my responsibility, and so far I have regarded the Institute's honor in this—"

"Honor!" Marilyn and Praed spoke nearly together. Praed went on when she hesitated.

"Sir, there can be no question of honor when someone has been killed. You assume now it has something to do with this other—but it may not. Had I known you had not called the police, I would have done so myself."

"I'm glad you didn't, Dr. Praed," said Jennicott heavily. "Very glad, for your sake—"

"Don't threaten me," said Praed. "Don't even try." Marilyn looked at him again, seeing the iron that had hidden so long in his meagre, colorless body. He gave her a sharp look that recognized her recognition and went on. "Sir, I was threatened before—before I ever came to this country, and perhaps you don't know that. I can be frightened, yes—but not by you. Death does not frighten me either; it is a warning, no more."

After that Jennicott seemed to crumple, returning to his usual dither, and dismissing them both after another look at the lists. But Praed refused to leave until Jennicott called the Security and told them to file Rickie's death. Marilyn stayed too. They walked back to the elevators and rode up together. Neither said much.

The police investigators, predictably, were furious with the delay. They appeared at the labs looking, as Dr. Padhari said, like tigers in a goat herd. When they heard the same story from Praed and Marilyn—that Jennicott had authorized the delay—they stormed out. Marilyn felt laughter tickle her mind for the first time in several days. Jennicott was in worse trouble than she was, if the police could manage it. It was too bad Tony couldn't be there to enjoy it too—she decided suddenly to call him. His wife answered on the second ring.

"Tony? Oh, he's outside. I'll get him." Grace Baker, Marilyn thought, always sounded as if she were in a bubble-bath. She heard footsteps on a wood floor, a sliding door scraping in its tracks, and Grace's voice, blurred with distance, calling. Then a long silence, and footsteps coming closer. The receiver rattled in her ear, and Tony's crisp cheerful voice.

"Marilyn—how's it going? Why don't you ever come visit the invalid?"

"You don't sound that sick," she said, already smiling.

"I'm not sick. I never was sick. My heart just decided to take a vacation, that's all." He sounded like the old Tony, wide awake and ready to take on whole Administrations, anyone's administrations, before breakfast. Not at all the way she had seen him last, leaning on his desk and muttering "awfully tired, m'dear—awfully, awfully tired."

"Mmm. Tony, have you heard about the—trouble out here?"

"Trouble? What's old goosefoot got into now? I told him to just hold things together lightly until I got back."

"He didn't tell you?"

"Tell me what? You want to send my BP through the roof, Marilyn? What is it?"

She took a long breath. What first? "You know the protein sensors," she began.

"Yeah," said Tony. "I approved those just before the attack—you know. It was in a memo."

"No," she said, wondering if he'd slipped a bit. "No, it wasn't. Maybe Jennicott forgot—"

"He didn't know," said Tony brusquely. "The memo was in my files—to go out that week, to all of you. But not Admin, not then."

"Oh. Well, anyway, it didn't come, and we only found out about it a few days ago." It was hard to think how few, right then. "He told us at one of the morning conferences—"

"The what?" Tony sounded angry, and Marilyn remembered that he had once sounded off about staff conferences at a national convention. Time-wasting idiocy, he'd called them.

"Jennicott," she said, starting to enjoy this, "has morning conferences two or three times a week."

"No!"

"Yes. All senior staff. And he told us about the protein sensors a few days ago, and we had a discrepancy."

A long silence; she could hear him breathing lightly. Then: "We—who had a discrepancy? A shortage? An overage? What?"

"Dr. Praed and I both. We had signed lab sheets recording embryo wastage that the protein sensors didn't pick up."

"Embryo wastage." A shorter interval. "You mean—by God, you do mean. You're missing human embryos, Marilyn? You and Praed both?"

"Apparently. We've isolated it to one eight-hour period on about fifteen occasions."

"And who worked those shifts?"

"In my lab? Kinsey and Dunkett worked second; Ellison and Peters worked third. And that's the other problem."

"There's more? Alan knew this and didn't call me?"

"I didn't know that," said Marilyn. She took another long breath. "Dunkett is dead."

"Dunkett—"

"The junior assistant on second shift. Under Kinsey—"

"I remember Kinsey. Tough girl. Smart."

"Yes. Rickie came this past fall. Grad student, starting his thesis work this summer. Seemed a good kid. Anyway, he died the night after Jennicott told me about the discrepancy. I'd been working on the figures, checking the protein sensors, and Ginger Harkness found him dead in an elevator."

"Not naturally, or it wouldn't be a problem."

"No. They haven't said what it was, but Ginger thinks poison." She went on describe what she had seen and done, and even (feeling guilty) Jennicott's reluctance to call in the police.

A long descending whistle, Tony's way of expressing emotion. "All I do is have a lousy heart attack, and the place starts busting out with organ stealing and murder. That damned Jennicott—"

"It's not all his fault, Tony—"

"The hell it's not. Nothing like this happened when I was around, now did it?"

But Tony always made her mind run faster. "So why did you agree to the protein sensors?"

"You're right. I wondered about things. I heard things. I knew we had a setup for implant thieves, if anyone thought of it."

"And someone did."

"Yeah. And Jennicott didn't tell me about it. And something else—Alan didn't tell you about the sensors until I told him."

"What?"

"That was—oh—two, three days ago. He called to ask about the quarterly grant report meeting, and I asked how the protein analysis of lab effluent was coming. He'd never heard of it—never bothered to query the computer, though it's one of the listed codes in my file. So I explained—and then apparently he got on it, and then jumped on you. Interesting."

"I suppose. But Tony, what now?"

"Now I think it's time for the eminent Dr. Anthony Baker to take up the reins he so carelessly dropped, that's what now."

"But you—"

"I was taking a vacation. I'm fine. I'll be there in two hours. Don't bother to tell Alan; I want to see his face." The phone clicked off, and Marilyn sat a moment, feeling a mixture of relief and apprehension. If Tony was really healthy, she wanted nothing as much as his reappearance—his usual quiet but effective leadership, his ability to make good decisions in a hurry. Tony's eruption later that morning eclipsed even Rickie's murder. Marilyn heard later how he had come through the main entrance, hardly slowing for the Security station, and stormed into an elevator. He had flung open the door of his office to find Jennicott sitting behind his desk and two policemen leaning on it. She had the rest from Praed, who had gone with the detective who questioned him to be sure Jennicott kept his story straight.

In only three sentences, Tony had Jennicott out of his chair, and Tony himself back in it. Praed said that Tony began questioning Jennicott, the police, and him, as if he were a detective himself. And Marilyn's phone rang a short time later.

"Staff meeting at two," Tony said. "Sorry, but this is necessary." And he hung up before she could reply.

Staff meeting was definitely the old Tony, who firmly shut the door on the police officer who wanted to sit in.

"You haven't the clearance," he said. Then he looked around the long table. "All right. Here's what we have. Two labs definitely have tissue missing: Lewis and Praed. Both have checked, confirmed the discrepancies, and isolated a time that whatever happened, happened. Three other labs may have tissue missing; the amounts are too small to be sure. Two labs have gross overloads. The most likely thing is dumping leftovers down the drains, but it may be that whoever took the tissue from the short labs dumped what they didn't want into these. Here are the figures." He handed out a single-page listing. "You also know that Rickie Dunkett, one of Dr. Lewis's assistants, was found dead in an elevator by Dr. Harkness. He was poisoned; I got confirmation from the police just now. Jennicott had sense enough to have the right tests run. It is possible, according to Dr. Lewis, that Dunkett was involved in the tissue loss from her lab. If so, it is possible that he was killed for that reason: either for doing it, not doing it well enough, or scaring a confederate." He sat down abruptly, but vigorously.

"I don't see any of my senior scientists selling illegal tissue," he said quietly. "If any of you are, I suggest you come to me quietly, in the next 24 hours, and we'll take care of it quietly. The police, of course, are investigating Mr. Dunkett's death, and any of you who have light to shed on that should speak to them. Those whose labs are not involved, try to keep your assistants out of the way, and get on with your research. Those whose labs are involved, if you need additional assistants to keep things on track while you investigate the problems, let me know. We always have kids looking for work in the Institute; we can help out. By the way, Dr. Lewis, I have a replacement for Dunkett—a third-year medical student, if that's all right. She's been working in Dr. Kearns's lab over there, and he says she's very good with embryo cultures. OK?"

"Fine." Marilyn wouldn't have argued then if he'd gotten her a computer technician.

"I'll be in my office, or available by intercom the rest of today," Tony said, standing once more. "And tomorrow, if anyone wants me. That's all."

With Tony back in his office, the Institute settled into uneasy routine. Tony and Marilyn made a brief news tape answering questions about the murder; she hated that sort of thing, but Tony insisted that she had to appear, however briefly. Marilyn found the medical student as good as

Tony had promised; Kinsey accepted her without comment, and by Saturday they were clearly on track for Tuesday's planned transfers. Marilyn accepted Padhari's offer to come in on Sunday, and took the whole day off.

Monday seemed almost normal. No morning staff conference, just an hour looking over the weekend reports. They had chosen to spread the transfers out more, just in case. Marilyn checked on supplies, and found that everything was ready—all the media made and autoclaved, all the glassware, all the instruments. Tony poked his head around her door shortly before noon to report that everything was quiet all over.

By midshift Monday, Kinsey had still heard nothing about Tuesday's embryo transfer and transplant. Surely it was cancelled—but why hadn't the boss said something? She did her work with only one corner of her mind on it, kept an eye on Laura, her new assistant, and tried to decide how to handle this. She couldn't believe the boss had killed Rickie. He wasn't the type for that—though poison, if he killed, would be his way. That doctor might, but how would he get in? They would have plenty of tissue tomorrow, and if the lab transfers were done on time, she'd have plenty of time to take a couple. But it was too dangerous; she didn't want to.

The police had questioned her closely about Rickie, but seemed to accept her meagre information. Perhaps they knew that in most labs an established assistant had little to do with students, who came and went every semester. They must have checked; they'd know that she lived alone, that she spent little, and nothing beyond her salary. The money the boss had paid her—a scant tenth of what he received—she'd given to Ann, in cash, the way she received it. Ann's husband made plenty, and the gifts to various charities would startle no computers coming from that house . . . not that anyone cared, since such gifts were no longer income tax deductions.

She had tried to see the boss several times, but she had no real business in Administration. She was not the sort to spend her break time chatting with secretaries, and everyone

knew it. Surely he would call her, tell her what to do—
Kinsey stared absently into space for a few moments. If she
failed him, he would expose her initial theft—that was the
threat that had kept her doing this so long, at least until
Ann's baby was born alive and well. But now Ann's baby
was alive. They couldn't destroy that—she was sure of it—
and now what could he do?

"Kinsey?" Laura's soft voice broke her concentration.

"Yes?"

"What do you use here for invalidation?" For a moment,
Kinsey didn't understand. Laura went on. "So far these
embryos are open, aren't they? The readouts look like it.
Don't you invalidate them before the gross transfers?" They
didn't call it that, in the Institute: they called it limiting.

That was what had alerted Rickie, too. By law, all research embryos had to be biologically unstable, incapable
of survival even if (by some remote chance, the lawmak-
ers intended) they got into a human uterus. But for Kinsey's
purposes, the embryos had to be stable, viable. Luckily, the
experiments Lewis was doing required open embryos most
of the way; they had agreed, with permission from Tony
Baker, to leave them open until the last transfer step. But
plating the clones out was intermediate, as she told Laura,
whose worried expression eased only partly.

"But couldn't they—I mean, what if someone took one,
or something?"

"They're open. They'd live—I guess. Though these are
sicklers, the alternate gene line to the one Perovski worked
with. But that's why we're so careful." She had said nothing to Laura about the missing tissue, and (according to
Lewis) no one else had either. Not officially at least. It
bothered her, though. Laura was too smart, smarter than
Rickie, a different kind of smart. She might even recognize that the blue threes weren't sicklers at all, but a line
known as Columbia-367, as clean a genome as you were
likely to find in North America.

"But legally—" Laura went on.

"Legally, the boss told me, we're clear because she
cleared it with the Ethics Committee and the Director, Dr.

Baker. We limit—invalidate—whatever—after the gross transfer, when we go to the artificial placentae; it's maintained by a non-physiologic zinc balance."

"Oh—that's neat. We use the old citrate trick."

"Well, that would foul up some of Lewis's work. She published an explanation about five years back, I think it was, in the Academy *Proceedings*. Ask her for the reference; she'll show you."

"She wouldn't mind?"

"No—not Lewis. She's very open." And that was true, though Kinsey had found that openness galling at times. How anyone could be so willing to discuss and explain, and so unwilling to listen . . . It was almost funny, in a strange way. Lewis had let her go early the day Ann had her baby, had wanted to see the pictures when they came back. Yet Kinsey was sure she'd never admit that it was right—or even possible. She shook her head, tightening her lips against the temptation to smile, and went on with her work.

On Tuesday morning, Dale decided what to do. He had heard about the murder at the institute; the victim's identity meant nothing to him, but the name of the lab he worked in did. That must have been the "trouble," that must be the connection. But it wasn't his fault, or Paula's, and the money had already been paid. On the phone, it had been a man's voice. The lab was run by a woman, according to news reports: Dr. Marilyn Lewis. She ought to understand, if she wasn't behind it anyway. He called the Institute. Dr. Lewis was working and could not be disturbed, but she would be free for appointments after 1630. Dale looked at the city map, and made an appointment for 1730. He had to give a reference, but his employers' firm, General Data Development, seemed to satisfy the secretary.

Marilyn and Padhari finished the last of the transfers on schedule. She had a four-hour break before the next sequence, several hours into second shift. They came out of the lab tired, stripping off their gowns and masks. Padhari refused a cup of coffee in her office—he wanted to be home in time for his son's game, he said. Marilyn sank into her chair and kicked off her shoes, gulping half a cup of coffee before she noticed the blinking light on her computer screen. Message waiting. With a sigh, she leaned forward and punched the keys.

Appointment for 1730 with a Dale R. Ivington, from General Data Development. She punched up the general information base, wondering what General Data could want. They weren't pharmaceutical, that she knew of . . . the screen filled with data. Modelling software for engineering firms, mostly, and graphics packages for science. Did they have her confused with Ginger Harkness? Perhaps they wanted to model embryonic development, though they'd have to work hard to better the MassGen system (misnamed, as many things were in science: it had been developed at Sloan-Kettering.) Or protein function; she remembered possible extrapolations of their last paper. She looked at the organization chart: Dale Ivington wasn't listed, but the chart was (she checked the date) almost a year old. A new man, then, looking for a new project to head. That made sense. She confirmed the appointment, which automatically cleared him with Security downstairs.

When Kinsey and the medical student arrived for second shift, Marilyn told them about the appointment. "We'll do the next transfers after that," she said. "Slow them down a little, Kinsey—just in case I'm delayed."

"Cool, or—"

"Cool. If we make the transfer later, that doesn't matter. I don't want to lose the whole batch, though, if this is important enough to stay with. It may be: usually their people don't work this late." Kinsey nodded, and withdrew.

The tap on her door came at exactly 1730. Marilyn had more coffee ready, and a plate of real chocolate brownies from downstairs. It never hurt to feed them, she'd noticed early in her career; as long as she didn't have to cook herself, she was willing. She called "Come in," and a tall, fit-looking man in a good suit entered with a briefcase.

"Dr. Lewis?" Dale had seen her on the telecast, saying that Rickie Dunkett had been a student assistant in her lab, and had appeared normal. She had conveyed authority then, in white lab coat and surgical cap, but now she looked more like his mother-in-law: an educated, cultured woman, fair-haired and slender. He knew he was sweating, and hoped it didn't show on his face.

"You must be Mr. Ivington," she said. He seemed nervous; had he thought up this by himself, and come to her without corporate approval? "Have a seat—would you like some coffee? Brownies?"

"Thank you." He accepted coffee, and sat on the edge of his chair. "Dr. Lewis—you work with human embryos, is that right?"

"Yes, of course. We have a number of projects in hand; right now the main thrust is on embryonic development of tissue-specific diseases. Of course we're trying to learn how to control those diseases."

"I see." He clearly did not understand a word of this, and Marilyn wondered again why he had come. He gulped coffee, then set the cup down. "Dr. Lewis, can you explain to me why Institute embryos are not made available for transplant?" He had thought this question out all day. If she were part of the deal, she should react—and if not, she wouldn't know that he was.

Marilyn stared at him. Her first thought was that he was a reporter, someone from the local TV station trying to get a surprise interview. She answered slowly, and thought how best to call for help.

"In the first place, Mr. Ivington, that would be illegal. A scientist who used research embryos for transplant to infertile women would be out of a job and in prison. In the second place, it would be unethical: a clear violation of my contract as a researcher, and of my duty to the world of science."

"How?"

She frowned, but went on. Surely he had a recorder in that briefcase. "You're aware, no doubt, of the law's intent. Research embryos have been changed by research: we treat them chemically, we do surgery on them. They aren't, in that sense, normal any more. Some people fear that the research we do on diseases would induce diseases, leading to problems in the human gene pool if these embryos were allowed to develop. Related to that is the idea that scientists are trying to breed a super-race. Of course, that's absurd. Evolution is doing quite well, has been for millennia. We do want to remove some dangerous genes, but no one's trying to make something new. But all this lies behind the law as it's written—concern that women who receive human embryo transplants will receive only natural embryos, unaltered by science: neither deformed, diseased embryos, nor supermen."

"I see." He seemed to have relaxed a trifle, and his face held intelligent interest. "But if there were no legal barrier to such action, would you still find it unethical?"

"Oh, yes," said Marilyn, nodding vigorously. "I am a research scientist, not a clinician in infertility. I must have thousands of embryos to work on, if I'm to find out anything. Suppose they were available for transplant. Every time something went wrong and we had wastage, I'd be defending myself against a charge that I murdered potential humans. Ridiculous, but that's how the public is. Right now, the law defines research embryos as human biological tissue, nonviable, and thus not human in the sense of human rights or responsibilities. That means that I can pursue my research—which may end in saving thousands of lives—without interference. And I am not tempted to make a profit off my work, as I might be if I could sell some of the embryos for transplant. As it is, I have grants that support so many embryos a year, and I make sure they're all used in the appropriate research." She leaned forward. "And now, Mr. Ivington, I'll have to ask you what you came for. We have more transfers to do this evening, and—"

She was looking into the end of a weapon. It looked exactly like the ones on TV and in movies: the round opening, the metallic, slightly greasy shine. She stopped, mouth open.

"I want an embryo," said the man, his voice shaking slightly. "I—I paid for it, and I want it, and you're going to give it to me." He would not have pulled the gun on her, but that voice—that tone—when she said the embryos weren't really human, and he thought of all the babies, the "wastage" as she'd called it, flushed down the pipes . . . it was too much.

Paid for it? thought Marilyn. *He's* one of them—one of them taking my embryos. Suddenly she was angry as well as afraid. "What do you mean you paid for it—as a taxpayer, or—?"

"I mean I paid—someone—in this lab—" He was sweating heavily, hardly able to speak. "He—he promised me. My wife—she's been on hormones, getting ready—we paid months ago, and she can't—I won't let it happen. You've got to give us one, you've got to!"

"Who? Who did this?" Marilyn reached for the phone buttons, but he waved the gun and she stopped, her hand in midair.

"I—I don't know. Some man—I've only talked to him on the phone, and the doctor—the one who'll do the transplant. But they called and said it was cancelled. Cancelled! You've no idea what that means—my wife—!" Now he was crying, tears streaking his face, but the gun still firm in his hand. Marilyn pulled her hand back down, clenched it with the other on top of her desk. This was the kind of person who wanted her embryos. This unstable, ignorant, fool! It made her sick. But he was still talking.

"You don't know—what we've tried. No adoptions—we tried the government transplant lottery; that took three years—*three years*, Dr. Lewis, and the fee isn't even refundable, and then we didn't get a chance. And you can't try again for ten years, and by then we'll be over the age limit. And it's not our fault! Me—chemicals, they said—showed me a list as long as my arm. Paula was molested in daycare, she was only a kid—was that her fault? No—but we want a kid, Dr. Lewis. Hell, my family, hers—all the way back to whenever men were men, our families have had kids, or we wouldn't be here—and now they say no." He bent his head, still crying.

She was appalled. She had never thought of it that way, never wanted to think of it that way. People who were infertile—she thought of drug addicts, hereditary genetic malformations, damage from gonorrhea (easily avoidable), chemical damage—but that happened to those who shouldn't have children anyway. The world was full of people—too full—and anyway, it wasn't her field.

She looked at the top of Ivington's head, the dark hair thinning on the crown. A good solid citizen, she had thought when he first came in. Three-piece suit, good-quality briefcase; he might have been a colleague. If he'd been approved for a government transplant, then he and his wife had passed a battery of physical and psychological tests. That's what she'd read. Either the tests had missed his craziness, or—she didn't like the alternative. And he still wanted a child that much—or his wife did. She wondered what his wife was like, surprised herself with that thought. His head came up slowly; she saw the quivering muscles of his cheeks.

"I want my child," he said firmly. Behind him, the door had opened, and Kinsey's startled face stared at Marilyn. "My embryo," he went on. "I paid—it's mine—and I'll blow you away, I swear I will, if you don't give me that embryo."

In that one startled look before she moved, Marilyn saw in Kinsey's face the full understanding of his speech. Then Kinsey jumped, wrenching his arm up and over his head, her other elbow slamming into the side of his neck. The gun flew wide, banging into a file cabinet, and the man slumped in his chair. Marilyn sat as if she'd been hit just as hard.

"Kinsey—"

"Yeah. Yeah, I heard. Someone offered him one of ours, and he took the offer and came to collect. And yes, Dr. Lewis, I did—" She turned, and shut the door firmly behind her. "I did take some embryos. I'll resign, or you can fire me, or whatever. But first let me tell you why."

"But Kinsey! I thought you—I thought you understood; you've worked in labs since you graduated, you—"

"I have a sister." Marilyn stopped, then, waved her hand, and settled back to listen. The man in the chair snorted, and shook his head. Kinsey walked over and picked up the gun distastefully, dropping it into the waste chute in the wall. "I have a sister who couldn't have kids. You don't know how that is, Dr. Lewis."

"He was telling me." It was hard to think. Kinsey, of all people!

"Yeah, well, it's that bad or worse. Ann—it wasn't her fault, or Tom's, or anything but the rotten world we live in." Kinsey paused and took a long breath, jamming her hands into the pockets of her lab coat. "You know, at first I didn't mind it here. I called it tissue, just like you did. I never thought of them as human. But when Ann told me what happened to them, when she kept asking why there weren't enough embryos to transplant—then it got where I could hardly flush them away."

"You should have told me."

"Told *you*? A staff scientist? After the lecture you gave when I started? You didn't want sentimentality, remember? And I needed the job; if I'd told you would you have recommended me for another?" Kinsey searched her face, and Marilyn knew she saw the truth: no. Kinsey nodded, as if Marilyn had answered aloud, and went on. "There was nothing you could do—or would do. So I dumped tissue, and thought I was killing babies, and Ann couldn't get an embryo. When you ordered those Columbia-strain clones, that finally did it. I told Ann I'd get her one. We practiced the transplant at her house—"

"You did it yourself?" Marilyn was stunned, but Kinsey merely smiled.

"Who else? We'd read up on it; you know I have good manual skills. It took several tries, even so. We had trouble getting her the right drugs to synchronize."

"Did she come here?"

"Oh yes. Once every week or so, to have supper with me on my break. Security never bothered us; they knew me, and Ann's IDs are current. We said her husband was traveling on business, and she'd show up with a pizza or something. Anyway, I did the transplant, and the last one took."

Suddenly Marilyn's mind jumped. "You—is that the baby *I* saw—the pictures you brought?"

"Yes." Kinsey's mouth twitched. "Normal. He's a month old." Kinsey looked down at the man slumped in the chair. "I don't know this one. He contacted someone else."

"It was a man," he said dully. "He called me, last week—"

"When?" asked Marilyn. Something gnawed the edges of her mind, demanding attention.

"Monday night—no, early Tuesday morning, about 0230, I think. A phone call, saying it was cancelled."

"But that's when—" Marilyn looked at Kinsey. "Was Rickie in this too?"

"Yes—he had to be, he started asking about the limiting factors, and why we put them in so late. The—the boss said he'd better know."

"Boss? I thought you said you did this for your sister—"

"Please." Kinsey sat on the edge of the desk, and looked down. "I started with Ann—my sister—and that's all I meant to do. But—I was caught. We were. The—the man—"

"Who!"

"I'm coming to that. He said he'd tell you—see that Ann was aborted and sterilized for getting an unlicensed transplant—unless I helped him. That was last summer, early in the summer."

Marilyn could think of nothing to say. Words she'd overheard and never thought of sprang up in her mind; for the first time she understood Ginger's occasional bursts of obscenity.

"You won't believe me when I tell you who it is," said Kinsey steadily. "But I had already decided, after last week, that it was too much. Ann's baby is alive—and by law it's hers, now. They can't change that. The doctor who followed her pregnancy doesn't know; he delivered her, signed the birth certificate. She's safe."

"I—shouldn't we call the police? Or security? Or—" She looked at the man sitting quietly in his chair, apparently harmless now.

"He won't do anything now, Dr. Lewis," said Kinsey. "Besides, we have no evidence—his weapon's down the chute. I'm not going to accuse him . . ."

Ivington looked up at her. "Were you the one—?"

"No. You must've talked to the boss. I got them out, but I didn't make any deals—didn't want to."

"But—" Marilyn shook her head, suddenly feeling completely helpless again. "Kinsey, don't you see? We can't let— you can't let things happen like this. Stolen embryos—they weren't meant to be people anyway. That's not your sister's child, not really—"

Kinsey's eyes flashed. "Dammit, Dr. Lewis! What good is your scientific training if you can't recognize a fact when you see it? 'Meant to be people'—that baby is a baby: you saw the picture. He cries, he nurses, he dirties his diaper, and his damn genome is as normal as anyone's! And how do you define 'your child'? She carried that embryo all the way to term; she's been pregnant with that child, she's nursing that child, she will care for that child until he's grown. If adoption makes a parent-child relationship, doesn't transplant?"

"But biologically—"

"Biologically be damned! People have adopted children for centuries, and considered the child theirs. We aren't just biology, Dr. Lewis. We're biology plus, and when you deny that you're denying facts. It's not sentiment, it's not silly emotionalism, it's a fact: genetic heritage is not the whole story. Besides, that's your argument against Dr. Murry. These embryos are biologically human, 100%; it's only legally that they're not." She looked down at Ivington. "I'm sorry—I wish I could bring you yours, too. But—"

"I still want to know who blackmailed you, Kinsey. And why."

"Dr. Jennicott." Kinsey waited for Marilyn's reaction, and seemed to enjoy it. "Yes, Jennicott. Acting director, and all that. I didn't know he'd bugged the staff lounge—that's where I did the transfer. Apparently he heard one of the first tries, and kept a tape on it. Then on the third, he was waiting when we came out."

"And threatened you."

"Yes. He had plans of his own, and a source of embryos fit in." Kinsey stopped and turned as a knock came on the door. Marilyn nodded, and she stepped over and opened it. Tony Baker stood outside, looking grim.

"Marilyn? I need to talk to you."

"Me too." She started to get up, but Tony seemed to realize that something had been happening, and he came in quickly.

"Trouble?"

"Of a sort."

"I think I know part of it. Miss Kinsey—and who is this?"

"Dale Ivington," said Marilyn neutrally. "He made an appointment to see me."

"I see." Tony pulled a card from his pocket, looked, and nodded. "Well, under the circumstances, nothing I would say would be new to anyone in this room but you, Marilyn. And, if you've been talking to Kinsey and Ivington together, maybe not even that." As always, it seemed Tony took control of any group of people. Kinsey had settled on the corner of Marilyn's desk, facing him; Ivington had turned his chair partway around.

"The police just arrested Alan Jennicott for the murder of your graduate student, Dunkett." He waited a moment, then went on. "Apparently Dunkett called him that night, concerned about the shortage you'd mentioned, and he told Dunkett to meet him in his office. He wasn't on the Security sheets, but the man who was on duty remembers that he came in with a plausible excuse, and was here less than five minutes. It was stupid of him to kill Dunkett; he claims Dunkett was trying to blackmail him, but I suspect he just panicked. The police found connections elsewhere, too. He had a contact in Praed's lab—and that tissue was going to an organ-clone scheme in Idaho. Praed, apparently, doesn't have any strains suitable for transplant. He admitted to arranging five transplants from your lab, Marilyn, but we suspect more; all those have already delivered healthy infants, and I'm sure some are in the pipeline. He did mention Mr. Ivington here, when he was still trying to put the blame on Kinsey."

"What?" Kinsey's ears turned red.

"Oh, yes. Clever Alan—he claimed he'd found out about the transplants, and was planning to confront Kinsey this evening when she brought the Ivingtons' embryo out. Had it all laid out, a careful plan—he had to do something, after he found out about the protein sensors. After all, I might have been getting those reports all along, for all he knew."

Marilyn shifted in her chair. "I simply can't imagine Jennicott—I don't like him, but—"

"Marilyn, he's not like us. You told me once he was a poor excuse for a scientist—and that's right. He's an administrator, a second-rate thinker, and a damn bad plotter; I'd have set my ring up so it couldn't be broken."

"But what about—" Her gesture encompassed Dale Ivington and Kinsey both.

Tony's smile was grim. "Kinsey's on the spot. Jennicott has already implicated her, and it's clear he'll try to make it all her idea. I doubt that myself. Was it, Miss Kinsey?"

"No—I told Dr. Lewis. The first one—that was my sister. I did it for her, and he found it out, and threatened to have her aborted."

Tony nodded. "I suspected something like that. But how are we going to prove it? Mr. Ivington, could you identify the person you contacted?"

He shook his head. "It was all over the phone. My wife's cousin, when her pregnancy got going, she told my wife. It was a doctor—my wife went to see him. He started her on the hormones, and then I got a phone call. How much it would be, where to take the money, and that. I never saw any of them, but I do know where the doctor's office is."

"So do the police; Jennicott told them that." Tony sighed. "And your wife—does she know yet?"

"That there's no—yes." He looked down, and his shoulders shook. Marilyn stared fixedly at the desk top.

"But so far all you've done is pay money and see a doctor—you haven't broken any laws. You're in the clear, Mr. Ivington." He sighed again. "You know, Dr. Lewis, there's been very lax supervision in this department since I got sick."

Marilyn looked up, startled, to meet Tony's dark gaze.

"We have a lot of tightening up to do. You're losing a good assistant, I assume—it might be natural for that assistant to . . . .mmm . . . make a last error or so." Now he was looking at Kinsey. "I doubt we'll ever know *every*thing that went on in this past week—or past few months—certainly we must do what we can to preserve the Institute's reputation for fairness and caring."

"Do you mean—?" Marilyn began to guess what he might mean, but he interrupted.

"I mean that perhaps we haven't convinced the public that we understand and care about their problems, as well as our own research interests. Perhaps Mr. Ivington should go home and bring his wife for a short visit, to tour the facilities—"

"Tonight? Paula? But if we can't—I mean she—"

"I think she might be fascinated," said Tony. He rocked back and forth, staring now at the ceiling. "You know, risk is a funny thing. Some people turn pale, sweat, back down. Others—they enjoy it. Call her, anyway. Suggest it."

"Tony, no!" Marilyn slapped her desk. "It's not right! It's—"

His face sagged a little, settling into the stony determination she had seen turned on others but never on her. "Marilyn, you can't hide from this. Eventually all research has human implications; there's no way to be safe. The proof is that those embryos—*your* embryos— are not only 100% human biologically, at least five of them are human in the full sense of the law. They are babies, Marilyn, with names and futures. Nobody knows what they'll grow into—unless someone transplanted a Columbia strain some years back—but there's every reason to believe they are perfectly normal human babies. It's illegal, yes—but what are you going to do? Kill Kinsey's sister's baby? And the others?"

"Of course not!" She felt tears stinging her eyes despite her anger, and hated herself for that. "I'm not a murderer! I—"

"They are traceable," Tony went on, his eyes distant. "Run a genetic check on all babies born in the past two months, say, and for the next six or seven—assuming all the recipients were in this metropolitan area. Then you could find them, I suppose. But then what?"

Marilyn shook her head, unable to speak. She glanced at Kinsey, and met a look of mingled anger and sympathy.

For her? She couldn't believe that, but she had always liked Kinsey. She shook her head again.

"We aren't hunting babies," Tony went on, finally. "It's a fact: they're human. It's not like someone had transplanted one of Ken's chimaeras. Then we might have to go looking. But these—no. So we let the ones in the pipeline alone, and we don't say a word about the ones already born. But that leaves Mr. Ivington."

"Who hasn't broken the law—yet." Kinsey's contribution was unexpected, her tone challenging.

"So you want me to approve of a last felony, is that it?" Marilyn was surprised that she sounded so calm, bringing it out in the open. Tony cocked his head, watching her.

"I want you to think beyond your next paper," he said quietly. "Beyond the feud with Ken Murry. You're a damn good researcher, Marilyn, but you won't go farther until you face what your research means."

"I don't want to!" She had found her shoes under the desk, and now stood abruptly. "Mr. Ivington isn't the only one who hasn't broken the law yet: I haven't. I'm doing important work, and I want to do it and be left alone!" She saw the naked pain on Ivington's face, and turned away. She heard Tony's sigh.

"It's too late for that. You've already lost embryos. You aren't going to be let alone—none of us is."

"So I should go over to the other side, break the law, just because—" She stopped suddenly, overcome by a sense of helplessness. No one would really believe she hadn't been involved, not if Tony chose to tell it that way. As if he'd read her mind, he answered.

"I'm not blackmailing you, Marilyn. I know you haven't broken any laws, and God knows Mr. Ivington can testify to that, and so can Kinsey. As far as I know you haven't so much as broken an anti-litter ordinance in your whole life. But being perfect by the law isn't always enough. What the hell is your research for—any of our research for—if we can't see the pain around us?"

"I hated gross anatomy," she said. No one answered, and she turned to face them. "I hated it: this woman with a tumor growing all over her guts . . ."

"So did I," said Tony. "Mine was a withered up old guy with prostate cancer, and I couldn't get it up for two months. Every time I peed I worried about mine. So you and I headed for a nice clean lab, right?"

She had not expected that; she had expected an attack. She stared at him, seeing no condemnation on his face. He went on.

"But Marilyn, that was years ago. I still don't want to dissect cadavers, or work with terminal cancer patients. But I know we have to face the results of our work."

"I don't know . . ." Even to herself, that sounded weak. She glanced at Kinsey, who was frowning at the desk, making patterns with the tip of her finger on its polished surface. "I still . . ." She looked then at Ivington, who flushed.

"I—I wish you'd look at a picture of Paula," he said softly. "It—she's such a—a good person." Before she could answer, he'd pulled out his wallet, slipped a photograph across the desk. She leaned over, looking. It was a snapshot, a laughing young woman with sadness lurking in her eyes. She looked normal, healthy, sane. Marilyn looked up to meet the same sadness, and no more anger, in Ivington's face. She felt her eyes watering again.

"Damn!" She turned away, fumbling for the desk drawer and the box of tissues. They were silent while she blew her nose, dabbed at her eyes. She faced Ivington again. "She's lovely," she said. "And you passed all the tests?"

"All of them." He drew a long breath. "We proved we were infertile, sane, stable in our relationship, financially responsible—" Marilyn held up her hand to stop him. She felt tired and slightly sick. Gun and all, craziness and all, he was so damned nice. If he'd passed the tests— She looked at Tony, who met her gaze steadily.

"Dammit to hell," she said without emphasis. "All right."

Ivington looked at Marilyn, eyes wide. She saw Tony's slight nod, and managed a smile as she slid the phone across her desk.

"You won't know until the tests come back," said Kinsey, stripping off her gloves. "Sometimes it doesn't work—sometimes they abort, partway along."

"But you tried," said Paula. Tears filled her eyes, and she blinked. "You tried to help." She had been as lovely as her picture suggested, even tense and frightened as she had been. Not a drug addict, not a prostitute, not an undesirable who shouldn't have had children—Marilyn could hardly bear to look at her.

"And we saw it," said Dale Ivington, his voice hushed. They had both looked through the microscopes, seen the tiny embryos in their cultures.

"Them," said Kinsey. "You have a better chance with more than one, so I gave you several."

"And now, fellow criminals," said Tony Baker, when Paula was dressed again and in his office. "This is where it must end. Until the laws change, no more: you have both promised not to set any more friends on us—the arrest of your doctor and Jennicott should provide ample excuse. If you lose this baby—and I hope you don't—we can't give you another."

Tony waited until everyone but Marilyn had gone to return to his main concern.

"You know, we haven't solved any problems," he said then. "We've eliminated a very nasty blackmailer—that's always good—but we haven't solved anything. People like the Ivingtons still want babies. We still have thousands of perfectly viable embryos. The world still has too many hungry people, people who wouldn't be at all happy to have Columbia strain embryos growing up. An excellent lab technician is out of a job and in trouble."

"I wish we hadn't done it," said Marilyn. Now that it was over, all her resistance had returned. She didn't wish the Ivingtons any more grief, but it was unscientific, somehow. "I still think—"

"You're a pure researcher, that's your limitation. Do you really think those babies won't grow up happy and healthy?"

"They should—biologically speaking. But if they do, then—"

"Then every embryo you dump is the same as dumping a baby. Right. Face that. If we can't face that, we shouldn't be doing the research in the first place. The whole natural world is like that—thousands dying, a few living—"

"But not on purpose, not—not knowing—"

"We don't know that." Tony stretched, and headed for the door. "We don't know that at all, Dr. Lewis. Maybe it *is* on purpose—did you ever think of that? No, I'm not advocating genocide or supermen: of course not. But honesty, yes. The same honesty that's served science from its beginning. We have to know what we're doing, and admit what we're doing, or we don't know what it means. Besides, one of the things that keeps me in science is sheer blind curiousity about what I don't know."

Marilyn shook her head, defeated but not convinced. "Well, what's going to keep me up the rest of the night is trying to salvage my project: all those transfers."

"You're the one who argued so long. If you don't watch it, you'll get as rigid as Ken about his chimaeras. It's too bad he had that early success with the protohoms. He's so damned convinced that he knows the only right way to set up a human disease system, and it's so obvious to everyone else that it's not . . ."

"Even after this?" Marilyn's gesture encompassed the whole miserable situation. Tony nodded.

"Yeah. They really shouldn't have outlawed the protohoms, I didn't think, but the chimaeras cost too much, are too unstable. Your work is really solving problems—like that thalessemia thing—"

"And creating problems."

Tony shrugged. Marilyn wondered if she'd ever have his attitude towards trouble. "The worst of the problems you create is that you don't see them coming. Learn to do that, Marilyn, and you'll never have to sit through another meeting listening to an Admin type like Jennicott: you'll be my successor." He flipped the light switch and waited until she came through the door before waving goodnight. Marilyn stared at his retreating back. Director? She'd never thought of that. It kept intruding the rest of the night, as she transferred embryos and made the delicate adjustments that kept them from being viable in someone's womb.

*Floods of one kind or another shape all our lives—floods of water, torrents of wind, currents of social change. Through all the floods, some human characteristics remain constant . . . and one of those is a farmer's love for his land.*

# TOO WET TO PLOW

Abel Jacobsen picked up the first warning on the weather-net well before dawn. He'd expected it. Winter snow accumulation was up—the highest in fifteen years, since the first Floatholes were installed—and starting to melt. They'd had plenty of rain already. Cloud patterns and the feel of his gimpy shoulder told him everything else he'd needed, without even the ring around the moon that Joey'd reported the night before. Rain, and plenty of it, and the river already set to bust loose.

They were eating breakfast when the alerts came through. A clamorous double ring on the emergency phone system; Joey answered, and listened, his mouth clamped tight. His eyes stared past them, seeing whatever the watch officer reported. Abel figured he could guess that well enough. Flood on the way. That damn river, he told himself, had a way of waiting until you just got brave enough to take out another mortgage, or just paid one off, and then ripped into everything, knee deep and a mile wide at best.

Joey hung up without saying a word, and sat back down to his food. They all waited a moment, but when he shoveled in a mouthful of hotcakes, Ben asked Abel about the shift to higher nitro in the weaner feed as if nothing had happened. You couldn't push Joey; he'd say it when he was ready. Abel fiddled with his calculator, checking the monitor readings in their silage against norm, and answered Ben, and Ben forked up two more sausages. Then Joey was ready.

"Flood," he said. They all stopped, watching him. They knew it already, being Abel's boys, and bred to that river. He took another hotcake, mopped the corn syrup off his plate with it, and stuffed it into his mouth. "Big one," he said around it. "It'll lift us for certain, that's what they said."

"How long?" Abel was already calculating loads and balances, what they might save, and what would have to go, part of the river's brown cargo.

"A week, maybe, for the crest. They've got two-inch rains all over the upper Ohio, and heavy stuff moving this way. Two or more to come. They say it'll take the snow with it." Joey quoted acre-feet, but Abel put fifty years of Mississippi flood-plain farming to work in his mind and converted it all to rise in feet. Plenty. More than knee-deep and more than a mile wide. He looked around at his sons and their families, the tightness around the eyes.

"Well," he said, as they waited for him, "I hope those damned idiots are right. I swear to God, if we float all the way to the Gulf, I'll swim back upstream and strangle 'em." He pushed back his chair, scraping Ellie's new vinyl flooring on purpose, and the others followed him out into the blowing wet.

It took the Corps of Engineers fifty years to tame the Mississippi, and it took the Mississippi five terrible years of death and destruction to destroy the Corps of Engineers. In the textbooks they called it the Forecast Flood Disaster. In southern Louisiana they don't talk about it. There's no one left to talk. The great shallow bay that replaced southern Lousiana has never been named.

After that, the arguments of the "idealistic" and "unrealistic" ecologists and hydrologists seemed to make more sense. Asked the right questions, inventive Americans answered with, of course, new technology. Hence the Floatholes. The name really didn't fit, since holes didn't float, but the rhyme with bolthole caught on, as did the near-rhyme float-hold. A floak-hold was an escape from the flood, and it floated, and it held—it wasn't a boat. It was anchored in place, held by cables tied to bedrock. It was anything that fit that description, and nothing that didn't fit the description could be built in the cleared area of the Mississippi Main Channel Project.

High above, the Mississippi Main Channel satellite, in geosynchronous orbit, was supposed to keep track of each beacon, notifying Main Channel Control if any one of them moved, came adrift. Only a few feet of downstream movement was allowable, since a drifting farmhouse or barn posed a threat to everyone moored downstream. That system had been tested in smaller floods, the annual spring rises, over the past few years. The beacons worked. The computers were able to track. But this was the first real test, the first major flood since the satellite went up.

Two days later Abel could look east across his farm and see the water. Instead of the dark line of a levee against the dawn, he saw silver, glinting in the first light. No more levees, he thought grimly. They say we don't need levees. I hope they're right. He and Ben drove that way, carefully, in the swamp buggy. Already the little grove of cottonwood and sycamore was half under, dark water swirling around slender young boles, tugging at the drooping sycamore twigs. Abel looked at the drifting trash, gauging the speed of it. He had to admit it was slower there than in the main stream beyond.

By noon it was closer. It was raining, too, a cold soaking rain that drummed on the cold soil. Abel and Joey started the pumps in the hog section, using the methane they'd stored over winter. Ben and Joanne were shifting feed, swinging the silos on their new pivots with the cranes that had cost as much as the whole farm—but on a special loan. If they failed, they wouldn't have to pay for them. Ellie was packing, moving everything in the deep cellar up, and balancing the load for a rise. Before dark, they all drove out to the last bit of dry ground east of the buildings, and picked up strays: three of their own cross-bred heifers that had wandered from the higher west lots, and a couple of hogs, and someone's fresh milk cow. Abel saw a bull stranded on a sandbar out beyond the young trees, bawling like a calf, but he couldn't do anything about it.

The buildings were all above water still, the hog section lowest, then the silos, then the equipment sheds and the house, with the cattle section a foot higher than the house. That wasn't the way Abel had built the farm in the first place, but that's what he had to live with now.

That night they listened to the weathernet all through supper, filling up on hot cornbread and baked beans and corned beef and cabbage. Joey made a bad joke about that meal giving them enough lift on its own, and Abel scowled at him. No sense being dirty-minded, just because there was trouble. He thought of his fields, now a bleak tannish gray with dead grass, the grass that had replaced his winter-sown grains. No more wheat, on this stretch, no more corn. Just the mat of mixed grasses the range biologists gave him. Soggy grass, right now, but supposed to hold even against the river. It didn't seem much like a farm, any more, and he suspected that the government hoped he'd quit, let them turn the land back into forest completely. But he wasn't about to quit. It was his land, and he'd stay on it even if it meant turning the barns into barges . . . even the house.

After supper, Louise called from New Bank. She and the kids had been there all winter; there were no more schools inside the Channel. Joey talked to her longest, then Ben and Joanne talked to their kids. Thirty miles seemed a long way away when they hung up.

Ben sat up that night, and caught the emergency phone on the first ring. He woke them all up: stage one flood, expect stage two by noon, stage three by day after. That took them off the phone system, and put them on radio linkage. Abel and Joey went out to check the hog section, and found that another sow had chosen exactly the wrong moment to farrow. She'd already rolled on three of her thirteen; Abel fished them out while Joey distracted her. They checked the weight distribution and cussed. They had to move two pens—never easy—and of course one shoat got loose in the confusion. Abel decided to eat more pork, no matter what the docs said. The damn pigs deserved to be eaten. They rechecked the balance, and the pumps, and turned on the running lights. Then Joey looked over, his face a question in itself, and Abel shrugged. One on each block and tackle, they set the lines that let the hog section float, lifting as the water came, moored to bedrock yards below, but with plenty of line.

Abel called in his first launch when he got back to the house. Three in the morning; he felt like an idiot on the radio, especially when the operator at Main Channel Control didn't understand "hog section" at first.

"Not 'house' section!" he bellowed back. "Hog—pigs—you know, bacon!"

"Pigpen?" asked the timid voice from miles away.

"No—oh, hell, call it a damn pigpen if you want!" A thirty-five thousand dollar hoghouse, set on a ninety thousand dollar barge, and they wanted to call it a damn pigpen. He gave them the beacon signal code. He felt the floor quiver; Ben had started the main pumps. A wet wind fanned his cheek: Joanne going out to check the silos. The radio buzzed at him, then another voice spoke in his ear.

"You'll have an eight-foot minimum, eleven-foot maximum for at least ten days. How about the house?"

"We're pumping now." Abel could feel the tremor as all four compressors lifted the house off its foundation. Ellie came panting up the cellar stairs, thumb high. That meant she'd sealed the lower cellar, and checked the inner locks. "Sealed and separated," he went on, smiling at her. "You want the house beacon now?"

"Yeah—go on. Give us a beep when you've launched."

Abel gave the number. Across the kitchen, the screen lit on the computer as Ellie hooked up the inboard power and switched it on. She punched in the beacon code. The screen flickered, then steadied, as the Channelmaster computer locked in. Abel gave the computer a grim smile. Something was working right, at least.

Then Joanne slammed in through the kitchen door, mud to the knees, and cussing like two regiments of Marines.

"Those . . . silos . . . " she finally said. Abel didn't hold with that kind of language, and not from his sons' wives especially, but when he saw the silos he could sympathize. One was safely down, resting in a cradle of inflated rubber, moored properly to upstream and downstream bedrock anchors. But the other two—including the big one—were in trouble. The crane had jammed, slipping in the mud as it was carefully designed not to do. Instead of lifting the silo off its locked base far enough for the lower curve to pivot through, it had caught it partway. The silo leaned at a highly unstable angle, downstream high.

"So why'd you pivot it that way?" growled Abel, still angry about the language. Joanne was his son's choice, an Oklahoma girl he'd met at the University, and Abel was still convinced those cowgirls grew up with barn dirt in their mouths.

"The house," she said shortly. Abel knew it as she said it, remembered too that it was his fault. The experts had told him to leave room to pivot all the silos with the upstream high, but he hadn't wanted to move either the house or the equipment shed. Nor had he wanted the silo on lower ground, or farther from the hog section. He snorted. Joanne gave him a worried look. "Listen, I can't free that thing. I've bounced the crane, but the footings are sagging."

He took his anger out on the contractor. "They told me they went to bedrock with those footings."

Headquarters, Mississippi Main Channel Control, occupied a squat block of new construction just outside the Channel markers in southern Indiana. Long before Abel launched the hog section, Channel Control had logged fifteen hundred-twenty eight launchings in the Ohio Valley. The first were on the small tributaries like the Miami, where three launchings were already back down, having floated for only thirteen hours. There the water rose and fell quickly. Downstream, as the swollen tributaries poured in yard after yard of turbid water, the floods came later, and lasted longer. Through the cold spring rains, monitor crews tramped woodland and pasture, checking the rise, the bank resistance, the current's velocity.

✧       ✧       ✧

With all of them working on it, the Jacobsen family got the smaller of the two stuck silos rotated and into its cradle of pontoons. That had been nothing worse than a jammed winch, and Abel had been clearing jammed winches since he first owned one. But the big silo still canted sideways, its high end looming over the walk between the house and the cattle section. It had to come up before it could come down— or it had to gouge a groove in its foundation. The cattle section was still unlaunched, but ready. Abel took another look at the silo, which looked too much like an Army rocket he'd once seen at the county fair, cocked up like that, and then at the water. Running lights on the house and hog section, and the worklights on the silos were all gleaming on a moving skin of black water that half-engulfed the house.

"Launch the cattle," he said to Ben, who nodded. Then to Joanne: "I don't know why everything that goes wrong out here has to go wrong in the damn dark. And you'd better excuse my French, Jo, after what you've been saying."

"I'm sorry, Pop Jacobsen," she said. She could be sweet when she wasn't cussing, and he knew exactly why the boy had married her. "I was just so mad . . . "

"Yeah. Well, now—so it's slipping on the foundations?"

"I think so. Look there." She pointed her worklight upward to the linkage of crane and pivot; raindrops glittered in its ray. Abel nodded. The angle was all wrong. Something had gone bad underneath; he could almost see, in his mind, the footing shifting slowly through the wet soil, forced by the unbalanced weight of the silo. "Worst thing is," Joanne said, "we pumped out of number two into the big one, to get the best average buoyancy. That's what they told us, remember?"

"Yeah. And we can't pump it back, now they're down. How full is it?"

"Twenty-two percent," she said. Quick as always, she anticipated his next question. "If we dump it, we'll be short 30 days. And even then it might not work."

"What if we put maximum lift under it—" Abel snorted as a swirl of wind sprayed heavier rain on his face. His feet were cold. He looked down and realized that the water had crept instep high on his boots.

Ben came jogging back, splashing with every step. "I'll check the hog section while I'm doing it," he called. "Last time on foot, I reckon." They heard the change of sound as the deeper water slowed him. Then a high yelp.

"You all right?"

"Yeah—water's deeper than I thought. Cold, too. Over my boot tops."

"Thirty days—the damn government ought to give us that, after OKing the contractor on that pivot job. If we save the silo itself, that's plenty." And the house, he thought privately, and whoever else is downstream.

"Can we pump from partway down?" asked Joey.

"Don't know. Might as well try." This approach had served Abel well, and he trusted it more than his sons' tendency to consult a computer at every move. Joey clambered up onto the silo's main foundation, and went to work.

They smelled it first, the sweet pungent stench of silage like a reminder of summer in the cold wet. Then the auger motor caught, adding its racket to the storm noise, and gouts of silage spurted out into the worklights. One of them smacked into the water only inches from Abel's feet.

"Aim it somewheres else!" he roared. He couldn't hear Joey's reply, and turned to Joanne, but she'd already left. He saw her lurching toward the hog section, already knee-deep. He yelled. Then he saw Ben wading toward her, and turned back to the silo.

Because of the angle, the augur couldn't empty the silo, but it was down to 12%. Abel helped rig the pontoons. He hoped the upward pressure would substitute for the crane's lift, hoisting the silo enough to clear the base, so it could swing down into the buoyant cradle. The water was knee-deep even on the silo platform, and he began to wonder if they should have brought the boat out for this chore. This water didn't seem to be moving fast, yet he found himself more than once near stepping off the downstream end of the platform when he hadn't headed that way.

Dawn showed a landscape more than half water by the

time they'd done as much as they could for the silo. They
held hands and waded back to the house, Joanne waist deep,
nearly swimming. Abel felt the cold strike clear to the bone.
They had trouble getting in; they were used to the porch
steps, and now the house floated a foot higher.

Ellie had hot coffee and oatmeal, and clothes warmed
by the oven. Abel hardly noticed that none of them had
bothered to leave the kitchen to change. They were all too
cold and wet to care, shivering and miserable. But coffee
and food brought them back quickly.

"It's not fixed," Abel told Ellie, as she put sausage on
to fry. "Damn thing won't go up, and won't go down. It's
just hanging there. What we did, we emptied it as much
as we could, and lashed the pontoons along it. We hope
maybe the river will lift it the rest of the way. Undogged
the cable—"

"No, dad," said Joey, suddenly alert. "I didn't. I left it
tight so it couldn't drop suddenly—"

Abel opened his mouth to say what he thought, and shut
it again. They'd all been tired, and he hadn't thought to
check it. "Undog it after breakfast," he said mildly. "It's got
to be able to come down."

"Think it'll be OK till then?"

"If we don't eat breakfast all day." He chuckled then,
and saw by Joey's puzzled look that he didn't understand.
Ellie did, reaching over with her long cooking fork to tap
his bald spot. She remembered the time they'd eaten breakfast all day—or that's what her folks had said.

During breakfast he noticed for the first time the floor's
gentle quiver under his feet. It made him uneasy. He'd
never been one for boating, though anyone along the river
had spent time in some kind of boat, some flood or other.
He saw Joanne steal a look at the floor when one corner
seemed to dip, and smiled at her.

"Like boats, Jo?"

"No." She shook her head. "I'm a dryland girl, remember?"

"I don't either, and I've lived by this river all my life.
But the way things went, we don't have much choice." He
pushed back his chair and went to the window. The rain

had stopped again. Nothing showed of the rosebushes in the front garden, the yard fence. They'd forgotten to take down the kids' tire swing, and the ropes dragged at the tree limb, the tire jerking against the current. He could see land, only a quarter mile away, range grass beaten flat by rain. Beyond that the road to New Bank showed as a silver stripe across the rising land, dipping and lifting again. North, the silo's looming presence blocked most of his view from the kitchen.

He went down the hall to the bedroom, and looked again. Now he could see the floating sections, each with a rippling wake behind it, widening to join other ripples before meeting the house. When he looked down, he could see that a curl of water rose around the blunt prow of the house barge where the cables held it against the current. North was almost all water, beyond his barges, but he thought he saw the wooded point in Armison's pasture, a dark blot against the brown water. East—nothing but river.

He shook his head, thinking. He'd been through many floods on this land, but this was the worst so far—and more was coming. In the old days, the levees held much of it back. His lower fields went under every year, and the house had had a foot of water in it once, but nothing like this.

"How's it look?" asked Ellie from behind him. He turned, seeing the same strain on her face.

"Like a lot of water," he said, shrugging. "I never really thought—" He didn't finish; she didn't ask. None of them had ever thought to see so much water right where the house was—where it would have been without the Floathole technology.

"How deep is it?" she asked.

"I don't know. There's nothing to tell by: everything's under." He led the way back to the kitchen, and peered at the several dials that had been installed. They'd explained all that at the time: the depth finder, the water velocity meter, all the things that made his house seem more like a boat, but he hadn't paid much attention. Now he found everyone clustered around, watching.

"Five feet," said Joey, and whistled. Ellie shivered; Abel

realized she was thinking of five feet of water *in* the house, how far up the wall it would be.

"Well," he said gruffly, "at least we're floating. They were right about that. Now let's get that cable fixed, so that monster can come down if it wants to."

Even without rain it was cold and raw outside. They wrestled the dinghy they'd been given off the wall of the porch, and checked the little motor. The government advisors had had plenty to say about landsmen, farmers, using boats on a flooding river, and now that he could see the river for himself, Abel decided to follow their advice. They launched from the downriver end of the porch, and hooked a clip on the cable that connected the house section to the highest Floathole, the number two cattle section.

"It's like a cable ferry," the government man had explained. "That way you can't drift too far away, and you'll use less fuel anyway. And with all the other sections upstream, you can clip to a cable and get back to the house without any power at all."

It had sounded unnecessary, but as the boat moved out into the current, Abel changed his mind. The current wasn't particularly fast, he thought, watching bits of trash drift by, but he could feel its grip on the little boat. Five feet of this water seemed more powerful than five feet of the river he'd fished last year. It was going somewhere, and determined. Their engine snarled, forcing them cross-current to the cattle section. From there, other cables led to the other Floatholes; from each a cable led back to the house. The silos, though, had no cables. Cables ran nearby, but not to, the silo foundations.

After that first ride, Abel decided to do the cow work first. "Otherwise," he explained, "we'll have to make the same trip over. If we feed and clean up now—" They all saw the reason behind that. Ben milked out the cow they'd found the day before, while the others spread hay in the feeders and shoveled manure into the chutes. From there it went below, to the big methane generating tanks. Abel hoped they'd be back down before they had to clean sludge: he couldn't imagine how they were going to get that stuff out while floating. Somehow all the advances that had come in his lifetime had done nothing to change the essentials: if you had animals at all, you had to feed one end and shovel up after the other. Nothing the biologists had done in breeding improved stock had changed that. Now they had methane generators, and automated feeders that weighed each animal and each ration, and all the rest—but in a flood, when anyone could see you needed *less* to do, you got more instead. With the silos disconnected, the automatic feeders didn't work, even though they'd moved enough feed to each floating section for the next two weeks. Back to buckets and barrows, and back to shovels—the tools of Abel's childhood, familiar as well to his father and grandfather.

It made sense to all of them to go on and do chores in the other sections before tackling the big silo: cattle section one, the hog section. It took longer than they thought it would. Rain started again while they were working in the first section, and they had a wet miserable trip over to the next. It was nearly noon—and again the rain had stopped for awhile—when they managed to snare the crane support on the silo while hooked to the house cable, and pulled themselves over to it. The inflated rubber sausages they had lashed under the low end of the silo bulged up, quivering with the current. Abel touched the leg of the pivot crane, felt the vibration in it. Water swirled around the inflated pontoons, tilting the dinghy at an angle away from the silo.

"I'll do it," said Joey, looking up at the locked winch some five feet above the bobbing boat.

Abel nodded. He didn't want to, not at his age, and Ben had never been as handy. Joey reached up and caught hold of the crane legs. The dinghy tilted back again with his shift of weight. Abel felt the sideways lurch when Joey put his weight on the crane, and left the boat. Ben shook his head.

"I hate boats," he said over the sound of water dragging at the pontoons and silo.

"So do I, but we couldn't do this without 'em." Abel peered upward, watching Joey climb toward the winch. He started to yell be careful, but Joey knew that metal was

slippery as well as he did. Better. From below, Abel's view
was obscured by Joey's boots and rain gear. He couldn't tell
what the boy was doing—not boy, he reminded himself. Not
any more, married and with kids in school. It seemed to
be taking a long time, though, and Abel began to wish he'd
gone up himself. They knew the river, his boys, and farming,
but it seemed sometimes they got slower every year. Joey's
elbow jerked outward, then down, then outward again. He
had to be through—

He felt it before he heard it, with that part of his mind
that had learned to feel trouble in time to jump away.
Then the sound: the whine of heavy steel cable unroll-
ing too fast from the drum, the incredible racket of metal-
on-metal that meant something loose, and the concussive
thump as the big silo slapped into the water all at once.
The far end went under, then bobbed up, and a wave
smashed into the house above the barge waterline. The
dinghy shook like a horse determined to ditch its saddle,
and all three of them grabbed for its sides. The half-
submerged pontoons rebounded, rocking, shaking the water
around them and the boat on its surface. Arm-wrenching
jerks, and then Ben and Joanne held it steady against the
rubber pontoons. Abel got his eyes straightened out and
looked up.

Joey still clung to the pivot crane support, but he wasn't
coming down. He wasn't moving at all.

"Joey!" Abel's voice didn't seem very loud to him. Nothing
seemed loud, after all that noise, and Joey didn't move. Abel
looked at Ben and Joanne, met their eyes wide with the
same fear, and heaved himself toward the crane support.

"Dad, you can't." Ben had his arm, hard, and Abel didn't
trust the boat enough to pull free.

"I can, and I will. Dammit, Ben, you have to make it."
Already he suspected he'd find something too far gone to
cure, but he knew Ben had to come home safe.

"Mom Jacobsen's at the window," said Joanne in a small
voice.

"After that crash she would be," Abel said. "Now listen—
don't either of you climb that thing, not until I say. That's

the first thing. Second thing is, if I fall, don't go up there, and don't bother chasing me. I've got a life jacket on. Just get back to the house and report."

"Yes, but—"

"Jo, no buts." Ben had already let go his arm, the habit of years, and Abel pulled himself slowly out of the boat, taking his time to be careful. Joey was on the maintenance ladder, taking up the whole thing, of course, and he had to figure out how to get past him. He didn't want to go up the inside of the support, between the crane and the silo. He'd learned early on not to get between something big and heavy and something hard and immovable. He climbed the ladder as far as Joey's feet. They were still planted on the ladder rail. That was something, he reckoned. He reached up and touched Joey's leg above the rubber boots.

"Joey?" He didn't expect an answer; when one came, he nearly fell with relief.

"Dad. I can't. Can't climb." The voice was one he hadn't heard in years, not since the time the boy had suffered a burst appendix. He'd wanted to play in the district championship game, and hadn't told anyone about his bellyache. Then he'd crumpled, just as the game started, and in just this tight colorless voice had told them he couldn't play. He was sorry, he'd said. "I'm sorry," Joey said now, and Abel grunted.

"What is it?" he asked.

"Arm."

"Winch?"

"Yeah." Abel nodded, having figured that much right. The winch had messed up, as winches so often did, and had either trapped Joey's arm, or ripped it off. Bad enough, but not as bad as what he'd feared, that the cable had snapped and hit Joey in the head.

"I'm here," he said, which was all he could offer right then. "We'll take care of it." Joey didn't answer. Abel hadn't expected him to waste that energy. He looked down into the boat, at the white faces staring up at him.

"He's alive," he said. Joanne's face crumpled a moment, and he turned his eyes to Ben. "I want that rope," he said.

Ben picked up the coil of rope, and tossed it upward, letting it roll open as it flew. Abel caught the loops easily, and nodded. "You get on back to the house," he said. "Check the moorings on this thing, call in a medical emergency, then get back out here with the boat and a jug of coffee."

"Right." Ben let go the pontoons, and let the current haul the boat along the current to the house. Abel turned back to Joey, and knotted the rope around the angle of support and ladder rail. Slowly, carefully, he worked his way upward, wrapping Joey onto the support with the rope. When he had to move between the silo and the crane support, he didn't even notice. From there he could see Joey's face, white around the mouth, eyes closed.

He looked up and sideways, but all he could see of the trouble was streaks of blood dripping down the metal. He sucked his cheeks tight against his teeth. Cursing wouldn't help, not now. A little higher, and he could see what had happened. Somehow the lower drum had released cable too fast when the winch unlocked, and the freewheeling motor had let a coil spin wide. That loop had caught Joey's arm and yanked it into a tangle of cable: luckily the arm had given. One of those splashes when the silo fell must have been his hand. It could have been his body, not his arm, if the arm hadn't gone. Now the stump lay crushed between the coils on the winch.

Abel looked back at Joey's face. This time the eyes were open. "Is it gone?" Joey asked in the same tight voice.

"Yeah." No sense in lying. "Stump's caught."

"I knew something was." He blinked, then went on. "Knife's in my pocket."

"Damn government," said Abel. He knew he'd raised good boys, but right then it was all he could say. They could think, they had guts, and a damn government contractor had stolen his boy's arm . . . "Tourniquet first," he said to Joey. Joey nodded. Carefully Abel hooked an arm into the maintenance ladder and felt under his rain gear for his own knife. He put it into his other hand, unsnapped his jacket, and pulled out his shirt tail. If he'd thought about it, he'd have said that cutting a strip off the tail of his shirt with one hand while clinging to a wet metal ladder was a tricky sort of thing . . . not safe, not good practice. He didn't think. When he had the strip of tough fabric, he shut his knife and replaced it, then moved to a better position.

"Going to tie it," he warned Joey, who nodded without words. It was hard to get his legs wrapped safely around the ladder, hard to get the right angle. He had the tourniquet tied before he remembered that he'd need a stick to tighten it. He didn't want to use the knife. He looked down and saw that Ben and Joanne were already back, with the boat tied on to the crane support. It had taken longer than he thought to climb that far.

"I'm going down," he told Joey. "Got to get a stick for that—"

"Wrench," Joey said, more faintly. "Hip pocket." Abel nodded, realized Joey wasn't watching, and touched his shoulder.

"Right. I'll get it." He felt his way gently along Joey's body, afraid he'd dislodge the wrench, but managed to lever it out from under the rain suit. When he tightened the tourniquet, he heard a faint sound from him, hardly speech. He didn't look. He'd had to place the tourniquet high, nearly at the shoulder. From just above the elbow the arm was either gone or mangled, locked into the coils of cable. He couldn't imagine how Joey had managed not to scream when it happened. Or had the sound been lost in all those other sounds? He pushed that thought aside, and got out his knife again.

"They said two hours, at least," said Ben when Abel clambered past Joey to pick up the coffee. "The nearest helicopter was already on a mission, and the next one is across—" Their eyes turned to the shoreless expanse of water to the east. "They've got more rain on the way, too. Anyway, they're sending a boat that was out, and the chopper. Whichever is first. Dad—"

"He's alive," said Abel, though he thought Ben knew that. "He's lost an arm in the winch. He can't stay there any two hours, though. We'll have to get him down."

"Is he conscious?"

"Off and on. We can't trust him to come down on his own, though." He noticed now, for the first time, that the boat was nearer Joey than it had been. "I've got a tourniquet on it, but it's high—it may not hold."

"You had to cut—?" Ben's eyes moved to Joanne, who had said nothing at all, hands clenched on the blankets she held. Abel nodded, and went on.

"I'll go back up—I know how I tied him on. Put a line around his chest—"

"No." They both stared at Joanne, surprised. "Not just that, Pop Jacobson." With quick gestures, she showed him what she meant. "Between his legs, and then up—and it's a sort of sling. Just around his chest, and with his arm gone it might not hold."

"You've done it, Jo?"

She shook her head. "No, but my roommate at college was from Colorado. She did rockclimbing, and she showed all of us."

"Okay." Abel thought a moment. "Like I said, I'll go up. I'll use Jo's idea, and then I'll run the line over the winch drum and drop the end to you. Then I'll unwrap what I've done, and you can lower him slowly while I come down on the other side, steadying. How about that?"

Ben nodded. "Joanne and I'll take him to the house. Boat won't hold all of us, with him down flat." Abel didn't like that: what if they lost him? But he saw the sense of it.

"Okay. Then you come back, Ben, and get me. Leave Jo with Ellie." He took the extra ropes and started back up.

He could not estimate how long it was taking. Joey roused to drink a mouthful of hot coffee, but choked on the second. Abel feared to give him more. He drank it himself, needing the bite of it, the heat and sugar: he'd felt his arms begin to quiver. Then he rigged the rope sling, explaining to Joey as he went. He didn't know if the boy was awake enough to understand. He dropped the rope's end to Ben, then started undoing his earlier work.

In the end, Joey was able to help, clinging to the ladder with his remaining arm, and lowering his feet one rung at a time, as Abel coached him. Joanne almost stood to reach him, but the boat rocked, and she sank back down. Abel watched as they wrapped Joey in the blanket and started back toward the house where Ellie stood at the kitchen door. They got Joey out of the boat, onto the porch, into the house, and then Ben came back, working his way against the current to pick Abel off the pontoon. He'd edged along the silo on top of them to cut the distance, hardly noticing the danger.

Joey lay on the bed in his room, gray-white around the lips. They had bound the stump of his arm tightly, following directions on the radio. He wasn't supposed to eat or drink, the doctor had said, because they'd want to do surgery. But Abel ignored that. The boy needed fluids, needed nourishment, same as a hurt animal, and he wasn't going to listen to someone miles away in a safe hospital. So a bowl of soup had gone into him, spoonful by spoonful, and then they'd let him rest.

Outside, the dull afternoon showed nothing but rolling brown water on every side. From time to time the radio crackled at them, reporting the location of the boat coming their way. Abel dutifully answered, reading off the depth and velocity of the water passing the house, when they asked, without thinking about the reasons. Fatigue weighed on his mind and shoulders, deadening even the sorrow he felt for Joey, even the worry. When he glanced out the windows at the blunt-ended silo, resting so innocently on its flotation cradle, he could hardly believe he had been up on the pivot crane himself, had managed to get Joey down.

Water depth hit eight feet, eight and a half. With no reference points but the trees in the front yard, their branches now drooping downstream, it was hard to estimate how steadily the water rose. Abel went back to Joey's room, settling into the old chair beside the bed. Ellie sat on the other side, checking his pulse, feeling his forehead from time to time. When the rain began, Abel hardly noticed. But when the wind rose again, and the fine drops ticked against the window, he looked up. Already it was darker. With rain and wind against it, with the river's current stronger every minute, how could a boat get to them? And even if the depth at the house were enough, what about the sandbars, and the young plantations of trees the forestry service had put in? Abruptly he stood, and went to the window. It wouldn't work, and he should have known it—would have known it, if he'd been thinking instead of letting himself sink into self-pity. They'd have to care for Joey themselves, alone, as farm people had always taken care of their own. He switched on the overhead light, ignoring Ellie's frown. Joey looked as bad as Abel felt.

In the kitchen, Ben and Joanne were head-to-head over coffee at the table. Abel could see the streaks of tears on Joanne's face. He glanced at the computer screen.

"When's that boat due?" he asked gruffly.

"They're having trouble," said Ben. "Cross-currents, and this wind and rain. Said they might not make it before dark, and they didn't dare come inshore without good visibility. Too many trees and sandbars and such."

"Always said those damn trees would cause trouble," said Abel without much heat. He saw in Ben's face the worry that this caused, the fear that his father had lost his ability to fight back, to think. For a moment he wondered if he had, but he knew better. He'd caved in like an old, untended levee for an hour or so—an hour they could not spare—but now the native stubbornness that had kept a Jacobsen on the land in the Mississippi floodplain for generations had caught its breath and taken hold once more. He wouldn't waste grief on the time he'd wasted, no matter what came of it. He turned away from the table, poured himself a cup of coffee, and took the last cold sausage from the drainer. As he bit into it, and remembered last night's fury at that miserable sow, he suddenly realized that he was hungry. They'd given soup to Joey, but no one else had eaten since breakfast.

He sat down heavily, mouth full of sausage, and waited until he'd swallowed before sipping the coffee. Ben and Joanne waited, silent. Then Abel looked at them, forcing himself to smile.

"Could be a whole lot worse," he said. "Could be, and isn't. You kids do the late chores yet?"

They looked shocked, both of them. Abel took strength from that, too. "Come hell or high water," he said, "stock's got to be fed, and that fresh cow needs milking."

"But we can't leave Joey—" began Ben.

"Your mother's doing the nursing," said Abel. "We've got to get the work done, and while we're doing that we can figure out what to do for Joey besides what we're doing."

"I wish we had a small boat we could take him in," said Joanne. "Something small enough to be safe going out through the trees, but big enough to be safe on the open river. Then we could meet that boat."

"That dinghy isn't it," said Ben. "Even if we were better at handling it, I wouldn't want to try it out on the river itself."

"Chores," said Abel again. He led the way to the door.

The chores had their own rhythm, enforcing a harmony on them. Abel leaned into the stray cow's flank, milking her out, and listened to the way Ben and Joanne moved in and out of step as they carried the feed, dumped it into the troughs, shovelled manure. By the end of the first cattle section, they were working smoothly together, a team that had functioned this way for years. They had come to the hog section before the thought that had struggled to come out broke free of his worry. He stopped, staring vacantly at the sow with her piglets. Then he went back to work, without saying anything, thinking it over. He foresaw the protests of the medical teams at the other end of the radio—but that's exactly where they were, out of reach.

Before they left the hog section, he took the vet kit off the wall and checked it.

"What are you doing?" asked Ben, coming up behind him. Abel said nothing, pointing to the nested vials of pharmaceuticals, the neat coils of tubing, the packets of needles. And the three large bags of saline solution in the bottom . . . recommended by their vet, to keep on hand for emergencies. He'd used them, too: twice on a calf, and once on a piglet.

"But—it's for animals," said Joanne. "We can't—we aren't doctors . . ."

Abel shrugged. "The doctors are a long way away, Jo. If I can start an IV on a pig, why not on Joey?"

"For one thing, they don't stick people in the neck," said Joanne. "You could tie that pig's snout down, but—"

"That vein in his arm is bigger than the pig's neck vein was," said Abel. "Besides—if it comes to that or letting him die, I'm not going to let him die." Before they could say more, he lugged the kit out to the dinghy and got in. They followed, silently, and said nothing on the way to the house. From that side, they could see the light in Joey's room, and Ellie sitting there like a painted picture.

Once back inside, Abel set the vet kit in the hall. The kitchen smelled of cooking food; he realized that someone— probably Joanne—had put something in the oven during the afternoon. Now she moved around the kitchen, heavily as an older woman, laying the table and opening cans of vegetables. Abel went back to check on Joey. He looked no worse, but didn't answer when Abel called his name softly. Ellie just shook her head.

Supper was a silent meal: pot roast, potatoes, carrots, peas, eaten quickly and with scarcely a word spoken after saying grace. Ellie came out, filled her plate quickly, and ate in Joey's room. Abel was thinking how he could ask on the radio for the kind of medical advice he wanted, when it erupted in a squall of static that stabilized into a voice. Abel grabbed the mike. The boat couldn't make it in, he was told, but they'd send the helicopter at daylight. If it wasn't storming too badly. Abel kept his temper, and asked his questions quickly. Their reaction was about what he expected. He kept asking, insisting that if they couldn't do anything, they ought to tell him how. Finally he worked his way up past the first level of emergency radio crew and advisors, to a voice he'd heard in the background. And that voice, quiet and precise, told him exactly what to do and how.

"If you miss," the voice said, "you realize you'll make things worse . . ."

"I realize." Abel bit back what he wanted to say, which

was that no one else was likely to realize as well as he did . . . he, after all, had held Joey as a newborn infant, slick and blood-streaked as he came from the womb. But the voice went on, asking now about the drugs in the vet kit, and Abel had to peer closely at the labels, spelling out the chemical names, and reciting the concentrations. He began to forgive the voice for its earlier arrogance: now that whoever it was had decided to cooperate, he was going farther than Abel had planned, beyond mere fluid replacement. Maybe he was a good doctor—by which Abel meant someone who agreed with him. If, that is, Abel could get the IV line in.

"Don't feel too bad if you can't," the voice finished up. "It takes most people quite a while to learn to do it consistently. And it's going to be harder on your own son."

It would be harder to *lose* my own son, Abel thought. He signed off the radio, and looked around at the others, who had listened to this exchange in silence. He thought about it. Would any of them do better? Ben's eyes dropped; Ben hated giving shots, and always let Joey do it. Joanne had her back to him, doing the dishes; that was a message in itself, since she hated housework. He'd seen the fear in her eyes, when she looked at the needles. And Ellie, too, looked away, shaking her head silently. Abel looked at his own hands: big, blunt, hard with years of work . . . but deft, skillful, obedient to his mind's command. He sighed, and picked up the vet kit.

"It won't get easier for waiting," he said. "You heard that." They nodded, still silent, and Ellie came with him.

He went slowly, all the same, careful with each step as the years had taught him. When he was ready, the bag of saline hung from the old hatstand, tubing full and carefully cleared of bubbles. Strips of tape lay ready to hand, stuck on the headboard of the bed. Ellie's narrow sewing ironing board was ready to stabilize Joey's arm after the line was in. He had scrubbed Joey's arm, wondering briefly why the big vein, usually so prominent, seemed half its size. But that was obvious when he thought of it . . . the difference between an empty sausage casing and a full one. He went over the doctor's instructions again, aloud, to Ellie, then opened the first of the needle packets.

It was harder than he would have believed to force himself to pierce Joey's skin . . . it seemed that half a life went by while he held the needle poised over the vein. Joey lay so still, so helpless . . . and the arm he held was so limp. Abel let out the breath he was holding, took another, and forced himself to slide the needle through the skin, straight at the vein he could see.

"It may roll sideways," the doctor had said. "And it may be collapsed. You should feel a sort of pop when it goes in, if you're lucky . . ."

He felt no pop, just a vague resistance, but Ellie's sudden gasp made him look at the back of the needle. A little blood ran out of it. Quickly Abel grabbed the end of the IV tubing and slipped it into the cuff on the back of the needle, only then remembering that he was supposed to slide the plastic catheter farther into the vein off the front. He pulled the tubing out, eased the catheter forward, got the inner needle out, and reinserted the tubing. Blood pooled in the end of the tubing, coloring the solution. Tape, he thought, and then—no, check to see if it will run. He nodded to Ellie, who carefully thumbed the flow control on. The blood in the end of the tubing disappeared, and he could see a steady flow from the hanging bag to the drip chamber underneath.

"Turn it off a second," he said. When the flow stopped, he reached over and got the first piece of tape. The doctor had said something about a fancy way to tape the catheter in place, which allowed the lines to be changed, but had finally agreed that simply taping the whole thing down tight would do. Abel finished with a soft cloth tie that held Joey's arm flat on the ironing board. Then he reached up and turned the drip back on, wide open as the doctor had told him.

After that, it was—as Abel liked to tell it later—no big deal to wait until dawn. He didn't admit how he'd felt when the first bag of fluid had no effect, when the first dose of drug the doctor had suggested didn't seem to do anything, when the whole day's tiredness fell on his shoulders all in a lump and he thought he could not do one more thing. But midway through the second bag, Joey had roused, briefly—long enough to complain. His arm hurt like hell, he said, and Abel gave him two of the pain pills the dentist had given Joanne the year before. He told the doctor afterward, and listened unmoved to the tirade that followed.

"He's got to rest," he said finally. "If he hurts too much, he'll thrash around and get worse . . . I've seen it with animals. Sometimes if you just knock 'em out so they don't hurt, they'll make it."

"Well, be sure he keeps breathing," said the doctor. "The big danger is respiratory depression—not breathing well—or nausea. If he vomits and chokes on it, we've got big problems."

"We've got problems already," said Abel testily. "He'll breathe. And he's never thrown up, not since he was six."

Joey kept breathing, and when the medical helicopter finally arrived, letting down two paramedics in a sling arrangement, he was, they agreed, stable enough for transport. So in the cold gray dawn, Abel watched a blanket-wrapped bundle being hauled into the belly of a helicopter, to be flown to the regional trauma center eighty miles away.

"I'll be back, Dad," Joey had said, moving his fingers in Abel's grip.

"We'll be here," Abel had answered. Promised. He saw in Joey's eyes that Joey took it that way, understood it. Then he pulled his hand away, and let the paramedics wrap Joey in a blanket and a waterproof covering, watched the hook on the end of its cable lock onto the suspension of the big basket-like thing Joey lay in.

And they still, he reminded the others when he came back inside, had the chores to do, flood or no flood. They'd have the flood all week, according to the forecast, and then they'd get to clean up after it, re-siting all the Floatholes back onto their foundations, clearing debris, restoring order.

"One hand short," he said, before he realized the double meaning of it. He saw them wince, and felt it himself.

"Sorry," he said. "I didn't mean—but it's true. And the stock can't wait." He felt that weight on his shoulders, the strength he'd transferred to his sons and would never get back, and wondered how he'd make it through the day. He was going to have to get back into that miserable little boat, and the last thing he wanted was a ride on those unquiet waters.

"Right." Ben laid a hand on his shoulder. Abel looked at it, and it seemed to glow with its own light. His son's hand . . . like his own, hardened with a lifetime of farmwork; unlike his own, belonging to a different self, a different time. He had a sudden vision of hands, passing the farm along: his grandfather's, his father's, his own, even Joey's hand somewhere in the cold floodwaters . . . they all belonged to the land, had served it, foolishly or well, had taken their strength from it, and given back what skill they had. He shook himself mentally, looked at the three of them: son, son's wife, wife of his own, and couldn't find any words for his thoughts.

"Damn government," he said, a lifetime's meaning in it. "Farming's a hell of a life . . . but there's nothing any better. And I'm not quitting for any miserable tree-farmers' theories, or anything else."

"No," agreed Ben.

"He'll come back," said Joanne. Firmly.

"We'll be here." Abel picked up his gloves again and headed out the door.

*Medical ethics from the viewpoint of the research sub-
ject, not the researcher . . . when you have changed
someone's life, what is your responsibility towards him?
When you have been changed, what is your responsibility
to yourself, to your world?*

# GUT FEELINGS

Leonard Sanders awoke the morning after the press
conference in a euphoric daze. He had done it. He—
Leonard Sanders, the wimp, the nerd, the perennial un-
derdog stepped on by everyone—*he* had been on national
television, alongside famous scientists and doctors. They had
praised his courage. They had talked about his contribution to research. And even though he knew they had done
most of the work, he also knew they were right: without
his contribution, his willingness to sacrifice for the good of
mankind, they would never have found, tested, and proved
effective the only chance for thousands of cancer victims.
Colon cancer was on the run because of him . . . and his
crabworms.

He sat up in bed, lifted his striped pajama top, and
patted his slightly rounded belly with complete approval.
His gut rumbled a little, and he chuckled.

"Hang in there, guys," he said. He imagined the odd-
looking little parasites (they'd shown him micrographs of
them) grazing happily along the walls of his gut, finding
every single cancer cell and gobbling it down so that it
couldn't grow into a big cancer and kill him.

His mood lasted through breakfast (bowl of bran cereal,
glass of fruit juice, three pills), through the early news
(displayed on the commuter-bus screen), and the first hour

or so at work. Mr. Stevens even spoke to him, patting his shoulder with approval.

"I never realized, Lennie, that you were helping out with something like that," he said. "Guess you don't need our health-insurance coverage, eh?"

"Well . . ."

"Fact is," Mr. Stevens went on, "if you'd been fully covered for that familial whatsis, you might never have gotten hooked in with that research group, right?" He nodded, patted Leonard's shoulder one more time, and went off smiling to himself. Ed Grantly grinned, a friendlier grin than usual.

"Old fart's always thinking of the bottom line, ain't he?"

"I guess," mumbled Leonard. He wasn't sure quite what Ed meant, but hated to admit it. It still wasn't *fair* that the company health plan wouldn't cover his genetic illness, but Mr. Stevens had a point: the research people hadn't charged him a cent. And he was going to live. He wouldn't die of cancer, be eaten out and rotted all through the gut, as his mother had described it . . . he was going to live. He could think of next year, and plan. He might get that transfer to inventory section . . . even a raise. Dr. Gerson was always telling him to plan ahead. Maybe he could. For a moment, shadowy in his imagination, he saw himself going somewhere with friends, laughing, talking, just like the people on television.

He had just come back from his morning break when the day abruptly changed direction. Sylvia Goldstein called him over to her desk.

"You got a call from those guys at the hospital." Leonard nodded, and took the slip of paper with the number. She put out her hand. "Listen, you're not going to be getting personal calls all the time now, are you? 'Cause if you are, you'll have to clear it with Mr. Stevens or somebody."

Leonard straightened. "Mr. Stevens said he appreciated what I'd done . . ."

"Appreciation's one thing; personal calls on company time's another. Remember." She turned away. Leonard stood there a moment, then headed for his own work station. He didn't have a phone there, but he could use Ed's. He dialled the number carefully while looking sideways at his own screen, to see if an urgent request came in.

They put him straight through to Dr. Gerson. He didn't have time to wonder about that; Gerson's soothing voice flowed into the phone line.

"Leonard? Now I don't want you to worry about a thing . . ." Leonard felt his gut twist in a spasm of panic. They never told you not to worry unless there was something to worry about. "It's just a little . . . uh . . . legal problem."

"Legal?" He didn't even have a lawyer, or know how to find one.

"Yes . . . it's just a formality, Leonard, but you'll be served some papers. A deputy or constable will come by to give them to you. Don't argue with him, and don't worry about it.

"Deputy? Constable?" Leonard could hardly say the words. "They're going to *arrest* me?" His mind built a picture of a prison cell (straight from video shows) with his meagre body cramped into it.

"No, no. That's not what I said. They're going to serve you— hand you some legal papers. Just take the papers, sign where they show you, and come on out to my office. That's what the papers will tell you to do, anyway. If worst comes to worst, we may have to go in and retrieve your . . . uh . . ."

"Not my *crabworms*!" He didn't realize how loud his voice was until he saw everyone's head turn, and Sylvia make an ugly face. "No!" he whispered then. "You can't!"

"Leonard, calm down. Please. Listen a moment." Dr. Gerson's voice went on, explaining something about federal regulations governing research animals, and the idiocy of some animal-rights group, and the courts, but Leonard could make nothing of it. His stomach churned, along with everything beyond it. As soon as the doctor's voice paused, he broke in.

"But you can't . . . please . . ." He choked back the tears. "*You* know—I thought everyone understood now. They're saving my *life*. They're eating my cancers out . . ." The weight of fear he'd lived with for years landed back on him, squeezing these past few weeks of hope into invisibility like a heavy weight crushing a light bulb. Was it that fragile? Could they send him back to that life without hope?

"I know, Leonard. And it won't be for long, I'm sure. Just a few days . . ."

"I won't let you." Leonard glanced around the room, already thinking about escape. "I don't . . . I can't . . ." Beyond the double half-glass doors to the main corridor, he caught a glimpse of movement, something that might have been a uniform. He saw someone from accounting stop, point to the doors.

"Leonard—" But he had already hung up, was now shutting down his own terminal.

"Lennie! What're you—" He ignored Ed and Sylvia, darting into the service stairway where Mr. Stevens never ventured, round and round to the fire door on the next floor down. From there he took a service elevator along with two bins of shredded paper trash and its guardian, a lanky maintenance engineer named Frank. Frank didn't say anything, just hummed a nameless tune. Leonard felt his heart beating wildly. He could imagine the flurry in his office, the sneer on Sylvia's face, the fingers pointing to the service stairs.

Outside, Leonard blinked at the late-morning sunlight. A tan car with a shield stood in the No Parking zone in front of the main entrance some yards to his right. He could see the wire mesh separating front from back seats. He turned to his left, and walked to the corner, where he darted onto a bus just before it whooshed away. He fumbled the fare out of his pockets, struggling with the change as if he'd never handled money before. The driver gave him one quick glance of contempt. The bus was nearly empty; Leonard sat near the front and stared blindly out at the busy streets.

He didn't want to die. He had never wanted to die, that was normal. The research doctors said no one wanted to die, even suicides, but Leonard was sure he himself didn't want to die. Not since he realized he *would*, that he'd inherited his father's disease, and his gut would fill up with cancers—hundreds of them—and eventually they'd get him.

He'd seen people dying of cancer, people getting treatment, all that, and to a scrawny young boy it had been a vision of the worst kind of death. If you don't go in for your checkup, his mother had threatened him, it'll just grow inside you, like rot in an orange, and someday you'll wake up with a hard knot of tumor and then . . . she'd coughed, then, her own face haggard with approaching death. And Leonard had gone to the doctor every three months, hating it, fearing it. He'd been upended on the procto table so many times, probed, scraped, sampled, and each time he came home with a painful, clenched gut and a new swelling on his personal growth of fear. Someday they wouldn't find one of the growths in time. Someday they'd miss one just a little too long, and it would turn cancerous, swell, seed itself.

He tried being good, the easy way for a boy with no talent for athletics, no personal beauty, and not enough belief in life to sample its pleasures. He did what he was told, behaved, wore a clean shirt every day. He never took drugs, got drunk, stayed out late with friends, stole or raped or vandalized. He followed the diet he'd been given, and went dutifully to each appointment. And two days after his seventeenth birthday, they'd found the first malignant growth.

"We got it all," the doctor had told him cheerfully. "Still very small. We're sure it didn't spread. But of course there might be others . . ." Leonard had nodded, all too aware of that. By then his mother was in the last stages of lung cancer, past all the chemotherapy and long past hope. He went daily after school to see her in the hospital, passing down a long hall from the elevator that stank of all the stale bodily fluids leached out by age and disease. With her last words, she reminded him that he would die the same way, and he believed her. He would die, and die horribly, and die horribly while young. So his father had died, and so he would die. He finished high school dutifully, took the first simple job he could find dutifully, and worked every day with the same blank obedience he had shown in school. He lived in the same bleak apartment, rode the same bus, watched the same old television every night. No use making plans: he was going to die anyway. No use making friends: they would have to watch him die, and Leonard, deeply honest, knew they wouldn't want to, any more than he'd wanted to watch his mother die. They would do it—friends did that sort of thing, at least on television—but they wouldn't want to, and he didn't intend to put anyone to any trouble.

Then had come the suggestion from his doctor that he apply to the new research project, and the project itself, and the sudden realization that he might *not* die—at least not for years. The parasites were working, eating away his cancers, and he had had, for those few months, the same feeling he got when a cloudbank suddenly lifted, letting sunlight slant under the gray and return color to the world. Dr. Gerson had pushed him to go on to night school, and he'd done it, even before he believed he had a chance. But he had had a chance: the treatment worked. And he'd felt so good, so *safe* waking up just that morning, comfortable and happy and knowing that the rumble in his gut was only hunger, not something wrong. And then . . . he pressed his head on the chill glass window, trying not to think about living with that fear again. He could not do it. He wouldn't let them . . .

After a few miles, he realized that he couldn't just ride the bus all day. For one thing, he didn't have enough change. He looked around. Two women sat up front, chatting. Someone slumped in the back corner seat. Leonard pulled out his wallet. Thirteen dollars and—he checked his pockets as well—sixty-two cents. No, he couldn't ride the bus all day, not without getting off and getting change somewhere.

They were out of the glittering downtown, and past a grimy intermediate space of failing businesses, pawnshops, and slightly shady light industry, into an older but still respectable residential section. The bus dipped its snout, approaching a stop at a small shopping center. Leonard had never seen it before. He stood up, letting his knees cushion the sway as the bus swerved and halted. One of the two women in front stood too, and he waited a moment, careful not to bump into her, before going down the steps.

"Hurry up, buddy," said the driver. "Don't have all day, y'know."

"Sorry," mumbled Leonard. The bus doors slapped shut just behind him. Across the parking lot was an old, small member of a large supermarket chain, a fabric shop, Crestview Music Center, Miss Lila's Dance Academy, Martial Arts Supreme, and a Christian bookstore, all sharing a sidewalk and overhanging arcade. Small concrete benches offered limited seating along the wall. The woman ahead of him had aimed straight for the fabric shop; Leonard wandered toward the supermarket.

Inside, airconditioning struggled against age. The store smelled of turnip greens, onions, spices Leonard never used. One aisle was given over to oriental foods, with banners in some kind of strange script: he had no idea if it was Chinese or Vietnamese or what. But the worn flooring was clean, the counters dusted. He bought himself a tangerine, a can of fruit drink, and a tunafish sandwich from the display cooler. The checkout girl pointed to the store microwave, but he preferred his sandwiches cold, and ignored it on the way out. He found an empty bench in front of the fabric shop (windows full of draped fabric swirling from bolts of cloth) and ate slowly, thinking.

He might have been fired for leaving so suddenly; people had been fired for less. Jamie Artwell hadn't done any more than call Mr. Stevens a bad name in front of everyone, that time he'd told her she'd have to redo the quarterly reports. If he'd been fired, then he wouldn't be paid at the end of the week, and he couldn't pay his rent without dipping into savings. Even his savings wouldn't keep him for long . . . not more than a month or two at most. The thought of being fired, being broke, having to move (and where?) made the tunafish taste funny.

Even if they didn't fire him, they'd be mad. He could just hear Sylvia Goldstein's voice, accusing . . . "and what did you think you were *doing*, Lennie?" just as if she already had her promotion to section manager. The others would laugh at him. He wouldn't have a chance at the new position opening in inventory section, the one he'd hoped for. And he couldn't imagine how much trouble he might be in with the law. Jail for years and years, probably, and never another good job like this one.

He tried to shrug off these thoughts. Dr. Gerson had told him—so had the others—that dwelling on all the things that *might* go wrong didn't help. Once you've made a decision and done something, they'd said, don't brood on the past. Easy for them. Their decisions were right, or nearly always, and even if they made mistakes they were big people, smart people, and they could talk their way out of things. He couldn't see anyone messing with Dr. Gerson.

And thinking of Dr. Gerson, there was another one who'd be mad at him. Mad at him for hanging up like that, and for not cooperating with whatever it was he'd meant. Leonard stared at the half tunafish sandwich remaining. Sylvia Goldstein was one thing, and Mr. Stevens was the same sort of person, only a man and older and richer, but Dr. Gerson . . . Dr. Gerson wasn't afraid of any of them. He didn't have to be. Leonard swallowed, thought about eating the rest of his sandwich, and decided against it.

He saw the blue-and-white police car turn into the shopping center parking lot as he stood up. How had they found him already? The car eased up a lane of parked cars toward the supermarket; the face Leonard could see gave him an impersonal, bored glance and moved on. Leonard forced himself to move slowly, casually, toward the doorway of the Crestview Music Center. Through smeared plateglass he could see two pianos and a row of electronic keyboards displayed on a stepped stand. He pushed the door, and heard the first four notes of the Beethoven Fifth (never forgotten from eighth grade music appreciation) clang overhead.

"Just a minute," came a voice from the back of the store. "Be right with you." Leonard said nothing. Along the wall opposite the pianos were long racks of sheet music and music books. He stared at them (*Music for Meditation*; *Three Chorales for Small Church Choirs*; *Bayley's Beginning Harmony Worksheets*) while trying to watch the police car out the window. It had stopped in front of the supermarket. A lanky black man got out, walked into the store. Leonard turned back to the music as a gurgling roar from the back of the store suggested its owner might be coming, and where he (or she) might have been.

She was a heavy-set gray-haired woman with bright blue eyes behind thick glasses. "Looking for anything in particular?" she asked, peering at him. She reminded Leonard of his third-grade teacher.

"Not really," he mumbled. "Just . . . just looking, really."

"Oh. Well, sacred choral's at the front, then popular choir and solo, then instrumental. I guess you're not looking to buy a piano, or anything?"

"No," said Leonard. She nodded as if she'd expected it.

"No one does, any more," she said. "Two or three keyboards a month, if we're lucky. I don't know why Mr. Parker bothers, but he says it's important to have a presence. His father had a store near here, you know: Parker Pianos. That was years ago, before the neighborhood changed, if you know what I mean." Leonard nodded, hoping she'd leave him alone. Instead, she let herself down on one of the piano benches with a little grunt; he noticed that her left knee was wrapped in an elastic bandage. "Used to be," she went on, "that all the nice children—at least the girls, and often the boys as well—all the nice children took piano. Some couldn't buy, of course, but that was no problem; Parker Pianos leased very good quality instruments. Every year, the piano classes . . . there were three teachers just in this neighborhood, you know, and those weren't the only ones. Piano music—we used to sell bundles of it. The Anderson series. Then the Purnel series. Exercise books. But not any more." She shook her head. Leonard looked away just in time to see the black policeman returning to the car with a sack. He waited for the car to drive away. It didn't.

"For awhile it was keyboards," the woman went on. "Parents kept insisting their child could practice just as well on a keyboard as on a piano. Ridiculous!" Leonard glanced at her politely, but she wasn't even looking at him, just staring at her knotted fingers spread on her thighs. He noticed the short, unpolished nails, the breadth of reach.

"You can't learn fingering for great music on something only that wide." Her nod toward the keyboards made Leonard look that way too. "You see?" she challenged. Leonard nodded. She took this as evidence of interest, and turned on the bench. "Listen to this, now," she said.

Leonard did not expect the explosion of sound that erupted from the piano. Dissonance in the bass slammed against ringing chords far up the keyboard; the woman's hands worked in complete independence, each finger an individual sledge-hammer. Before Leonard could react, she'd stopped, and turned to face him. "You see?" she said again. "You can't do *that* on an electronic keyboard."

He tried to think of something polite to say, and couldn't. "It . . . it's loud," he offered.

She chuckled. "Why do you think it was called a piano-forte? It's louder than that when I really let go. You liked that?"

"Uh . . ."

"Too strong for you, probably. You're like the rest, think piano music should be sweet, tinkly music: Chopin, maybe, or Debussy. That was Prokofiev, if you didn't recognize it . . ."

Leonard didn't recognize even the name, let alone the music. He saw a puff of smoke come out the exhaust of the police car, and watched it move slowly away. He knew he should wait a minute or so before leaving.

"You know," the woman was saying, "you remind me of someone . . . have you been in here before? Are you in some kind of trouble? My eyes are getting so bad . . ." Leonard was already out the door.

He started back toward the supermarket end of the center, wondering about an intersecting bus line on the other street, but saw the police car make a loop at the end of the parking lot and swing back toward him. He reversed. The woman was watching out the window of the music store; he couldn't go there. Next was the Dance Academy, its windows screened to head height with posters of ballet and jazz dance performances. "Back at two—Call Cathy if you need anything" read the scrawled notice on the door.

Leonard felt the back of his neck prickle. Surely they were watching him. He dared not glance around to see where the police car was.

Martial Arts Supreme had its glass door painted red on the inside, with gold and black spiky-looking letters on the outside, and oriental characters down one edge. At some point its window had been bricked in; the new brick was pale gray, not tan. A neatly lettered sign beside the door offered classes for beginners, intermediates, and advanced in a variety of things Leonard had only heard of on television. Behind him, Leonard heard the purring of an engine coming closer. Then the abrasive squawk of a car radio turned to loud: "All units. All units. Fugitive suspect, a white male . . ." He pushed the door, half-expecting it to be locked, but it yielded to his hand. He was through the door and leaning against it as it closed when the radio outside blasted the morning with his name. " . . . Leonard Sanders, age 23, height . . ." The door shut with a final click, shutting the sound outside. He blinked.

The large room was brightly lit with three rows of overhead fixtures. Along both side walls were neatly stacked mats covered in faded gray canvas. To Leonard's left, under what had been the window, a low bench of polished wood ran the width of the room. At the far end, a panelled partition cut off the rear of the place, with a narrow hall separating several smaller rooms. Leonard stepped forward, onto a narrow rug that ran along the near wall to the first stack of mats. At once a soft gong rang in the distance. He heard a door open, and a man in pajamas appeared in the passage.

Of course they weren't pajamas. Leonard realized that in his second glance. They were those white baggy things worn by martial arts people, the ones who broke boards with their bare hands, and (in video adventures) tore up whole battalions of normally armed troops. Only then they wore black pajamas, not white ones, and had black scarves tied around their heads.

Leonard had assumed that all—or nearly all—martial arts instructors were Oriental: Chinese or Korean or Japanese or something. That's what he'd seen on television. Also they were small. But the blunt-faced man who stood silently at the end of the room was dark, bearded, and big. Very big. Leonard swallowed. The silence stretched. Leonard could heard a faint buzzing from one of the fluorescent light fixtures. He could hear his own heart, the blood roaring in his ears. What could he say to this man—how could he explain that he'd come to the wrong place? He glanced at the bare wooden floor, the stacked mats, and finally at the dark man again. He stood, perfectly relaxed, and as solid as a tree. Leonard could not imagine him moving. Then he moved.

With the same relaxed solidity, he moved smoothly, silently. Leonard thought vaguely through his terror of waves on the shore, rising and falling in quiet power. He stopped again about ten feet away, his dark eyes holding Leonard's gaze easily. When he smiled, suddenly, mouth full of uneven teeth flashingly crowned in brilliant metal, Leonard felt his heart race even faster. Sweat slicked his back, trickled down his ribs. The man's smile faded, and he shook his head.

"I never saw anyone who needed martial arts training more," he said. His voice was warm, humorous, slightly accented. "But what are you doing here? You didn't come here to learn self-defense."

"No." Even to Leonard, his voice sounded odd and squeaky. He tried again. "No, I . . . I was eating lunch . . . I mean late breakfast. And I saw your sign . . ."

"Cops after you?" inquired the man. Leonard stared at him. How had he known? "You don't look like a thief . . . not a regular . . ." the man mused. "You sure ain't streetwise, not standing there with your pulse pounding twice normal and your sweat screaming fear at me. But a whitecollar type—you get caught shorting deposits or something?"

"No!" Even frightened, Leonard couldn't stand that accusation. "No—I never took anything. Never! It's not that, it's—" And then, of course, realized what he'd said. The dark man was already nodding.

"They after you right now? 'Cause if so, I can't afford trouble, but if not, it's none of my business. I'm a neutral, if you know what that means."

"I don't know." Leonard went back to staring at the floor. "I didn't think . . . I mean, I've never . . . I don't know what they know, or where they think I am."

"Umph." Something in that grunt prompted him to go on.

"I . . . they were going to make me go to the doctor." He couldn't explain about the crabworms, the bioengineered parasites that now lived in his gut and grazed the walls for cancer cells, the tiny carcinomas that had been fatal for so many of his family. "So I left work early, before they came, and I guess they're looking for me."

"Make you go to the doctor? Are you a crazy or something?"

"I'm not crazy. It's—they want me to have an operation. They want to cut me open . . ." Leonard shuddered again at the thought. It was bad enough to have had to swallow the crabworm capsules, knowing what was inside the gelatin that would protect them until they were past his acidic stomach. But the thought of being cut open, having them scoured out, was terrible.

"Not crazy, but they want to cut you open?" The dark man shook his head. "That doesn't sound right. Cops don't care if someone needs an operation or not." He shrugged. "Well, did they follow you here?"

"I . . . don't think so," said Leonard carefully. "I saw a police car, and heard their radio, but they weren't looking at me . . ." The man nodded, and waved Leonard toward the bench.

"Sit down before you fall down," he said. Leonard sat, and looked up. "I'm Hank Esper," the dark man said. "I'm a black belt . . ." He paused. "Hell, you don't know what all that means, do you?" Leonard shook his head. The man sighed. "If I agreed with my teacher, I'd say your fate brought you, but I reckon neither of us believes that . . . do you?"

"I don't know." Leonard sagged on the bench. His neck hurt when he kept looking up.

"Keep your spine straight," said the dark man. Hank, thought Leonard, reminding himself. He tried to sit up straighter. His knees hurt. His shoulders hurt. Hank sighed. "I wish you *had* come for instruction," he said. "You're the worst-scared rabbit I've seen yet . . . worse than the Archer boy when his mother dragged him in . . ." He turned away, seeming to glide across the floor rather than walk. Leonard watched, unable to do anything else. Then he turned back. "You know, you're lucky you came in here. Did you try any of the other stores?"

"The music store," said Leonard. To his surprise, his voice seemed to be working well again.

Hank grinned. "Ha! What'd you think of Alicia? What'd she say?"

Leonard stared at him. "She . . . she played the piano."

Hank's eyebrows went up. "Did she, now! Something that sounded like hell warmed over?" Leonard nodded. "Must have been that Russian stuff again. You should hear her when she's warmed up. She's pretty sharp, for a lady her age. She guess you were on the run?"

"She did ask if I was in trouble, just as I left."

"I'm not surprised. She—" Hank stiffened. Before Leonard realized he'd moved, Hank had grabbed his arm and shifted him halfway across the room. "Get in there and change!" he ordered, giving a final shove that sent Leonard almost through the closed door to one of the rooms. Leonard fumbled with the doorknob, and rushed in. Behind him, he heard the solid smack of mats hitting the floor. He was in a room lined on two sides with lockers: in front of him was a clothes rack full of white pajamas, from tiny toddler-size outfits on the right to voluminous garments big enough for Hank on the left. As he tried to guess where his size would be, he heard the melodious gong again and guessed that someone had come in and stepped on the rug inside the door. He heard Hank's footsteps, then his voice.

"Hello, sergeant. Anything I can do for you today?"

"Naw . . . keeping fit, eh? Got any strange customers this morning?"

"Not out of the usual. Looking for someone?" Leonard clawed at his shirt, got it off, and found an open locker.

He pulled on one of the loose white tops quickly, then unfastened his trousers, still listening. The cop laughed.

"Well, yeah . . . sort of crazy case. There's a court order out on this guy that was on TV last night: the one those docs were doing cancer research on. You see that?"

"That guy with the tapeworms or whatever they are?" Hank asked. Leonard started to yell out that they weren't tapeworms, they were crabworms, but he caught himself.

"That one. Seems there's this animal rights group that's got an injunction—thinks it's cruel that those whatever-they-are have to eat cancer cells—and this Sanders fellow is supposed to report to the hospital to have his removed. Only he panicked when the deputy tried to serve the papers on him and took off. Just remembered we saw someone sorta like his description half an hour ago or so—wondered if he'd stopped in here. Real little rabbit, this guy is—scared to death of everything, his doc says."

"Well . . ." There was a pause. Leonard pulled on a pair of loose white cotton pants and tied the drawstring snugly around his waist. Rabbit. That's what he was, all right . . . a scared rabbit. He felt odd and even more vulnerable in the strange white clothes. He kicked off his loafers, peeled off his socks, and tucked the socks neatly in his shoes before putting everything in the locker. His bare feet looked pale and ridiculous, toes still cramped together.

"Thought we'd look around," the cop said, with no edge in his voice but immense certainty. "Unless you want we should get a warrant . . ." That had the edge, a threat Leonard could hear easily."

"No problem," Hank said. "I do have one student right now, but he's no rabbit . . . just another out-of-shape beginner." His voice came nearer. "Ken Jones . . . he's a computer operator, I think." He rapped on the door. "Hey—Ken—you still having trouble getting that thing tied right?"

"Yeah." Leonard tried to copy that casual tone.

"Well, at least get the right color this time . . . on the last peg, remember?" On the last peg beside the clothes rack were strips of cloth of various colors, printed with strange designs. Leonard grabbed one at random, just as

Hank opened the door, talking over his shoulder to the cops. "The office isn't locked, or the storeroom—go on and look. I'll be just a second . . . let me get Ken started." He pushed Leonard into the corner. "My God, Ken, you'll never get anywhere with your sash tied like that. If I were my teacher you'd be black-and-blue already." He flipped a sash around Leonard's waist and tied it with quick hands. Then he grabbed another strip of cloth from another peg Leonard hadn't seen, and wrapped it around his head. "The sweat band has to be tight enough to stay on when I flip you," he said roughly, and swung Leonard around. "Now let's go."

Leonard had a quick glimpse of two uniformed backs opening a door down the passage, and then he was tumbling onto one of the mats lying in the center of the floor. Quickly, Hank shoved, prodded, and pulled him into a variety of strained postures, complaining loudly that he was the stiffest, slowest, and least-likely 19-year-old he'd ever taken on. Leonard thought of explaining that he was 23, but the look in Hank's eye kept him quiet, even when he remembered that his wallet—with his IDs—was in the locker.

But the cops only glanced in that room, returning to watch as Hank urged Leonard through a stretching exercise on the mat. Already he was red-faced and out of breath. When the sergeant asked his name, his gasped "Ken . . . Jones . . ." didn't get a reaction. With a final word to Hank, the cops left. Leonard lay breathless on the mat, and waited for Hank's next suggestion. Instead, the dark man came and squatted easily on the end of the mat.

"You're that guy that was on TV? The cancer research guy?"

Leonard nodded. "They aren't tapeworms, though. They're crabworms."

Hank shrugged. "No difference to me. But that's a bum deal—didn't it say last night that you'd likely die of cancer before 30 if you didn't have those things?"

"Yeah . . . my father did." Leonard did not remember his father; he had run out on the family long before his final bout with gut cancer.

"Hmph. It's a damn shame they want to cut you up.

But—" He looked around the room for a moment, then directly at Leonard. "Did it ever occur to you that you might be better off dead?"

"What? No!" Leonard managed to sit up straight, ignoring the protest of his abdominal muscles. "I—"

"Look what you are now," Hank went on. "A rabbit—that's what those cops called you—"

"I am," said Leonard, slumping again.

"Do you like it?"

"What?" Leonard couldn't quite straighten again, but he tried. "Of course not . . . but it's what I am." He'd heard it often enough. Every P.E. teacher from junior high on up had called him rabbit or worse. So had the school toughs. He'd grinned nervously and taken his lumps before they got tired of messing with him. Other targets were more interesting, were cause for pride if defeated, but Leonard was the kid all the kids could beat.

Hank looked him up and down. "What you are is a grown-up man acting like a rabbit. Are you really stupid?"

Leonard felt the heat rising in his face. "I don't . . . I don't know. Some of my teachers said I wasn't, but . . . I never did have much initiative." Initiative was for people with a future, people who would live to profit from it.

"I'll believe that. But—what are you going to do now?" Leonard said nothing, feeling the same hopeless fear he always felt. Hank leaned forward. "Going to let them cut you open and take those things out?"

"No." He didn't know how to prevent it, but he clenched himself around that decision.

"A stubborn rabbit." Hank smiled slightly. "Listen—you need muscles, rabbit, if you're going to be stubborn."

"I'm no good," muttered Leonard.

"Stop saying that. It doesn't help."

"That's what Dr. Gerson said."

"He's right about that, anyway. So stop it. I'll give you something better to say." Hank stood, then came back down again, folding himself into something that Leonard remembered having seen on television. "Sit like this," Hank ordered. Leonard looked again and tried. His knees felt twisted sideways; his thighs ached. He didn't want to do this, but Hank was a lot bigger, and the police were outside, and . . . Hank unhooked one foot from one thigh. "Like this, then, for now. Now—I want you to straighten up . . ."

Two hours later Leonard was wondering if jail wouldn't have been easier. That's when Hank helped him into his own clothes and passed him out the back door of Martial Arts Supreme and into the back door of Lila's Dance Academy. He had heard only a little of the hissed conversation between Hank and Cathy, the senior instructor.

"You want me to what?"

"Just till my classes are over—"

"What about my classes? I've got all those little girls . . ."

"He's not gonna bother your little girls. He's not that kind—"

"Oh ho!"

"Nor that kind either. Just . . . let him do your books or something, okay?"

Cathy stared at him; Leonard was too miserable to do more than stare back.

"Can you?" she asked. "Do books, I mean?"

"Yes," he said. He had, after all, hoped for that transfer to inventory, and he had made a 97 on his final in basic accounting practices last summer. So when the shrill voices discovered a man in Cathy's office, and demanded to know who it was in there, he heard her explain that it was an accountant. By then he was deep in the intricacies of Cathy's private system: she didn't trust the computer, and had a duplicate set of figures kept in an old spiral notebook. He looked up from time to time, out the window of the tiny office, to see spindly girls teetering on tiptoe. As the afternoon went on, the girls got taller and less spindly.

He expected Hank to come back, but when Cathy took a supper break (no classes from 5:30 to 7, she explained) she handed him over to Alicia the music saleswoman.

"Just for supper," Cathy said severely. "Alicia will bring you back around nine." By this time Leonard could hardly move, let alone resist. He was almost too tired to be frightened—at least he hadn't thought about the police, or the jail, or the crabworms, or the cancer while Hank was folding him into impossible shapes and yelling at him to jump or twist or move faster. And Cathy's bookkeeping had demanded all his attention since then. Alicia's eyes twinkled behind her thick glasses.

"I thought you were in some kind of trouble," she said, leading the way along the alley behind the shopping center. "Looking out the window every second at that police car . . . and you didn't know anything about music at all."

"I do," said Leonard, stung. She was old enough to be his mother, if not his grandmother, and she walked so fast he was breathless. Whatever she had a bandage on her knee for didn't slow her down at all. "I know your door chime does that opening from Beethoven."

Alicia gave him a smile over her shoulder. "That's something. Did you have that in school?" Leonard nodded at her back, unable to speak, and she went on as if he'd answered aloud. "You've probably never heard anything but those little snippets they give school kids. We'll take care of that." Leonard thought of the torture she'd inflicted on his ears in the music store and shuddered.

Alicia lived only two blocks from the shopping center, on the sort of quiet street Leonard had never seen except on television. She walked the whole way at the same fast pace, using the alleys as if they were her private paths—he supposed they were. Alicia's house had an unkempt backyard with shaggy grass, weedy flowerbeds, and an immense sycamore tree surrounded by humped and broken paving. The back door of her two-story house was shadowed under an overgrown rambler rose, long past blooming. She had her key out while Leonard was still looking around the yard, and motioned him in.

The tiny back porch was crowded with washer, dryer, sink. The kitchen, large but bare, smelled of herbs. Alicia brushed past Leonard to turn the lights on. "Go on in the front," she ordered. "In the music room." And as he hesitated in the doorway, "Left," she said. "Do you like tabouli?"

"Tabouli?" He had never heard the word, and wasn't sure

if it was a style of music, a kind of embroidery, or had something to do with food. She made an exasperated noise behind him, something of a snort crossed with a sniff, and he went on through a dim hall to a large room walled with tall windows. Here a grand piano centered the room, its burnished flanks gleaming in the late afternoon light. He had never been that close to a grand piano, though he'd seen them, of course, on television. He edged close to it, almost forgetting his sore muscles and aching back in his curiosity. The top was open: he looked in to see the ranked strings. A table to one side was covered with music books, sheet music, much of it yellowed with age, but some obviously new. Bookshelves lined the inner walls of the room. A litter of books and papers covered every horizontal surface, including an old chintz-covered couch across one corner. Leonard edged along the bookcases, trying to read the titles in the fading light. He'd never heard of most of the books, and the ones he had heard of (from English classes) he'd never read. He thought only libraries had books like that, not people at home.

Alicia appeared in the hall and sniffed again. "You could turn on the lights," she said, flicking a switch. "And move some things off the couch and sit down." She gathered an armload of books, dumping them onto another stack, swept papers aside, and gestured. Leonard sat down nervously. The couch was comfortable, and he found himself leaning back into its cushions before he realized it. She had gone to the bench of the piano, and now looked back at him. "I'll give you something easier to like than Prokofiev," she said, and set her hands on the keyboard. Again he was surprised— astonished—at the sound that came out. He had no idea what she played, but the sound ravished him, struck into him almost forcibly. He could hardly remember what the piano in the music store had sounded like: this one seemed to contain a waterfall, chiming bells, thunder, and ribbon-like ripples of sound, cascades of sound . . . he didn't realize he was crying until he felt the tears on his face.

"Real music," Alicia said softly. She had stopped play-ing, but was looking through a stack of sheet music. "Real

music has real power . . . and great music, like that, casts
out all sorts of devils."

"Devils?" Leonard felt his stomach turn at that. Who *was*
this strange woman? Did she really believe in devils? His
mother had warned him that some people really did, even
in this day and age: she herself wasn't superstitious, she'd
told him, but those who were could cause a lot of trouble.

"Figure of speech," Alicia said, shaking her head at him.
"Once people believed that all bad emotions, bad thoughts,
were evil spirits inside. Even then they knew music eased
sorrow and pain and anger . . . so they thought it charmed
or tamed the demons. My point is that whether you call
it devils or hormones, music has the power to ease the pain
inside."

"Even for rabbits?" Leonard found himself asking.

"Especially for rabbits." Alicia turned again to the keyboard, and in seconds Leonard found himself swinging his
foot to the beat, tapping fingers on the arm of the couch.
Tired and sore and scared as he was, he felt like jumping
up and following that rhythm around the room . . . or
anywhere. She glanced back at him, grinning. "It works,
doesn't it?"

"Yes," he said, surprised at the firmness of his own voice.
"I guess it does." She played again, something cheerful and
spirited, though not quite as rousing as before. Leonard
relaxed. Surely nothing bad would happen within that music's
spell.

Nothing bad happened, but he didn't realize he'd fallen
asleep until he woke to Alicia's prodding finger. "Supper-
time," she said. "You'll need it."

He was stiff, arms and legs seizing when he tried to
move. She didn't say anything, and when he finally stood
led him back through the archway into the kitchen. A large
blue-striped bowl centered the kitchen table, a loaf of brown
bread beside it. Two blue-striped plates, two fluted blue
glasses, blue napkins folded in neat triangles, and—Leonard
stared: was that *real* silver? It didn't look anything like his
own knives and forks.

Tabouli, he discovered, looked like a disgusting mess and

tasted like nothing he'd ever had in his mouth. "Mint?" he asked once, and Alicia nodded.

"And other things," she said. "Olive oil, lemon juice, any herbs you like, but always mint. You know what the grain is?"

"Rice?" he guessed. It wasn't like any rice he'd had, but that was the closest he could imagine. On the whole he liked it, to his surprise, but he wasn't sure if the crabworms would. He was supposed to stick to a defined diet, something from the lists he'd been given.

Alicia laughed. "Wheat," she said. "The same as in wheat flour for bread, but this isn't ground to flour. I learned about this from—" A bell chimed, somewhere in the house, and Alicia stood quickly. "That's Hank, I hope. If not, you're . . . Ken Jones, right? Computer operator?"

"Uh . . ."

"Remember it." She bustled out of the kitchen, pulling the swing door closed behind her. Leonard couldn't hear anything from the front of the house until she pushed it open again. Hank's big frame filled the doorway behind her. He carried a big grocery sack, which he set on the white tiled counter before looking at Leonard. Then he grinned.

"You like tabouli?" he asked. "I taught Alicia to make it—and dammit, Lish, you're not supposed to eat it with ordinary bread."

"And you're not supposed to swear at me in my own kitchen," snapped Alicia flicking her fingers at him. "I didn't have any pita, and you'd dumped your rabbit on me—"

"Sorry." Hank started unloading the sack. "Just teasing, that's all. Here's the pita . . . some olives . . . cheese . . ."

By the end of that strange meal, Leonard had quit worrying about his crabworms. He hadn't known such flavors existed. As Hank wolfed down his own meal, and Alicia warned about the effects of Lebanese cuisine on the unaccustomed stomach, he ate until he could eat no more. Then he sat, torpid as an overfed cat, while they discussed what to do with him. Right then Leonard didn't care what anyone did with him. He felt almost as safe and comfortable as he had that morning.

"He can't stay here," said Alicia firmly. "Not that I worry

about him, but everyone in the neighborhood saw him arrive, from old Mrs. Sayers to the Villegas youngsters. Someone'll have to see him leave."

"So I'll take him home with me—no—" Hank paused, eyes narrowed. "Not tonight, I can't. Well, he can stay in the office—if we're careful."

Careful, Hank explained to Leonard on their way back to the shopping center, included not flushing the john after he was left alone. "Lights can get left on by accident, but johns don't flush themselves. It's a noise you can hear all over the building, and any cop would be dumb to ignore it."

"But if I have to—"

"Then don't flush it. Just wait till morning. I'll be there with you for a half-hour or so anyway."

They met no one on their walk back, and only a few cars clustered around the lighted supermarket on the far end of the building. Hank led the way into the well-lighted alley, and unlocked his back door without even looking around for watchers. Leonard felt invisible eyes peering at him, and barely restrained himself from pushing past Hank to get inside, out of sight.

Hank had dragged the mat into the dressing room for him, told him which door was the john and reminded him not to flush it after he left. Leonard used it then, and made his way back to the dressing room.

"I'll be back around seven or eight," Hank said. "You be OK until then?"

"Sure," said Leonard, trying to match that casual tone. Hank nodded, and went on, flicking the light off as he shut the heavy back door.

He had never slept on the floor in his life. A mat was not a mattress, not a proper bed, and he found himself turning over and over, restless. It was the darkest place he'd ever been in, too. No light seeped past the red paint on the front door, and the back door was solid steel. Darkness pressed on his eyeballs, and when he blinked little wavery shapes of pale light floated across his vision.

The hours wore on. He had plenty of time to imagine

what had happened after he fled from work: the contempt on Sylvia's face, the distaste on Mr. Stevens's already austere countenance. He imagined the word coming down from Administration: Sanders is fired. The obligatory green slip, the termination paycheck with its notice of the amount in his Employee's Retirement Account. He wondered what Ed thought, and who had taken over his work station. He couldn't remember if he'd bolted in the middle of a transaction . . . and struggled with the memory until he was sure he hadn't done any harm. Beyond work, there were the doctors at the medical center. He could almost see the raised eyebrows, the pursed lips, almost hear the shocked murmurs. Sanders, do such a thing? *Leonard* Sanders? For one moment he felt almost smug about it—surprising the doctors like that—but his mood soon sagged again. He wasn't really the adventurous type, he told himself. It was one thing to swallow a capsule of bioengineered parasites, and another to be a police fugitive, with armed men searching for him. He had done just what he'd always done: taken the easy way out, run away. He was a coward, a rabbit: not a brave renegade.

Yet even as the thought made him shiver, something warmed his cold, tense feet, and he slept, waking stiff and sore and frightened at the sound of Hank's key in the back door.

"I expect you're stiff," said Hank, before he even looked. Leonard was discovering that nothing wanted to move, and it hurt to lie still. He rolled his eyes toward the door, where Hank stood with a big brown sack that gave off a delicious aroma. "Go on," Hank said. "Get up . . . you'll get worse if you lie still." Leonard clambered up. His clothes felt strange—more comfortable, yet somehow *different*, for having been slept in.

An hour later, he was back at Cathy's desk in the dance studio. Hank had insisted on a brief workout: painful as it was, Leonard could now move his arms and legs much better. After that had come breakfast from the sack—fruit-filled pastries still warm from the oven—and a shower. Hank had brought clean clothes from his place—not his, he explained carefully, but his younger brother's—and Leonard's own clothes, with the labels carefully removed, were now on their way to a cleaner's three blocks away. Leonard felt very strange in a rust-colored shirt and a gold and green striped tie, but at least he had his own shoes. What really bothered him was the way these people were taking over his life, just as firmly as Mr. Stevens and Sylvia Goldstein. Tabouli was an improvement on frozen Salisbury steak with green peas, but was it worth it? Alicia's music . . . Cathy's smile . . . they were more pleasant than his workstation, but he felt the same dominating attitude underneath. What would happen when he wanted to do something else? Where could he run?

When the front door crashed open, Leonard looked up to see a huge black-haired woman in a black leotard and purple wrap skirt confronting Cathy.

"You think I'm cheating you, is that it?" Her voice matched her size; it rolled through the dance studio, bouncing off the walls. "You thought you could sneak in your own accountant . . . ."

"That's not it, Miss Lila," said Cathy, throwing a nervous glance behind her toward the office window. Leonard hunched his shoulders, feeling the sweat break out under his arms. Another one of *this* kind!

"You didn't think anyone'd notice," Miss Lila went on. She moved, now, and Leonard noticed that she managed her heft lightly, as if she were full of helium like a balloon. She circled Cathy and came toward the office. Leonard stared at the books, unable to bolt for cover. "You think those girls never tell me anything?"

"I'm sure they do," said Cathy sharply. "But it's not what you think."

"A boyfriend?" boomed Miss Lila in the office doorway. Leonard looked up and saw the expression on her face. "Not a boyfriend," she said then. "An accountant." She sat down on the corner of the desk, overflowing half the papers Leonard had laid out. "Find anything crooked?" she asked. Before Leonard could answer, she had turned on Cathy again. "Girl, I thought we understood each other—if you're not happy with the deal, you can get out."

"It's not that!" Cathy slammed a pair of ballet slippers onto the other desk. "Will you listen, for once?"

"I'm listening." Miss Lila, this close, had the body of a dancer upholstered with several inches of foam: an erect back towered above Leonard's hunched shoulders, and her arms did not hang at her sides: they were poised, alive to the carefully placed fingertips. Silence held the room, thickened there, clotting in Leonard's ears. Cathy looked like someone trying out several stories in her mind, unsure which would serve. Finally she sighed.

"It has nothing to do with the school," she said finally. "I—a friend of mine was looking for somewhere to stow someone for a few days . . ."

"You?" Leonard looked up to find himself impaled by two glowing dark eyes lined in black and shadowed in purple and gray. Beneath them a wide mouth stretched. He managed a nod. "A crook?"

"No." Cathy shook her head vigorously, and Miss Lila looked away, to Leonard's relief. "He's not a crook. He's that man on TV—the one they're looking for because the medical center's in trouble. It was on the news last night— the animal rights group thinks they've broken some law about cruelty to research animals or something. Like not giving them fresh air, and clean cages and stuff. Because they have to live inside him . . ."

Again Leonard suffered Miss Lila's intense gaze. This time she rotated slowly on the corner of the desk to face him. Fascinated, he watched the smooth movement, unable to see how she could do that without any hitches or jerks. "You have those *things* in you," she said.

"Yes." Leonard's mouth had been dry; now it was full, and he swallowed.

"Horrible things . . . they showed the pictures, the most disgusting, ugly creatures. Can they get out?"

"They're not horrible," Leonard said, almost forgetting his fear in his enthusiasm. "They're saving my life. See, I have this kind of cancer that runs in families, and if you have it—"

bright blue eyes twinkling, sat squarely on her folding hands on knees. Rose clasped her hands together ; Leonard was not fooled. In some way she was the here, the person to convince. She had listened to ard's story, then Alicia's, then Hank's, and at no point Leonard tell what she was thinking. Now, after a long e during which everyone stared at nothing in particu- she spoke again.

In ten days—no, nine days, now, the injunction will ire. I saw on the news this morning that the medical center seeking a counter-injunction to prevent Mr. Sanders's necessary surgery, but they don't have it yet. And besides, e's broken the law by fleeing, even if they get it . . ."

"So we keep him hidden," Hank broke in. Rose raised her hand, and he subsided.

"We can't keep him hidden forever," she said sweetly, "unless you're planning to change his identity permanently— are you?" Hank shook his head. "No, I shouldn't think so. He's hardly at risk of serious punishment, once this surgery isn't a threat any more." She looked at Leonard. "And you, Mr. Sanders—what are you planning to do when you turn yourself in or the police find you?"

Leonard couldn't answer; he wasn't sure if she meant to call the police herself, or what.

"Will you go back to your job?" she asked. "Or will they re you?"

Leonard had not thought about his job for several hours, ce Miss Lila's arrival in fact, but Rose's reminder sent spirits plummeting. "I expect they'll fire me," he said wly. "I did leave without permission, and they've fired rs for less."

What kind of work do you do? Are you in a union?" eonard shook his head. "No, I'm a shipping clerk for ities, Inc. I have a terminal, you know, and just enter elete orders, and transfer them to the right depart-

ee. Is that what you *want* to do?" Leonard stared and she gazed back, her faded gray eyes showing ession at all.

"Cancer," announced Miss Lila, "is a failure of faith." She moved to the other chair in the office and sat down, crossing strong ankles demurely. "If you have faith in the spiritual unity of all beings, your cells will never rebel. It's that simple."

"Miss Lila . . ." began Cathy, with a glance at Leonard.

"Oh, well, you can't expect everyone to have faith." Miss Lila shrugged, the movement flowing from shoulders to fingers in one long wave. Leonard's mouth dried again. It was so beautiful. "It takes a strong mind." She tilted her head slightly. "So you don't think those worm things are horrible, eh?"

"No . . . they're not really worms, you know."

"Whatever they are. So long as they can't get out."

"Oh, no."

"But—" she gave Cathy a hard look. "He is fugitive, and we do have a responsibility to our students."

Cathy looked determined. "Miss Lila, we can't turn him in. They want to cut him open, and—"

"Surgery!" Miss Lila's bellow stunned Leonard's ears. "That's ridiculous. That's worse than drugs. It's faith—faith, and thinking healthy thoughts—"

"So all I did was give him a place to stay in the day-time, and tell the girls he was an accountant because it seemed the best thing . . ."

"Of course you couldn't turn him in," said Miss Lila, still quivering with indignation. "Not if they were going to violate his bodily integrity. But he's been pawing through the books . . . you don't really know anything about accounting, do you?"

"In a way," said Leonard. "I mean, I've studied it at night school. And so far everything's fine."

"Well, good," said Miss Lila. "That's that, then. But we can't have you here day after day, or the girls will be tell-ing their mothers I have financial trouble, and the next thing you know we'll be losing students."

"I never thought of that," said Cathy.

"I realize that. And besides, they'll have seen him on TV last night—if he's here, someone will remember." She turned to Leonard. "Your name is Sanders, then? I'm Lila Courtney." She seemed poised, one arm lifted toward her ample bosom and when Leonard said nothing went on. "Are you a dance fan?"

"No . . . not really. I guess I've seen it on TV."

Miss Lila's arm sagged. "Oh. Well, I used to be quite a dancer, but if you never heard of me, you never heard of me." She heaved a vast sigh and stood. Leonard remembered distant courtesies and stood also. "I'm going to see Alicia and the girls down the row, and we'll find you something, Mr. Sanders, but not here. Just put all the papers back where you found them, OK?" She swept out, purple skirt swirling.

Cathy grinned at him. "Something, isn't she? Would you believe she's over fifty?"

"She's . . ." Leonard tried to think of a tactful term, and avoided looking at Cathy's skinny torso. "I thought ballerinas were all thin," he said finally. Cathy laughed.

"When she was dancing professionally, she was thin. She hated it, she told me—dieting, and all that. When she quit, she ate what she pleased and gained forty pounds in one year. But she can still do things I can't: I didn't start early enough."

Leonard started putting the papers back into Cathy's notebook, and closed down the computer. Another boss, another person making plans for him, when all he wanted was to be left alone . . . he wished Cathy would leave. He might make it out the back door. But Cathy lounged in the doorway, apparently relaxed and willing to chat. The last thing Leonard wanted was more chat.

The door chimed. Miss Lila, Alicia, and a woman Leonard had never seen came in together. Alicia smiled and nodded; Miss Lila looked grim.

"You didn't tell me it was Hank that brought him," she began. Cathy turned red.

"You didn't ask, and I don't see why it matters. Hank happened to have him first . . ."

"I told you I don't want you hanging around with that no-good Arab and his Jap-style fighting school—"

"Lillian!" Alicia interrupted with a w
"That's ridiculous. Just because Hank is

"I even like him," said the strange w
colorless person of indeterminate age.

"It's not being Lebanese, though that's a

"Careful, dear," said the stranger. This ti
turned red.

"Rose, that's not what I was going to say."

"No, but it's what you were thinking. All of us
so to speak." She turned to Leonard. "I'm Rose
by the way, from the Sunrise Christian Bookstore (
row. And before you make any rash assumptions,
Christian: I'm Jewish." Leonard started to murmur
greetings, but Rose had turned back to Miss Lila. "An
should remember, because I know he's explained it,
he doesn't fight Japanese. It's oriental martial arts, and so
of them are Korean or Chinese, and the Koreans and Jap
nese don't like each other anyway."

"He's trouble," said Miss Lila stubbornly. "Him and that
bunch he runs with, those motorcycles and all that. We run
a clean business here—"

"And so does he, here," said Rose. "What he does over
there is his business . . . the same as yours." Miss L
turned even redder, which Leonard had not believed
sible. Rose ignored that and went on. "He knows th
about hiding fugitives that the rest of us have forg
if we ever knew them. We'll need his help."

"Not in here," said Miss Lila.

"Then in there." Rose turned to leave. Miss L
again.

"All right. In here. Cathy—"

"I'll get him."

Leonard stared at the row of faces, one
and Miss Lila, two antagonistic giants, anc
of the arc, carefully not looking each other
wore spotless white pajamas (as they
Leonard) and a rakish glint in his eye
blonde, had left a distinct space betwee

He thought, while she held the silence unbroken around him. What did he want to do? He wanted to live, first off, with no cancers eating out his guts, and no pain, and no fear of it. He wanted to . . . beyond that was a shadowy place of half-formed dreams. He wanted people to be nice to him: no more sneers and jibes from Sylvia Goldstein or Mr. Stevens. He wanted people to quit telling him what to do all the time. He wanted to make enough to live on, and maybe enough to go out now and then, and he wanted . . . he didn't really want anything at all but that. He looked again along the faces: Hank's dark, amused, dangerous glance; Cathy's bright professional smile now sobered into concern; Alicia's stubbornness clear in every line of her body, but lightened by humor; Rose's strange remoteness that held a strength he'd never seen before; Miss Lila's flamboyance of makeup and expression overlaying conventional propriety. He did want something else, Leonard realized. He wanted these people—these strange people, odd and frightening as they were. He wanted to stay near them, but . . . but he didn't want to be their pet, their project-of-the-week or whatever they thought he was.

There were no words for that, and he struggled with the rest of it. "I want to live," he began, miserably. "I want a job—"

"As a shipping clerk?" asked Rose, inexorably. That was the voice his junior-high math teacher had used, accusing his lack of ambition.

"He can do accounting," Cathy put in. Rose glanced at her, and Cathy, like Hank, subsided. Rose let her eyebrows ascend her forehead. Leonard nodded. He would like to have said it to the teacher.

"I can do accounting. I took a course, even. I was hoping for a transfer to inventory, but now . . ."

"But you wouldn't mind an accounting job?"

"Oh, no." He was startled out of his confusion. "I'd like that." Hank stirred, and this time Rose gave him permission with an eyebrow.

"You need more than that," Hank said. "All sorts of things you need to know, like what we said yesterday." Leonard started to nod agreeably, but his stiff neck caught him. Besides . . . he didn't want martial arts training, not really. He'd rather everyone left him alone so he wouldn't need it.

"And music," Alicia put in. "He's got an ear, but no training. It's a shame for someone like that, with the ability to hear and no chance to. He ought to have a chance—"

"Chances," said Rose, in a voice that made the hair stand up on Leonard's arms. "He's had the chances anyone has— more than some—"

Hank mumbled something and she glared at him, then nodded. "I said," Hank said loudly, "that he's acting like a scared rabbit because someone told him when he was a kid that he was doomed—what else can you expect. Even me, if someone had told me from first grade I was going to die of cancer, how much time would I have spent learning to fight?"

Rose smiled, a quick twitch of her whole face that gave it color and life for a moment. "You? You'd have fought anywhere and any time—but I'll grant that it's a bad way for a child to grow. But what now?"

Everyone looked at Leonard briefly, then away. He could almost hear the gears turning in their heads, see the plans being laid out, imagine the way they would set things up for him: go here, stay with so-and-so, study this, take this job, buy these clothes . . .

"It's not your decision," he found himself saying. The heads swung toward him, astonished. Their startled silence gave him the courage to go on. "It's *my* life. My crabworms, my cancers, my gut . . . that's why I ran."

Only Rose moved; she nodded, her gray eyes warming slightly. Leonard sat up straighter, feeling the pull of sore muscles in shoulders and chest. They were listening . . . listening to *him*, almost the way the reporters had listened.

"You all helped . . . and I thank you . . . but I want to make plans for myself."

"But you don't have—" began Hank; Rose's gesture hushed him, and he looked down.

"I'm not big," said Leonard. "And I'm not strong, and I'm not very brave, but I can do some things. I can keep books straight, and I can—I did—decide to be a volunteer in medical research. Dr. Gerson told me that took a lot of courage, the same as climbing a mountain." He looked at all the faces again: Hank, doubting but silent; Cathy, sympathetic; Alicia, interested; Rose, approving; Miss Lila, unconvinced. "Maybe it's not the same," he went on, "but it's something. And I didn't let them catch me like they wanted to. That's something. Maybe I shouldn't have run, but I made that decision myself, and did it. If I hadn't done it, I wouldn't ever have come here. And—and I like you all, but I want to like you as a person, not a . . . a pet."

Stiff muscles and all, he was able to stand and walk to the door before the others shook themselves into action. "Thanks again," he said, and went out into the bright sunlight of the parking lot.

He made it all the way into the hospital lobby before being spotted. He always thought afterwards that it was Hank's brother's choice in clothes—not Leonard Sanders's style at all. It was Dr. Akers who recognized him, the lanky red-headed endocrinologist; she grabbed his arm and whisked him into a staff elevator before the police guard noticed.

"Where have you *been*?" she hissed. "Gerson's been hunting all over. Don't you realize how much trouble you've caused?"

Leonard felt the familiar twinge of panic, the runnels of sweat creeping down his ribs. He swallowed a mouthful of bile and said nothing. Dr. Akers finally turned away to study the level indicator as the elevator slid upward. It stopped on 19, opening its door onto the familiar gray-panelled lobby of the research unit's section. He followed Akers out, and across the lobby. She paused to tell a wide-eyed receptionist to keep her mouth shut, and then waved Leonard ahead of her down the hall to Gerson's office.

Through the glass panel beside the door, Leonard could see Gerson and another person in a white coat, leaning over something on Gerson's desk. Dr. Akers leaned past him to knock at the door and push it open quickly. Gerson looked up.

"Hi, Ann, we were—my God, it's Lennie!" Gerson's tufted gray eyebrows shot up the slope of his brow. He looked more startled than angry. "Where did you come from? Did you see the latest newsbreak?"

Leonard shook his head. "No, sir. I—I just thought I should come in . . ."

"I'm glad you did. I—Ann, Pete, if you'll excuse us, I think Lennie and I need to have a talk . . ."

"Sure." The other man, someone Leonard had seen around the hospital but never met, turned to go, snagging Dr. Akers as he went. Gerson moved around behind his desk, and waved Leonard to the comfortable chair beside it.

"Lennie, I understand you were frightened and upset, but I wish you'd come here first . . ."

Leonard felt his determination wavering. Dr. Gerson had been so thoughtful, all along, and so encouraging. But a remnant of the strange mood he'd felt the night before in the Martial Arts Supreme storeroom stayed with him. "I don't want anyone to cut me open," he said.

"There's no question of that," said Gerson smoothly. "A court can't make you submit to surgery when you haven't committed any crime. It would have been easier if you hadn't run from the police, but . . ."

"I didn't exactly run from the police," said Leonard. "I just left the office . . . the police hadn't arrived. So I wasn't ever charged with anything, or arrested . . ."

"Yes, but—" Gerson chewed his lip a moment. "Look, Lennie: they know I called you to tell you about the summons . . . so they assume you ran away to avoid it. Now that's illegal—trying to avoid a legal summons. And they put it on the news—"

"I didn't watch the news." All his stubbornness had returned in force. "It's not against the law to not watch the news for one night."

"No. It's not." Gerson sighed. "Lennie . . . I've got to tell the court where you are. I'll be compounding the crime if I don't."

"I know that." Leonard looked up, meeting Gerson's gaze squarely. "I know you have to tell them, and maybe I have to go to jail. But I wanted to see you first, and tell you something. I won't agree to having an operation, and I won't agree to give up my crabworms. And if they try to make me do it, I want you to help stop them."

"You could have another dose later . . ."

"No." Leonard shook his head, not even wincing at the pain in his stiff neck. "They might not let you give me another dose. I won't take that chance. My crabworms are eating up my cancer cells—you proved that—and I don't want to die."

Gerson sighed again. "I know. I know, and you're right. It would be easier if you just . . . but I guess if it were my gut, I wouldn't either. OK, Lennie . . . we'll see what we can do, and I promise you I'll stand between you and the knife. Right?"

"Right." Leonard sat still, astonished at himself, while Gerson put in the call to the hospital legal department. He had actually done it. He had actually made it back to the hospital on his own, and talked to Gerson, and Gerson had listened to him. Listened to him almost as if he were worth listening to. He listened to Gerson explaining that Leonard had come to the hospital on his own, and was ready to come into court when called. When he finally put the phone down, he was shaking his head slowly.

"You have to stay here, they said, and they'll send someone over around three. There'll be a hearing. You heard me say we'd post bond for you . . ." Leonard hadn't heard it, really, but he nodded. "I think—if you don't mind my giving advice—that if you tell the judge you were afraid of your cancer erupting, and that's why you ran, she may be lenient."

"She?" Leonard still thought of judges as gray-haired serious men in long black robes. That's what he saw on television.

"Judge Lane. Our lawyers got the case transferred from Pearson's court; he was obviously prejudiced, and we could prove it. Anyway, I'll have lunch sent up. Our lawyer will be here in a few minutes." Gerson leaned back in his chair. "Do you want me to call your office, let them know you're all right?"

"No." He had thought about the office all the way to the hospital, to keep himself from thinking about the police. "I don't want to go back there. I want to find another job."

"Hmm. Any idea what?"

"Accountant," said Leonard. "I took a course . . ."

"Do you want to work here, in the medical center?"

"I—hadn't thought about it. Are there jobs?"

"I don't know. Have to check. But there might be."

The court was unimpressive compared to the sets on television dramas. The judge's desk ("bench," explained the lawyer) sat on a raised dais; the tables for counsel were plain, and the seating behind was only cramped folding chairs. The hospital lawyer, a large pink man with silver hair in a careful wave, nudged Leonard to his feet when Judge Lane came in. She looked, to Leonard, like someone who should have had five children clustered around her: a comfortable, middle-aged woman with an expressive mouth and bright eyes. Alicia would like her, he thought to himself, and wondered if she lived anywhere near the Crestview Music Store.

"Mr. Leonard Sanders," she said, and Leonard stepped forward before the lawyer could nudge again. She had that sort of voice.

"Yes sir . . . I mean, ma'am."

She smiled briefly. "Your Honor is the usual form of address. You are aware, Mr. Sanders, that you have broken the law by running away when a summons was being served?"

"They explained it to me," Leonard said.

"Who?"

"The lawyer at the hospital," Leonard said. "He said it was against the law to run like I did."

"You didn't know that before?" Her voice held polite disbelief.

"No . . . I mean, I knew I shouldn't, but not that it was against the law, when I hadn't broken a law. If I stole something, and then ran away, it would be different."

"I see." She looked down at papers on her desk, and then back at him. "The law, Mr. Sanders, is quite specific on this. Evading the officers sent to summon you to court—intentionally evading them—is against the law, and constitutes contempt of court. Now I understand you didn't actually see the officers coming, is that right?"

"Yes, Your Honor."

"But you knew about them . . ."

"Yes, I did. Dr. Gerson called me to say they were coming to take out my crabworms, and—"

"You thought the officers would do that?"

"No . . . I meant, he said that's why I had to come with them, and they'd take me to jail, and then to the hospital . . ."

"To jail!" Judge Lane leaned forward. "Mr. Sanders, did you seriously think that a summons to appear in court was the same thing as an arrest?"

"Isn't it?"

Her gaze stabbed beyond him. "Why didn't you tell him the truth?" she asked Gerson, obviously angry.

"I hung up," said Leonard quickly, before Gerson could answer. "He tried to say something more, and I just hung up and bolted . . ."

"Is that true?" she asked.

"Yes," said Gerson. "I was trying to reassure him and explain what would happen, when the connection blanked. I thought maybe he'd fainted, or dropped the phone, and called back. They told me he'd suddenly run out of the room."

"You should have been more careful," she said, then looked back at Leonard. "How old are you, Mr. Sanders?"

"Twenty-three."

"And I already know you have no record . . . have you ever been in court before?"

"No, Your Honor."

"Hmmph. All right. Let's get the rest of this cleared up, and then I'll see about your contempt citation."

The opposing attorneys, nearly identical in their dark suits, started to unpack several briefcases, but the judge stopped them.

"Gentlemen, I've read your material already, and this is only a preliminary hearing on the validity of the original injunction and the request for counter-injunction filed by the medical center. The question here is whether the organisms presently residing in Mr. Sanders' digestive tract need to be removed for safekeeping until the matter of the applicability of the Animal Rights Act comes up. According to briefs submitted by the medical center, Mr. Sanders requires these organisms in his intestine to destroy cancerous tissue and sustain life. These organisms were designed to live in the human gut, and cannot easily be maintained except in this environment. They are safe where they are, and Mr. Sanders is safe where they are, and I need a fairly compelling legal reason to order their removal."

"But how do we *know* they'll be there when the main trial comes?" asked the taller attorney. "They could flush them out and we'd have nothing . . ."

"It's an inhumane environment," added the other. "Confined in darkness, without fresh air or freedom of movement . . ."

The hospital's attorney bounced to his feet and was recognized. "Your Honor," he began, "many organisms have their natural habitat in the human gut. This one, though not originally found there, is designed for it. And we can certainly agree to keeping the organisms there until such time as the matter comes to trial, if that happens. We have no intention of removing them; it would be dangerous for Mr. Sanders, and probably fatal to the organisms themselves."

The opposing attorneys both stood, and the judge recognized the taller one again. "It is ridiculous to allow someone charged with maltreatment of an organism to retain control over it. We feel that unless the organisms are under court supervision, there's an excellent chance they will not survive to the later trial. The defendants have every reason to get rid of them—"

"I do not!" said Leonard. Dr. Gerson hastily pulled him down as the judge banged her gavel.

"Mr. Sanders, you are stretching my sympathy to the limit," she said. "You are not to speak unless called on— is that clear?"

"Yes, ma'am," he mumbled.

She turned to the opposing attorneys. "If the court should order the organisms removed from Mr. Sanders's gut, just exactly how would you think they should be cared for?"

"Well . . . in a laboratory, under proper supervision— which must, Your Honor, include supervision by either the court or by our representatives. Given plenty of light, fresh air, the appropriate food . . ."

She looked back at the hospital's attorney. "And you say this would be impossible? Can you explain?"

Leonard, watching her as the hospital's attorney stood to speak, had the feeling that she already understood both sides as well as he did, if not better—she had her own reasons for making them go through it all. The hospital's lawyer was going through it carefully, in detail, but without a trace of patronization in his tone. The organisms' requirements, which included no oxygen, no light, a diet rich in certain fatty acids and not others . . .

"—in other words," the judge broke in smoothly, "they must live in someone's gut?"

"It is *possible* to maintain them in the laboratory," said the lawyer, "but very difficult." The judge turned to the opposing side.

"You gentlemen have the right kind of environment for these things?"

"Well, I'm sure we can arrange something, Your Honor," began one, but the judge waved him to silence.

"When I give custody of an abused animal—a horse, say—to someone other than the owner, I make sure that person has adequate facilities. Your initial argument suggests that you do not, in fact, have facilities for this organism—unless one of you was planning to volunteer?"

"Volunteer, Your Honor?"

"To let them live in *your* innards," said the judge sweetly.

"I don't know how it could be arranged, but that would insure that they would be under the supervision of your society, wouldn't it?"

The attorneys had turned several interesting colors, ending in greenish gray. "But—" one of them managed to gasp.

"I thought not." Judge Lane smiled. It was not a friendly smile. "You want to subject an adult citizen to exploratory surgery to recover intestinal organisms which you supposedly want to protect—but you have no place to keep them and care for them properly, and you aren't about to volunteer to use your own bodies as a receptacle—is that true?"

"Well, no. But we—"

"Let me put it this way." She leaned forward. "I will not agree to putting these organisms anywhere but in a human gut. As far as I'm concerned, Mr. Sanders' gut is simplest. Mr. Sanders has reason to keep his organisms alive and healthy: they're keeping him alive and healthy. I don't think he's going to kill them off just to spite your organization. But if you're willing to volunteer your own, I will might consider a motion to transfer at least some of the contents of Mr. Sanders' gut to your gut. Not a hired gut, you understand—yours."

A brief muttered conversation, during which the two opposing attorneys scowled at each other, glared at each other, and finally faced the judge with expressions of anger tempered with caution.

"Your Honor," said the short one, "if the court is prepared to require Mr. Sanders to swear to produce these organisms later, if required . . ."

"Fine," said the judge. She nodded at Leonard. "Mr. Sanders—come up here."

Leonard got to his feet, and made his way to the bench.

"Mr. Sanders, you have said that you think the organisms in your intestinal tract are all that keep you alive: is that right?"

"Yes, Your Honor."

"And you will adhere to whatever medical regimen is required to keep those organisms in good health until this matter is finally decided?"

"Yes, Your Honor." Leonard's gut rumbled; he saw the corner of the judge's mouth twitch. It was the tabouli, he thought to himself, and he'd have to ask Dr. Gerson what all that strange food might have done to the crabworms.

"And you will present yourself in court, when summoned, without any shenanigans of the sort you pulled this time?"

"You mean when I ran?"

"Yes, when you ran. I want you to swear that you will appear, without having to be chased all over the city, whenever the court requires."

"Yes, Your Honor. I will."

Judge Lane looked up at the others. "I need to speak to Mr. Sanders on the matter of his contempt of court. Court is adjourned; Mr. Sanders, come to my chambers." Leonard cast a frantic glance toward Gerson and the hospital's attorney, but both of them shook their heads, and made pushing motions: he had to go. Nervously, sweating already, Leonard followed the judge to her office next door to the courtroom, a small, cluttered room with one bookcase and a desk overflowing with papers and books. A notebook-size computer lay open on her desk.

"Sit down," said Judge Lane. She was already in her own chair behind the desk, flipping the sleeves of her judicial robe out of her way. Leonard sat on the edge of the other chair. "I asked your employers about you," she said, as she flicked the computer on. Her fingers danced across the keys; she looked over the top of the display at him. "They said you were unstable, immature, and unsuitable for re-employment."

"Re-employment?" Leonard repeated the word mechanically, almost without thinking.

"Yes. My clerk was told they'd fired you, and when I pointed out that this was a violation of the Fair Employment Practices Act, and that all you had done was evade a summons to be a witness—that you had not been charged with anything—they said they'd assumed you were quitting when you left. Your final paycheck is supposed to be in the mail."

"Already?" Leonard had been sure they'd fire him, but

he'd thought someone would do it when he came back, in person.

"Already. Do you know a Sylvia Goldstein?" Leonard nodded. "And a Mr. Stevens?" Another nod. "Poisonous, those two. If you'd been charged with a felony, they couldn't have been more eager to see you gone. I think you probably have a case against them, under the Act, but it would cost a lot to pursue it, and I doubt you'd find it a pleasant place to work after all this."

"It wasn't pleasant before," said Leonard, surprising himself.

"Are you unstable, immature, and so forth?"

Leonard looked at her. Another Alicia, or Rose, or maybe even Hank . . . he tried to sort out his thoughts. "I . . . I was always afraid of the cancers," he said. "I mean, my father died, and my mother had lung cancer and died, and she'd told me I would. So it never seemed worthwhile to try for anything big. I wasn't that smart, or talented, or anything. But after Dr. Gerson picked me for the research . . ." He paused, remembering that first faint glow of self-esteem, the day Gerson had signed him as a research subject. "I did have something," he went on. "They needed me; they said I could help a lot of people by helping them. And they started talking to me—" He told the judge about the people he'd met at the medical center: their encouragement, when he mentioned taking a night class in accounting, their friendly questions.

"I knew it wasn't really a friendship," he said. "I mean, I'd never try to go to Dr. Gerson's house or anything like that. But they were just—just nice to me. Cindy, in the lab, the one who did my tissue samples, and Bill, in the animal labs, where they keep the guinea pigs . . . they'd tell me about their work, and their families. It made me feel good. At work, it was all 'Lennie, do this' and 'Lennie, do that'; no one cared. Anyway, I took the course, and passed it—" He remembered the brighter glow when he got his first exam back, with "Excellent" scrawled on the top. And making an A on the final. He told the judge all this, and finished up with—

"But I never had a girlfriend, or anything, and I'm still scared a lot. I've always tried to do what they told me to—"

"They?"

"Anyone like teachers, or my boss. That's why—" He stopped again, watching her face. She looked a *lot* like Alicia. "I guess—I mean I *know* I was wrong, to run away, but—but it was one time I just did something myself. Without asking anyone, all on my own. I went places I've never been—"

"I was going to ask you about that. Would you tell me where you were, and what you did?"

"I—I guess. Will it get them in trouble?"

The judge's eyes twinkled. "You don't have to tell me any names, you know."

"I hadn't thought of that." Leonard took a breath and plunged in, telling her everything from Gerson's phone call on: the janitor in the service elevator, the rude bus driver, the patrol car at the supermarket parking lot, his adventures in the shopping center (without names) and his sudden decision to turn himself in. "I just realized I could do things," he said finally. "Dr. Gerson had told me that before, but it came clear suddenly. I think maybe because my neck hurts."

"Hmmm." Judge Lane was tapping on the keyboard again. "So you aren't sorry you ran away? Even though it was a crime?"

Leonard felt sweat prickle his neck again. "I'm sorry I ran . . . I mean, I'm sorry I wanted to run, that I was that scared, but I'm not sorry I did something *myself*."

"Suppose it did get those people in trouble—would you be sorry about that?"

"Oh, yes. They didn't mean to do any harm; they just tried to help me. They're *nice* people."

"I see. So what you're saying is that you wish you hadn't been so frightened, but you feel just a little proud of yourself for doing something—even something wrong—on your own. Is that it?"

"I think so. Yes. I know you have to punish me for doing wrong, but—" Leonard's gut rumbled again, comfortably, and he laid his hand against it. "I'm really somebody now. I'm not going to die—at least, not from the cancers—and I can plan things, and do things, and—"

"All right, Mr. Sanders. Let's get this straightened out. You admit that you ran away from the court's summons, and you knew it was wrong. I'm still not sure you had the right idea of what the summons meant, but that's not the main point here. The point is that you did something wrong, and you knew it was wrong. On the other hand, you thought the court order might result in your death, and you have a disease which made that fear reasonable, or at least understandable, and you're very young and inexperienced in the world. Now. The law is quite firm on what constitutes contempt of court, and what you did qualifies; you were ruled in contempt of court, in fact, before you appeared. But you turned yourself in, and you have a convincing explanation of your actions. Also, you've lost your job over this. I'm going to consider that a lost job is ample punishment for your panic, but—" She leaned forward, her face now serious. "You're going to have to grow up, Mr. Sanders, and learn to make good decisions for yourself. Fear of death is an excuse—a powerful one, but not compelling—for blind panic. Dr. Gerson thinks you can do better—and from what you tell me, so do you. And I think you owe those people who took you in an apology for risking their legal standing, and a better explanation than you probably gave them. I want you to promise me that you will go back there and talk to them. Will you?"

"Yes, Your Honor," said Leonard, his heart thudding painfully.

"Soon," she said, her eyes dropping to the computer display. "I'll want you to let me know when you've done it."

"Yes, Your Honor."

"Then you may go. I've entered it on your record as 'dismissed for extenuating circumstance,' which is the best I can do."

With his first paycheck from his new job, Leonard filled two grocery sacks with pita, ground lamb, fresh vegetables, and a wine recommended by the delicatessen owner ("A party for who?" he'd asked. Leonard had explained, in some detail, and the man had shaken his head, but helped anyway.) He lugged them aboard a crosstown bus, having had to look up the route (two transfers) to the shopping center. When the bus finally curtsied to a halt in front of it, Leonard managed to get down the steps without spilling anything out of the bags. It was just after noon on a Saturday; more cars were in the parking lot than he'd seen before. A patrol car was stopped, lights flashing, at the far end of the parking lot where a crowd had gathered. Leonard glanced at it, and felt no fear. Whatever had happened was no threat to him. He headed for the strip of stores.

Through the smeared glass of the window, he saw Alicia talking to a pair of gray-haired women by the music display racks. He hitched the sacks up in his arm and wandered down to the dance studio, just as a raft of giggling pre-teen girls in baggy leg-warmers converged on the door. A minivan pulled up and disgorged an even shriller group. Another hitch of the sacks, and he headed for the Martial Arts Supreme. But here a group of older boys lounged against the door, occasionally feinting kicks at each other, hooting with glee. Leonard thought of pushing through them, and going inside, but it was probably busy in there, too.

That left the bookstore. He hadn't been inside before. He looked past the window display of books with glowing rainbows or praying hands on the covers, and saw Rose sitting at a counter, reading something. He couldn't imagine her reading anything that would have a rainbow on the cover.

When he leaned on the door, it opened slowly. Over his head a chime jangled. Rose looked up. Her expression did not change, but her eyes seemed to flicker.

"Ah . . ." she said softly. "Is it—?"

"Leonard Sanders," he said.

"You're not really a rabbit," she said, as if to continue the conversation of weeks past.

"No," he said. "Not any more." He set the sacks down on her counter.

"Did you get in a lot of trouble?"

"Not as much as I'd been afraid of." He took a breath, and faced her eyes, the challenging eyes of someone who has seen worse than this. "I shouldn't have run—but since I did run, I'm glad I ran here."

"I'm glad you stopped running," she said gravely. "And I'm glad you came back to tell us about it. We'd worried."

"I know. It helped." He grinned at her. "I—I wanted to give a party, but my place isn't big enough."

"I think we can find a place," she said. Now her face was changing, into that warmth he had glimpsed once before. "Just let me call the others." She turned to the phone, then glanced back at him. "You realize we'll try again—to run your life for you, I mean. We're like that, when we care."

"I know," said Leonard. "I won't let you."

"Good." She winked at him, and started dialling.

*Some people never learn, and sometimes their not learn-
ing is what makes a story. I love this story for several reasons, and one of them is that my mother said no one would
ever publish it.*

*Another? Well, a urologist wrote to tell me he couldn't
believe a woman understood about all "that."*

# THE GENERIC REJUVENATION
## OF MILO ARDRY

Before his first rejuvenation, Milo Ardry had not been
concerned with the cost. The procedure itself had been new
enough, risky enough, and—perhaps most important—*exclusive* enough to justify any expense. He had been seventy,
a sleek and pampered seventy but seventy nonetheless, with
all that implied about, for example, his prostate. A chance
to become thirty again was worth a few millions. He chose
*Reverberations*, the first licensee of the procedure, and
already establishing itself as the top of the line.

He was one of the lucky ones who sailed through rejuvenation with hardly any trouble. They told him when he
woke that it would be the same every time. Either your
body took to rejuv easily, or it didn't, and that's the way
it went. So Milo went back to his remaining millions with
the healthy thirty-year-old body he remembered so well, and
rode it hard until he reached nominal fifty. At that point
he couldn't see why he should live through the fifies and
sixties again, going downhill all the way, and bought his
second rejuvenation from *Reverberations*.

He was mildly annoyed to find that they charged as much

to return him to nominal thirty from fifty as they had from seventy, but—cushioned in one of their famous consultancy suites—thought it too much effort to check out and find another company. Even though it would take most of his reserves, and his children (approaching the need for their own rejuvenation procedures) would complain bitterly, he still felt that he deserved the very best. After a few sarcastic remarks which the *Reverberations* valet, immaculate in formal dress, received in respectful silence, Milo fell asleep and woke up thirty.

The good years returned: the strength, the concentration, the taste of good food and drink, the delight in women. He hadn't lost *much* between thirty and fifty, but that little was the difference between good enough and splendid, between coming off the court after a fast eight-goal game with the pro, still ready for all night on the town, and deciding to play a couple of friendly goals with another fifty year old. Or even deciding not to play deven at all, to sit out the games and watch.

Musing on this, he decided to rejuv oftener. After all, why not? Why not live at his peak all the time, and not just for the few years it lasted each cycle?

He thought about it, off and on, until the year he reached nominal thirty-five and found himself breathless after water-wrestling Heather and Jeri Brannon (ages 27 and 29) in the Maelstrom. That night he called up his whole financial setup, from asteroid mining to zoological park. He wanted to rejuv every five years . . . at most every ten, if he reverted to twenty-five, but he'd still had a bad complexion at twenty-five. Say seven years. Rejuv every seven years to age twenty-eight, and live until thirty-five, and then another cycle. Why not?

Money, that's why not. He called up the latest *Reverberations* advertisement, fed it into his computer, and stared in complete shock at the display. At those rates, he would be bankrupt in three—at most four—cycles. His net worth still hadn't recovered from his second rejuv; he had to live out at least nineteen years between cycles.

Close after shock came anger. It simply was not fair.

*Reverberations* charged a flat fee for rejuv, expensive enough if it meant reversing thirty or forty years of aging, but outrageous when the body had only suffered through five or six. Milo grumbled, watching the display, and called his advisors.

They couldn't give him a different answer. At the current rate, he'd be completely bankrupt after a few more rejuvs, and—his legal staff had pointed out—his heirs would almost certainly declare him incompetent for wasting the family fortune to keep one old man young. Milo had glared for thirty seconds at the fancy-pants youngster the legal department had put on the line before realizing that it was the same old Charles Raymond Coatesworth, fresh out of rejuv and a nominal thirty at most.

"I suppose you'd help them," he said sourly.

Coatesworth smiled. "I should have to state my opinion, Milo, and that's what it was the last time. Under present law—"

"Which can be changed," said Milo.

"Which hasn't been changed yet," Coatesworth pointed out. "And that's the law we're under. Your heirs have a right to petition the court to have you declared incompetent any time you act in an irrational, unbusinesslike way with their heritage. And *Farnton vs. Kansas*, if you read my memo on it, sets a precedent that your heirs could use to advantage."

"All right, all right." Milo cut everyone off the circuit, and brooded. He hadn't read Coatesworth's memo; he never read Coatesworth's memos. He thought of querying the computer, but it really didn't matter. If his own legal staff were ready to cooperate with those fortune hunters, his miserable whining sons and daughter, he might as well give up the idea of a *Reverberations* rejuv. But that didn't mean aging for twenty or thirty years before rejuv, not any more. Other companies had moved into the expanding market. He toed the control, and called up the figures on them. Holenew . . . he'd heard a few stories about them. An accountant at the home office had rejuved with them, and died six months later, in agonizing pain from the bone cancers. OverEasy had a good reputation, but their prices were only 10% under *Reverberations*. He watched as the list scrolled by alphabetically, then called it again, sorted by price. Never buy cheapest, he'd always believed, so he ignored the bottom five. The sixth lowest was *Revibrations*.

Milo grinned. That kind of humor got to him. He found himself nodding as he read the rest of the listing. Licensed both nationally and locally, as a Class B rejuv service. That meant nothing, really—only the top three firms were Class A, and B ran from "almost as good" to "really sleazy." There were Class C firms that charged more. He suspected that *Revibrations* was about to move up . . . he might be getting one of the last good, cheap rejuvs around. He chuckled all the way to bed.

*Revibrations* was housed in a plain brick building in what Milo considered "secondary" property. Instead of the white glazed tile entrance, with a blue canopy over carpet, with which *Reverberations* welcomed its clients, the cheaper rejuv service had a strip of green fake grass on either side of a stone-flagged walk. Its door was blacked-glass; Milo had to push it open himself.

But once inside, it was luxurious enough. A uniformed guard bowed at him; a receptionist (female, he noted with approval) came forward smiling. In less than a minute he was relaxing in a comfortable leather chair, sipping antique coffee while the Director explained the procedure. Milo concentrated on the flavor in his mouth, and paid little attention. After all, he'd been rejuved before, and at the best place: what could *Revibrations* tell him about it? When the Director fell silent, Milo smiled and signed on the dotted line. He did read the contract—or at least looked at every paragraph—for that basic survival skill of business had never deserted him. But a rejuv contract was full of words he didn't know; all he did was note that it looked much like the *Reverberations* contract which he'd had his legal staff go over the first time. It didn't have any of the "siren" clauses—any claim on his inheritance, any authorization for use of *his* body parts—so he signed.

He gave his medical history to a someone in a white uniform, and his credit card to someone with a portable BankChek, and finally his clothes to someone in rumpled green surgical scrubs. He noticed, at points in the procedure, that the *Revibrations* facilities were not as luxurious as those he enjoyed elsewhere. The toilets were clean, but plain and functional: white porcelain and steel. The chairs were a little too firm, not completely shaped to his individual back; the clothes closet was more like a locker. The personnel, too, while competent and polite, showed no desire to give extra service: they almost seemed hurried. But after all, he was paying less than half what *Reverberations* charged.

Milo woke with his usual ease, and knew at once that rejuv had occurred. The light was just that fraction brighter, sounds just slightly clearer. He wore a plain, not-very-comfortable hospital gown, and a technician was only then slipping the last needle from his arm. Milo settled back, ready for a final nap, but felt an insistent tug.

"Come on, sir, up you go." The technician had grasped his shoulder.

"I think I'll just lie here," Milo started to say, but he felt himself heaved upward.

"Come *on* now, sir. Time to go." Before he could protest, he was in a wheelchair, floating down the corridor with the technician's hand on the back cushion. Milo blinked. He saw two litters along one wall, each with its sleeping occupant. Had *he* been left out like that for anyone to stare at? He had no time to ask. The technician twirled the wheelchair into a curtained cubicle, and decanted Milo onto a padded shelf along one wall. "Clothes in there, sir," he said, pointing at a locker that made no pretense of being a closet. "Nurse'll be along to sign you out."

Milo felt the cold draft along his naked back and glared at the cheap green curtain the technician had pulled across the opening. He hadn't been treated with such complete callousness since his father's death, when his uncle had sent him to Camp He-Man, guaranteed to change spoiled rich boys into tough, cooperative, independent young men. As a result of that experience, Milo had thrown his uncle off the Board of Directors as soon as he'd gotten on it himself, and his cousins still wondered why "Dear Milo" never had time to see them or an available job in his companies. He did not put up with this sort of thing. Not now. He sat on the shelf, smouldering, until someone called him from outside.

"Mr. Ardry? Aren't you ready yet? Dr. Allison's waiting."

"Let him wait," growled Milo. "I need help—where's a valet?" He hoped the nurse would be pretty—her voice didn't sound it, but voices could lie. But he heard the squeak of her shoes on the floor as she moved away. "Nurse!" he yelled, but got no answer. He was almost angry enough to storm after her, open-back gown and all. His dignity prevented him—young and handsome he might be, rejuved to thirty, but no man looked his best in what was no more than a modified apron.

After another fuming minute or two, when he heard nothing from the hall outside, Milo gave up. He might as well get dressed himself, because he wanted to waste no time before entering a complaint. He stood up, finding himself slightly shaky on his feet, and opened the locker. He had just dropped the hospital gown on the floor, and reached for his LeGentilhomme silk underwear when someone jerked the curtain aside, and he felt a heavy fat hand on his shoulder. What followed was the most humiliating experience since camp, an experience made worse by Dr. Allison, who, when he finally met her, insisted on treating his justifiable anger as a psychological symptom of rejuvenation. "Now, now, sir," she kept saying, and handed him a packet of pills to take. Milo finally stormed out to his waiting limousine, ready to throw several shelf-loads of books at *Revibrations*, just as soon as he could get his legal staff onto the job.

His private medical exam at home, however, was reassuring. Nominal thirty. Milo registered with the government, as the law required, and received his new IDs a few minutes later: the pictures showing a crisp jawline, dark hair, unclouded eyes. He relaxed, then, in the gray velvet chair he favored (recovered, of course, during his rejuvenation: so careless to let the wear on one's furniture reflect one's true age.) Despite the disgusting lack of courtesy shown by the *Revibrations* staff on the way out, he was nominal thirty, and he felt nominal thirty, and a long life was, after all, the best revenge. He took a long, satisfied breath, and notified all departments that the Chief was back in command. That evening, when he still had the energy for a double trip through the Maelstrom (in a new black suit that left nothing to the imagination), was the high point of his cut-rate rejuv.

The next morning his troubles began.

In the first place, the old Milo Ardry—the original, who would now, without rejuv, be a nominal ninety-odd—had had prostate trouble. Many 70-year-old men do, and being rich is no help. There are only a few ways to correct the problem, all of them unpleasant. He had—in those days—been resigned to shortness of breath, crepy skin hanging in loose folds from his arms and legs, wrinkles everywhere, long gray hairs on his back, the bald spot (concealed under an implant, but still bald in his mind). But not to that personal and very humiliating difficulty, the proper revenge (his then mistress had snickered before he dismissed her) of Mother Nature on all arrogant males who survive long enough. A "good stream" was something boys were proud of as soon as they learned to aim it more or less; even Rembrandt had done etchings showing that proud difference between men and women. And now—then—at seventy, he no longer had that good stream or anything like it. He strained. He struggled. He—not to put too fine a point on it—dribbled. A function easy—almost thought-less—for two thirds of a century became an act hard to begin, hard to continue, and excruciating to withhold. Not to mention sex, which he didn't out loud but thought about bitterly.

He had tried the pills, when the first trouble came on at fifty-seven. He had considered—and shied away from— the recommended surgery. But just before his rejuvenation, he had decided to go through with it . . . let himself be reamed out, so to speak, and then implanted with a surgical assist for his pleasure. Luckily the rejuv had taken easily, and he had no more need for urological consultation. His second rejuv was done before he had any difficulty at all. He had no idea just how rejuv worked, or how an old, enlarged prostate became once more the smooth, snug gland he had once had: it worked, and that was all he cared about.

Until the morning after he came home from *Revibrations*. It had been, by this time, twenty-five years since the last time he'd noticed his prostate or—except in delight—any of the attendant organic apparatus. So when he threw off his robe and discovered a haze of blue fur, he was, to say the least, appalled. His own body hair, what there was of it, was black. Not rich, lustrous, brilliant electric blue fuzz.

He touched, pinched, tugged gently. Attached, and evidently growing in place. In the mirrored wall of his refreshment suite, he could see the expression on his face, mingled smirk and snarl. *Revibrations* would never be the same; he would pluck those responsible from their snug little racket as a gull plucks snails from their shells. Blue fur indeed. Then, admiring past the blue haze on his body the taut line of his nominal thirty belly, he braced his legs and aimed.

And nothing much happened.

Milo frowned, and tried again. Quickly connected two and two, and attempted a test of his hypothesis on the expected sum. Sure enough, despite the lean belly and springy feel of his muscles, the clear sight and undimmed hearing, something was missing. Something *important* to Milo, one of the things he wanted a rejuvenation of . . . and for.

Now his face in the mirror was grim, and he dressed quickly for the day's business, of which the first item was the total, complete, absolute beyond all doubt annihilation of *Revibrations*. At his desk, he called up a copy of the contract, and then called Charles Coatesworth for a live conference.

Coatesworth was not as sympathetic as he should have been. "You did not have the legal department check that contract for you . . ."

"No, but it was the same old thing, and I did look for the clauses you'd warned me about."

"Some of them, yes." Coatesworth pointed to a subparagraph. "Notice this?"

Milo peered at it. He didn't really understand all that legal nonsense. "Hold harmless" and "generic substitution of equivalent bioactive material" . . . what was that? There was no way that *Revibrations* could claim that blue fur and urological problems were "equivalent" to the nominal-thirty rejuvenation he'd been promised. Coatesworth cleared his throat, regaining Milo's attention, and explained.

"This right here says that they can use generic genetic material in the carrier viruses as well as the bioactives."

"Is that bad?" To no one but Coatesworth, who had been with him from the beginning, would Milo have revealed his ignorance so freely. Now he wished he had not made an exception. The expression on Coatesworth's face had far more contempt than was comfortable.

"Milo, I know you're bright. You always were. But you also always hated to study hard enough to actually learn anything. And what it sounds like now is that you haven't the faintest idea how a rejuvenation works, despite having undergone three of them and signed papers each time that said you did."

"I'm not a doctor," said Milo. "Get to the point."

"The point is that they used generics. Which means we really don't know exactly what they did use, because they didn't have to specify, except in the most general terms. At *Reverberations* and the other Class A licensees, you're guaranteed nothing but pure human-genome, cloned culture material, for both the carrier virus and the bioactives themselves. This means, for one thing, that you don't sprout blue feathers . . ."

"It's not feathers; it's fur," said Milo. Coatesworth folded his lips together for a moment.

"Have you looked lately?"

"What—?" Milo stared, with dawning suspicion. "No . . ." Coatesworth nodded. Milo keyed a command into his desk and a mirror slid out of the left-hand side, lifted to face-height, and tilted. There, where the morning's surprise had been a thin blue fuzz on his cheeks, was a fluff of something clearly not hair. Down? He peeked down into the neck of his low-cut raw silk shirt. The heavier growth on his chest was a stage beyond down . . . little blue pinfeathers sprouted, their tips just starting to open. "No!" said Milo with feeling. "Not feathers!"

Coatesworth had fixed his eyes on a sheaf of printouts. "I put this together even before I saw you. The feathers are some kind of interaction between your native hair follicles and the new genetic overlay. It's not as simple as if they'd used bird genes for feathers instead of mammalian genes for hair . . . that we could nail them on. Your feathers are an idiosyncratic symbiotic synthesis . . ." Coatesworth was clearly enjoying rolling those long words off his tongue; Milo clenched his fists. What he could understand of it sounded as if his hair follicles had rejuvenated all the way back to a primordial nonmammalian ancestor who had feathers. Blue feathers. When Coatesworth looked up, he glared at him; Coatesworth merely looked sober. "We can't do a thing about the feathers," he said. "It's a risk you undertook, in writing, without the advice of your legal department, which you chose to ignore." His eyes dropped back to the printouts he held. "But I think we can argue with them about the other problem. You paid for a nominal-thirty rejuvenation, and a urological study will no doubt indicate that your function is not within normal limits for nominal thirty."

"But they can't—I can't—"

"Milo, I'm terribly sorry, but all we can do legally is file for a refund of that part of the procedure detailed as urological. Unless you want to let them try again . . ."

"NO!"

"I thought not. I've already contacted other firms about a partial rejuvenation, limited to urological. *Reverberations* won't touch it; they say that they can't afford to handle clients who have been contaminated with generic genetic material. Their experts feel that once such material has been incorporated into your body, there's no way to be sure it's all eliminated. And their guarantee would make them liable for any future problems. They did, however, recommend a firm which does partial rejuvenations for medical reasons, when a single organ system has been damaged by disease, for instance. It's going to cost you—"

"It's going to cost *them*," said Milo grimly, his fingers catching on the fuzz of his chin.

"*You*. You're the one who signed that contract. I don't know how many times I've told you not to sign contracts without the legal department's approval . . ."

"I'm sorry." Milo glared at Coatesworth, who gave him a level look back.

"The firm I'm talking about will do a complete urological rejuvenation to nominal 30, and they *think* they can isolate and uncouple the insertion that caused the trouble, so it should be a permanent fix, and not something you'll have to deal with in each rejuvenation process."

Milo could think of nothing scathing enough, and was silent, his rejuvenated innards seething.

"They're not so sure about your fertility," Coatesworth said.

"I've got enough damn children," said Milo.

"Then shall I schedule you with them?"

"Yes. As soon as possible. And see if there isn't something they can do about these feathers."

Coming out of a partial rejuvenation was far worse than the whole process. Milo felt as if he'd had major surgery, which even at nominal thirty is not a pleasant feeling. He ached. He throbbed. Parts of him felt compressed and cramped, and other parts felt distended. But as he shifted in his bed, he heard around and above him the kind of deferential, low-voiced murmur he preferred. When he opened his eyes, the gowned nurses at his side had sympathetic smiles. In a very short time, he was able to tell that the procedure had been a complete success. So far as it went.

When Coatesworth came in to see him, Milo was propped up in a comfortable bed eating real oysters (cloned and grown in saltwater tanks far from any contamination) on toast. Coatesworth stood by the door, obviously wary.

"I feel very well," Milo said, in answer to Coatesworth's polite inquiry. He was sure that Coatesworth had access to his medical records anyway. "But what am I going to do about this?" *This* being the blue feathers, now fully sprouted and forming a lush blue covering for his chest under the brocade dressing gown, and a very odd-looking arrangment on his lower face and throat—apparently his distant ancestor had had a metallic purple gorget.

"I suggest using a depilatory," said Coatesworth. "It's bound to clog a razor." And he ducked out before Milo could say anything, or even throw an oyster-laden square of toast.

*This is the original ending of the story, but not the one that saw print . . . you can find that one in the back of the book, and decide which you like best.*

*The impractical artist is such a stock figure of political thought that I love to put a spanner in the works now and then. What are the reciprocal bonds that connect an artist to his culture, and the culture to the artist? What happens when they fray?*

# NEW WORLD SYMPHONY

It was his first world. On the way out, resting in the half-doze of transfer, he imagined many things. A fire world, all volcanic and rough, showers of sparks against a night sky, clouds of steam and ash, firelit. Or a water world like Pella, with all the endless quivering shades of color, the blues and silvers, purples and strange greens. It might have mountains like Lelare, a purple sky, six moons or none, rings like golden Saturn's, rainbowed arcs . . . he saw against the screen of his mind these and other worlds, some seen once in pictures, others created from his mind's store of images.

All he knew for certain was that no one yet had set foot on it. Only two probes had been there: the robot survey, which had noted it as a possible, and the manned scout, which had given it a 6.7, a marginal rating, out of 10. He didn't know why the rating was 6.7; he knew he might not have understood it even if they'd told him. It had been approved, and then assigned, and he—just out of the Academy, just past his thesis—he had been given that assignment.

He half-heard something in his chamber, felt a pressure on his arm, hands touching his face. He struggled to open his eyes, and heard the quiet voice he had heard so far ago.

"Please, sir, wait a moment. It's all right; you're rousing now. Take a deep breath first . . . good. Another. Move your right hand, please . . ."

He felt his fingers shift, stiffly at first, then more easily. More than anything else, the reported stiffening had frightened him: his hands were his life. But they'd explained, insisted that it was no more than missing a single week of practice, not the three years of the voyage. He moved his left hand, then tried again with his eyelids. This time they opened, and he had no trouble focussing on the medical attendant. Gray hair, brown eyes, the same quiet face that had put him in his couch back at the Station.

He wanted to ask if they had arrived, and felt childish in that desire. The attendant smiled, helped him sit and swing his legs over the edge of the couch. "Your first meal, sir; it's important that you eat before standing." He pushed over a sliding table with a tray of food. "Do you recall your name, sir?"

Until he was asked, he hadn't thought of it. For a moment the concept of his name eluded him. Then he remembered, clearly and completely. "Of course," he said. "Georges Mantenon. Musician-graduate."

"Yes, sir." The attendant fastened a strap around his left arm while he ate with his right. "I must check this, just a moment."

Mantenon paid no attention to the attendant; he knew the man wouldn't answer medical questions, and even if he did it would tell him nothing. He had an appetite; the Class Three food tasted the same as always. His hands felt better every moment. He held his left arm still until the medical attendant was through with it, and went on eating.

When he'd finished, the other man showed him to a suite of rooms: bath, workroom, sitting room. Along one wall of the workroom was the keyboard/pedal complex of a Meirinhoff, the same model he'd used for his thesis. He made himself shower and change before climbing into it. He adjusted the seat, the angle of keyboard and pedal banks, the length of cord from the headpiece to output generator. Then he touched the keys, lightly, and felt/heard/saw the Meirinhoff awake.

His fingers danced along the keyboard, touching section

controls as well as pitch/resonance indicators. Woodwinds, brass—he felt festive, suddenly aware that he'd been afraid, even during the transfer dreams. He toed a percussion pedal, tipped it off. Wrong blend, wrong tempo. For a long moment he struggled with the pedals, then remembered what was wrong. He'd put on exactly what the attendant laid out, which meant he had on slippers.

Slippers! He scraped them off with his toes, and kicked them out of the way. His toes, surgically freed at the metatarsal, and held for walking by special pads in his shoes (not that he walked much), spread wide. Years of practice had given him amazing reach. He tried again for the percussion he wanted, toed cymbal on delay, pitched the snares down a tone, added the bright dash of the triangle. He played with balance, shifting fingers and toes minutely until the sound in the phones matched that in his head. Then he paused, hands and feet still.

His head dipped, so that the subvoc microphone touched the angle of his larynx. His hands lifted briefly, his toes curled up. Then he reached out, curling his tongue up in his mouth to let the clean sound come free, and put the Meirinhoff on full audio/record. He could feel, through his fingers, his feet, his seat, the wave of sound, the wave he designed, drove, controlled, shaped, and finally, after two glorious minutes of play, subdued. He lay back in his seat, fully relaxed, and tapped the system off audio.

"Sir?" The voice brought him upright, the short cord of the headset dragging at his ears.

"Klarge!" It was the worst oath he knew, and he meant it. No one, *no one*, not even a full professor, would walk in on someone who had just composed. And for someone who had had no outlet for years—! He pulled off the headset and glared at the person standing in the doorway. Not the medical attendant; that blue uniform meant ship's crew, and the decorative braid all over the front probably meant some rank. He forced a smile to his face. "Sorry," he said, achieving an icy tone. "It is not usual to interrupt a composition."

"I didn't," the person pointed out. He realized she was

a woman. "You had finished, I believe; I did not speak until you had turned off the audio."

Mantenon frowned. "Nonetheless—"

"The captain wishes to speak with you," said the woman. "About projecting all that without warning."

"Projecting—?" He was confused. "All I did was compose—that's my job."

"You had that thing on external audio," she said, "and you nearly blasted our ears out with it. You're not supposed to be hooked up to the ship's speakers without permission."

"Was I?" He remembered, now he came to think of it, something the attendant had said about the bank of switches near the console. He had been so glad to see the Meirinhoff, he hadn't paid much attention. He gave a quick glance at the recording timer: two minutes fifteen seconds—quite a long time, actually, if they didn't know it was coming or how to interrupt it.

"You were." Her mouth quirked; he realized she was trying not to laugh at him. "Your suite has an override for anything but emergency; that's so we could hear if anything was wrong." She nodded at the Meirinhoff. "That was more than we bargained on."

"I'm sorry. I—it had just been so long, and I didn't know the hookup was on . . ." He hadn't felt so stupid since his second year in the conservatory. He knew his ears were red; he could feel them burning.

"All right. I understand it wasn't intentional. I'd thought maybe you were going to insist that we listen to every note you played—"

"Klarge, no! Of course not. But the captain—?"

She grinned at him. "I'm the captain, Mr. Mantenon. Captain Plessan. You probably don't recall meeting me before; you were sedated when they brought you aboard."

"Oh." He couldn't think of anything to say, polite or otherwise. "I'm sorry about the speakers—"

"Just remember the switch, please. And when you've recovered fully, I'd be glad to see you in the crew lounge."

"I'm—I'm fine now, really—" He started clambering free of the Meirinhoff, flipping controls off, resetting the recorders, fumbling for his slippers. He'd like to have stayed, listened to his composition, refined it, but everything he'd been told about shipboard etiquette urged him to go at once. He'd already insulted the captain enough as it was.

He had hoped the lounge viewscreens would be on, but blue drapes with the Exploration Service insignia covered them. The captain waved her hand at them. "You were probably hoping to see your world, Mr. Mantenon, but regulations forbid me to allow you a view until your initial briefing is complete. You must then sign your acceptance of the contract, and acknowledge all the warnings. Only then can I allow you to see the world."

"And how long will that be?"

"Not long. Only a few hours, I expect." A chime rang out, mellow, with overtones he recognized at once. Several others came into the lounge, and the captain introduced them. Senior crew: officers, the Security team, medical, heads of departments. These would see to his needs, as well as the ship's needs, in the coming months. He tried to pay attention to them, and then to the final briefing the captain gave, but all he could think of was the new world, the unknown world, that hung in space outside the ship. He signed the papers quickly, glancing through them only enough to be sure that the Musician's Union had put its authorization on each page. What would that world be like? Would he be able to express its unique beauty in music, as his contract specified, or would he fail?

At last the formalities were over. The other crewmembers left, and the captain touched controls that eased the curtains back over the viewscreens and switched video to the lounge.

His first thought was simply *NO*. No, I don't like this world. No, I can't do this world. No, someone's made a mistake, and it's impossible, and it wouldn't take a musician to express this world in sound. A large crunching noise would do the job. His trained mind showed him the score for the crunching noise, for both Meirinhoff and live orchestra, and elaborated a bit. He ignored it and stared at the captain. "That?" he asked.

"That," she said. "It's going to be a mining world."

That was obvious. Whatever it was good for, anything that disgusting shade of orange streaked with fungus-blue wasn't a pleasure world, or an agriculture world. That left mining. He forced himself to look at the screens again. Orange, shading from almost sulfur yellow to an unhealthy orange-brown. The blue couldn't be water, not that shade . . . he thought of bread mold again. Something vaguely greenish blue, and a sort of purplish patch toward the bottom . . . if that was the bottom.

"Does it have any moons or anything?" he asked.

"All that information is in the cube I gave you, but yes, it has three of them. Let me change the mags, here, and you'll see . . ." She punched a few buttons and the planet seemed to recede. Now he saw two moons, one small and pale yellow, the other one glistening white. "I'll leave you now," she said. "Please don't use the ship speakers for your composition without letting me know, and if you need anything just ask." And without another word she turned and left him.

Monster, he thought, and wasn't sure if he meant the planet or the captain. Ugly bastard—that was the planet. Someone must have made a mistake. He'd been told—he'd been *assured*—that psych service had made assignments based on his personality profile and the planet's characteristics. The planet was supposed to represent something central to his creativity, and draw on the main vectors of his genius. Or something like that; he couldn't quite remember the exact words. But if he hated it from the beginning, something was wrong. He'd expected to have to court a reaction, the way he'd had to do with so many projects: the Karnery vase, the square of blue wool carpet, the single fan-shaped shell. Each of those had become an acceptable composition only after days of living with each object, experiencing it and its space, and the delicate shifts his mind made in response.

But he saw nothing delicate in that planet. And nothing delicate in his response. It hung gross and ugly in the sky, an abomination, like a rotting gourd; he imagined he could smell it. He could not—he *would* not—commit that atrocity to music.

In spite of himself, a melodic line crawled across his brain, trailing harmonies and notations for woodwinds. He felt his fingers flex, felt himself yearning for the Meirinhoff. No. It was ridiculous. Anything he might compose in this disgust would be itself disgusting. His study was beauty; his business was beauty. He glanced at the viewscreen again. The white moon had waned to a nail paring; the yellow one was hardly more than half-full. He wondered how fast they moved, how fast the ship moved. How could they be in orbit around the planet, and yet outside its moons' orbits? He wished he'd paid more attention to his briefings on astroscience. He remembered the cube in his hand, and sighed. Maybe that would tell him more, would explain how this world could possibly be considered a match for him.

But after the cube, he was just as confused. It gave information: diameter, mass, characteristics of the star the planet circled, characteristics of atmosphere (unbreathable), native life forms (none noted by surveys), chemical analysis, and so on and so on. Nothing else; nothing that gave him any idea why the psychs would pick that planet for him.

Restless, he moved over to the Meirinhoff. He couldn't tell the captain no, not after signing the contract. He had to compose something. He checked to make sure he was not hooked into the speaker system and climbed back into his instrument. At least he could refine that *crunch* of dismay . . . it might make an accent in something else, sometime.

With his eyes closed, he stroked the keys, the buttons, the pedals, bringing first one section then another into prominence, extrapolating from what he heard in the earphones to the whole sound, once freed. The crunch, once he had it to his satisfaction, became the sound a large gourd makes landing on stone . . . he remembered that from his boyhood. And after, the liquid splatter, the sound of seeds striking . . . in his mind a seed flew up, hung, whirling in the air like a tiny satellite, a pale yellow moon, waxing and waning as his mind held the image. He noted that on subvoc, recorded that section again.

The melody that had first come to him, the one he'd suppressed, came again, demanding this time its accompaniment of woodwinds. He called up bassoon, then the Sulesean variant, even deeper of pitch, and hardly playable by a human. Above it, the oboe and teroe. He needed another, split the oboe part quickly and transposed pedals to woodwinds, his toes and fingers racing while the thought lasted. He wasn't sure it had anything to do with the planet, but he liked it. He paused, then, and called the recordings back into the earphones.

The crunch: massive, final, definitive. A long pause . . . he counted measures this time, amazed at the length of it before the splattering sounds, the flute and cello that defined the seed/satellite. He stopped the playback, and thought a moment, lips pursed. It was a conceit, that seed, and maybe too easy . . . but for now, he'd leave it in. He sent the replay on. The melody was all right—in fact, it was good—but it had no relation to the preceding music. He'd have to move it somewhere, but he'd save it. He marked the section for relabelling, and lay back, breathing a little heavily and wondering what time it was.

The clock, when he noticed it on the opposite wall, revealed that he'd spent over three hours in the Meirinhoff. No wonder he was tired and hungry. He felt a little smug about it, how hard he'd worked on his first day out of transfer, as he levered himself out of the instrument and headed for the shower.

In the next days, he found himself working just as hard. An hour or so in the lounge alone, watching the planet in the viewscreen, changing magnification from time to time. Disgust waned to distaste, and then to indifference. It was not responsible, after all, for how it looked to him. The planet could not know his struggles to appreciate it, to turn its mineral wealth, its ugly lifeless surface, into a work of art.

And when he could look at it no longer, when he found himself picking up what little reading material the ship's crew left lying about, he returned to his instrument, to the

Meirinhoff, and fastened himself into that embrace of mingled struggle and pleasure. His mind wandered to the Academy, to the lectures on esthetic theory, on music law, all those things he'd found so dull at the time. He called up and re-read the section in General Statutes about colonization and exploitation of new worlds, until he could recite it word for word, and the rhythm worked itself into his composition.

"It is essential that each new world be incorporated into the species ethic and emotional milieu . . ." Actually it didn't make much sense. If it hadn't been for whoever wrote that, though, most musicians wouldn't have a job. The decision to send musicians and artists to each newly discovered, rated world, before anyone actually landed on it, and to include artists and musicians on each exploration landing team had provided thousands of places for those with talent. Out of that effort had come some superb music and art—Keller's "Morning on Moondog," and the ballet *Gia's Web* by Annette Polacek—and plenty of popular stuff. Miners, colonists, explorers—they all seemed to want music and art created for "their" world, whatever it was. Mantenon had heard the facile and shallow waltzes Tully Conover wrote for an obscure cluster of mining worlds: everyone knew "Mineral Waltz," "Left by Lead," and the others. And in art, the thousands of undistinguished visuals of space views: ringed planets hanging over moons of every color and shape, twinned planets circling one another . . . but it sold, and supported the system, and that was what counted.

Georges Mantenon had hoped—had believed—he could do better. If nothing as great as *Gia's Web*, he could compose at least as well as Metzger, whose *Symphony Purple* was presented in the Academy as an example of what they were to do. Mantenon had been honored with a recording slot for two of his student compositions. One of them had even been optioned by an off-planet recording company. The Academy would get the royalties, if any, of course. Students weren't allowed to earn money from their music. Still, he had been aware that his teachers considered him especially gifted. But with a miserable, disgusting orange ball streaked with blue fungus—how could he do anything particularly worthy? The square of blue carpet had been easy compared to this.

He tried one arrangement after another of the melody and variations he'd already composed, shifting parts from one instrument to another, changing keys, moving the melody itself from an entrance to a climax to a conclusion. Nothing worked. Outside, in the screens, he saw the same ugly world; if his early disgust softened into indifference, it never warmed into anything better. He could not, however calmly he looked, see anything beautiful about it. The moons were better—slightly—and the third, when it finally appeared around the planet's limb, was a striking lavender. He liked that, found his mind responding with a graceful flourish of strings. But it was not enough. It fit nowhere with the rest of the composition—if it could be called a composition—and by itself it could not support his contract.

He had hardly noticed, in those early days, that he rarely saw any of the crew, and when he did, they never asked about his work. He would have been shocked if they had asked: he was, after all, a licensed creative artist, whose work was carried out in as much isolation as Security granted any of the Union's citizens. Yet when he came into the crew lounge, after struggling several hours with his arrangement for the lavendar moon, and found it empty as usual, he was restless and dissatisfied. He couldn't, he thought grumpily, do it *all* himself. He lay back on the long couch under the viewport and waited. Someone would have to come in eventually, and he'd insist, this time, that they talk to him.

The first to appear was a stocky woman in a plain uniform—no braid at all. She nodded at him, and went to the dispenser for a mug of something that steamed. Then she sat down, facing slightly away from him, inserted a plug in her ear, and thumbed the control of a cubescreen before he could get his mouth shaped to speak to her. He sat there, staring, aware that his mouth was still slightly open, and fumed. She could at least have said hello. He turned away politely, shutting his mouth again, and folded his arms. Next time he'd be quicker.

But the next person to come in ignored him completely, walked straight to the other woman and leaned over her, whispering something he could not hear. It was a man Mantenon had never seen before, with a single strip of blue braid on his collar. The woman turned, flipped off the cubescreen, and removed her earplug. The man sat beside her, and they talked in low voices; Mantenon could hear the hum, but none of the words. After a few minutes, the two of them left, with a casual glance at Mantenon that made him feel like a crumpled food tray someone had left on the floor. He could feel the pulse beating in his throat, anger's metronome, and a quick snarl of brass and percussion rang in his head. It wasn't bad, actually . . . he let himself work up the scoring for it.

When he opened his eyes again, one of the med techs stood beside him, looking worried.

"Are you all right, sir?"

"Of course," said Mantenon, a bit sharper than he meant. "I was just thinking of something." He sat up straighter. "I'm fine."

"Have you been overworking?"

He opened his mouth to say no, and then stopped. Maybe he had been.

"Are you feeling paranoid, sir?" asked the med tech.

"Paranoid?"

"Does it seem that everyone is watching you, or talking about you, or refusing to help you?"

"Well . . ." If his bad mood was a medical problem, maybe they would give him a pill or shot, and he'd be able to compose something better. He nodded, finally, and as he had hoped, the med tech handed him a foil packet.

"Take this, sir, with a cup of something hot—and you really ought to eat your meals with the crew for a day or so."

Med could override his artist's privileges, he remembered suddenly—if they thought he was sick, or going crazy, they would tell Security, and he'd be put on full monitor, like everyone else.

He made himself smile. "You may be right," he said. "I

guess I started working, and just forgot about meals and things."

The med tech was smiling now, and even brought him a hot drink from the dispenser. "Here. You'll feel better soon. Shall I tell the captain you'll be eating with crew today?"

He nodded, gulping down the green pill in the packet with a bitter cup of Estrain tea.

He showered and changed for the next meal, unsure which it would be, and walked into the crew mess to find himself confronted with piles of sweet ration squares and fruit mush. He forced himself to smile again. He had hoped for midmeal or latemeal, when the ration squares were flavored like stew of various kinds. Sweets made his head ache. But the med tech, halfway around the ring, waved to him, and Mantenon edged past others to his side.

"The yellow ones aren't sweet," the med tech said. He handed over a yellow square and a bowl of mush. "You'll like it better than the brown ones."

Mantenon found the yellow squares similar to the ones he had had delivered to his suite: those were orange, but the taste was the same, or nearly so. He ate two yellow squares while listening to the others talk. None of it made sense to him. It was all gossip about crewmembers—who was sleeping with whom, or having trouble with a supervisor—or tech talk, full of numbers and strange words. Finally someone across the ring spoke to him, in a tone which seemed to carry humor.

"Well, Mr. Mantenon—how's your music coming?"

He choked on his bite of ration, swallowed carefully, and folded his hands politely to answer.

"It's . . . well, it's coming. It's still unsettled."

"Unsettled?" The questioner, Mantenon now realized, was the same stocky woman he'd seen earlier in the lounge.

"Yes, it—" His hands began to wave as he talked, mimicking their movements on the Meirinhoff. "It's got some good themes, now, but the overall structure isn't settled yet."

"Don't you plan the structure first?" asked someone else,

a tall person with two green braids on his collar. "I would think rational planning would be necessary . . ."

Mantenon smiled. "Sir, your pardon, but it is not the way creative artists work. We are taught to respond to a stimulus freely, with no preconceptions of what form might be best. When we have all the responses, then we shape those into whatever structure the music itself will bear."

"But how do you know . . . ?"

"That's what our training is for." He dipped a bite of fruit mush, swallowed it, and went on. "Once we have the responses, then our training shows us what structure is best for it."

The tall man frowned. "I would have thought the stimulus would determine the correct structure . . . surely anything as large as a planet would call for a serious, major work—"

"Oh no, Kiry!" That was a young woman who hadn't spoken before. "Don't you remember *Asa's Dream*? It's just that short, poignant dance, and yet the planet was that big pair of gas giants over in Harker's Domain. I've seen a cube of them: it's perfect."

"Or the truly *sinister* first movement of Manoken's 5th Symphony," said Mantenon, regaining control of his audience. "That was not even a planet . . . he wrote that it was inspired by the reflections of light on the inside of his sleepcase." They all chuckled, some more brightly than others, and Mantenon finished his breakfast. The med tech seemed to be watching him, but he expected that.

That day he incorporated the bits he'd scored in the crew lounge—the "anger movement" as he thought of it—into his main piece. It was the planet's response to the insult of his initial crunch; for a moment he wondered about himself, imputing emotions to planets, but decided that it was normal for an artist. He wouldn't tell Med about it. And at latemeal, several crew chose to sit near him, including him casually in their chatter with questions about well-known pieces of music and performers. He felt much better.

Still, when he decided, several days later, that his composition was complete and adequate, he had his doubts. The planet was ugly. Had he really made something beautiful out of it—and if he had, was he rendering (as he was sworn to do) its essential nature? Would someone else, seeing that planet after hearing his music, feel that it fit? Or would that future hearer laugh?

That doubt kept him doodling at the console another few days, making minute changes in the scoring, and then changing them back. He spent one whole working shift rooting through the music references he's brought along, checking his work as if he were analyzing someone else's. But that told him only what he already knew: it had a somewhat unconventional structure (but not wildly so), it was playable by any standard orchestra (as defined by the Musicians Union), it could be adapted for student or limited orchestras (for which he would earn a bonus), none of the instruments were required to play near their limits. It would classify as moderately difficult to play, and difficult to conduct, and it contained all the recommended sections for a qualification work (another bonus): changes in tempo, changes from simple to complex harmonics, direct and indirect key changes.

He played it back, into the headphones, with full orchestration, and shook his head. It was what it was, and either it would do, or it wouldn't. And this time he could not depend on a panel of professors to check his work and screen out anything unworthy. This time, if he judged it wrongly, the whole CUG system would know. He frowned, but finally reached for one of the unused memory cubes and slid it into place. And punched the controls for "Final Record: Seal/No Recall." It was done.

With the cube in hand, and the backup cubes in his personal lockbin, he made his way to the lounge area once more. The curtains were drawn; the captain sat on one of the couches. He opened his mouth, and realized that she already knew he'd finished. Security must keep a closer watch on musicians than he'd thought. He wondered if they'd listened to his music as well . . . he'd been told that no one did, without permission of the artist, but Security was everywhere.

The captain smiled. "Well—and so you've finished, Mr. Mantenon. And we've not heard it yet . . ."

"Do—do you want to?" He felt himself blushing again, and hated it. Yet he wanted her to hear the music, wanted her to be swept away by it, to see and feel what he had seen and felt about that planet.

"It would be an honor," she said. He watched the flicker of her eyelid. Was it amusement? Weariness? Or genuine interest? He couldn't tell. He wavered, but finally his eagerness overcame him, and he handed her the cube.

"Here," he said. "It runs about 29, Standard."

"So much work for this," she said, with no irony, holding the cube carefully above the slot. "Twenty-nine minutes of music from—how many weeks of work?"

He couldn't remember, and didn't care. Now that she held it, he wanted her to go on and play the thing. He had to see her reaction, good or bad, had to know whether he'd truly finished. "Go on," he said, and then remembered that she was the captain. "If you want to." She smiled again.

Played on the lounge sound system, it was different, changed by the room's acoustics and the less agile speakers which were not meant to have the precision of the Meirinhoff's wave generators. Even so, and even with the volume held down, Mantenon thought it was good. And so, evidently, did the captain; he had been taught to notice the reactions of the audience to both live and replayed performances. Smiles could be faked, but not the minute changes in posture, in breathing, even pulse rate that powerful music evoked. In the final version, his original reaction framed the whole composition, the *crunch* split, literally, in mid-dissonance, and the interstice filled with the reaction, counter-reaction, interplay of themes and melodies. Then the crunch again, cutting off all discussion, and the final splatter of the seeds—the moons. As the cube ended, Mantenon waited tensely for the captain's reaction.

It came, along with a clatter of applause from the speakers—she had switched the lounge sound system to transmission, and the crew evidently liked it as well as she did.

Mantenon felt his ears burning again, this time with pleasure. They were used to hauling musicians; they must have heard many new pieces . . . and he . . . he had pleased them.

The captain handed his cube back to him. "Remarkable, Mr. Mantenon. It always amazes me, the responses you artists and musicians give . . ."

"Thank you. Is it possible—excuse me, Captain, but I don't know the procedure—is it possible to transmit this for registry?"

Her expression changed: wariness, tension, something else he couldn't read, swiftly overlaid by a soothing smile. "Mr. Mantenon, it *is* registered. You mean you weren't aware that immediate . . . transmission . . . for registry was part of the Musicians Union contract with this vessel?"

"No. I thought . . . well, I didn't really think about it." He was still puzzled. He remembered—he was sure he remembered—that the licensed musician had to personally initiate transmission and registration of a composition. But Music Law had always been his least favorite subject. Maybe it was different the first time out.

"You should have read your contract more carefully." She leaned back in her seat, considering him. "Whenever you're employed to do the initial creative survey, you're on CUG Naval vessels, right?"

"Well . . . yes."

"It's different for landing parties, though not much. But here, all communication with the outside must be controlled by CUG Security, in order to certify your location, among other things. In compensation for this, we offer immediate registration, datemarked local time. You *did* know there was a bonus for completion within a certain time?"

"Yes, I did. But—does this mean we aren't going back soon?"

"Not to Central Five, no. Not until the survey's complete."

"Survey?" Mantenon stared at her, stunned.

"Yes—you really didn't read your contract, did you?"

"Well, I—"

"Mr. Mantenon, this was just the *first* of your assignments. Surely you don't think CUG would send a ship to each separate planet just for artistic cataloging, do you? There are seven more planets in this system, and twelve in the next, before we start back."

"I . . . don't believe it!" He would have shouted, but shock had taken all his breath. Nineteen *more* planets? When the first one had taken . . . he tried to think, and still wasn't sure . . . however many weeks it had been. The captain's smile was thinner. She held out a fac of his contract.

"Look again, Mr. Mantenon." He took it, and sat, hardly realizing that the captain had settled again in her seat to watch him.

The first paragraph was familiar: his name, his array of numbers for citizenship, licensure, Union membership, the name of the ship (CSN *Congarsin*, he noted), references to standard calendars and standard clocks. The second paragraph . . . he slowed, reading it word for word. " . . . to compose such work as suitably expresses, to the artist, the essential truth of the said celestial body in such manner . . ." was a standard phrase. There was specification of bonuses for instrumentation, vocal range, difficulty, and time . . . but where Mantenon expected to find " . . . on completion of this single work . . ." he read instead, with growing alarm, " . . . on completion of the works enumerated in the appendix, the musician shall be transported to his point of origin or to some registered port equidistant from the ship's then location as shall be acceptable to him, providing that the necessary duties of the CUG vessel involved allow. In lieu of such transportation, the musician agrees to accept . . ." But he stopped there, and turned quickly to the appendix. There, just as the captain had said, was a complete listing of the "celestial bodies to be surveyed musically." Eight of eleven planets in the CGSx1764 system, and twelve of fifteen planets in the CGSx1766 system. It even gave an estimated elapsed time for travel and "setup," whatever that was . . . cumulative as . . . Mantenon choked.

"Twenty-four *years*!"

"With that many planets in each system, Mr. Mantenon, we'll be traveling almost all the time on in-system drive."

"But—but that means by the time we finish, I'll be—" he tried to calculate it, but the captain was faster.

"By the time we return to Central Five, if we do, you'll be near sixty, Mr. Mantenon . . . and a very famous composer, if your first work is any indication of your ability."

"But I thought I'd—I planned to conduct its premier . . ." He had imagined himself back at the Academy, rehearsing its orchestra on their first run through his own music. If not his first contract composition, then a later one. "It's not fair!" he burst out. "It's . . . they told us that Psych picked our first contracts, to help us, and they gave me that disgusting *mess* out there, and then this!"

"To help you, or best suited to you?" The captain's lips quirked, and he stared at her, fascinated. Before he could answer, she went on. "Best suited, I believe, is what you were told . . . just as you were told to read your contract before signing it."

"Well, but I—I assumed they'd screened them . . ."

"And you were eager to go off-world. You requested primary music survey; that's in your file. You asked for this—"

And with a rush of despair he remembered that he had, indeed asked for this, in a way he hoped the captain did not know—but he feared she did. He had been too exceptional . . . he had challenged his professors, the resident composers, he had been entirely too adventurous to be comfortable. When he looked at the captain, she was smiling in a way that made her knowledge clear.

"The Union has a way of handling misfits, Mr. Mantenon, while making use of their talents. Adventure, pioneering, is held in high esteem—because, as a wise reformer on old Earth once said, it keeps the adventurers far away from home." And with a polite nod, she left him sitting there.

He knew there was nothing he could do. He was a musician, not a rebel; a musician, not a pioneer; a musician, not a fighter. Without the special shoes to counteract the surgery on his feet, he couldn't even walk down the hall. Besides, he didn't want to cause trouble: he wanted to compose his music, and have it played, and—he had to admit—he wanted to be known.

And this they had taken away. They would use his music for their own ends, but he would never hear it played. He would never stand before the live orchestra—that anachronism which nonetheless made the best music even more exciting—he would never stand there, alight with the power that baton gave him, and bring his music out of all those bits of wood and metal and leather and bone, all those other minds. By the time he returned—if they ever let him return—he would be long out of practice in conducting, and long past his prime of composing. He would know none of the players any more: only the youngest would still be active, and they would be dispersed among a hundred worlds. That was the worst, perhaps—that they had exiled him from his fellow musicians.

He came to himself, after a long reverie, sitting with clenched hands in an empty room. Well. He could do nothing, musician that he was, but make music. If he refused, he would be punishing himself as much as he punished the government or the Union. So . . . George Mantenon rose stiffly, and made his way back to his quarters. So he would compose. They thought he was too good to stay near the centers of power? They would find out how good he was. Anger trembled, cymbals lightly clashed, a sullen mutter of drums. Outrage chose a thin wedge honed by woodwinds, sharpened on strings. They would refuse power? He would create power, become power, bind with music what they had forbidden him to hold.

His mind stirred, and he felt as much as heard what music was in him. He had not imagined *that* kind of power before. Hardly thinking, he slipped into the Meirinhoff's embrace, thumbed it onto the private circuit only he could hear, and began. He had plenty of time.

When he spoke to the captain again, his voice was smooth, easy. He would not repeat, he said, his earlier mistake of isolation and overwork . . . he requested per-

mission to mingle with the crew, perhaps even—if it was
permitted—play incomplete sequences to those interested.
The captain approved, and recommended regular Psych
checks, since the mission would last so long. Mantenon
bowed, and acquiesced.

He began cautiously, having no experience in deceit. He
asked the crew what they'd thought of Opus Four, and what
they thought he should call it. He chatted with them about
their favorite musicians and music. He told anecdotes of
the musicians he'd known. And he composed.

He made a point of having something to play for them
every few days . . . a fragment of melody, a variation on
something they already knew. One or two played an instrument as a hobby. Gradually they warmed to him, came to
ask his advice, even his help. A would-be poet wanted his
verses set to music to celebrate a friend's nameday. The lio
player wondered why no one had written a concerto for lio
(someone had, Mantenon told him, but the lio was simply
not a good solo instrument for large spaces.)

In the weeks between the first planet and the next in
that system, Mantenon did nothing but this. He made
acquaintances out of strangers, and tried to see who might,
in the years to come, be a friend. He knew he was being
watched for a reaction, knew they knew he was angry and
upset, but—as he told the most clinging of his following
with a shrug—what could he do? He had signed the contract, he was only a composer (he made a face at that,
consciously seconding the practical person's opinion of
composers), and he had no way to protest.

"I could scream at the captain, I suppose," he said. "Until
she called Med to have me sedated. I could write letters
to the Union—but if in fact the Union wants me out here,
what good would that do?"

"But doesn't it make you *angry*?" the girl asked. He was
sure it was a Security plant. He pursed his lips, then shook
his head.

"I was angry, yes—and I wish I could go back, and hear
my music played. It doesn't seem fair. But I can't *do* anything, and I might as well do what I'm good at. I have a

good composing console—that's a full-bank Meirinhoff they gave me—and plenty of subjects and plenty of time. What else could I do?"

She probed longer, and again from time to time, but finally drifted away, back into the mass of crew, and he decided that Security was satisfied—for a time. By then they were circling the second planet he was to survey.

This one, luckily for his slow-maturing plans, was one of those rare worlds whose basic nature was obvious to everyone. Habitable, beautiful, it was the real reason that the system was being opened; the other worlds—like the marginal mining planet he had begun to call "Grand Crunch"— were merely a bonus. It had three moons, glinting white, pale yellow, and rosy. Its music had to be joyous, celebratory: Mantenon thought first of a waltz, with those three moons, but then changed his mind. Three light beats and a fourth strong, with a shift here to represent that huge fan of shallow sea, its shadings of blue and green visible even from orbit. It wrote itself, and he knew as he wrote it that it would be immensely popular, the sort of thing that the eventual colonial office would pick up and use in advertising.

So light-hearted a work, so dashing a composition, could hardly come from someone sulking and plotting vengeance. Mantenon enjoyed the crew's delighted response, and noted the captain's satisfaction and Security's relaxation. He was being a good boy; they could quit worrying. For awhile.

One solid piece of work, one definite hit—he wished he could see his credit balance. It hadn't occurred to him to ask earlier, and he was afraid that if he asked now, he'd arouse their suspicions again. But—assuming they were registering these as they were supposed to, he would end up as a *rich* old man.

The next worlds were each many weeks apart. Mantenon wrote an adequate but undistinguished concerto for one of them; a quartet for woodwinds for another; a brass quintet for the crazy wobbling dance of a double world. Week after week of travel; week after week of observing, composing, revising. Even with his music, with the Meirinhoff, it was monotonous; he had been accustomed to the lively interaction of other musicians, people who understood what he was doing, and appreciated it. He had enjoyed afternoons spent lazing in the courtyards or gardens, listening to others struggling in rehearsal halls.

Without the music he knew he would have gone mad. CUG ships used a seven day week and four-week month; since there was no reason to worry about a planetary year (and no way to stay in phase with any particular planet), months were simply accumulated until mission's end, when the total was refigured, if desired, into local years. Mantenon felt adrift, at first, in this endless chain of days . . . he missed the seasonal markers of a planet's life, the special days of recurrent cycles. Surely by now it was his birthday again. He asked one of the med techs about it during one of his checkups . . . surely they had to keep track of how old people were?

"Yes, it's simple really. The computer figures it—ship time, background time, factors for deepsleep. Most people like to choose an interval about as long as their home planet's year, and flag it as a birthday."

"But it's not their *real* birthday . . . I mean, if they were back home, would it be the same day?"

"Oh no. That's too complicated. I mean, the computer could do it, but it's not really important. The point is to feel that they have their own special day coming up. Look— why don't you try it? What day of the week do you like your birthday to come on?"

"Well . . . Taan, I suppose." The best birthday he'd ever had fell on Taan, the year he was eight, and his acceptance to the Academy was rolled in a silver-wrapped tube at one end of the feast table.

"Taan . . . right. Look here." The tech pointed out columns of figures on the computer. "Your true elapsed age is just under 30." Mantenon had to force himself to stay silent. Thirty already? He had lost that many years, in just these seven planets? The tech noticed nothing, and went on. "Today's Liki . . . what about next Taan? That gives you three days to get ready. Is that enough?"

There was nothing to do to get ready. Mantenon nodded,

surprised to feel a little excitement even as he knew how artificial this was. A birthday was a *birthday*; you couldn't make one by saying so. But then there were the birthdays he had already lost—that had gone unnoticed. The tech flicked several keys and one number in one column darkened.

"Now that's marked as your shipday—your special day. The interval will be about what it was on Union Five, because that's given as your base, and next time you'll be given notice four weeks in advance. Oh—you get an automatic day off on your shipday . . . I guess it won't mean much to you, you don't have crew duties. But you get special ration tabs, any flavor you like, if it's on board, and a captain's pass for messages. You can send a message to anyone—your family, anywhere—and for no charge."

Mantenon's shipday party enlivened the long passage between worlds, and he ended the lateshift in someone else's cabin. He had dreaded that, having to admit that he was a virgin, but, on the whole, things went well.

The last world of that system was a gas giant with all the dazzling display of jewelry such worlds could offer: moons both large and small, rings both light and dark, strange swirling patterns on its surface in brilliant color. Mantenon found himself fascinated by it, and spent hours watching out the ports, more hours watching projections of cubes about this satellite or that. Finally the captain came to see what was wrong.

"Nothing," he said, smiling. "It's simply too big to hurry with. Surely you realize that an artist can't always create instantly?"

"Well, but—"

"I'm starting," he assured her. "Right away." And he was, having decided that he was not about to wait the whole long sentence out. They couldn't be planning to stay in deep space for that long without resupply, with the same crew growing older along with him. They must be planning to get supplies and replacements while he was in deepsleep, while he thought they were using the deepspace drive. And he intended to be free of this contract at the first stop.

He had written a song for the poet: three, in fact. He had taken a folksong one of the lifesystems techs sang at his shipday party, and used it in a fugue. He listened to their tales of home, their gossip, their arguments and their jokes, saying little but absorbing what he needed to know. Gradually the crew were responding to him, to his music; he heard snatches of this work or that being hummed or whistled, rhythmic nuances reflected in tapping fingers or the way they knocked on doors. Everything he wrote carried his deepest convictions, carried them secretly, hidden, buried in the nerve's response to rhythm, to timbre and pitch and phrase. And gradually the crew had come to depend on his music, gradually they played their cubes of other composers less. But he knew his music could do more. And now it would.

Mantenon sat curled into the Meirinhoff's embrace, thinking, remembering. He called up his first reaction to his contract, refined it, stored it. Then he began with his childhood. Note by note, phrase by phrase, in the language of keychange, harmonics, the voice of wood and metal and leather and bone, of strings and hollow tubes, vibrations of solids and gases and liquids, he told the story of his life. The skinny boy for whom music was more necessary than food, who had startled his father's distinguised guest by insisting that a tuning fork was wrong (it was), who had taught himself to read music by listening to Barker's *Scherzo To Saint Joan* and following the score (stolen from that same guest of his father's, the conductor Amanchi.) The youth at the Academy, engulfed for the first time in a Meirinhoff, able for the first time to give his imagination a voice.

He stopped, dissatisfied. It wasn't only *his* dilemma. He had to make them understand that it was theirs. He couldn't take the ship; they had to give it to him; they had to want him to go where he wanted to go. Either they would have to understand his need for music, or he would have to offer something they wanted for themselves.

He let himself think of the different homeworlds he'd

heard of. The famous worlds, the ones in the stories or songs. Forest worlds, dim under the sheltering leaves. Water worlds. Worlds with skies hardly speckled with stars, and worlds where the night sky was embroidered thick with colored light. And in his mind the music grew, rising in fountains, in massive buttresses, in cliffs and shadowed canyons of trembling air, shaping itself in blocks of sound that reformed the listening mind. Here it was quick, darting, active, prodding at the ears; there it lay in repose, enforcing sleep.

In the second week, the captain came once to complain about the fragments he'd played in the crew lounge.

"It's unsettling," she said, herself unsettled.

He nodded toward the outside. "That's unsettling. Those fountains . . ."

"Sulfur volcanoes," she said.

"Well, they look like fountains to me. But clearly dangerous as well as beautiful."

"No more, though, to the crew. Check with me, first, or with Psych."

He nodded, hiding his amusement. He knew already that wouldn't work. And he kept on. The music grew, acquired complex interrelationships with other pieces . . . the minor concerto, the brass quintet, the simple song. Humans far from home, on a ship between worlds, with a calendar that accumulated months and gave no seasons, what did they want, what did they need? The rhythmic pattern gave it, withheld it again, offered it, tempting the listener, frustrating the ear. Yet . . . it *could* satisfy. It wanted to satisfy. Mantenon found himself working until his arms and legs cramped. To hold that power back, to hold those resolving discords in suspension, took all his strength, physical as well as mental.

He knew, by this time, that Security had a tap in his Meirinhoff. They monitored every note he brought out, every nuance of every piece. He did what he could: kept the fragments apart, except in his head, and devised a tricky control program, highly counterintuitive, to link them together when he was ready. It disgusted him to think of someone

listening as he worked; it went against all he'd been taught—
though he now suspected that Security had taps in the Academy as well. If they wanted to, they could make him look
ridiculous all over CUG, by sending out the preliminary drafts
under his name. But they wouldn't do that. They wanted his
music. So they had to monitor everything. Someone was
having to listen to it, all of it; someone whose psych profile
Mantenon was determined to subvert.

First he had had to learn more about it. The Central
Union boasted hundreds of worlds, each with its own culture . . . and in many cases, multiple cultures. The same
music that would stir a Cympadian would leave a Kovashi
unmoved. For mere entertainment, any of the common
modes would do well enough, but Mantenon needed to go
much deeper than that. He needed one theme, one particular section, that would unlock what he himself believed
to be a universal desire.

It was the poet who gave him the clue he needed. At
latemeal, he hurried to sit beside Mantenon, and handed
over four new poems.

"For Kata," he said. "She's agreed to marry me when
we—" He stopped short, giving Mantenon a startled look.

"When you get permission, Arki?" asked Mantenon. He
thought to himself that the poet had meant to say " . . .
when we get back to port." He wondered which port they
were near, but knew he dared not ask.

"Yes . . . that is . . . it has to clear Security, both of us
being Navy."

"Mmm." Mantenon concentrated on his rations; Arki
always talked if someone looked away.

"It's Crinnan, of course," Arki muttered. "He'll approve,
I'm sure—I mean, he's from Kovashi Two, just as we are."

"You're from Kovashi?" asked Mantenon, affecting surprise.

"I thought I'd told you. That's why I write in seren-form:
it's traditional. I suppose that's why I like your music, too
. . . all those interlocked cycles."

Mantenon shrugged. "Music is universal," he said. "We're
taught modes that give pleasure to most."

"I don't know . . ." Arki stuffed in a whole ration square and nearly choked, then got it down. "Thing is, Georges, I'd like to have these set to music . . . if you have time . . ."

"I've got to finish this composition," Mantenon said. "Maybe before I go into deepsleep for the outsystem transfer . . . how about that?" He saw the flicker in Arki's eye: so they really were close to a port.

"Well . . ." Arki said, evading his glance. "I really did want it soon . . ."

"Klarge." Mantenon said it softly, on an outbreath, which made it milder. "The second movement has problems anyway—maybe it'll clear if I work on your stuff briefly. But I can't promise, Arki—the contract has to come first."

"I understand," said Arki. "Thanks, and—oh, there's Kata." He bounced out of his chair to greet the woman who'd just come in.

Mantenon hugged the double gift to himself. Now he knew the home system of the senior Security officer aboard, and, thanks to the poet, had an excellent excuse for composing highly emotional music designed to affect someone from that system. If Arki was telling the truth: if that whole conversation were not another interlocking scheme of Security. Mantenon glowered at the Meirinhoff's main keyboard, now dull with his handling. It would be like Security, and like any Kovashi, to build an interlocking scheme. But—he thought of the power hidden in his composition—it was also a Kovashi saying that a knifeblade unties all knots.

As if Arki's poems were a literal key for a literal lock, he studied them word by word, feeling how each phrase shaped itself to fit into a socket of the reading mind. And note by note, phrase by phrase, he constructed what he hoped would be the corresponding key of music, something that fit the words so well it could not have been meant for anything else, but which acted independently, unlocking another lock, opening a deeper hidden place in the listener's will. Briefly, he thought of himself as a lover of sorts: like Arki's penetration of Kata, opening secret passages and discovering (as the Kovashi still called it) the hidden treasures of love, his penetration of Crinnan's mind searched secret byways and sought a hidden treasure . . . of freedom. The songs—asked for by crew, and therefore surely less suspect—could be played openly, without Psych review, and he hoped by them to stun Crinnan and the captain into musical lethargy long enough to play the whole song of power that would free him.

It was hard—very hard—to stay steady and calm, with that hope flooding his veins. Against it he held up the grim uncertainty of success, the likely consequence of failure. He could be killed, imprisoned, taken to a mining planet and forced into slavery. He might live long and never hear music again, save in his own ears . . . and they might twist his mind, he thought bleakly, and ruin even that. Surely others had tried what he was trying. In all the years the artists and musicians had gone out, surely some of them had tried to use their art to free themselves. If Crinnan were chuckling to himself now, listening to his work through a tap, he was doomed.

But he wanted out. He had to keep going. And shortly after that he had finished the work. The knife, a mere three minutes of Arki's lyrics set to music, lay at hand: the heavy weaponry was loaded, ready to play on his signal. Mantenon called Arki on the intercom.

"Want to hear it?" he asked.

"It's ready? That's good, Georges; we don't have much— I mean, I've got a few minutes before the end of shift. Can you send it along?"

"Certainly." His finger trembled over the button. He could *see* the music, poised like a literal knife, heavy with his intent. He pushed the button, positioned his hand over the next control, the one that would send the main composition over the main speakers. And thumbed with his other hand the intercom to Security. Crinnan would be listening— had to be listening—and if asked *while* he was listening . . .

Crinnan's voice was abstracted, distant. Mantenon reported that the planetary composition was finished at last. He requested permission to play it, as he had all the others, on the main speakers. Crinnan hesitated. Mantenon visualized the speaker tag in his other ear, could see the flutter of his eyelid as the song slipped through the accumulated tangle of CUG regulations and Security plots, straight for the hidden center of his life, the rhythm woven in it by his homeworld and its peoples. "I suppose . . ." he said, a little uncertainly. "You've always done that, haven't you?"

Mantenon answered respectfully, soberly. Now the song would be at *this* phrase; Crinnan should be nearly immobile. He heard in his ear a long indrawn breath, taken just as he'd designed. For a moment the sense of power overwhelmed him, then he heard Crinnan grant his request. More: "Go on—I'd like to hear it," said Crinnan.

The interval between song and main composition was crucial. Those who heard both must feel the pause as an accent, precisely timed for the composition on either side of the interval. Those who were not in the circuit for the song must have no warning. But for someone whose fingers and toes controlled whole orchestras, this was nothing: Mantenon switched his output to full ship, and pressed the sequence for the linking program.

Even though he'd written it—even though he knew it intimately, as a man might know a wife of thirty years, sick, healthy, dirty, clean, sweet, sour, fat or lean—even so, its power moved him. For twenty bars, thirty, he lay passive in the Meirinhoff, head motionless, toes and fingers twitching slightly, as the music built, with astonishing quickness, a vision of delight. Then he forced himself up. He, alone, should be proof against this: he could give it a formula, dissociate from its emotional power. And he had things to do.

Their farewells were touching, but Mantenon could hardly wait to be free of them. His new world seemed huge and small at once: a slightly darker sky than Central Five's, a cooler world of stormy oceans and great forested islands. A single continent fringed with forest, its inner uplands crowned with glacial ice, and a broad band of scrubby low growth—for which he had no name, never having seen or studied such things—between. He had seen it on approach, for an hour or so, and then been landed in a windowless shuttle. At the port, green-eyed dark men and women in dark lumpy garments had scurried about, complaining to the shuttle's crew in a sharp, angular language as they hauled the Meirinhoff across to the blocky shelter of the single port building. He himself shivered in the chill wind, sniffing eagerly the scent of his new prison: strange smells that brought back no memories, mixed with the familiar reek of overheated plastics, fuel, and ship's clothing. He wondered—not for the first time—if he'd done right. But at least he would have the Meirinhoff. Or the planet would. He didn't yet know what his status would be, after all the turmoil on the ship. He'd had no chance to play the cube the captain had given him.

"Ser Mantenon?" It was a narrow-faced, dour man whose CUG insignia had tarnished to a dull gray. His accent was atrocious; Mantenon could just follow his words. "It is our pleasure to welcome such an artist as yourself to the colony. If you will follow . . ."

He followed, down a passage whose walls were faced with rounded dark cobbles. Around a turn, left at a junction, and the walls were hung with brilliant tapestries, all roses, pinks, reds, glowing greens. Into a room where a cluster of people, all in dull colors, waited around a polished table. He was offered a chair: richly upholstered, comfortable. His escort found a chair at the head of the table.

"So you are a rebel, Ser Mantenon?" the man asked.

Mantenon pondered his reply. "I am a musician," he said. "I want to make music."

"You suborned an official vessel of the CUG Navy," the man said. "This is not the act of a musician."

"How he did so . . ." interrupted a woman near Mantenon. He looked at her. Her eyes were the same green as the others, her dark hair streaked with silver.

"How he did so is not the issue, Sera. *Why* he did so matters to me. What he will do in the years ahead matters to me. Will he bring trouble on us?"

your music. And you destroyed us, and we honor you
that. A worthy enemy; a worthy loss. If you ever believe
t, and understand, write us another song, and send *that*."
And nothing lay between his hands but empty air. After
long moment he breathed again. In the silence, he heard
e beginnings of that song, the first he would write on his
ew world, the last gift to the old.

"No," said Mantenon firmly. "I will not. I am not a rebel
that way—stirring up trouble. I only want to make music:
write music, play music, conduct—"

"Your music makes trouble." That was a balding man
halfway around the table. "Your music made them bring you
. . . it might make us go. If you have that power, you must
have plans to use it."

"To give pleasure," said Mantenon. Suddenly the room
felt stuffy. He'd been so sure anyone living on a planet
would understand why he *had* to get off that ship. "I don't
want to control people with it. I only did it because it was
the only way."

"Hmmm." Eyes shifted sideways, meeting each other,
avoiding his gaze.

"Pleasure," said the woman who'd spoken. "That's a good
thought, Ser Mantenon. Do you like this world?"

"I hardly know it yet, but it seems . . . well, it's better
than the ship."

She chuckled. "I see. And you want to give *us* pleasure—
the colonists?"

"Yes. I want to make music you will enjoy."

"And not to send us to war with Central Union?"

"Oh, no." This time, after his answer, he felt an odd
combined response: relaxation and amusement both rippled
around the table.

"And you are willing to work?"

"At music, certainly. I can teach a number of instruments,
music theory, conduct, if there's an orchestral group with
no conductor, as well as compose. But I have had surgical modifications that make some kinds of work impossible."

"Of course. Well." She looked sideways; heads nodded
fractionally. "Well, then, we are pleased to welcome you.
We think you will find a place, though it will not be what
you're used to."

And from there he was led to a ground vehicle of some
kind (he noticed that the shuttle had already been canted
into its takeoff position), and was driven along a broad hard-
surfaced road toward a block of forest. Within the forest

were clearings and buildings. Before he had time to wonder what they all were, he found himself installed in a small apartment, with clean bedding stacked on the end of a metal bunk, and the blank ends of electrical connections hanging out of the walls. His original escort yelled something down the passage, and two men appeared with utility connections: cube player, speakers, intercom.

"We have not installed your machine . . . your composing machine . . . because we do not yet know if you will stay here, or prefer to live somewhere else."

"That's fine," said Mantenon absently, watching the men work.

"The group kitchen is on the ground floor, two down," the man said. "If you think you will wish to cook here, we can install—"

"Oh, no," said Mantenon. "I don't know how to cook." The man's eyebrows rose, but Mantenon didn't ask why. He was suddenly very tired, and longed for sleep. The workers left, without a word, and the escort twitched his mouth into a smile.

"You are tired, I'm sure," he said. "I will leave you to rest, but I will come by before the next meal, if that is all right."

"Thank you." Mantenon didn't know whether to wave or not; the man suddenly stepped forward and grasped his hand, then bowed. Then he turned away and went out the door, shutting it behind him.

Mantenon spread a blanket over the bunk and lay down. Something jabbed him in the ribs, something angular. The captain's message cube. He sighed, grunted, and finally rolled off the bunk to stick the cube in the player.

It was a holvid cube, and the captain's miniature image appeared between his hands. He stepped back, slouched on the bunk.

"Mr. Mantenon," she began, then paused. Her hair was backlit by the worklight on her desk, her face the same cool, detached face he'd known for these years of travel. "You are an intelligent man, and so I think you will appreciate an explanation. Part of one. You resented being tricked, as all young artists do. You were smart enough to avoid

violence, and obvious rebellion. I suspect you ___ of we had experienced attempts to use art against ___ fo And I know you suspected that I knew what you w___ th If you are as smart as I think you are, you're w___ now if you're in prison or free, if you've won ___ a thought you were winning. And the answer is yes, ___ t answer is no. ___ r

"You are not the first to try what you tried. You ___ the first to succeed. Most do not. Most are not good e___ Your music, Mr. Mantenon, is worth saving . . . at th___ of risking your effect on this colony. Although you will ___ be allowed to leave that planet, for you I think it w___ freedom, or enough to keep you alive and well. Stud___ to teach, music to play . . . you can conduct a live orche___ when you've taught one. You were not ambitious, ___ Mantenon, and so you will not miss the power you mi___ have held at the Academy. You can curse me, as the re___ resentative of the government that tricked you, and go o___ with your life. But there's one other thing you should know.___ Again she paused, this time turning her head as if to ease a stiff neck.

"You can think of it as plot within plot, as your music wove theme within theme. The government removes the dangerous, those who can wield such power as you, and protects itself . . . and yet has a way to deal with those who are too powerful for that isolation. But the tr___ Mr. Mantenon, that you *did* overpower my ship. Y___ free; we must return, or be listed as outlaws, and ___ return, our failure will cost all of us. You hoped we ___ rebel, and follow you into freedom. You did not kn___ our ship is our freedom . . . that I had worked ye___ this command, and you have destroyed it. You ___ government as an enemy—most artists do—but to ___ all that keeps the worlds together, providing things ___ other that none can provide alone. Like the Academ___ you may send a student someday. Like my ship, ___ we traveled freely. I don't expect you to believe ___ now. But we were honored to have you aboard, ___ first: truly honored. And we were honored by t___

*Sometimes . . . very rarely, but sometimes . . . a story arrives in my head ready all in one piece. Even more rarely, it's this short.*

# JUST ANOTHER DAY AT THE WEATHER SERVICE

I caught the phone on the second ring. "National Weather Service," I said. "UFO Clearinghouse, George Karantzopoulin speaking."

"I'm sorry to bother you," said the voice in my ear. Male, middle-aged, and embarrassed. "This is Professor Garris, of the science department at Owen Junior College . . ."

"Yes, sir," I said. "What can we do for you, Professor?"

"Well." He cleared his throat. "I'm sure it's just a weather balloon, or something . . ." That trailed away, then he spoke with more confidence. "You know, you people sent me a schedule at the beginning of the year, so that I wouldn't have students calling you up for no reason . . ."

"Yes?"

"But—well—the schedule didn't mention last night. Three students—and I saw it myself . . . I'm sure it wasn't anything . . . you know . . . but still, if I don't check, they'll say I'm narrow-minded, and . . ."

"You're saying you saw an unidentified flying object?" I hardly waited for his answer. "What time, sir, and where were you, and what was its course?"

With a total of eight "institutions of higher learning"—universities, colleges, and junior colleges—within fifty miles, it's a rare week that we don't get a UFO call. And a rare semester when some enterprising youth doesn't build a UFO and send it up just to see what his or her peers will say. That's why I have an extension of the National Weather Service number. I'm supposed to prevent panic and national network news coverage of an innocent weather balloon or research rocket launch. I have a form to fill out, for every "sighting", which asks for more details than most callers have even thought of. It's wonderful what large computers can do in storing all those data, and routing all UFO calls right to my desk, from all over the country.

Professor Garris could answer all the questions; he was an amateur astronomer who'd been star-gazing with the Space Club of the college. He gave it to me in great detail: the apparent size, the exact location of the observers, the azimuth and bearing, and the course the thing appeared to take. I went "Mmm" at intervals, to assure him I was listening. Then he said, "Of course, I know it wasn't a—well, anything odd—that is . . . you know . . ."

"From outer space?" I asked, making a joke of it. His chuckle in response was feeble. "Just a second," I went on. "I'll check the master file. Sometimes, you know, someone has a permit to send up a research balloon, and they don't bother to tell us . . . they're supposed to, but . . ."

"I understand," he said eagerly. He wanted me to know he was sane, plain, and sound. He was also scared stiff, and sounded it. I rambled on.

"Yeah—if we complain, it could cost them a grant—it's nearly always a government grant—but unless a citizen is really riled, we—"

"You mean do I want . . . ? Oh, no, Mr. Uh—"

"Call me George," I said. "No one but my family can pronounce the other." And that was true enough, even in the Anglicized version. George is a good name. John or Jim is almost too all-American. George is the kind of name that no one would pick, and yet it's not peculiar.

"George," he agreed. "I'm not filing a complaint, you understand. If it's someone's research—"

"They're supposed to file a flight plan with us. Just to keep people from worrying."

"Yeah, but—"

"Oh." I let my voice express finding something. "Here it is. Sorry—they did file. It's a university out west, Professor Garris. Research on high-altitude gas exchange and something about wheat. Wonder how that works. Anyway, it was launched yesterday, and just let me check the wind drift . . . .yes. It sure could have been visible when you saw it. I'm sorry, sir. Someone should have sent you an updated schedule."

"That's fine," he said. "That's just what I told them—just what it had to be. It's only—you know, you get to depending on the schedules, and then when something comes up different . . ."

"Yeah," I said. "I understand. We're always glad to chase these things down, Professor. Don't hesitate to call."

"Thanks," he said. "I really—I was afraid you'd think I was some crank or something."

"Oh, no," I said, "we aren't like that." And he thanked me again and hung up, obviously relieved.

So was I. The last thing our space program needed was another outbreak of the sort of hysteria I'd seen in the '70s. Half the population out at night, looking for odd lights, and that sort of thing. Fear of aliens, fear of space itself. I leaned back in my chair, promising my transfer crew a real scolding when they returned. They know they're supposed to stick to the schedule, or update it. All it takes to mess up our whole program is some halfway intelligent and articulate observer—a professor would be the worst—spotting a "weather balloon" off the schedule. Of course, it *was* a weather-balloon all right—but not theirs, any more than I work for the National Weather Service. It's really wonderful what those big computers can do, routing all those UFO calls right to my desk, and storing all the reports I file.

*"Politics" and "In Suspect Terrain" were written for Bill Fawcett's The War Years anthologies. They are the first stories I wrote "to order," as it were. Bill wanted "a Marine landing" for The Far Stars War and "a sort of last-ditch Siege of the Alamo" for Siege of Arista. I galloped into this project not knowing that my mind reacts skew-ways to declared themes in anthologies. "Politics" is a "Marine landing" story, but it's also the story of how character impacts events. Tinker, Dietz, and Sewell are only as fictional as they need to be.*

# POLITICS

Politics is always lousy in these things. Some guy with rank wants something done, and whether it makes any sense or not, some poor slob with no high-powered friends gets pushed out front to do it. Like Mac . . . he wants a fuzzball spit-polished, some guy like me will have to shave it bare naked and work it to a shine. Not that all his ideas are stupid, you understand, but there's this thing about admirals—and maybe especially *that* admiral—no one tells 'em when their ideas have gone off the screen. That landing on Caedmon was right out of somebody's old tape files, and whoever thought it up, Mac or somebody more local, should've had to be there. In person, in the shuttles, for instance.

You know why we didn't use tanks downside . . . right. No shields. Nothing short of a cruiser could generate 'em, and tanks are big enough to make good targets for anyone toting a tank-bashing missile. Some dumbass should have thought of shuttles and thought again, but the idea was the cruisers have to stay aloft. No risking their precious tails downside, stuck in a gravity well if something pops up. Tradition, you know? Marines have been landed in landing craft since somebody had to row the boat ashore. Marines have died that way just about as long.

Now on Caedmon, the Gerin knew we were coming. Had to know. The easy way would've been to blast their base from orbit, but that wouldn't do. Brass said we needed it, or something. I thought myself it was just because humans had had it first, and lost it; a propaganda move, something like that. There was some kind of garbage about how we had this new stealth technology that let the cruisers get in real close, and we'd drop and be groundside before they knew we were there, but we'd heard that before, and I don't suppose anyone but the last wetears in from training believed it. I didn't, and the captain for sure didn't.

He didn't say so, being the hardnosed old bastard he is, but we knew it anyway, from the expression in his eyes, and that fold of his lip. He read us what we had to know— not much—and then we got loaded into the shuttles like so many cubes of cargo. This fussy little squirt from the cruiser pushed and prodded and damn nearly got his head taken off at the shoulders, 'cept I knew we'd need all that rage later. Rolly even grinned at me, his crooked eyebrows disappearing into the scars he carries, and made a rude sign behind the sailor's back. We'd been in the same unit long enough to trust each other at everything but poker and women. Maybe even women. Jammed in like we were, packs scraping the bulkheads and helmets smack onto the overhead, we had to listen to another little speech—this one from the cruiser captain, who should ought to've known better, only them naval officers always think they got to give Marines a hard time. Rolly puckered his face up, then grinned again, and this time I made a couple of rude gestures that couldn't be confused with comsign, but we didn't say anything. The Navy puts audio pickups in the shuttles, and frowns on Marines saying what they think of a cruiser captain's speechifying.

So then they dropped us, and the shuttle pilot hit the retros, taking us in on the fast lane. 'Course he didn't care that he had us crammed flat against each other, hardly breath-room, and if it'd worked I'd have said fine, that's the way to go. Better a little squashing in the shuttle than taking fire. Only it didn't work.

Nobody thinks dumb Marines need to know anything, so of course the shuttles don't have viewports. Not even the computer-generated videos that commercial shuttles have, with a map-marker tracing the drop. All we knew was that the shuttle suddenly went ass over teakettle, not anything like normal re-entry vibration or kickup, and stuff started ringing on the hull, like somebody dropped a toolshed on us.

Pilot's voice came over the com, then, just, "Hostile fire." Rolly said "Shut up and fly, stupid; I could figure out that much." The pilot wouldn't hear, but that's how we all felt. We ended up in some kind of stable attitude, or at least we weren't being thrown every which way, and another minute or two passed in silence. If you call the massed breathing of a hundred-man drop team silence. I craned my neck until I could see the captain. He was staring at nothing in particular, absolutely still, listening to whatever came through his comunit. It gave me the shivers. Our lieutenant was a wetears, a butterbar from some planet I never heard of, and all I could see was the back of his head anyway.

Now we felt re-entry vibration, and the troop compartment squeaked and trembled like it was being tickled. We've all seen the pictures; we know the outer hull gets hot, and in some atmospheres bright hot, glowing. You can't feel it, really, but you always think you can. One of the wetears gulped, audible even over the noise, and I heard Cashin, his corporal, growl at him. We don't get motion sickness; that's cause for selection out. If you toss your lunch on a drop, it's fear and nothing else. And fear is only worthwhile when it does you some good—when it dredges up that last bit of strength or speed that we mostly can't touch without it. The rest of the time fear's useless, or harmful, and you have to learn to ignore it. That's what you can't teach the wetears. They have to learn for themselves. Those that don't learn mostly don't live to disagree with me.

We were well into the atmosphere, and dropping faster than my stomach liked, when the shuttle bucked again. Not a direct hit, but something transmitted by the atmosphere outside into a walloping thump that knocked us sideways and halfover. The pilot corrected—and I will say this about the Navy shuttle pilots, that while they're arrogant bastards and impossible to live with, they can pretty well fly these shuttles into hell and back. This time he didn't give us a progress report, and he didn't say anything after the next two, either.

What he did say, a minute or so later, was "Landing zone compromised."

Landing zone compromised can mean any of several things, but none of them good. If someone's nuked the site, say, or someone's got recognizable artillery sitting around pointing at the strip, or someone's captured it whole (not common, but it does happen) and hostile aircraft are using it. What landing zone compromised means to us is that we're going to lose a lot of Marines. We're going to be landing on an unimproved or improvised strip, or we're going to be jumping at low level and high speed. I looked for the captain again. This time he was linked to the shuttle com system, probably talking to whatever idiot designed this mission. I hoped. We might abort—we'd aborted a landing once before—but even that didn't look good, not with whatever it was shooting at us all the way back up. The best we could hope for was an alternate designated landing zone—which meant someone had at least looked at it on the upside scanners. The worst—

"Listen up, Marines!" The captain sounded angry, but then he always did before a landing. "We're landing at alternate Alpha, that's Alpha, six minutes from now. Sergeants, pop your alt codes . . ." That meant me, and I thumbed the control that dropped a screen from my helmet and turned on the display. Alternate Alpha was, to put it plainly, a bitch of a site. A short strip, partly overgrown with whatever scraggly green stuff grew on this planet, down in a little valley between hills that looked like the perfect place for the Gerin to have artillery set up. Little colored lines scrawled across the display, pointing out where some jackass in the cruiser thought we ought to assemble, which hill we were supposed to take command of (that's what it said), and all the details that delight someone playing sandbox war instead of getting his guts shot out for real. I looked twice at the contour lines and values. Ten-meter contours, not five . . . those weren't just little bitty hills, those were going to give us trouble. Right there where the lines were packed together was just about an eighty-meter cliff, too much for a backpack booster to hop us over. Easy enough for someone on top to toss any old kind of explosive back down.

And no site preparation. On a stealth assault, there's minimal site preparation even on the main landing zones—just a fast first-wave flyover dropping screamers and gas canisters (supposed to make the Gerin itch all over, and not affect us.) Alternate strips didn't get any prep at all. If the Gerin guessed where alternate Alpha was, they'd be meeting us without having to duck from any preparatory fire. That's what alternate landing sites were like: you take what you get and are grateful it doesn't mean trailing a chute out a shuttle hatch. That's the worst. We aren't really paratroops, and the shuttles sure as hell aren't paratroop carriers. Although maybe the worst is being blown up in the shuttle, and about then the shuttle lurched again, then bounced violently as something blew entirely too close.

Then we went down. I suppose it was a controlled landing, sort of, or none of us would have made it. But it felt, with all the pitching and yawing, like we were on our way to a crash. We could hear the tires blow on contact, and then the gear folded, and the shuttle pitched forward one last time to plow along the strip with its heatshield nose. We were all in one tangled pile against the foreward bulkhead by then, making almost as much noise as the shuttle itself until the captain bellowed over it. With one final lurch, the craft was motionless, and for an instant silent.

"Pop that hatch, Gunny." The captain's voice held that tone that no one argues with—no one smart, anyway—and Rolly and I started undogging the main hatch. The men were untangling themselves now, with muttered curses. One of the wetears hadn't stayed up, and had a broken ankle; he bleated once and then fell silent when he realized no one cared. I yanked on the last locking lever, which had jammed in the crash, just as we heard the first explosions outside. I glanced at the captain. He shrugged. What else could we do? We sure didn't have a chance in this nicely marked coffin we were in. Rolly put his shoulders into it, and the hatch slid aside to let in a cool, damp, breath of local air.

Later I decided that Caedmon didn't smell as bad as most planets, but right then all I noticed was the exhaust trails of a couple of Gerin fighters who had left their calling cards on the runway. A lucky wind blew the dust away from us, but the craters were impressive. I looked at the radiation counter on the display—nothing more than background, so it hadn't been nukes. Now all we had to do was get out before the fighters came back.

Normally we unload down ramps, four abreast—but with the shuttle sitting on its nose and the port wing, the starboard landing ramp was useless. The portside hatch wouldn't open at all. This, of course, is why we carry those old-fashioned cargo nets everyone teases us about. We had those deployed in seconds (we *practice* that, in the cruisers' docking bays, and that's why the sailorboys laugh at us.) Unloading the shuttle—all men and materiel, including the pilot (who had a broken arm) and the wetear with the bad ankle—went faster than I'd have thought. Our lieutenant, Pascoe, had the forward team, and had already pushed into the scraggly stuff that passed for brush at the base of the nearest hill. At least he seemed to know how to do that. Then Courtney climbed back and placed the charges, wired them up, and came out. When he cleared the red zone, the captain pushed the button. The shuttle went up in a roiling storm of light, and we all blinked. That shuttle wasn't going anywhere, but even so I felt bad when we blew it . . . it was our ticket home. Not to mention the announcement the explosion made. We had to have had survivors to blow it that long after the crash.

What everyone sees, in the videos of Marine landings,

is the frontline stuff—the helmeted troops with the best weapons, the bright bars of laser fire—or some asshole reporter's idea of a human interest shot (a Marine looking pensively at a dead dog, or something.) But there's the practical stuff, which sergeants always have to deal with. Food, for instance. Medical supplies, not to mention the medics, who half the time don't have the sense to keep their fool heads out of someone's sights. Water, weapons, ammunition, spare parts, comunits, satellite comm bases, spare socks . . . whatever we use has to come with us. On a good op, we're resupplied inside 24 hours, but that's about as common as an honest dockside joint. So the shuttle had supplies for a standard week (Navy week: Old Terra standard—it doesn't matter what the local rotational day or year is), and every damn kilo had to be offloaded and hauled off. By hand. When the regular ground troops get here, they'll have floaters and trucks, and their enlisted mess will get fresh veggies and homemade pies . . . and that's another thing that's gone all the way back, near as I can tell. Marines slog through the mud, hump their stuff uphill and down, eat compressed bricks commonly called—well, you can imagine. And the next folks in, whoever they are, have the choppers and all-terrain vehicles and then make bad jokes about us. But not in the same joint, or not for long,

What bothered me, and I could see it bothered the captain, was that the fighters didn't come back and blow us all to shreds while all this unloading went on. We weren't slow about it; we were humping stuff into cover as fast as we could. But it wasn't natural for those fighters to make that one pass over the strip and then leave a downed shuttle alone. They had to know they'd missed—that the shuttle was intact and might have live Marines inside. All they'd done was blow a couple of holes in the strip, making it tough for anyone else to land there until it was fixed. They had to be either stupid or overconfident, and no one yet had accused the Gerin of being stupid. Or of going out of their way to save human lives. I had to wonder what else they had ready for us.

Whatever it was, they let us alone for the next couple

of standard hours, and we got everything moved away from the strip, into a little sort of cleft between two of the hills. I wasn't there: I was working my way to the summit, as quietly as possible, with a five-man team.

We'd been told the air was breathable, which probably meant the green stuff was photosynthetic, although it was hard to tell stems from leaves on the scrub. I remember wondering why anything a soldier has to squirm through is full of thorns, or stings on contact, or has sharp edges . . . a biological rule no one yet has published a book on, I'll bet. Caedmon's scrub ran to man-high rounded mounds, densely covered with prickly stiff leaves that rustled loudly if we brushed against them. Bigger stuff sprouted from some of the mounds, treelike shapes with a crown of dense foliage and smooth blackish bark. Between the mounds a fine, gray-green fuzz covered the rocky soil, not quite a lush as grass but more linear than lichens. It made my nose itch, and my eyes run, and I'd *had* my shots. I popped an broad-spectrum anti-allergen pill and hoped I wouldn't sneeze.

Some people say hills are the same size all the time, but anyone who's ever gone up a hill with hostiles at the top of it knows better. It's twice as high going uphill into trouble. If I hadn't had the time readout, I'd have sworn we crawled through that miserable prickly stuff for hours. Actually it was less than half a standard when I heard something click, metal on stone, *ahead* of us. Above and ahead, invisible through the scrub, but definitely something metallic, and therefore—in this situation—hostile. Besides, after DuQuesne, we knew the Gerin would've wiped out any humans from the colony. I tongued the comcontrol and clicked a warning signal to my squad. They say a click sounds less human—maybe. We relied on it, anyhow, in that sort of situation. I heard answering clicks in my earplug. Lonnie had heard the noise, too (double-click, then one, in his response) which figured. Lonnie had the longest ears in our company.

This is where your average civilian would either panic and go dashing downhill through the brush to tell the captain there were nasties up there, or get all video-hero and run screaming at the Gerin, right into a beam or a slug.

What else is there to do? you ask. Well, for one thing you can lie there quietly and think for a moment. If they've seen you, they've shot you—the Gerin aren't given to patience—and if they haven't shot you they don't know you're there. Usually.

It was already strange, that the Gerin fighters hadn't come back. And if Gerin held the top of this hill—which seemed reasonable even before we went up it, and downright likely at the moment—they'd have to know we got out, and how many, and roughly where we were. And since Gerin aren't stupid, at least at war, they'd guess someone was coming up to check out the hilltop. So they'd have some way to detect us on the way up, and they'd have held off blowing us away because they didn't think we were a threat. Neither of those thoughts made me feel comfortable.

Detection systems, though . . . detection systems are a bitch. Some things work anywhere: motion detectors, for instance, or optical beams that you can interrupt and it sets off a signal somewhere. But that stuff's easy enough to counter. If you know what you're doing, if you've got any sort of counterhunt tech yourself, you'll spot it and disarm it. The really good detection systems are hard to spot, very specific, and also—being that good—very likely to misbehave in combat situations.

The first thing was to let the captain know we'd spotted something. I did that with another set of tongue-flicks and clicks, switching to his channel and clicking my message. He didn't reply; he didn't need to. Then I had us all switch on our own counterhunt units. I hate the things, once a fight actually starts: they weigh an extra kilo, and unless you need them it's a useless extra kilo. But watching the flicking needles on the dials, the blips of light on the readouts, I was glad enough then. Two meters uphill, for instance, a fine wire carried an electrical current. Could have been any of several kinds of detectors, but my unit located its controls and identified them. And countered them: we could crawl right over that wire, and its readout boxes wouldn't show a thing. That wasn't all, naturally: the Gerin aren't stupid. But none of it was new to our units, and all of it could fail—and would fail, with a little help from us.

Which left the Gerin. I lay there a moment longer wondering how many Gerin triads we were facing. Vain as they are, it might be just one warrior and his helpers, or whatever you want to call them. Gerin think they're the best fighters in the universe, and they can be snookered into a fight that way. Admiral Mac did it once, and probably will again. It would be just like their warrior pride to assign a single Gerin triad to each summit. Then again, the Gerin don't think like humans, and they could have a regiment up there. One triad we might take out; two would be iffy, and any more than that we wouldn't have a chance against.

Whatever it was, though, we needed high ground, and we needed it damn fast. I clicked again, leaned into the nearest bush, and saw Lonnie's hand beyond the next one. He flicked me a hand signal, caught mine, and inched forward.

We were, in one sense, lucky. It was a single triad, and all they had was the Gerin equivalent of our infantry weapons: single-beam lasers and something a lot like a rifle. We got the boss, the warrior, with several rounds of rifle fire. I don't care what they say, there's a place for slug-throwers, and downside combat is that place. You can hit what you can't see, which lasers can't, and the power's already in the ammo. No worry about a discharged power-pack, or those mirrored shields some of the Gerin have used. Some Navy types keep wanting to switch all Marine forces away from slug weapons, because they're afraid we'll go bonkers and put a hole in a cruiser hull, but the day they take my good old Belter special away from me, I'm gone. I've done my twenty already; there's no way they can hold me.

Davies took a burn from one of the warrior's helpers, but they weren't too aggressive with the big number one writhing on the ground, and we dropped them without any more trouble. Some noise, but no real trouble. Lonnie got a coldpak on Davies, which might limit the damage. It wasn't that bad a burn, anyway. If he died down here, it wouldn't be from that, though without some time in a good hospital, he might lose the use of those fingers. Davies being Davies, he'd probably skin-graft himself as soon as the painkiller cut in . . . he made a religion out of being tough. I called back to our command post to report, as I took a look around to see what we'd bought.

From up here, maybe 70 meters above the strip, the scattered remains of the shuttle glittered in the sun. I could see the two craters, one about halfway along, and another maybe a third of the way from the far end. Across the little valley, less than a klick, the hills rose slightly higher than the one we lay on. The cliffs on one were just as impressive as I'd thought. The others rose more gently from the valley floor. All were covered with the same green scrub, thick enough to hide an army. Either army.

I told the captain all this, and nodded when Skip held up the control box the Gerin had used with their detectors. We could use the stuff once we figured out the controls, and if they were dumb enough to give us an hour, we'd have no problems. No problems other than being a single drop team sitting beside a useless strip, with the Gerin perfectly aware of our location and identity.

Brightness bloomed in the zenith, and I glanced up. Something big had taken a hit—another shuttle? We were supposed to have 200 shuttle flights on this mission, coming out of five cruisers—a fullscale assault landing, straight onto a defended planet. If that sounds impossibly stupid, you haven't read much military history—there are some commanders that have this thing about butting heads with an enemy strength, and all too many of them have political connections. Thunder fell out of the sky, and I added up the seconds I'd been counting. 10,000 meters when they'd been blown—no one was going to float down from that one.

"What kind of an *idiot* . . . ?" Lonnie began; I waved him to silence. Things were bad enough without starting that—we could place the blame later. With a knifeblade, if necessary.

"Vargas . . ." The captain's voice in my earplug drowned

out the whisper of the breeze through stiff leaves. I pushed the subvoc microphone against my throat and barely murmured an answer. "Drop command says we lost thirty cents on the dollar. Beta-site took in four shuttles before it was shut out." Double normal losses on a hostile landing, then, and it sounded like we didn't have a secure strip. I tried to remember exactly where Beta-site was. "We're supposed to clear this strip, get it ready for the next wave—"

I must have made some sound, without meaning to, because there was a long pause before he went on. If the original idea had been stupid, this one was stupid plus. Even a lowly enlisted man knows it's stupid to reinforce failure, why can't the brass learn it? We weren't engineers; we didn't have the machinery to fill those craters, or the manpower to clear the surrounding hills of Gerin and keep the fighters off.

"They're gonna do a flyby drop of machinery," he went on. I knew better than to say what I thought. No way I could stop them, if they wanted to mash their machinery on these hills. "We're going to put up the flyspy—you got a good view from there?"

"Yessir." I looked across the valley, around at all the green-clad slopes. The flyspy was another one of those things that you hated having to take care of until it saved your life. "By wire, or by remote?"

"Wire first." That was smart; that way they wouldn't have a radio source to lock onto. "I'm sending up the flyspy team, and some rockers. Send Davies back down." Rockers: rocket men, who could take out those Gerin fighters, always assuming they saw them in time, which they would if we got our detection set up.

Soon I could heard them crashing through the scrub, enough noise to alert anyone within half a klick. The rockers made it up first, four of them. I had two of them drag the Gerin corpses over to the edge and bounce 'em over, then they took up positions around the summit. Now we could knock off the Gerin fighters, if they came back: whatever's wrong with the rest of Supply, those little ground-air missiles we've got can do the job. Then the flyspy crew arrived, with the critter's wing folded back along its body. When they got to the clearing, they snapped the wings back into place, checked that the control wire was coiled ready to release without snagging, and turned on the scanners.

The flyspy is really nothing but a toy airplane, wings spanning about a meter, powered by a very quiet little motor. It can hold an amazing amount of spygear, and when it's designed for stealth use it's almost impossible to see in the air. On wire control, it'll go up maybe 100 meters, circle around, and send us video and IR scans of anything it can see; on remote, we can fly it anywhere within line-of-sight, limited only by its fuel capacity.

Soon it was circling above us, its soft drone hardly audible even on our hilltop, certainly too quiet to be heard even down on the strip. We didn't know whether the Gerin *did* hear, the way we hear, but we had to think about that. (We know they hear big noises, explosions, but I've heard a theory that they can't hear high-pitched noises in atmosphere.) The videos we were getting back looked surprisingly peaceful. Nothing seemed to be moving, and there was only one overgrown road leading away from the strip. Garrond punched a channel selector, and the normal-color view turned into a mosaic of brilliant false colors: sulfur yellow, turquoise, magenta, orange. He pointed to the orange. "That's vegetation, like this scrub. Yellow is rock outcrops—" The cliff across from us was a broad splash of yellow that even I could pick out. "Turquoise is disturbed soil: compacted or torn up, either one." The strip was turquoise, speckled with orange where plants had encroached on it. So was the nearly invisible road winding away from the strip between the hills. So also the summit of the hill which ended in cliffs above the strip . . . and the summit of our own hill. Another outpost, certainly.

But nothing moved, in the broad daylight of Caedmon's sun. According to briefing, we'd have another nine standard hours of light. None of our scanners showed motion, heat, anything that could be a Gerin force coming to take us out. And why not?

It bothered the captain, I could see, when he came up

to look for himself. Our butterbars was clearly relieved, far too trusting an attitude if you want to survive very long. Things aren't *supposed* to go smoothly; any time an enemy isn't shooting at you, he's up to something even worse.

"An hour to the equipment drop," said the captain. "They're sending a squad of engineers, too." Great. Somebody else to look after, a bunch of dirtpushers. I didn't say it aloud; I didn't have to. Back before he saved Admiral Mac's life and got that chance at OCS, the captain and me were close, real buddies. Fact is, it was my fault he joined up—back then they didn't have the draft. Wasn't till he started running with me, Tinker Vargas, what everyone called gypsy boy—gambler and horsethief and general hothead—that Carl Dietz the farmer's son got into any trouble bigger than spilled milk. He was innocent as cornsilk back then, didn't even know when I was setting him up—and then we both got caught, and had the choice between joining the offworld Marines or going to prison. Yet he's never said a word of blame, and he's still the straightest man I know, after all these years. He's one I *would* trust at poker, unlike Rolly who can't seem to remember friendship when the cards come out.

And no, I'm not jealous. It hasn't been easy for him, a mustang brought up from the ranks, knowing he'll never make promotions like the fast-track boys that went to the Academy or some fancy-pants university. He's had enough trouble, some of it when I was around to carefully not hear what the other guy said. So never mind the pay, and the commission: I'm happy with my life, and I'm still his friend. We both know the rules, and we play a fair game with the hand dealt us—no politics, just friends.

In that hour, we had things laid out more like they should be. Thanks to the flyspy, we knew that no Gerin triads lurked on the nearest two hilltops, and we got dug in well on all three hills that faced the strip on the near side. There was still that patch of turquoise to worry about on the facing hill, above the cliffs, but the flyspy showed no movement there, just the clear trace of disturbed soil. Our lieutenant had learned something in OCS after all; he'd picked a very good spot in a sort of ravine between the hills, out of sight beneath taller growth, for the headquarters dugout, meds, and so on.

Then the equipment carrier lumbered into view. I know, it's a shuttle same as the troop shuttle, but that's a term for anything that goes from cruiser to ground. Equipment carriers are fatter, squatty, with huge cargo doors aft, and they have all the graceful ease of a grand piano dumped off a clifftop. This one had all engines howling loudly, and the flaps and stuff hanging down from the wings, trying to be slow and steady as it dropped its load. First ten little parachutes (little at that distance), then a dark blob—it had to be really big if I could see it from here—trailing two chutes, and then a couple more, and a final large lumpy mass with one parachute.

"I don't believe it!" said the captain, stung for once into commentary. But it was—a netful of spare tires for the vehicles, wrapped around a huge flexible fuel pod. Relieved of all this load, the shuttle retracted its flaps, and soared away, its engines returning to their normal roar.

Already the lieutenant had a squad moving, in cover, toward the landing parachutists. I watched the equipment itself come down, cushioned somewhat by airbags that inflated as it hit. Still nothing moved on the hilltop across from us. I felt the back of my neck prickle. It simply isn't natural for an enemy to chase you down, shooting all the while, then ignore you once you've landed. We know Gerin use air attack on ground forces: that's how they cleaned up those colonists on Duquesne.

Yet ignore us they did, all the rest of that day as the engineers got themselves down to the strip from where they'd landed, and their equipment unstowed from its drop configuration and ready for use. One grader, what we called back on my homeworld a maintainer, and two earth-movers. The whole time the engineers were out there getting them ready, I was sure some Gerin fighter was going to do a low pass and blow us all away . . . but it didn't happen. I'd thought it was crazy, dropping equipment that had to be prepped and then used in the open, but for once high command had guessed right.

By late afternoon, the engineers had their machines
ready to work. They started pushing stuff around at the far
end of the strip, goudging long scars in the dirt and making mounds of gravelly dirt. The captain sent Kittrick and
one platoon over to take a hill on the far side; they got up
it with no trouble, and I began to think there weren't any
Gerin left there at all. Half that group climbed the hill with
the cliff, and found evidence that someone had had an
outpost there, but no recent occupation.

We were spread out pretty thin by this time, maybe thirty
on the far side of the strip, the rest on the near side, but
stretched out. We'd rigged our own detection systems, and
had both flyspys up, high up, where they could see over
the hills behind us. What they saw was more of the same,
just like on the topo maps: lots of hills covered with thick
green scrub, some creeks winding among the hills, traces
of the road that began at the landing strip. Some klicks east
of us (east is whatever direction the sun rises, on any world),
the tumbled hills subsided into a broad river basin. The
higher flyspy showed the edge of the hills, but no real detail
on the plain.

Meanwhile the engineers went to work on that strip just
as if they *were* being shot at. Dust went up in clouds, blown
away from our side of the strip by a light breeze. Under
that dust, the craters and humps and leftover chunks of our
troop shuttle disappeared, and a smooth, level landing strip
emerged. There's nothing engineers like better than pushing
dirt around, and these guys pushed it fast.

By dark they had it roughed in pretty well, and showed
us another surprise. Lights. Those tires we'd laughed at each
held a couple of lamps and reflectors, and the coiled wir-
ing that connected them all into a set of proper landing
lights controlled by a masterboard and powered from the
earthmover engine. By the time everyone had had chow,
the first replacement shuttle was coming in, easing down
to the lighted strip as if this were practice on a safe, peaceful planet far from the war.

None of us veterans could relax and enjoy it, though.
The new arrivals had heard the same thing I had—thirty

percent losses on the initial drop, sixty shuttles blown. No report from anyone on what we'd done to the Gerin, which meant that the Navy hadn't done a damn thing . . . they tripled their figures when they did, but triple zilch is still zilch. So how come we weren't being overrun by Gerin infantry? Or bombed by their fighters? What were the miserable slimes up to? They sure weren't beat, and they don't surrender.

During the night, five more shuttles landed, unloaded, and took off again. Besides the additional troops and supplies, we also had a new commanding officer, a mean-looking freckle-faced major named Sewell. I know it's not fair to judge someone by his looks, but he had one of those narrow faces set in a permanent scowl, with tight-bunched muscles along his jaw. He probably looked angry sound asleep, and I'd bet his wife (he had a wide gold ring on the correct finger) had learned to hop on cue. His voice fit the rest of him, edged and ready to bite deep at any resistance. The captain had a wary look; I'd never served with Sewell, or known anyone who had, but evidently the captain knew something.

Major Sewell seemed to know what he was doing, though, and his first orders made sense, in a textbook sense. If you wanted to try something as impossible as defending a shuttle strip without enough troops or supplies, his way was better than most. Soon we had established a perimeter that was secure enough, dug into each of the main hills around the strip, each with its own supply of ammo, food, and water. Besides the original headquarters and med dugout, he'd established another on the far side of the strip. All this looked pretty good, with no Gerin actually challenging it, but I wasn't convinced. It takes more than a few hundred Marines to secure an airstrip if the enemy has a lot of troops.

Shortly after sundown, one of the squads from the first replacement shuttle found ruins of a human settlement at the base of a hill near the end of the strip, and had to get their noses slapped on the comm for making so much noise about it. Not long after, the squad up on that clifftop put two and two together and made their own find. Having heard the first runkus, they didn't go on the comm with it, but sent a runner down to Major Sewell.

There's a certain art to getting information, another version of politics you might call it. It so happened that someone I knew had a buddy who knew someone, and so on, and I knew the details before the runner got to Major Sewell.

We'd known the strip itself was human-made, from the beginning. What we hadn't known was that it had been privately owned, adjacent to the owner's private residence. It takes a fair bit of money to build a shuttle-strip, though not as much as it takes to have a shuttle and *need* a shuttle strip. The same class of money can take a chunk of rock looking out over a little valley, and carve into it a luxurious residence and personal fortress. It can afford to install the best quality automated strip electronics to make landing its fancy little shuttle easier, and disguise all the installations as chunks of native stone or trees or whatever. The Gerin had missed it, being unfamiliar with both the world and the way that humans think of disguise. But to a bored squad sitting up on a hilltop with no enemy in sight, and the knowledge that someone might have hidden something . . . to them it was easy. Easy to find, that is, not easy to get into, at least not without blasting a way in . . . which, of course, they were immediately and firmly told not to do.

Think for a little what it takes to do something like this. We're not talking here about ordinary dress-up-in-silk-everyday rich, you understand, not the kind of rich that satisfies your every whim for enough booze and fancy food. I can't even imagine the sort of sum that would own a whole world, hollow out a cliff for a home, operate a private shuttle, and still have enough clout left to bribe the Navy in the middle of a desperate war. This was the sort of wealth that people thought of the military-industrial complex having, the kind that the big commercial consortia do have (whether the military get any or not), the kind where one man's whim, barely expressed, sends ten thousand other men into a death-filled sky.

Or that's the way I read it. We were here to protect—to get back—some rich man's estate, his private playground, that the Gerin had taken away. Not because of colonists (did I see any colonists? Did anyone see any evidence of colonists?) but because of a rich old fart who had kept this whole world to himself, and then couldn't protect it. That's why we couldn't do the safe, reasonable thing and bomb the Gerin into dust, why we hadn't had adequate site preparation, why we hadn't brought down the tactical nukes. Politics.

I did sort of wonder why the Gerin wanted it. Maybe they had their own politics? I also wondered if anyone was hiding out in there, safe behind the disguising rock, watching us fight . . . lounging at ease, maybe, with a drink in his hand, enjoying the show. We could take care of that later, too. If we were here.

Sometime before dawn—still dark, but over half the night gone—the higher fly by reported distant activity. Lights and nonvisible heat sources over at the edge of the hills, moving slowly but steadily towards us. They didn't follow the old road trace, but kept to the low ground. According to the best guess of the instruments, the wettest low ground. I guess that makes sense, if you're an amphib. It still didn't make sense that they moved so slow, and that they hadn't come to hit us while we were setting up.

The next bad news came from above. Whatever the Navy had thought they'd done, to get the Gerin ships out of the way, it hadn't held, and the next thing we knew our guys boosted out of orbit and told us to hold the fort while they fought off the Gerin. Sure. The way things were going, they weren't coming back, and we wouldn't be here if they did. Nobody *said* that, which made it all the clearer that we were all thinking it. During that long day we made radio contact with the survivors at Beta Site. They were about 80 klicks away to our north, trying to move our way through the broken hills and thick scrub. Nobody'd bothered them yet, and they hadn't found any sign of human habitation. Surprise. The major didn't tell them what we'd found, seeing as it wouldn't do them any good. Neither would linking up with us, probably.

The smart thing to do, if anyone had asked me, was for us to boogie on out of there and link with the Beta Site survivors, and see what we could do as a mobile strike force. Nobody asked me, at least nobody up top, where the orders came from. We were supposed to hold the strip, so there we stuck, berries on a branch ready for picking. I know a lot of the guys thought the same way I did, but hardly anyone mentioned it, seeing it would do no good and we'd have a lot more to bitch about later.

Slow as the Gerin were moving, we had time to set up several surprises, fill every available container with water, all that sort of thing. They ignored our flyspy, so we could tell where they were, what they had with them, estimate when they'd arrive. It was spooky . . . but then they didn't need to bother shooting down our toy; they only outnumbered us maybe a hundred to one. If every one of our ambushes worked, we might cut it down to ninety to one.

Gerin ground troops might be slow to arrive, but once they were there you had no doubt about it. Just out of range of our knuckleknockers, the column paused and set up some tubing that had to be artillery of some sort. Sure enough, we heard a sort of warbling whoosh, and then a vast *whump* as the first shells burst over our heads and spit shards of steel down on us. After a couple or three shots, fairly well separated, they sent up a whole tanker load, and the concussion shuddered the hills themselves.

We watched them advance through the smoke and haze of their initial barrage. They were in easy missile range, but we had to save the missiles for their air support. Everyone's seen the news clips—that strange, undulating way they move. They may be true amphibians, but they're clearly more at home in water or space than walking around on the ground. Not that it's walking, really. Their weapons fire slower on automatic than ours, but they can carry two of them—an advantage of having all those extra appendages. And in close, hand-to-hand combat, their two metal-tipped tentacles are lethal.

They came closer, advancing in little bobbing runs that

were similar to our own tactics, but not the same. It's hard to explain, but watching them come I felt how alien they were—they could not have been humans in alien suits, for instance. The very fact that I had trouble picking out the logic of their movements—why they chose to go *this* way up a draw, and not that—emphasized the differences.

Now they were passing the first marker. Rolly tapped me on the shoulder, and I nodded. He hit the switch, and a stormcloud rolled under them, tumbling them in the explosion. Those in the first rank let off a burst, virtually unaimed; the smack of their slugs on the rocks was drowned in the roar and clatter of the explosion, and the dust of it rolled forward to hide them all. Chunks of rock splattered all around; a secondary roar had to mean that the blast had triggered a rockslide, just as we'd hoped. When the dust cleared a little, we couldn't see any of the live ones, only a few wet messes just beyond a mound of broken stone and uprooted brush.

One of the wetears down at the far end of the trench stood up to peer out. Before anyone could yank him back, Gerin slugs took his face and the back of his head, and he toppled over. Then a storm of fire rang along the rocks nearby while we all ducked. Stupid kid should have known they wouldn't all be dead: we'd told them and told them. Our flyspy crew concentrated on their screens; at the moment the critter was reading infrared, and the enemy fire showed clearly. Garrond gave us the coordinates; our return fire got a few more (or so the flyspy showed—we didn't stand up to see.)

But that was only the first wave. All too soon we could see the next Gerin working their way past the rockslide toward our positions. And although I'd been listening for it, I hadn't heard an explosion from the other side of the strip. Had they been overrun, or had the Gerin failed to attempt an envelopment?

Suddenly the sky was full of light and noise: the Gerin had launched another barrage. Oddly, the weapons seemed to be intended to cause noise as much as actual damage. And they were noisy: my ears rang painfully and I saw others shaking their heads. Under cover of that noise, Gerin leapt out, hardly ten meters away. Someone to my left screamed; their slugs slammed all around us. We fired back, and saw their protective suits ripple and split, their innards gushing out to stain the ground. But there were too many, and some of them made it to us, stabbing wildly with those metal-tipped tentacles. One of them smashed into Rolly's chest; his eyes bulged, and pink froth erupted from his mouth. I fired point-blank at that one. It collapsed with a gasping wheeze, but it was too late for Rolly.

Even in all the noise, I was aware that the Gerin themselves fought almost silently. I'd heard they had speech, of a sort—audible sounds, that is—but they didn't yell at each other, or cry out when injured. It was almost like fighting machines. And like machines, they kept coming. Even in the dark.

It was sometime in that first night when I heard the row between the captain and the major. I don't know when it started, maybe in private before the Gerin even got to us, but in the noise of combat, they'd both raised their voices. I was going along, checking ammo levels, making sure everyone had water, and passed them just close enough to hear.

"—You can't do that," Major Sewell was saying. "They said, hold the strip."

"Because it's that bastard Ifleta's," said the captain. He'd figured it out too, of course; he didn't turn stupid when he got his promotion. I should have gone on, but instead I hunkered down a little and listened. If he talked the major around, I'd need to know. "So no heavy artillery, no tactical nukes, no damage to his art collection or whatever he thinks it is. And it's crazy . . . listen, the Gerin are amphibs, they even have swim tanks in their ships—"

"So? Dammit, Carl, it's the middle of a battle, not a lecture room—"

"So they're territorial." I could hear the expletive he didn't say at the end of that . . . Sewell was a senior officer, however dense. "It's part of that honor stuff: where you are determines your role in the dominance hierarchy. If we move, we're no threat; if we stay in one place they'll attack—"

"They *are* attacking, in case you hadn't noticed, *captain*. We're dug in here; if we move they can take us easily. Or were you suggesting that we just run for it?" The contempt in Sewell's voice was audible, even through the gunfire.

The captain made one more try. I knew, from our years together, what it took for him to hold his temper at the major's tone; the effort came through in his voice. "Sir, with all due respect, after the massacre on Duquesne, there was a study of Gerin psychology in the *Military Topics Review*— and that study indicated that the Gerin would choose to assault stationary, defended positions over a force in movement. Something about defending certain rock formations in the tidal zone, important for amphibians . . ."

"Yeah, well, what some egghead scientist thinks the slimes do and what the slimes out here in combat do is two different things. And our orders, captain, say stand and defend this shuttle strip. It doesn't matter a truckful of chickenshit whether the strip is Ifleta's personal private hideaway or was built by the Gerin: I was told to defend it, and I'm going to defend it. Is that clear?"

"Sir." I heard boots scrape on the broken rock and got myself out of there in a hurry. Another time that I'd heard more than I should have, at least more than it would be comfortable to admit. Not long after, the captain met me as I worked my way back down the line. He leaned over and said in my ear, "I know you heard that, Gunny. Keep it to yourself."

"You got eyes in the dark?" I asked. It meant more than that; we'd used it as a code a long time ago. I didn't think he'd choose that way, but I'd let him decide.

"No," he said. A shell burst nearby, deafening us both for a moment; I could see, in the brief glare, his unshaken determination. "No," he said again after we could hear. "It's too late anyway."

"Ifleta's the owner?" I asked.

"Yeah. Senior counselor—like a president—in Hamny's Consortium, and boss of Sigma Combine. This is his little hideaway—should have been a colony but he got here first. What I figure is this is his price for bringing Hamny's in free: three human-settled worlds, two of 'em industrial. Worth it, that's one way of looking at it. Trade a couple thousand Marines for three allied planets, populations to draft, industrial plants in place, and probably a good chunk of money as well."

I grunted, because there's nothing to say to that kind of argument. Not in words, anyway. Then I asked, "Does the major know?"

The captain shrugged. "You heard me—I told him. I told him yesterday, when they found the house. He doesn't care. Rich man wants the aliens out of his property, that's just fine—treat Marines like mercs, he doesn't give a damn, and *that*, Tinker, is what they call an officer and a gentleman. *His* father's a retired admiral; he's looking for stars of his own." It was a measure of his resentment that he called me by that old nickname . . . the others that had used it were all dead. I wondered if he resented his own lost patrimony . . . the rich bottomland farm that would have been his, the wife and many children. He had been a farmer's son, in a long line of farmers, as proud of their heritage as any admiral.

"Best watch him, captain," I said, certain that I would. "He's likely to use your advice all wrong."

"I know. He backstabbed Tio, got him shipped over to the Second with a bad rep—" He stopped suddenly, and his voice changed. "Well, Gunny, let me know how that number three post is loaded." I took that hint, and went on; we'd talked too long as it was.

So now I knew the whole story—for one thing about Captain Carl Dietz, he never in his life made accusations without the information to back them up. He hadn't accused me when it might have got him a lighter sentence, all those years ago. If he said it was Ifleta's place, if he was sure that our losses bought Ifleta's support, and three planets, then I was sure. I didn't like it, but I believed it.

The pressure was constant. We had no time to think, no time to rest, taking only the briefest catnaps one by one, with the others alert. We knew we were inflicting heavy losses, but the Gerin kept coming. Again and again, singly and in triads and larger groups, they appeared, struggling up the hills, firing steadily until they were cut down to ooze aqua fluid on the scarred slopes. Our losses were less, but irreparable.

It was dawn again—which dawn, how many days since landing, I wasn't at all sure. I glanced at the rising sun, irrationally angry because it hurt my eyes. What I could see of the others looked as bad as I felt: filthy, stinking, their eyes sunken in drawn faces, dirty bandages on too many wounds. The line of motionless mounds behind our position was longer, again. No time for burial, no time to drag the dead farther away: they were here, with us, and they stank in their own way. We had covered their faces; that was all we could do.

Major Sewell crawled along our line, doing his best to be encouraging, but everyone was too tired and too depressed to be cheered. When he got to me, I could tell that he didn't feel much better. One thing about him, he hadn't been taking it easy or hiding out.

"We've got a problem," he said. I just nodded. Speech took too much energy, and besides it was obvious. "There's only one thing to do, and that's hit 'em with a mobile unit. I've been in contact with the Beta Site survivors, but they don't have a flyspy or good linkage to ours—and besides their only officer is a kid just out of OCS. The others died at the drop. They're about four hours away, now. I'm gonna take a squad, find 'em, and go after the Gerin commander."

I still didn't say anything. That might have made sense, before the Gerin arrived. Now it looked to me like more politics—Sewell figured to leave the captain holding an indefensible position, while he took his chance at the Gerin commander. He might get killed, but if he didn't he'd get his medals . . . and staying here was going to get us all killed. Some of that must have shown in my face, because his darkened.

"Dammit, Gunny—I know what Captain Deitz said made sense, but our *orders* said defend this strip. The last flyspy

image gave me a lock on what may be the Gerin commander's module, and that unit from Beta Site may give
me the firepower I need. Now you find me—" My mind
filled in "a few good men" but he actually asked for a squad
of unwounded. We had that many, barely, and I got them
back to the cleft between the first and second hills just in
time to see that last confrontation with the captain.

If I hadn't known him that long, I'd have thought he
didn't care. Sewell had a good excuse, as if he needed one,
for leaving the captain behind: Deitz had been hit, though
that wound wouldn't kill him. He couldn't have moved fast
for long, not without a trip through Med or some stim-tabs.
But they both knew that had nothing to do with it. The
captain got his orders from Sewell in terse phrases; he
merely nodded in reply. Then his eyes met mine.

I'd planned to duck away once we were beyond the Gerin
lines—assuming we made it that far, and since the other
side of the strip hadn't been so heavily attacked, we probably
would. I had better things to do than babysit a major playing
politics with the captain's life. But the captain's gaze had
the same wide-blue-sky openness it had always had, barring a few times he was whacked out on bootleg whiskey.

"I'm glad you've got Gunny Vargas with you," the captain said. "He's got eyes in the dark."

"If it takes us that long, we're in trouble again," said the
major gruffly. I smiled at the captain, and followed Sewell
away down the trail, thinking of the years since I'd been
in that stuffy little courtroom back on that miserable back-
water colony planet. The captain played fair, on the whole;
he never asked for more than his due, and usually got less.
If he wanted me to babysit the major, I would. It was the
least I could do for him.

We lost only three on the way to meet the Beta Site
survivors, and I saved the major's life twice. The second
time, the Gerin tentacle I stopped shattered my arm just
as thoroughly as a bullet. The major thanked me, in the
way that officers are taught to do, but the thought behind
his narrow forehead was that my heroism didn't do him a
bit of good unless he could win something. The medic we

had along slapped a field splint on the arm, and shot me up with something that took all the sharp edges off. That worried me, but I knew it would wear off in a few hours. I'd have time enough.

Then we walked on, and on, and damn near ran headlong into our own people. They looked a lot better than we did, not having been shot up by Gerin for several days; in fact, they looked downright smart. The butterbar had an expression somewhere between serious and smug—he figured he'd done a better than decent job with his people, and the glance I got from his senior sergeant said the kid was okay. Sewell took over without explaining much, except that we'd been attacked and were now going to counterattack; I was glad he didn't go further. It could have created a problem for me.

Caedmon's an official record, now. You've seen the tapes, maybe, or the famous shot of the final Gerin assault up the hills above the shuttle strip, the one that survived in someone's personal vicam to be stripped later by Naval Intelligence after we took the hills back, and had time to retrieve personal effects. You know that our cruisers came back, launched fighters that tore the Gerin fighters out of the sky, and then more shuttles, with more troops, enough to finish the job on the surface. You know that the "gallant forces" of the first landing (yeah, I heard that speech too) are credited with *almost* winning against fearful odds, even wiping out the Gerin commander and its staff, thanks to the brilliant tactic of one Marine captain, unfortunately himself a casualty of that last day of battle. You've seen his picture, with those summer-sky-blue eyes and that steadfast expression, a stranger to envy and fear alike.

But I know what happened to Major Sewell, who is listed simply as "killed in action." I know how come the captain got his posthumous medals and promotion, something for his family back home to put up on their wall. I know exactly how the Gerin commander died, and who died of Gerin weapons and who of human steel. And I don't think I have to tell you every little detail, do I? It all comes down to politics, after all. An honest politician, as the saying goes, is the one who stays bought. I was bought a long time ago, with the only coin that buys any gypsy's soul, and with that death (you know which death) I was freed.

*I had just read an article in* Nature *on avalanches caused by slippage along tilted formations, and the way noise can trigger them, especially in wet weather. But in the course of the story, slippages of character overtook the ending I had in mind, and the triggering of catastrophic failure— and the survival of it—became the real story.*

# IN SUSPECT TERRAIN

Morning light poured between the peaks, pummeling the mist hanging over the creek until it gave up and floated away in tatters. The air smelled of spicewood and hawberry, deep leaf-mold under the trees, fresh-broken rock where a slide had come down almost to the pasture level. Armitage lay back against cool wet grass, careless of the chill, and let his eyes rove the brightening sky. Maybe he'd see a reiver a-wing, even this early, hunting the slopes. The ground beneath him trembled . . . hoofbeats? He raised his head, looking for the horses, and saw a line of them coming, all at a gallop, all tossing heads and hooves, manes flying wildly, great round bodies red and brown and bright gold. . . .

It was dark, and cold, and the air in his helmet stank of death. What shook the ground left gaping holes in the dark, brilliant flashes of violent light too bright for vision, and then too dark afterward. His head ached savagely, whether from the bad air or a blow he could not tell. Had he slept, or been knocked loopsided?

He reached out to either side, and felt only the slimy sides of the hole. It must have been raining again. Armitage carefully did not let himself remember rain falling on green pastures where his father's draft horses had grazed. That was gone, wiped out, never to return, and if some other place clean rain fell on green grass, it was for someone else, not for him. His world was here, wherever this was . . . he would remember, in just a bit, if he lived that long.

He did remember the war. The Hothri, who had violated someone's biological rule (he had never had the chance to learn what it was, only that it existed) about the maximum size of insectoids, and had also violated, in the process, some considerable number of rules and laws and planets and systems. They didn't like bright light, cool water rain falling on green grass, big gentle drafters who ate lumps of beetroot and carrot out of your hand . . . but he wouldn't think about that. Automatically, his hands found his weapons, and felt their way around the controls. As his fingers caught on the knobs and twirls that gave him control even with gloves, his mind cleared a bit more. The troopship, on its way . . . but he couldn't remember where from or to, if they'd even been told . . . the attack that broke up their convoy, which they'd known only by being slammed from side to side in the webs . . . the forced landing that left them somewhere . . .

It had to be Arista, because the gravity felt right, and he remembered that they'd been in suborbital transports, not deepspace. Yet the barren expanse of potholed mud and shattered rock had none of the amenities of a habitable planet. Except mud, which somehow the universe seemed to supply whenever and wherever a war was going on. The bit of his mind that remembered his father's library managed a wry chuckle at that, but the chuckle didn't make it to his mouth.

Another brilliant flash of violet-white, throwing his shadow onto the mud before him. The cold mud shook around his suited legs; he was massaged by the dying rumble of the explosion. He couldn't see anything useful before the light was gone, and the broad-scan sensors that should have been in his helmet, with replay facility for just such times, had gone out days ago. So had the suit radios. So had half the fancy junk that was supposed to make him able to go one-on-three with Hothri in their own ships.

With the next flash of light, he remembered that he was supposed to be anchoring the end of a defensive line. The Hothri had tried an assault landing—that's why they'd been hopped around the planet's curve. They were to counterattack, wherever it was—somewhere he'd never seen. Now, with the troopship blown, the colonel had said they'd try to set up somewhere, with the light artillery they'd taken off the ship, blow the Hothri that came after them. *Stupid idea*, his sergeant had muttered, *but there aren't any smart ideas left. Gonna die, men, no use fretting about it. Nobody's coming out here to rescue us, not with the war going on where it matters*. Armitage had wanted to say "We matter, too," but knew that was nonsense. His D.I. had always said they were born to die, and so far his D.I. had been right all the way.

Armitage managed to tongue the right control in his helmet and got a warm mouthful of obviously recycled water. It tasted like the air smelled, and the ration chunk he got next wasn't much better. These combat suits weren't supposed to be good for much more than 48 hours, although they'd tanked up with air enough for lots longer. How much longer he wasn't sure, but the glowing control—one of the few telltales still working—was green. He checked his weapons controls again. He had ammunition, if only he could see a target. But he saw nothing move, in the flashes of light that seared his eyes, nothing that looked like a Hothri ship or Hothri themselves.

The slap on his back brought a scream to his mouth before he could choke it off. He tried to whirl, staggered in the mud, and nearly fell. In the next flash, he knew the shape of the suit was human. A helmet clanked against his, and a distorted voice said "Pull back—come on!" The heavy powered gauntlet of the other's suit grasped his arm and tugged. It was—it had better be—Garamond, the corporal. He felt someone else bump into him and slide into the hole he'd just vacated.

With the voice, with an order to follow, his mind abruptly recovered itself. They had, in fact, kept the Hothri busy; he remembered now that the bugs had a reputation for being unwilling to leave live enemies behind. While the Aristans couldn't quite surround the Hothri ground forces, the Hothri had chosen to stand and fight when they had every chance to disengage and do more damage elsewhere. For eight days, now, they had fought, and for eight days the Hothri transports had dared their meagre but accurate artillery to land more troops. They had destroyed one transport before it landed, and cheered when it crashed and exploded. Two others had been disabled after landing, with casualties. Many Hothri—how many Armitage had no idea, for they seemed to come in endless streams or waves when they attacked, and when they fell, their angular bodies collapsed in irregular heaps, like ants swept before a broom—many Hothri had died, shattered by rifle fire or the few remaining plasma guns or the various explosive rounds lofted into their formations by the mortars and antitank guns.

And every Hothri who landed there, who fell to their weapons, was a Hothri not landing in some more vulnerable area. It had cost them dearly; they had lost more than half their men; but it had cost the Hothri more.

Now they were falling back, to another set of holes dug by those on the off rotation. And the colonel had had something in mind, he was sure, in the pattern of their withdrawal. The transport had gone down in the foothills of the Greater Alps, a vast mountain range on Arista's less populated hemisphere. Each withdrawal had moved them toward the escarpment that blocked the horizon toward the equator. Armitage knew little about this hemisphere, and nothing of the mountains besides their name. He had grown up with the Lesser Alps rising over the sweet green pastures of his father's farm. Walking or driving a team up the winding road to Elise's farm (Entremont's farm, he corrected himself; she was only the third daughter) he had often looked up to those majestic slopes, thinking them the perfect frame for the fields and vinyards that lay around him. So they had been, but the fields and vinyards were gone, blasted into ash along with Elise and the rest of the Entremonts, and his own parents and younger sister.

Armitage tore his mind away, once more, from the

memory of those times, when Elise had reached up a basket of berries, and he had given her his first man's kiss in reply. He focussed desperately on the mountains. These were higher, wilder, than those of home, the treeline barely up to their knees, from whence long slopes of gray rock rose to the ice-capped summits. Glaciers lurked there, the peculiar green-blue color obvious against the snowfields.

Armitage grunted as he climbed along behind the man who'd summoned him. He had always loved mountains, or thought he had, but this everlasting uphill slogging, always uphill with each shift, got to him. It would have been bad enough if he'd been able to breathe the chill mountain air instead of the ripe brew the tanks fed him, and if he hadn't had to lug his weapons with him. He had no breath for grumbling, this way, and it seemed most unfair of all to be deprived of a soldier's favorite recreation.

Colonel Casagar, a tough little man with bright gray eyes and a deceptively soft voice, glanced from his topo maps to the mountains, their shapes just returning with daylight from the massive dark block they'd appeared at dawn.

"If the surveyors were honest, this is our best bet." His finger tapped precisely, and Major Perralt nodded. Perralt was a big man, whose strength and willingness to work hard had made him invaluable to a series of commanders. Now Perralt was hoping that the colonel didn't realize that to him all those mountain valleys looked the same: narrow and steep. He realized that Casagar was waiting for a comment of some sort.

"If you pull this off, you'll be a general."

"If I pull this off, I'll be dead." It was said without drama, the plain truth of a plain man, but a man utterly determined. Perralt glanced at him.

"Surely you can get high enough . . ."

"Someone may. But it's going to be chancy, at best. I will be with the lowest; it's only fair." At Perralt's continued look, he gave a quick lift of the shoulders. "Come now, you knew the situation when we came here. Even if they hadn't blasted our troopships, even if everything had gone perfectly, we'd have been in the same fix, only days or weeks later. No reinforcements, and orders to hold them as long as possible. Headquarters hoped they'd react just as they have, sending more of their troops here, relieving pressure back home—"

"I still don't see why the Hothri are wasting time on us."

Casagar shrugged again. "Nor I. You know the theory, that it's a biological imperative for them to follow up any resistance. Why they're doing it is immaterial. The point is, the more of them land here, and the more of them we keep busy, the fewer can be attacking the heartlands. But we can't keep them busy and escape safely at the same time." He sighed, looking out toward the distant plains, where the Hothri ships slid out of the sky each night, and where by day the shattered hulls of their own troopships glittered in the sunlight that broke through every morning between the squall lines.

"We'll need to move faster," Perralt commented. "Once we pull back out of range—and that won't be far—we'll be unable to damage their landers. Unless you're going to use the last of the Esprit rockets—"

Casagar shook his head. "No. We'll need those later. And we can't move too fast—we want them to follow, to think they're pushing us back. I know it means more casualties, but it's the only way. If they give up on us and go away, we've failed." He grinned. "But we won't. For whatever reason, they've decided to go this far, and they'll want to finish, and we'll give them reasons to go on."

Perralt wondered, not for the first time, just where Casagar had come from. His name was not Aristan, nor his accent, yet he knew all the current Aristan slang, and seemed to know all the right people. And he had a certain edge—more than military discipline, more than being used to authority. Perralt had known men of courage before, and had been under fire more than once himself . . . it was not courage, in Casagar, but something else. A brightness, a brisk cheerfulness, a settled refusal to be dour or grim, when dourness and grimness could be expected. Not flippancy, just . . . certainty? If anyone, thought Perralt, can somehow entrap a small army of Hothri in a mountain valley with our few remaining troops, this one can. He wanted to be skeptical—it was in his family's traditional way to be skeptical—but Casagar elicted trust. Not feverish fanaticism, not that kind of blind loyalty, but trust.

Part of it was Casagar's broad knowledge of things Perralt had never thought to learn. When the Hothri attack on the troopships destroyed the holomap projectors, Casagar had had old-fashioned topo maps, the kind Perralt hadn't seen since his first year in the Academy, rolled into an equally old-fashioned mapcase. He also had geological maps of the region, and while Perralt could read topo maps, he was at a loss to follow the meaning of the dashed and solid lines, the tiny arrows, the curious hatchings and colors, of the geological maps. Casagar had shrugged off Perralt's surprise with the quiet comment that no knowledge was useless to the military.

So now they were committed to leaving the more open country, in which they could maneuver, and would climb into a steep, narrowing valley. An obvious trap. The Hothri, Perralt understood, were supposed to think it was a trap for humans. He thought that himself, as he looked at the topo maps and mentally pictured the impassible walls of rock those stacked contour lines represented. Never go to ground without a back door to your burrow, his father had often said, when they were out hunting and he could see for himself what happened to animals that didn't have one. Once in that valley, there were no back doors, only the uncaring rock. Would they really be able to surround the Hothri pursuers, and do them any significant damage? He shrugged, silently, realizing that he had, after all, known he was going to die on this mission. He had not admitted it to himself, but the knowledge had been there, a subtle tension in his mind. Now it was out in the open, the tension eased, and he found himself very alert, very aware of the shapes of clouds, the color of light, the dirt ground into the skin of his own fingers.

"All right?" Casagar was watching him, and he wondered how much of his thoughts had shown on his face.

"I'm fine." Perralt found himself smiling more easily than he would have expected. Odd how many worries vanished, once he admitted the knowledge of death's certainty. Odd that he'd never achieved this calm before, in any of his other combat experiences. Surely he'd always known he could die—why was this different?

"We'll start moving back today, in whatever sunlight we get. I'd like to be here—" Casagar's finger tapped the map, "—in three days."

Armitage had six hours in the dugout, six hours of what passed for real sleep, in which he knew he was not responsible for anything. The medics had looked him over, after Garamond noticed the dint in his helmet. He had the mud to thank for his life, he was told, and the suit; he should have had a broken neck at the least, but the suit had protected his neck at the cost of throwing him violently on the ground—and the ground had been mud. He might have nightmares, the medics said, shaking their heads. He did not dream at all. When he woke, he could see daylight at the entrance, a pale colorless light that offered neither hope nor beauty. He felt as stiff as his suit, but he could move, and even think. He sniffed, finding no taint of halogens in the air, and wondered if he'd have to put the heavy stinking helmet back on. Probably. In the meantime, he dipped a cup of unrecycled water (or at least, not recycled in *his* suit), and took a chunk of the tinned meat laid out on an ammunition box. He had once thought it was bland and leathery; now it tasted better than any meal he could remember.

Garamond met him at the entrance. "Sarge bought it," he said. He didn't have to say more; he had moved up. Armitage nodded. Garamond led him to the others who would go back to the front. Armitage hoped he looked more alert than the others but knew he didn't. Everyone seemed to be staring at some infinite distance; a few twitched or shivered enough to make their suits hitch nervously. Garamond himself looked nothing like the suave ladies' man who had taken his squad through the bars outside the base

and parted half of them (Armitage included) from their
money playing his own demonic brand of baccarat. His
bright black eyes were red-rimmed and looked bruised; he
moved as stiffly as any of them. "The bugs have overrun
the flanking positions, and they've landed another transport.
Had to withdraw, or they'd have gotten in behind the lines.
We can't reach the landing site now with anything we've
got, so we're beginning a slow withdrawal on a narrower
front."

"Helmets?" asked Armitage.

"Yeah. Captain thinks they're using some gas weapons—
just their own breathing canisters and a little explosive's bad
enough." Most of them groaned or spat eloquently into the
mud. Garmond looked at Armitage. "You're in the middle
this time, and be ready to pull back on the signal." He
handed Armitage a narrow gray box. "*This* radio works—
whoever's center gets it, and then you have to tap the two
on either side. We're going to withdraw up there." He
pointed, and Armitage looked up . . . and up . . . into
mountains much nearer than he remembered.

For once it was not raining, and the clouds had lifted
enough to show the valleys cut into the mountain wall.

"We're going into one of those?"

"Mmm. So I hear. The colonel has a plan, though what
it is, I don't know. Maybe the bugs can't stand high alti-
tude."

"And we can?" The thought of more uphill slogging
appalled him; he had been this high before, but up there
was the very home of mountain-sickness.

Garamond scowled at him, but answered. "We've got the
suits. Freibourne has the apparatus set up to recharge the
tanks—as you'll find when you get your hoses hooked up
again."

"I can hardly wait," muttered someone behind Armitage. "Freibourne—!" Freibourne was not the senior suit
technician, who'd been killed in the landing, nor yet the
second senior, but merely a teenage apprentice welder
who'd been drafted and given six weeks instruction in suit
repair.

"It means we'll have the high ground," Garamond said sharply. Armitage could sense his uncertainty. Looking around, he saw that they all did.

"They've got flyers," said someone tentatively. "They could strafe . . ."

Garamond shrugged. "If they could, they haven't. We'll have the rains another week or so; they don't like to fly in daylight anyway, and night flying in this weather, in the mountains . . . it's the best we can do. If they start using the flyers, well . . . then they do, that's all."

Armitage snapped his helmet closed and checked the hose connections before he stood. Garamond had been right about one thing; the air smelled better. Then he headed for his post, the others trailing. It was only a short hike downslope this time. Behind him, the sleepsite emptied, the two remaining crawlers loaded with the heavier gear. Already the head of the retreating column was several klicks closer to one of the valley entrances.

The dull background crump of Hothri indirect fire sharpened as he got closer. At midday, the bugs rarely stirred, but they had their long-range guns on automatic to keep the Aristans at a safe distance. No one seemed to know how the things aimed—if they used temperature sensors, or what—and on the days with heaviest rainfall the barrage was far from accurate. Today, though it wasn't raining, most of the fire seemed to be concentrating on the far right. Armitage spared little sympathy for the recipients; he'd been there only twelve hours before, and he'd earned his respite in the center. If they just wouldn't shift to pound the center for a few hours . . .

He made it to his post without much trouble, and slid into the comfortable excavation Delacrosse and Virain had occupied for two nights. Comfortable being a relative term, but muddy rock to stand on rather than mud alone was a definite improvement. He banged helmets with the former owners of this prime real estate, and sent them back up the slope. Dubarry slid into the hole behind him, and Meroux; they would operate the antitank gun. Half the hole was taken up with them, their weapon, and the stacked rounds for it. He had time, then, to arrange his own weapons, his ammunition, and even think, before the silvery draperies of the afternoon rains swept up from the distant coast and shut him into a little room walled with falling water and furnished with tedium and fear.

About midafternoon, as the rain fell more heavily and he could feel the rocks beneath his boots sinking into the mire, the Hothri moved up. First he saw the bright muzzle flashes from their weapons through the rain, and then the mud splashing up, steaming, where their rounds fell. He looked sideways, where he could just make out a dimple on either side—Poroully to the left and Schnasser to the right. He waved, and they waved back, and so the signal passed. He remembered his working radio, clicked it on, and reported the renewed assault.

"Hold the line." Those orders hadn't changed. A thousand men had died, following those orders, and the rest of them would die, in time . . . but that didn't bear thinking of. Armitage looked at the antitank crew, busy with their weapon, and then ahead again. More muzzle flashes, brighter now. Mud gouted up not a meter in front of his face, splattering his faceplate. Rain sluiced it away instantly. A thin fog crept along the ground, almost invisible in the spray the hard rain threw up about its feet. But the fog wasn't rain-colored. Armitage swallowed hard, very glad that Freibourne had recharged the tanks, for as sure as horses ate oats, that was gas. His throat felt tight; he told himself it could not be the gas, for he was safely inside his suit. He hoped.

Next he felt a vibration in his boots, carried through the rain-soaked soil. At first the bugs had attacked on foot (or claw, as some of the wits insisted on calling it), but in the past two days they'd begun to use their own tracked assault vehicles to lead an advance. These were smaller and flatter than the Aristan tanks, and mounted with a single laser atop and two machine guns on the forward deck. Each one trailed one or two armored troop carriers, "so the bugs don't get their feet wet," someone had explained. As the Aristans didn't have enough antitank guns for the entire line, it had become a guessing game. Where would the Hothri send the main column today, and could the Aristans position the antitank crews so they wouldn't have far to travel?

Today they were fortunate, for out of the rain's shadow came another, low and dark. Meroux touched his helmet to Armitage's.

"Straight into the lion's mouth—couldn't be better." Then he turned away, and despite his ear protectors Armitage flinched as the antitank gun fired. He had barely seen the target, and the shell's passage through the rain distorted those smooth brushstrokes to a wild flurry. Then a colorful flare brightened the distance, and the ugly brownish stain of ruptured Hothri breathing tanks colored the clean blues and grays. Meroux held up one finger before turning back to his weapon.

That was but the first of many; the stack of antitank shells in the hole dwindled steadily. Apparently the Hothri had decided to throw the main force into the center this time, rather than trying to turn a flank. Twice one of the Hothri assault vehicles got within fifty meters of the line, and Hothri troops, their four jointed walking legs carrying them lightly over the mud, made it closer than that. Armitage fired mechanically, without thought, picking out of the falling rain the staccato movements imposed by Hothri structure, aiming, firing, finding another target . . . and beside him, the antitank gun bucked and lurched in the mud, as Meroux and Dubarry struggled to keep the braces even.

Armitage called back to HQ for more ammunition before dark, and it came as the last of the light faded from the sullen clouds. With it came orders—written orders, signed by the colonel—to withdraw "as soon as possible and maintain radio silence" which made Armitage furious. In the dark, in the mud, with the Hothri hot on their tails, they were supposed to slog uphill into unfamiliar country? And why send down more heavy ammunition if they were supposed to carry it back up? As if to emphasize the ridiculousness of the orders, the rain lifted as a gust of wind rolled along the ground, and then swatted down again with renewed intensity, but this time angled by the wind.

The ammunition bearers were already straggling away, upslope to the old camp; Armitage managed to grab one arm and hold a brief, intense, and unsatisfactory conversation with a sulky private he knew only by name. His orders were to return at once; he had no orders to return carrying ammunition, and he wasn't about to involve himself in any affair between Armitage and the colonel. Before Armitage could marshal the words he wanted to use, the man was gone into the darkness, and he realized that he was being left to make a decision no one in his position should have to make.

"Generals make decisions," he muttered to himself in the privacy of his helmet. "Colonels make decisions, even captains . . . even sergeants. But privates make no decisions, that's what they always told me, and now—" Now, he would decide when the line moved back . . . and if he made that decision wrong, it could not move back. The orders said "as soon as possible," which meant if he didn't think it was possible to carry back with them all that newly delivered ammunition in the blowing rain (for the wind had risen), then they wouldn't, yet. How long should he wait? What had the colonel meant?

A gust of wind slapped his suit hard enough that he felt it, even down in the hole. The bugs had trouble in high wind; they could cling with their clawed feet, but when they tried to move rapidly, they sometimes overbalanced and tumbled along the ground. He peered into the dark, seeing the random spots and blotches visible to anyone who strains to see on a dark night. No muzzle flashes, no flares. Of course the bugs didn't need as much light, and preferred it in the red range; they could be creeping close even now. He found one of the flare rounds (he had eight of them) and fitted it in his rifle, then aimed high and upwind. It functioned perfectly for once (some of them acted like tracer rounds which the bugs were particularly good at tracking. They'd learned early not to use tracers with bugs.) But all he could see, in the few second of light, was falling rain and the usual messy wet jumble of mud and rocks and broken machinery. Nothing that looked like a Hothri moved out there. He fired a few quick rounds. Nothing in response, but the wind buffeted harder as he tried to see.

It was two hours before Armitage managed to pass the word to everyone, and get the withdrawal underway. The Hothri artillery had begun to lay down patterns all along the line, but nothing seemed to be moving forward under it. This was small comfort when the ground leaped and jiggled from a near miss, when the suit's override dampers suddenly held Armitage rigid. But for whatever reason—rain, wind, or incompetence—the shells reached little beyond the line itself, and once the men could overcome their reluctance to leave perfectly good holes and venture into the open, they had only a short distance to go before they were beyond the shell patterns.

Not that it went without losses. On the far right, Marchant—who had been Armitage's bunkmate in boot camp—had lost suit integrity and half an arm to the same shell fragment. His partner Jeffries had a field clamp on the arm, but neither of them would leave. "We'll confuse them," Jeffries had explained. "They will follow, and then we'll fire into their flank—" Near them, two positions had been wiped out completely, although the bugs, concentrating on the center, hadn't taken advantage of the gap. All along the line, there were perhaps thirty wounded, and all but two chose to stay behind. So did their partners. They did not bother to explain. The realities were obvious without discussion. Anyone who had lost suit integrity, or power, could not make it where they were going. A partner's knife gave quick ease to those unable to fight or walk, but those who could still fight preferred a chance. Armitage argued with no one, and when the Aristans moved back, cloaked in night and blowing rain, he felt less guilt than he expected. The way things had gone so far, those who died tonight or tomorrow were the lucky ones.

For hours they struggled uphill, first to the old sleepsite, where they found a guide who led them on. Behind them, only the rain and wind moved; they heard the shells exploding, but that sound faded. It seemed forever that they had slogged through wet and wind and chill, their suits humming and clanking, the air in their helmets hissing. Finally they rested, still in their suits, huddled together with only the barest watch . . . for this the guide insisted was all that was needful, and they were all too tired to argue. When dawnlight seeped into the blowing rain, they could see nothing but tumbled rock and mud, none of it familiar, and no sign of the rest of the defenders. That day, they continued, coming at last into forested country where they went in single file beside a brawling stream brown with runoff. Often enough they had to walk in it, with its eager current tugging at their ankles or knees, for the way the guide led them was choked with huge boulders and slippery steep bluffs of mud. Around noon, the rain stopped as usual, but the wind continued, moaning in the trees. They had taken their helmets off, since no one had seen any sign of Hothri on their track. The fresh air smelled wonderful, full of growing plants, flowers, and the rich earthy smell of the mud and rotting leafmold.

"Too bad there's a war," said Dubarry, plucking a delicate red flower that hung from a niche in a boulder. "This would be a good place for a picnic . . ."

"In sunshine," said Meroux firmly. Like the others, he was looking around warily. Armitage was as puzzled as the rest; surely they'd have seen some sign that the rest of the column had passed this way? Even heavy rains couldn't destroy all sign. He watched their guide, a heavy-browed man he couldn't remember seeing more than once or twice. The man looked at no one, munching his ration bar steadily. Could the guide be a deserter? A traitor of some kind? Armitage had just made up his mind to ask him some hard questions when the man stood, refastened his helmet, and gestured for them to follow.

Perralt had no idea how to go about it, but it had to be done. Too many others were wondering the same thing, and rumors had begun to spread where even he could hear them. He could see trouble coming, beyond the Hothri, when a few more became convinced. He straightened his shoulders, wished desperately for a clean uniform, and ducked into the command dugout.

Casagar was, as usual, bent over the maps, this time with dividers and pen in his hands. He glanced up as Perralt came in, and went back to the map.

"Sir . . ."

"Yes, Major?" Whatever it was on the map, Casagar seemed fascinated.

"Sir, I need to talk with the colonel."

At that, Casagar looked up, nodded, and laid the dividers precisely on the map. He capped his pen, folded his arms, and said "Go on, Major."

"Sir, I hope the colonel will realize that my questions have nothing to do with his honor . . ." That was ridiculous; you could not ask a man if he were an enemy agent without insulting his honor. But Perralt made himself plunge on. "It's only that the colonel isn't well known . . . I mean none of us know you . . ."

The bright gray eyes met his steadily. Whatever a traitor looked like, surely this wasn't it, a trim, fit, little man with honest eyes. "And you're wondering where I came from, is that it?"

"Well . . . yes, sir." That was part of it.

"You've recognized that I'm not Aristan by birth—my accent's pretty strong, I suppose. I was born on Dessalles, one of the out-colonies. Came here for my degrees—Dessalles never did have a university—and went home to join the Home Guard. When the war broke out, I transferred to offplanet duty with the Fleet."

Perralt remembered Dessalles, one of the first planets lost to the Hothri, but knew nothing else about it or any of the other out-colonies. If Casagar's name and accent were Dessallian, he would not know.

"It's just that we knew the other senior officers . . . General Duarte, Colonel Marish, Colonel Pachek, and then when they were all killed—"

"There was this stranger, not even Aristan, in command. And it bothered you. What did you think, that the Hothri had planted a turncoat among you?"

This was so exactly what he'd suspected that he could not keep from flushing; he felt the heat on his face. "Not only me, sir."

Casagar's eyebrows went up. "Oh? And is it a common topic of discussion, your turncoat colonel?"

"Sir, I never mentioned it. Whatever I thought myself . . . one does not speculate on such possibilities in such a dangerous situation. But some of the men and junior officers . . . they wonder, sir . . . all the familiar commanders dead, and your choice of tactics . . ."

Casagar cocked his head on one side. "Tell me, Major, do you have an armed squad waiting to arrest me if you decide I'm a traitor?"

Perralt felt a wave of anger; it was nothing to joke about. "With all due respect, sir, I thought this could be handled between officers and gentlemen."

"Major Perralt, I am not making fun of you. It would have been an intelligent thing to do, if you seriously believed I was a traitor, and I would not have been insulted, whether I was guilty or innocent. I suppose it would do no good to show you the original orders . . . ? No, of course not. If the Hothri could supply a traitorous colonel, they could supply me with fake orders, and personnel lists, and anything else to make me seem legitimate. And if you're so convinced, then the loss of our communications equipment and computers, and the equipment failures, all of that is part of the same scheme." Casagar squeezed his eyes closed, and when he opened them looked around as if he saw a new world. Perhaps, Perralt thought, he did, having found suspicion where he was accustomed to trust.

"I have made bad mistakes," Casagar said, almost to himself. "I thought it was so clear, the only thing to do under the circumstances, and even you—" He looked straight at Perralt again, and his voice strengthened. "Even you, Major, have not really understood, have you?"

"No, sir," said Perralt, not giving in.

Casagar sighed, and hitched one hip up onto the table. "Very well. Let's try to clear this up. I'm not native Aristan, and I'm from a planet you know was taken by the Hothri.

You can't get at the Fleet records to see my date of transfer, and you might not believe the records if you saw them. I've been on Arista only eight months, came in with the Seventh . . . you'll know Admiral Koch by name, and if you've met him you'd remember the scar on the back of his left hand—but I could have got that from a photograph. I had met Colonel Marish and General Duarte; when the landing response teams were being formed, they asked if I'd care to serve there. General Duarte checked my background with Admiral Koch. Of course, he's not alive to explain that, and you could choose to believe I made it up." For the first time, anger leaked into his usually level voice. "I'm helpless to clear myself, for exactly those reasons you'd expect a guilty person to have devised."

"It is not only the opportunity," said Perralt, still stiffly.

"No. I see that. If I had chosen to throw all my forces at the Hothri landing site, however foolishly, or if I'd chosen to retreat into the forest and try to escape, I suppose you'd have fewer doubts."

The tone was crisp, once more devoid of anger, and Perralt couldn't help smiling. "Sir, in the first case I'd be dead, and have no worries. In the second . . . well . . . it would be less wasteful."

"Would it?" Casagar beckoned. "Come here and look at this, and this time *listen* to what I'm telling you. And no, I won't take this opportunity to knock you on the head."

Perralt flushed again but moved up to look at Casagar's hand holding the dividers on the stacked lines that meant the mountain escarpment.

"Major, we had orders to prevent the Hothri landing, if we could, or engage and occupy them if we couldn't stop them. As you know, our transports were attacked even as we landed, and we lost men and vital equipment immediately—with more to come in the first hours. We did not have enough left to prevent a Hothri landing. But we could—and did—harry them. Smart human commanders who found a remote landing site infested with troublesome defenders would just pull out and go land somewhere else, but the Hothri are—luckily for Arista—different. They kept coming, and we kept killing them. That worked as long as we had enough men and materiel to keep them boxed near their landing site."

"I understand *that*," said Perralt grumpily.

"If you do, then you understand that we had to pull back, or be wiped out with decreasing Hothri losses. The question facing me then was how to pull back, and where, and how we could do the most damage to the Hothri in the process."

"I still don't see why we could not operate as a mobile strike force. There's plenty of rough country at hand."

"Because the rains will stop any day now, and once the Hothri have control of the air—which they will, because we don't have adequate anti-aircraft weapons—our so-called mobile strike force is dead meat."

"How do you know the rains will stop?" asked Perralt.

"First, it was in the briefing given to the senior officers, and second, I make it a practice to know something about *all* the environmental components of a field of battle. Third, the end of the rains is signalled by increasing winds—as we've had the past day or so. The more you know, the less chance there is to be caught in someone else's trap. Besides, the Hothri aren't going to be moving from here on the ground—they wanted this as a secure landing site for their spacecraft, and they'd use suborbital and aircraft to transport their troops from here to the cities. So a mobile strike force would have nothing to do but snipe at the landing site, and we had dropped below a size that could do that effectively."

Put that way, it made sense, but Perralt still had questions. "But why this retreat into a blind trap?"

"It's either that, Major, or wander around in the brush and trees waiting to be picked off by the Hothri flyers. Or even a stray column that just wants to go human-hunting. We'd do no good, in the sense of keeping them busy or doing them harm, and in six months—actually much less—we'd all be just as dead. This way . . . this way we make them pay for our deaths, at ratios that may do them enough harm to help Arista. Can't you see that?"

Perralt could, but he could also see how hard it was going to be to convince the others. His face must have shown that, because Casagar sighed again.

"If they're all about to plot a mutiny, I suppose I'd better take the time to convince them otherwise. What do you think it will take?" Perralt noticed that this assumed he himself no longer thought Casagar a traitor. He didn't want to ask himself, because he could see no clear alternative to Casagar's plan. No better ideas rose up to suggest themselves, no brilliant tactical coups popped out of his memory of military history lectures.

"Well," he said at last, "You're going to have to talk to them. The officers, at least."

"And you?" Casagar put the question Perralt had hoped to escape. He spread his hands.

"Sir, I can't think of anything else. You've answered my objections. Actually—if you *were* a Hothri plant, you've been doing them a lot of damage, and aside from retreating as soon as we landed, trying to save ourselves by hiding in the hills—" He shook his head. "No, I can see that wouldn't have done Arista any good, while what we did may have helped. It's not like anything I ever read about, but it's the best choice out of bad ones, I suppose. I don't like it, but then . . . war's full of things I don't like. If you'll excuse me—" Casagar nodded, and Perralt went back out, his mind in a whirl. Would it seem so sensible the next day or the next, when they had their backs to a stone wall and the Hothri moving in on them?

Casagar had gathered all the remaining officers. Perralt watched their faces as they listened to the colonel's final explanation of his plan. Fatigue, despair, sullenness, confusion, and, on two or three, growing comprehension that turned to horror.

Casagar paused, reading the same signals as Perralt. "You don't think it will work, I gather?"

Girond, lately a captain and now a major, clambered up. "Begging the colonel's pardon, but it seems too simple to work—like trying a rabbit snare on a cow."

Casagar smiled in a way that Perralt had learned meant he was pleased. Why now? Perralt wondered. "It's a matter of scale, Major Girond," Casagar said. "This is really nothing more than the classic battle of Marathon, only we haven't the human reserves in the wings. We have the planet itself, the mountains."

"But sir . . . rockslides? I've seen rockslides, and yes, they'll kill a few, perhaps block pursuit behind us for awhile, until the bugs climb over. But the colonel seems to think they'll act like a couple of thousand reinforcements—"

"Five thousand fresh men couldn't do what those slopes will do," said Casagar briskly. "Come—none of you are geologists, nor have any of you done fieldwork in these mountains." He nodded at Captain Solomon, who had once boasted of his mountaineering skills. "Tell them Eugene—what velocity will an avalanche reach down a slope like these?"

"It depends," began Solomon cautiously, but at Casagar's nod he went on to speak of snow avalanches and mudslides, rockfalls and rockslides, describing how they moved down-slope at more than 100 kilometers per hour, splashing high on opposite slopes, veering wildly down narrow mountain valleys to destroy everything in their path.

"And that's the smaller ones," Casagar said. "There are records—all the way back to Old Earth—of slides so huge, so destructive, that they reshape not only the valley and valley walls, but extend beyond that valley to its outwash. It requires very large, very steep mountains, with very unstable rock strata. The steeper the slope, the faster the slide travels, the more rock it can move, and the farther it goes."

"Wait—you're not thinking of making a slide that could reach to the Hothri landing site—?"

"No—probably not. But it may spill out a kilometer or more—the outwash fan from this valley is steep; it's one reason I chose it. No, what I intend is to destabilize both valley walls, in sequence from the head of the valley to its outlet. Right now, at the end of the rains, those steep-pitched shales and slates are full of water. Water reduces friction between rock strata just as it does between your boot and the rock. I once saw a shaped charge shake loose a ten-meter thick layer and send it sliding on a month's worth of heavy rains. Not here, but the principle's the same. The Hothri can't fight gravity, any more than we can. Even a ship's shields would have trouble with that much mass moving that fast."

"So all that rock—whole or broken, is supposed to come crashing down on the Hothri and their equipment, and send them tumbling down the valley under it?" asked Barthe, whose family had been rich, and who could not let any discussion go on long without his contribution. Casagar nodded. "And—where will we be? If it can splash as high as Solomon said, can we climb above it?"

"Most of us, no. The rocket crews maybe, although being above the splash puts you in the zone where separation occurs. The thing is, gentlemen, the concussion of the explosions and other slides may—and probably will—induce sympathetic slides everywhere in the valley. There will be no safe place."

"But sir—" Girond stopped abruptly, and reddened.

"It's all right, Major; all the rest are thinking the same thing. Why would I choose a plan that is almost sure to kill all of us?" Casagar smiled again, a slightly challenging smile. "I'm sure you've all read your military history, and I assume you remember the Iron Duke of Wellington." No one answered; he nodded as if in answer to a question of his own and went on. "At Waterloo, when hard-pressed by Napoleon's forces, his comment was 'Hard pounding, gentlemen; we shall see who pounds longest.' You would understand calling in artillery or airstrikes on our position, if it were necessary." Heads nodded. "We have had hard pounding, and I am calling in the hardest pounding, the best and only reinforcements, we can get. We have eroded their forces considerably—amazingly, I think—but from here on the Hothri can kill more of us with less risk to themselves. Unless we stake all on this trap, and let the mountains of Arista join the defense. If with loss of our last hundreds, we can destroy their thousands, it is worth that loss. I myself will be on the valley floor."

He paused for that to sink in, and when the faces were thoughtful but calm, he went on. "There is one thing. Our rear-guard was directed not to this valley, but to another nearby. I believe, in the storm that night, the Hothri will be unable to trace them. If they do, they'll be no worse off than we are. But if the Hothri do not trace them, they're in a smaller, shallower, valley with more cover and more stable rock. They may survive. I have sent with them a written report of this entire expedition, and my plans. It may be that if the Hothri are defeated, these men will be found alive, and our work known. At least the report may be found, even if they do not survive."

Up the valley the Hothri came, the tracked assault vehicles lurching over the smaller boulders, between the larger ones. Skirmish teams afoot flanked them. There had been no rain since the previous morning, and the Hothri had probably moved all day and night. Through his scopes, Perralt could see the shiny carapaces bob over the uneven ground, even though sunlight barely touched the highest peaks he could see. He had gone up one of the terraces, with a functioning radio, to keep track of the Hothri advance. From here, forty meters above the valley floor, he had an excellent view of the colonel's plan. At the head of the valley, as if hopelessly trapped but determined to fight to the death, the Aristans had clumped their forces beneath a three hundred meter cliff. If a Hothri had been where he was, it could have seen how few they were—and with a scope could have seen how ragged, how many suits were holed, how many wounded, how few heavy weapons remained to them. Given that view, a Hothri might decide to drop a few shells on them, and let be.

But all the Hothri were down in the valley. A *lot* of Hothri were in the valley; a column that ran all the way back to the entrance, and perhaps beyond. A trail of ants on a line of honey, he thought bitterly, looking for the honeypot at the end. They could never have defeated this many Hothri, could not have held them even another day, in straight fighting.

The colonel was right about one thing, and Perralt had the grace to admit he might be right about many others. *I was never the officer I thought I was*, he admitted to himself, *despite my rank in the Academy, despite my combat experience. I am not bad—I am brave enough, and I care for my men, but—but Casagar is right. If we had all known all we could know, if we humans would ever realize that all knowledge really is connected, and useful, and that recognizing a trap before you're in it is better than having the courage to chew off your leg, or even lie in wait for the trapper* . . . His thoughts cut off abruptly as he caught a light signal from one of the rocket teams on the opposite slope.

The Hothri were still entering the valley, apparently determined to overmatch the humans enough to need no second battle. An observer even nearer the valley entrance reported that a ring of tanks had made it to the top of the outwash slope and come to a stop. More infantry were coming in. Perralt looked back to the valley floor, and saw that the Hothri were almost in close-firing range. He had worried that they might try an artillery barrage before the rocket teams could set off the slides, but the colonel said that would do almost as well.

"As long as they are in the valley—whoever makes the first loud noise will set it off. The rockets are probably not necessary, but I want to be certain."

Perralt thumbed the radio's control. "Colonel?"

"Here. How close?"

"Their advance lines are perhaps 200 meters; the main body is a few hundred meters behind that, and it's solid from there back. They've brought up heavier vehicles— tanks, the observer says—to the outwash slope. My estimate is well over two thousand, maybe as many as four . . ."

"Artillery?"

"Nothing but the guns on their assault vehicles, that I can see. None reported."

"Very good, then—"

"Colonel Casagar," Perralt interrupted hastily. "Before you give the order, sir, there's something I must say. I'm sorry

I suspected you of being an enemy agent; I'm honored to have served under you."

There was a pause, then Casagar replied. "Perralt, you have nothing to apologize for. You've been supportive, you've followed what must have seemed cockeyed orders, you are brave and you care for your troops. Times like these breed suspicions. Besides . . . you ought to know . . . the Hothri think I *am* their agent."

"What!"

"We have only moments, but you deserve the truth, Perralt, before we die. In one way only your suspicions were correct: I was a reserve officer on Thormelde, captured in a Hothri attack. They wanted a prisoner, and despite all I could do . . . Anyway, they 'converted' me, and to make my long story short, planted me on Arista to do just what they think I've done—bottle up a regiment and deliver at least 500 prisoners."

"But—"

"Let me finish, Perralt. They think this valley is safe; they expect to launch gas canisters and knock us out, because they think our suits are no longer operational. They think they can convert the others as easily as they converted me." A brief pause, in which Perralt stared fixedly at the sunlight touching the top of the slope across from him, his mind blind with panic. "They're angry, that I cost them so many casualties in the past few days, just to convince you that I was really what I claimed; they would probably have followed us here for that only." Another pause, and then Casagar's voice regained its wonted brisk cheerfulness. "They don't know I was a geologist before I was drafted into the reserves; they don't know one damn thing about the geology of terrestrial planets. They had to believe I was truly their turncoat, to fall for this rather obvious trap, and I hope you'll forgive what I had to do for that. But I am human, though not Aristan; my death will prove what loyalty I have."

"You . . . you lied," breathed Perralt.

"Yes. And you, with your blunt honesty, felt it. But under that lie, Perralt, was the truth you wanted. As you saw on down below; we hurt them badly. As you will see, in the few minutes left to us. God bless you, Perralt, and Arista."

Perralt could neither bless nor curse in reply; fury and sorrow and amazement struggled for dominance in his mind, trapping his tongue.

"And now it's time, Perralt, and I must know if you trust me enough to follow this last command."

"I . . . if I don't, you'll signal from down there, won't you?"

"Yes."

Perralt drew himself up, wondering if Casagar peered upward with his scope, or if this was an empty gesture, and saluted briskly. "Sir, I'm waiting . . ."

"Go ahead, then."

"On your order."

The shadow of the ridge behind him was fleeing down the opposite slope as Perralt picked up his own rifle and sighted at the leading Hothri team. "Fire," came the word from the radio, and he squeezed the trigger. His aim did not matter; it was the sound, the flat crack of the rifle, that signalled the rocket teams. From above and to his left he heard the pop and roar as the first team on his side launched their Esprit; a few seconds later, when the crack of his rifle had crossed the valley floor, he saw the plume of vapor from the first team opposite. Immediately behind him, a brisk rattle of loose scree began, triggered by his shot and the Esprit launching.

He could see the white vapor trail of both Esprits crossing the valley, making an X against the dark rocks. He followed the one from his side to its impact just below the ridge-top; a massive roiling ball of flame and vapor obliterated his view of its target before the wind blew it away. Then the thunder of it came to him, just as the roar of an impact on his side of the valley made him grab for his ear protectors.

Across the valley, he saw dust still rising, and then realized that the explosion had triggered a rockslide. It looked pitifully small, and much slower than he expected, no more than the slithering of sand down the side of a sandpile when children are playing. Sorrow clenched his heart, as much for Casagar's lie as for the failure of their plans. He had wanted so to believe in one last truth before he died. But the ground rumbled beneath him, so heavily that his ear protectors couldn't handle it. He glanced left, and saw boulders the size of tables jouncing down the slope beyond the terrace; when he looked up, he saw an immense bulge of broken rock and soil hanging in midair, hardly seeming to fall except that individual pebbles grew into house-sized blocks as they approached.

He tore his gaze away from this to the opposite side, just in time to see the vapor trails of two more Esprits crossing farther down the valley. He looked down; the Hothri advance had stopped, and the neat column seemed to be breaking up. Across . . . across was a gray-brown wave that fell endlessly, slowly and then faster, so fast it was no longer visible as a mass of rock or soil, but a smooth blurred surface that rippled like muddy water pouring down a gully.

Dust rose from its leading edge now, clouding his vision, but he felt in his bootsoles the rising rumble, like twenty thousand organs all playing their longest pipes. When he glanced upvalley to see what was happening to the pitiful clump of human fighters, he was just in time to watch the slow fall of part of the cliff behind them, a great chunk of rock that crumbled as it fell . . . he could not see its final fall, because now the froth of those immense avalanches, great spurts and clouds of rockdust, rose higher than his terrace. The noise was vast, beyond comprehension; his mind seemed to turn into itself and hide. He had retreated to the middle of the terrace, half-hoping that the approaching chaos would miss him, though he had no idea what he would do if he survived. See how much damage had been done, he supposed, though it was clear that Casagar's plan was working.

And then a tongue of wet rock and mud slopped up across the terrace, and gathered him in, one more bit of organic debris, on its way to scour the valley and its outwash slope.

❖     ❖     ❖

Morning light blazed upon the peaks, swept down the western slope of their valley, and swallowed the mist hanging over the noisy little river. The air smelled of spicewood and hawberry, leafmold under the needled mountain trees, unknown flowers starring the lush grass. Armitage lay back against the grass with the others, free of the encumbering, smelly combat suit. They had all bathed in the river, braving its chill and the uneven rolling rocks of its bed. Now, damp and chilly, but welcoming the sunlight and its promise of a warmer day, they sprawled in forgotten luxury, scratching and stretching at will. No Hothri had found them yet, and the rearguard said none had followed them—they had seen the hordes going by in the distance, all headed for another valley entrance. So for this day, they counted themselves safe—and if they died later, they'd have had one last day of pleasure.

Armitage lay his head on his arms, and let the grass tickle his ears and forehead. He wondered if the pink starry flower in front of his nose were related to the white starry flower that had grown in their upper fields. He wondered what the others thought about the letter the colonel had written them, the one he'd opened yesterday and shared around. No one had said anything about it at all. It was safer to wonder about botany.

The ground beneath him trembled, a faint quiver that grew stronger for several minutes, then died away. All the men were looking at each other. Armitage looked west, to the valley's sheltering ridge. A roiling cloud rose at some distance beyond, and blew away on a wind from the mountains. Reivers rose from the high ground, lifting easily on air currents, to circle gradually in that direction. Armitage watched their dark wings silently.

"Was that it?" asked Meroux after awhile, as they all watched the cloud disperse.

Armitage shrugged. "What else? It is not a cavalry charge."

"Do you suppose it worked, what he said? Trapped the bugs in there too?"

"Probably. We have to hope so, or they'll be hunting us."

None of them said what Armitage was thinking, what they were probably all thinking. They were the witnesses, but the glory belonged to those in the other valley, buried under rocks where no reiver could find them.

Armitage lay back down, squinting against the sunlight that now warmed his cold skin. As he closed his eyes, he thought again of his father's farm, and their horses, this time without as much pain. It was gone; it would never come again; but he was alive in another mountain valley, and if Arista survived he would farm again. He would find another woman to love as he had once loved Elise, and they would have children. He owed the others that.

*This is another of the rare stories that arrived in my head all of a piece. It's one of my favorites, perhaps because it gives me a mellow feeling when I read it. Some people think fiction shouldn't give you a mellow feeling, but then some people put catsup on everything they eat, too. I like fiction, as well as food, to have a variety of flavors and textures.*

# THE HAPPY FROG

Once there was a frog who lived in a large pond at the edge of the forest. His broad back was patterned with dapples of gold and black on shining green; his belly was smooth and silvery. Long legs thrust him from bank to lily pad, and from lily pad far into the clear green waters of the pond. Great eyes like crinkled gold foil, the pupils black wells, showed him a world fit for such a prince of frogs: small creatures of the air to catch with a flip of his long and agile tongue, small creatures of the water to gulp and swallow when he swam. Broad lily pads and half-sunk logs to sun on; shady shallows where a frog could bask safely, eyes only showing above the water's skin. He had survived the dangers of his youth: the supple snakes who feasted on young frogs, the herons who hunted the water's edge and speared his kin with savage beaks, the great fish at the pond's bottom, who would take frog when he could not find a smaller cousin, the quick-pawed mink and otter. Now, grown broad and bitter, long hind toes clawed, he sent his richly patterned song throbbing into the evening air. Here, here, here, he sang. Great frogs, spotted frogs, here, here, here.

In all this idyll, only one recurring problem. Far away, some fool (as the frog would have said it) sang a tale, and in that tale a witch's curse shriveled a prince into a frog. Eventually a princess kissed the frog, broke the enchantment, and freed the prince. A story, the frog would have said, of surpassing foolishness, the sort of thing one might expect of idle humans who knew nothing of frogs but their croaking in the night. Ridiculous, foolish story, and (above all) absolutely and completely impossible.

But no one asked the frog's opinion. The story spread. In a realm where eligible princes were few, and princesses many, a fashion arose of searching for such enchanted mortals. Frog-hunts, with all the panoply of royal venery: the huntsman, the beaters, the music, the companions of the chase, ribbons and laces and little frog-stickers bound in silver. The castle ponds were soon depleted, for of course it quickly became obvious that to release an unenchanted frog meant chancing a catch of the same unenchanted frog on the next hunt. Unenchanted frogs became froglegs, a new and fashionable item at the feasts that followed the hunt (although two years before, froglegs had been a peasant dish, too coarse to be mentioned by persons of quality.) If one could not have a verifiable disenchanted prince bowing over one's hand, one could devour the faithless (and luckless) frogs so unwise as to be mere frogs, and slow enough to be caught.

When the castle ponds yielded only small, furtive brown frogs (obviously not princes: no one would kiss such a thing lest it be an enchanted servant) the princesses moved on to farm ponds. Soon the farm ponds were all empty of great, green, speckled or spotted frogs suitable as enchanted princes, and the search spread to woods and pastures and distant lakes.

The first princess found the pond by the forest on a hot summer afternoon when the great frog was lying in shady water, eyes nearly shut, half-thinking about letting the mosquito hovering in front of him live another day. A loud thumping downhill opened his eyes wide. Horns brayed, dogs barked, and human voices chattered through it all. His eyes flipped open, he gulped a great gulp of air, and slid underwater, swimming with long, easy kicks to the clump of cattails that ran out into the pond. From there, screened by the shaking shadows, he could watch unseen.

What he saw was appalling. First the dogs, dashing to the water's edge and slavering into the pond, splashing and yelping with glee. Then the huntsman, all in green with a red feather in his peaked cap, and the beaters in russet, with green feathers. Then the musicians, on spotted ponies, beating their drums and blowing their horns with more energy than harmony. And then the bevy of ladies, their sweaty horses decked with ribbons and bells and bits of braided yarn, and leaning toward the water eagerly. A few knights as escort, including one old gray-beard, grim and watchful, who clearly thought the entire expedition was a mistake. And behind, on foot, gasping and struggling, the servants bearing the picnic.

All—dogs, horses, huntsman and beaters, ladies, knights, and servants—came to the water. Horses and ponies churned the grassy verge into a mucky mess; the frog could smell it all the way across the pond. Servants dipped cans into the pond (carefully away from the horse-churned shallows); a bright taste of copper made the frog's mouth ache. The huntsman and his beaters knelt to drink from the pond's edge, as did the servants; the ladies and knights drank water from the copper cans, mixed with wine in tankards the servants unpacked along with all the other paraphenalia of a royal picnic.

As bad as the roiling of the water was the noise. Splashing, crashing, thudding of hooves, loud voices, clinking tankards and knives and plates. The frog blinked, wondering what they could possibly be up to. When they had finished eating, tossing their scraps messily into the pond itself, he found out.

Among his many relatives, some hardly smaller than himself had survived the snakes, the herons, the old great fish in the bottom of the pond. One of these, more curious than wise, bobbed up scarce a single leap's length from shore to examine a crust of bread. The ladies shrieked. "A

frog! Bigger than the one at Miller's pond! Bigger even than
the one at Appleford. Surely this is a prince!" Then the dogs
barked, and the huntsman blew his whistle, and the beaters rolled up their russet trousers, picked up strange fan-
shaped objects, and waded into the water. His relative, the
younger frog, had already dived, making for the water lilies.

Two lines of beaters entered the water, while the ladies
stood on dry grass and waved encouragement. Slowly they
dipped their mysterious handfuls into the pond, slowly drew
them along, and lifted them with a quick twist of the wrist—
and there, in one, the frog saw a fish struggling, a small
fish of silver streaked with red and yellow. The frog gulped;
he was himself particularly fond of small silver fish streaked
red and yellow, and hated to see that delicacy slide into
another throat. But the beater tossed the fish aside, into
the water, and again stroked the water with what the frog
now realized was a catcher of some sort.

As the beaters worked along the shallow water, a young
frog panicked, and leaped from bottom mud to shore in one
wild splashing arc. At once the beaters flung themselves after
it, great floundering creatures that they were, and the
knights on shore grabbed for it. Finally someone—the frog
could not see who—made the catch, and held the struggling creature aloft. "A frog, a frog!" cried the ladies. "A
kissable frog!" And then they drew back into a crescent,
and allowed one of their number the center. The frog could
see nothing different about her except the shining metal
circlet on her head. His young relative gaped, terrified, in
the strong hands that held him aloft; that lady then came
forward and carefully, almost studiously, put her lips to the
frog's head.

From the frog's point of view, what followed was more
of the same incomprehensible nonsense. A cry of dismay,
from the ladies; covert grins from the servants, knights,
beaters. A look of disgust on the face of the lady who had
kissed the frog, and then a look of calculation. She reached
out her hand. The huntsman drew from a forest-green
sheath a little silver frog-sticker (the frog stiffened in outrage and astonishment: a *frog* hunt? Was that was this was

about? But only peasants hunted frogs, and they never had time to come this far; their own ponds held all the frogs they needed.) While the great frog watched, disgusted and fascinated all at once, his young relative was stretched on the sorry, trodden ground, and pierced by the pretty weapon. His legs were torn off and dropped in a sack, and his tattered remains thrown into the center of the pool, where their rich smell brought the great fish up from the bottom, his long tail stirring and stirring the water as he climbed almost to sunlight.

This would have been bad enough, an afternoon to blight a whole moon of summer, but it was not over yet. The beaters returned to the water, once more sweeping back and forth with their nets. Again a young frog broke, this time leaping and swimming frantically for safe water, but so disoriented by the foot-churned mud that he zigged stupidly back toward them. The beaters thrashed after, flailing at the water with their nets. Another fish was caught, thrown back. A net's edge hit one young turtle, shattering its shell. And in the pond's deep center, the old fish circled, alarmed and wary both.

The great frog could stand it no longer. He swam in three long kicks from the cattails to the lily-pads, slid himself onto the largest of these, and CROAKED. "Stop!" screamed the princess. The beaters had already stopped, recognizing that croak for what it was, the croak of a large and vigorous frog in the prime of life. "Where?" asked the huntsman. The frog croaked again, louder, and saw all those pale and foolish human faces turn to him. "There!" yelled and shouted and cried and screamed the humans. "It must be a prince," said one lady. The younger frog, forgotten, swam in jerky strokes to the lilies, and hauled himself gasping onto a smaller pad. "Forget the little one," said the huntsman. "It's the big one we want."

But it was the big one they could not get, not then. For those lily pads grew on the far side of the pond, and between the beaters and the lilies were many yards of deep green water. They waded out, deeper and deeper, and realized they could not wade across. Cursing, they went around. The frog and his relatives retired to the deep center, risking the old fish (who had gone into a sulk and returned to the bottom to put his nose in the cold spring that fed the pond.) And although the huntsman threw rocks at them, and his beaters thrashed the shallow water near the shore, they were safe. At last, as the sun declined, the whole party withdrew: hunter, beaters, dogs, servants, ladies, knights, ponies, horses, and all. It was over.

Until, that is, the next fine day. This time the frog knew what to expect when he heard the drums, the horns, the horses' hooves and dogs' barks, and all those discordant human voices. It had been talked about. All the frogs swam at once to the center of the pool, and hung in the water, eyes bulging up like so many floating eggs. The great frog kicked, and they croaked derisively, in unison.

Unfortunately, it seemed the humans were neither amused nor deterred. Idly, the frogs watched them unpack the picnic, this time carried in long wooden boxes instead of baskets. Idly, they watched as servants dragged the boxes to the water's edge. Idly, they watched the beaters roll up their russet trousers and wade into the water carrying those selfsame nets.

And then the boxes moved on the water, two beaters in each box, sliding along the surface like large but very stiff water snakes. The frogs were so amazed they almost forgot to dive, and the nets caught one. The others scattered, frantic, beneath the surface, feeling the water roil around them as the nets reached and waved. They came up all around the pond, breathless with astonishment and terror, and watched as the box bore their comrade to the same fate: a kiss, and then death, and then dismemberment. Only the terror, with its instinctive power, saved them from the beaters who were *not* in the boats, who had crept around the pond to wade in and scoop up those who fled from deep water. They dived again, swam four or five wild kicks, and surfaced. Again the beaters in the floating boxes dipped and swayed; again a single victim rose dripping and forlorn from the water.

Even so, four men in two small boats on a large pond

are no match for free frogs, and a half-dozen or so on the shore can cover only a part of the shallow water. Now that they understood, the frogs stayed in that middle zone—too deep for wading, but out of reach of the boatmen. Back and forth the men rowed, and back and forth the men on shore waded, and up and down and back and forth the frogs swam. It was, in a perverted sort of way, *fun* to dodge beneath the boats, feel the pressure wave of water as the net stroked nearby, slip aside into safe darkness, then rise (but carefully, watching for the shadow of the boat, and carefully, watching for the rising gleam of the great fish) to put narrow nostrils and bulging eyes out of water. If the humans' backs were turned, then a quick swelling of the throat, a quick croak and quicker dive. Not natural fun, like catching a juicy moth or tasty fish fry, but fun.

Eventually, before dark, the humans tired of this, too, and they all went home. The great fish had eaten the sorry remains of three young frogs and retired to his cool haven, and the rest were feasting on evening flies. They were safe.

But the next night men came with torches, great flaring stalks of fire set on iron posts all around the pond. Musicians played tinkling tunes under the forest edge, while the ladies lounged on carpets spread on the grass. The frogs could hardly see even this much. Glittering light washed over them, blinding even underwater with its flickering, unsteady gleam. Again a boat moved out—only one, a black shadow darker than the night sky—and this time lamps hung low along its sides, and from a pole before it. The frogs swam jerkily around the pond, uncertain.

Then a harsh croak, most unfroglike, sent them all to the bottom. A cormorant! Minute after minute they lay, colder than the cold water with fear. But air-hunger had its way with them, and slowly, carefully, one by one they drifted toward the surface. Hardly had the first wave taken a cautious breath, noses barely out into the air, when a black shadow thrust among them, a gaping beak hungry for prey. And one luckless frog was caught, brought to the surface by that captive bird with a ring around its neck, and a long cord tied to one bony leg. Hands plucked the frog from that beak, bore it to the princess . . . and to the usual doom, save that the mangled remains were tossed into the boat, to feed the cormorant when its night's work was done. Meanwhile the cormorant dove again, caught another frog, to repeat the cycle.

How this might have ended, none of them could imagine, but the light and furor drew the old fish. Up he came, slow and easy as a rising current of water, uneven light making him waver like a vision in blowing mist. His long snout opened, tasted the water, the frogs' terror, the swirl and plunge of some hunter in territory he considered his own. In one dive, the bird raked the fish's side with its beak . . . and in that same dive the fish took the bird, and dove back to the pond's bottom, jaws clenched around a hot, feathered prize such as he had not enjoyed since the ducks quit nesting there.

The beaters yanked on the bird's leg-cord, jarring the old fish's descent; in memory of old wounds and battles, the fish let go briefly, then followed the dead bird up, taking chunks and feathers from it until the beaters saw that mysterious shape rising out of darkness and panicked, stabbing with net handles. The fish rolled, swerved beneath the boat—he had no love for boats—and lay there, concealed. A net handle poked his side; he humped, and the boat bobbed. The beaters cried out, dropped their nets. The fish considered the cormorant corpse, now hanging temptingly from the boat near his nose. But hooks . . . he remembered hooks, all too well, and the cormorant smelled of metal, from the ring on its neck. The fish bumped the boat again, harder, then took the cormorant's loose wing in his mouth and wagged it back and forth. Above him, in the boat, the beaters screamed. From the angles the light made in the water, the great fish looked even greater, a monster of legend, all iron scales and fins of steel and crystal. Onshore, one of the knights threw a light lance that scraped the fish's tail. The beaters cried out again, in warning, but it was too late. The fish had mastered this pond, and had no mind to have humans invade it; certainly not in the peaceful night, when he most felt secure. With a lunge and a plunge, he rocked the light boat, then drenched it as he breached beside it. Another plunge, a shove on the side that suddenly seemed higher, and the boat went over, spilling two terrified humans into the water. The fish sank, spiralling down to his favorite resting place, and ignored the chaos above. Eventually the water quieted, and did not, he was sorry to notice, smell of drowned humans. He enjoyed the bits of dead frog that had fallen out when the boat went over.

Although the night frogging party left when the two beaters finally floundered to shore, it was clear to everyone that the humans were not going to give up. The resident water snakes moved downstream "for the duration" as they put it. Dogs, they said vaguely, making sinusoidal patterns without going anywhere, and then suddenly going, without appearing to move. The remaining heron packed his long crooked neck into a tight wedge and flew away. For some days nothing happened. The great frog relaxed enough to send his booming call out into the night: Here, here, here . . . here. But no one came, no one he wanted to speak to. Their reputation had spread. No one was going to move to that pond, until the humans gave up on it. The great frog began to realize that he was getting sidelong looks, even from his own kin . . . his own offspring.

When the next trouble came, it was worse than anyone had imagined. The noisy procession seemed familiar, but what was this rumbling thing on wheels (they knew about wheels: mills had wheels) pulled by two hefty, hairy-ankled horses? A box, set down heavily at the foot of the pond, just where it spilled into a stream. A long snake-like thing, trailed out (a HUGE snake, the frogs noted nervously) into the pond water. A shorter snakelike thing run down the stream a little. Beaters by the shore, their trousers rolled, with nets—more than ever before. And two huge, sweating peasants, who began to haul and shove on sticks coming from the box, up and down, up and down, up and down.

It made a horrible noise, obscene: slobbering and sucking and groaning all at once. Worse than that, as the noise went on, the water near the mysterious snake turned brown, as mud and slime and fluff off the bottom rose, churned, and slid inexorably toward the end of the . . . hose. Thump and thud, slurp and slobber, the two-man firepump sucked water from the pond. It was then early morning; the princess and her ladies had not arrived. But by midmorning, all the creatures in the pond knew what was happening. The pond was being killed, sucked away by that horrible box and those sweating peasants, who worked in shifts, without pausing. Inch by inch the water went down, and the beaters moved a little farther into the water, churning up yet more mud, blinding those creatures with eyes, and smothering those who depended on smell. Already five crayfish holes were exposed to the drying sun.

The pump went on, its throbbing palpable to the old fish down by the spring. Exquisitely sensitive to the water's messages, he felt the lessening pressure, knew the spring was pouring in less than the pump was taking out. Worse was to come. Another pump arrived by noon. The pond shrank visibly. Bundles of frog spawn rose into the light and air, to die. Tadpoles were stranded in old footprints, trodden underfoot by the beaters.

In the cool afternoon, the princess came to see what progress had been made, came with a pavilion in which to spend the night, if necessary. By then the frog had made his decision. Freedom was not worth the loss of all his progeny, the destruction of his lifelong home. He did not wish to die, but he would let the human touch her lips to his, and trust in his strength and speed to escape. So when the princess strolled down to the grass verge, now some feet from the water, he rose to the surface and croaked. She pointed. He swam nearer, arrowing straight for her feet. A net swooped at him, but her command halted it. Behind her, her ladies murmured, awed. Surely so bold a frog . . . surely so large and handsome a frog (for a frog) . . . surely so *unnatural* a frog must be a prince.

At the water's edge, he hopped onto stinking mud, as lightly as he might, and then to her feet. Looking up, he croaked again. The princess crouched down, and offered her hand. The frog waddled onto it; she lifted him to her

For the frog, who had never been told about enchantments, it was a startling experience. Under his lips, her soft, warm, human-smelling lips turned cool and rubbery. Her chin shrank away, her face receded, and two huge luminous green eyes rose scarcely a head-length from his own. And she hopped out of the tangle of her discarded clothes, a sleek, green, black-and-gold-spotted frog, whose breath was clean and froglike, whose long legs folded and unfolded in a great leap that ended in a splash.

It did not take him long to follow, and though he never completely understood what it had been about, they lived happily ever after in that pond by the forest edge. As for the minstrel who had so garbled the story he heard from the naiad who lived in the witch's well, he lived long and happily on his own version, although none of the princesses who went frog-hunting ever found a prince in a pond. What had a frog-maid done, to be cursed into the shape of a human princess all those years? That's another tale altogether.

face, and, with a frown of concentration, touched her lips (hot, dry, unpleasant lips) to his cool, slick ones.

And of course he remained what he had always been: a large, handsome, spotted frog, a prince among frogs, but entirely batrachian. Furious, for having been so visibly convinced, so publicly fooled, she clutched at him, eager for sacrifice, but he thrust his long, sharp, breeding claws into her wrist. With a shriek, she dropped him, and he leaped instantly as far as he could. Feet, sticks, and nets thrashed around him. He leaped again, wildly, anywhere, as deaths pursued. Screams from the princess, from the other ladies, bellows and curses from the men. But at last he leaped straight over a net, high and clean, and landed with a splash in water just deep enough for swimming.

She would have had the pool drained to kill him, the frog who so humiliated her, but the knights prevailed. If that frog, the biggest anyone had seen, was not a prince, then no lesser frog in that pond would be, and she could not reasonably waste the labor of so many peasants with the harvest in progress. Forget the stupid thing, the knights said . . . one of them crooned, stroking her disordered hair. We need the firepumps back in the castle, said another. And as it was coming onto sunset, and she had no wish to spend the night here, in sight of so insolent a frog, she let herself be persuaded. The ladies rode off first, with light chatter and edged merriment, escorted as always by the knights, then the beaters, muddy to the knees, grinning slyly at each other, and finally the peasants, cursing quietly about the time lost from harvest, the labor it would take to drag these miserable stinking firepumps back where they should never have been taken from, did the king have the sense the gods gave . . . they paused, spat severally into the pond, and ended . . . frogs. Damned frogs, and they'd be switched if they ever ate another frog leg.

By the end of summer, the spring had managed to refill the pond, although the lost frog spawn and tadpoles couldn't be replaced. The watersnakes had moved back upstream. And it all seemed to be over.

It was on a hot, dry, dusty day at the ragged end of

summer, when the pond's skin was dusted with goldenrod pollen, that the next princess arrived. No procession, this time: a tired donkey, whose red saddle had faded from exposure and no proper oiling. And on the donkey, a sad-faced young woman who hardly merited the title of lady . . . not after the royalty the frog had seen that summer. Her dress had once been green, but was weatherworn into blotches of brown and dull yellow. Bright metal on her head, yes, but no finery, no ribbons, laces, jingling bells . . . no jewels. No servants to carry her picnic luncheon, no knights riding escort, no ladies in waiting, no musicians, no carpet and cushions, no pavilion, nothing. Frogs have no conception of human beauty; the girl might have been ugly, plain, or pretty—to him she was a human, a pale-faced, huge, smelly creature about to cause trouble. The frog broke off his musings when the donkey came to water. The princess— if indeed that bright metal meant a princess—had thrown herself carelessly on her stomach at the water's edge, alongside the donkey, and was resting her cheek on the water, as if her skin burned.

The frogs stayed in the middle of the pond. Who could know what tricks she might have? She sighed, pushed herself up, looked around, and burst into tears. The donkey backed up a few steps and brayed. Still crying (a disgusting sound, the frog thought), she tended to the donkey, unfastening the girth of the red saddle, pulling off the bridle. The donkey shook itself, doglike, and ambled off to find a good place to roll. The girl came back to the water's edge, sank down in the nest of her shabby skirts, and cried.

Terror lasts only so long. When the girl didn't move, but continued to sob, the frogs returned, one by one and cautiously, to their own activities. Late flies, careless moths, butterflies worn to tatters by a summer's life: all were prey, delicious to frogs fattening for winter endurance. The great frog slid onto the largest lily pad and watched. No beaters crept out of the woods . . . no danger at all. Only the girl, whose sobs gradually died away as she fell asleep in the last light.

Dusk thickened and a chill mist formed over the pond,

warning of autumn to come. The frog swam stealth through the warm surface water, closer and closer to sleeping girl. He could hear the donkey ripping into a be vine under the forest edge, hear the tiny patter of nigh hunters' paws in leafmold now crisping in the turning ye And he could hear the deep, quiet breathing of the gi the rustle of her clothes as she shivered in the mist.

His feet found mud, and he crouched. Her hand was onl a leap away, just on dry ground. The frog considered. So fa she had not been much trouble, but experience was agains her. It had worked before: the best plan was to let her pu her lips on him quickly, and then go away. He was sure h could escape a single human with no trouble at all. Behind him, one of his relatives offered a tentative croak. He let his own throat swell into a glorious round, so big he could see it himself, and expelled a powerful reply. Here, he said. Here, here, here. Frog . . . frog, frog, frog. I know what I'm doing, he said, bracing his hindlegs. He had heard her indrawn breath as she woke in chill, damp, darkness with a booming bullfrog near at hand, and prepared to leap if necessary.

But her voice came on a warm gust, somewhat less smelly than the other princess's breath. "A frog!" she said. It was the same, the frog thought, as the other one. For some reason, they wanted to kiss a frog. It made no sense at all. He didn't want to kiss a human . . . in fact, frogs do not kiss frogs. But he felt that he understood the routine, now. He croaked more softly, and hopped forward. As he had hoped, she stayed where she was, lying down with her face near the ground. It was not *quite* dark, even with mist, for the starlight suffused it. He could see the white blur of her face, and finding her mouth was no problem, with that warm, odorous breeze coming from it. And she saw him, for she said again, "A frog! A huge frog! Then maybe it's true . . . all that about enchantments . . . ' This the frog did not understand, but he waddled forward anyway. She held still, poised. He waited, one long moment after another. Why didn't she . . . ? With t' suggestion of a sigh, the frog stretched slightly a his cool, damp mouth to hers.

*When I was a very small child, the people next door owned a couple of parade horses. It was my (unfulfilled) dream to ride one of them down Main Street, carrying one of the flags. This story started out as an ordinary main-stream story about the limitations of acceptable ambitions and the way society looks at girls and horses . . . until one of the horses came close enough to show me its wicked emerald eye. The mental equivalent of a dust devil blew through my mind and twisted the story quite a few degrees darkward.*

# HORSE OF HER DREAMS

It was just another little wide spot in the road. One of those towns with a hot shadeless Main Street, some old brick or rock buildings on each side, and a big ugly new government building intended to look modern and urban and progressive, but clunky as a cinder block in a display case of Chinese porcelain. Here it combined City Hall, Fire Station, Library, and Community Center, all in one big chunk of beige precast-concrete panels that hadn't had time to mellow, but had been there long enough for rust streaks to come down the sides. Three spindly little oaks in planters out front hadn't really taken hold.

We knew the town's reputation as the county scapegoat—it's our business to know—but that's not why we came. We—the Frontline News team, Channel 8—had come to cover their annual festival, producing a 30-second clip for our Weekend Previews on the Friday night six o'clock news. So on this July Wednesday there we were square in the middle of that two blocks of Main Street, in trouble.

What you want is local color, and what the locals think is color isn't what you want. Which meant the big sign draped across the City Center saying "Welcome Frontline News!" wasn't it. Nor the pair of girls in shorts and clogs who stared at us through the windows of Clara's Cafe and then sauntered out, flipping their long out-of-date hair and pretending to ignore us. Obviously they didn't understand what a long lens does to a rear view . . . anyone's rear view.

Main Street had been modernized back in the fifties or sixties, more stucco and plate glass than stone or brick. No old hitching rails, no antique street lights. There weren't any shady benches for old men to sit and talk and look rural on—so of course we didn't see any local-color kind of old men. The fiberglass horse over the door of Sim's Western Wear and Saddlery would have done, except that the week before we'd used a fiberglass horse over the door of another western wear somewhere else. And *that* one had had a fancy saddle on it.

Aside from Main Street, all two blocks of it, the town had something under 2000 inhabitants living on maybe 16 miles of streets. I know, because we drove up and down every single damn street, looking for local color. We found what you always find: a few neat brick houses maintained by fanatics (curtains matching, grass plucked with tweezers at the sidewalk, freshly tarred drive), many more comfortable looking old brick or frame houses with shaggy yards and big hairy dogs lying in the shade, a few backyards enlivened by a sheep, calf, or pony, and some much older but very dilapidated old shacks that were the wrong sort of local color if we ever wanted to come back.

Then Joe stepped hard on the brakes and said "God bless," under his breath, which isn't his usual expletive.

She was the kind of local color you almost never find. Not too young, not at all old, shaped perfectly for the camera, and a true honey blonde. She moved well, too, and she was heaving a big old parade saddle (black with silver trim) onto a palomino horse as pretty as she was—for a horse, that is. White blaze and four white stockings, and they sure looked like a pair, her in those tight jeans and tall white boots and blue western shirt with a little white pinstripe.

There's a lot that happened later that I don't understand, but I can't believe that it was Kelly's fault. She's just a normal, healthy, flat-out *gorgeous* hunk of Texas womanhood, getting ready to lead a parade in three days and happening to catch our eye. Which of course she did.

Turned out she was a junior (at the University, I figured) and wanted to be a school teacher, and thought her mom and dad were wonderful, and wouldn't miss a—well, I can't tell you the name of the festival, or you could find the town, now, couldn't you? But she wouldn't miss it, and if she married and had to move to (her blue eyes rolled up as she thought about someplace outrageous) to *New York*, even, she'd come back every summer and lead the parade the way she had since . . . a short pause, and I thought she was counting years, but she said "Since I got Sunny." Well, people do tend to name horses stupid things like Brownie and Black Beauty and Sunny, and you don't have to have more sense than that to be married in your senior year to someone headed for law school or medical school, which was clearly her destiny.

She wasn't camera shy at all—knew all the tricks, and no wonder, having led the parade all those years. She clucked, and Sunny put those ears forward like a pro. Joe got her talking to the horse, and waving at her mom on the porch. Her mom didn't look anything like her, but lightning doesn't strike twice in families, either. My wife's a showstopping redhead, but our daughter has my hair. And nose. Then he asked her if she'd ride for us, and she beamed, and bounced up on that horse as slick as butter, and pranced him back and forth. It was then I noticed the spurs.

I don't pretend to be much of a cowboy, but one thing I do know is that those big old rowelled spurs you see pictures of aren't in use any more. The humane society had something to say about it, I think. But she had these bluedsteel spurs with rowels as long as my fingers, and needlesharp, or looked like it. Wicked things, that could have hurt if you'd just bumped into them. And she was digging them into that sleek golden horse like he had no nerves at all, with a pretty smile on her lovely face. I looked at the bridle. Sure enough, hung on that fancy black and silver parade bridle was a blued-steel bit that would have held a charging grizzly.

Funny thing is, that gold horse just pranced back and forth, never jumping sideways when she jabbed the spurs in, never gaping its mouth when she gave a little yank to the reins. And that's not natural. A horse that'll prance like that is usually the kind that's pretty touchy about having its reins yanked and spurs stuck in its sides. I wondered did she have it tranquilized, but the horse's eye was a clear shining . . . *green*.

It's a wonder I didn't grab Joe's arm in the middle of a shot. Green! Horses don't have green eyes, and if they did it wouldn't be that bright, clear, emerald green, wickedly alight with mischief. Horses are (forgive me, ladies) *stupid*. I mean, any animal that could buck people off, but prefers to carry them around on its back . . . any animal that runs back into a burning barn and sticks its dumb legs in fences and then fights to get loose, tearing itself to shreds . . . that's *stupid*. Black Beauty and all those horse stories aside. Besides, my cousin Don's horse ran under a tree with me and scraped me off when I was ten or so, and any animal with brains would have known that I was lighter than anyone else around, and if it got rid of me it would only mean more work. I live on the edge of the city, and my ranchette came with a two-stall stable and corral (courtesy of the previous owners who had two teenage daughters) but we don't have a horse even though Marcy's as horse-crazy as any other girl.

Joe didn't notice, but then Joe's from Houston, and where he grew up he never saw a horse in real life till he moved away. For all Joe knows, horses might have eyes every color of the rainbow. Joe just nodded and swung the camcorder around as usual, and let me do the interview.

Kelly kept chattering away, telling us about her friend named Charlene—she thought maybe we'd like a shot of both of them on their horses. Charlene had always ridden right behind her in the parade, she said. I guess Joe and I both were thinking the same thing: girls like Kelly had girlfriends with names like Charlene, and the girlfriends were always a lot less pretty but very energetic and *sweet*. Sweet, out here, means nothing to look at, and not enough spunk to leave. I tried not to let myself think about Marcy, my Marcy, who was born to be sweet. . . .

Charlene, Kelly went on, wrote poetry and painted pictures, and was going to be a famous writer someday. Joe and I looked at each other and managed not to sigh, and said Sure, we'd be glad to meet her friend, but the folks back at the station couldn't ever use all we'd shot. We always had that excuse. So Kelly rode off down the street, and for once a back view looked good in the long lens. Joe caught some of it, just for us.

When she came back, we had another shock. Charlene could have been Kelly's twin for size and shape, with long curly black hair and a face out of an art book. Kelly was pretty—Kelly was typical golden-girl all-American longlegged gorgeous—but Charlene had bone to keep her beautiful for years, while Kelly would find out in her thirties that a round chin can double all too easily. Charlene had a black horse to match her hair, the blackest, shiniest horse I ever saw outside of a china figurine, not a brown hair on him. And green eyes.

Now one green-eyed horse would be a marvel, the sort of thing that's a freak. *Two* green-eyed horses—one black, and one palomino and both with the prettiest girls I'd seen in years on their backs—that's something else. The black horse gave me the same mischievous sidelong glance as the golden one had, and I noted that Charlene also wore wickedly rowelled spurs and had one helluva long-shanked bit, like Kelly's, in that beast's mouth. I got a cold feeling on the back of my neck, and decided not to worry about it; it wasn't my business, and the girls were easy to look at. That was our business.

"Charlene used to lead the parade," said Kelly, throwing her friend one of those smiles that cuts your hand if you touch it. "But then I got Sunny."

I think I'd have let them lead it together—it must be spectacular anyway, with two gorgeous girls on those two handsome horses—for horses—and why not both in front? But Charlene was giving Kelly a smile to match the one she'd been given, and her voice, when she spoke, was husky and warm and in keeping with that face.

"I didn't want to hog it forever," she said. "Besides, the Texas flag looks better with a black horse. And I know you'll be just as generous when someone else is ready to take over." Kelly smiled back, a little stiffly, and I figured they weren't really friends. How could they be? Two pretty girls in such a small town are born rivals, and if they don't know it everyone makes it clear to them. About the time that one beat the other out for class sweetheart or most beautiful, *friend* had become an empty term. You don't, right out loud, talk about enemies.

When I got home, I told Marcy about the horses. Like so many girls her age, she thinks anything with four legs and a mane is wonderful. For years she's been saving her allowance and birthday money to buy her own horse and take lessons at the stable up the road.

"Could we go see them, Daddy?" I should have expected that. I looked at Denise. Mothers have rights, I'd learned, and besides we had planned to go to Hal's poolside barbecue on Saturday. I had hoped Marcy would learn some things from his daughter. Suzi wasn't a patch on those gorgeous girls with their horses, but she did have style, and Marcy was going to need all the help she could get.

Denise gave me one of those inscrutable glances she'd been giving me lately and shrugged. "If you want . . ." She'd already told me she didn't much like the party idea, back when I made the mistake of saying I thought Suzi was pretty sharp for a kid her age. Denise said yes, like a knife, and Marcy was a wonderful girl who needed to be recognized for what she was. We hadn't exactly argued, but I'd felt uncomfortable. She should know I love Marcy more than anything else; I just want her to have a happy life, and pretty girls are happier. Denise should know that; she was a stunner.

So I said, "If it's clear," and Marcy grinned at me, half braces and half teeth.

We ran the spot Friday, on schedule. I'd noticed on the monitor that the horses' green eyes didn't show up well, and decided not to mention it. The girls were pretty enough, one all gold and blue on a gold and white horse, and one all black and green (did I mention that Charlene wore a green western shirt, something that glittered, with black jeans and boots?) on a black horse. Not quite as gorgeous as I remembered—in fact, not more than middling pretty—but things rarely look the same on tape and I'm used to it. After all, we'd had to shoot the spot in midafternoon in July. Maybe those little lines came from squinting at the bright sun—the camera sees what's really there; it doesn't make allowances for lousy lighting. Kelly's voice I'd figured wouldn't tape well—breathy, a little too high—but I was surprised at Charlene's—it sounded more hoarse than husky. But again—a hot day, midafternoon—maybe she'd been thirsty. Marcy thought the horses were great; I don't know if she even looked at the riders.

Saturday morning, traffic held us up north of the city, and if Marcy hadn't been humming tunelessly beside me, I'd have turned back. It was nothing but a little pissant country town with two pretty girls riding horses in a tacky parade; we'd get hot and dusty and eat too much cheap greasy food—Hal's pool would be a lot more fun. But Denise had sent us off smiling; she wouldn't like it if I changed plans on her now.

We had to park at the far end of a dusty field beside the town's rickety little football stadium, crammed in between a pickup truck with its bed full of assorted junk, and a rusty barbwire fence. It was a two block walk to the parade route, nothing much in the city, but here a hot, sweaty trek past sunburnt yards and houses flaking ancient paint. They looked even older, more faded, today than they had on the Wednesday before. Two people came out of one house, and glanced at us without speaking.

We got to the main street a little late, and had to crowd

in behind a double row of others. A little boy rode by on
a bicycle decorated with crepe paper, holding a red ribbon
in his teeth. I glanced at my watch. Time and more for the
parade to start. Sweat trickled down my sides; I could smell
the hair spray from the huge bouffant arrangment on the
tall woman next to me. A puff of wind blew a wiry strand
of it across my nose; I batted it away, blinking at the dust,
just as another, sharper puff spanked my other cheek. Marcy
shook her head, but when I looked down she flashed her
metallic smile at me. One thing about her, she's no com-
plainer, our girl. If she had the looks she deserves, she'd
be a match for anyone. I squeezed her shoulder, and felt
my heart contract at the look she gave me. I didn't deserve
that kind of trust—no man could.

More little gusts of wind, carrying the smells of a summer
celebration: bubblegum baked on the pavement, horses,
barbecue. Scraps of paper lifted from the street; a small
child chased one, was captured by a tired-faced woman
wearing an apron over her dress. It crossed my mind I
hadn't seen a woman wear an apron like that in years. Then
the dust hit, a soft fist pummeling our faces, our eyes,
stinging; wind jerked my shirt and hair first one way then
the other. Marcy grabbed my arm and squealed "Daddy!"
then coughed. I could hardly breathe myself. For an instant,
sight and hearing blurred, caught in a whirl of wind noise
and grit. Then I could hear the chokes, coughs, children
crying, even screams.

The wind went as it had come, without warning or
reason; I watched the tawny blur of the dust-devil follow
the road out of town, as steadily as a drunk driver trying
to be careful.

But the crowd's noise yanked my attention back to the
street. Something had happened. I cursed myself for coming
without even a pocket 'corder, but I'd promised Denise the
trip was for Marcy. Still I edged us leftward, back toward
the disturbance.

Another news team stood where I usually stand, in the
middle of things. How was I going to explain *this* at work?
With Marcy clinging to my hand, a little nervous in the

crowd, I couldn't push my way through as I usually did. I
went up on tiptoe, trying to see. There was an opening:
that usually meant someone was on the ground. Just beyond
the gap, a well-polished pickup had both doors open; behind
it was the parade's first float, and the girl who should have
been perched on a throne waving was stepping across the
trailer hitch from the float to the pickup, hampered only
slightly by her formal gown, intent on seeing what had
happened.

Suddenly a siren went off in my ear, and I jumped. It
was the fire engine that should have cleared the way for
the parade; we had come around it, with the rest of the
crowd, hardly noticing it—now its lights flashed, and the
siren beeped and squealed. The volunteers, in their blue
shirts with lots of insignia, began pushing the crowd back,
and I saw another flashing light coming along a side street:
the ambulance.

Of course everyone was talking about what happened,
but already there were five or six stories just in those few
minutes. Only a few, it seemed, had been on the spot, and
they'd been squinting against the sudden dust storm the
same as anyone else. The girls were hurt, the girls were
killed, the girls had been bucked off, the horses had run
away . . . I figured then who it had to be, of course. We
backed up with the others, as requested, and let the ambulance through; I couldn't see any more than the stretch-
ers being loaded aboard it. Then the siren whooped again,
and the parade went on, just as parades always do go on
in spite of accidents.

Marcy was less disappointed than I'd expected. There
were other horses to exclaim over, and after all she never
had seen the palomino and black that weren't there anymore except on tape. I felt it more; I'd really looked forward to seeing those two girls ride by, all proud and
beautiful in the sunlight, and without them the parade was
a predictable mixture of sentimentality and cheap glitter.
The girls on the homemade floats, the pride of each little
town in the festival circuit, were pretty enough, but nothing
like Kelly and Charlene on horseback.

But I set myself to being a good father, and Marcy enjoyed herself. I even waited patiently while she walked around talking to the people who had ridden in the parade. She petted their horses, flashed that metallic grin more than I'd seen in months. I caught myself thinking that if she looked like Kelly, I'd buy her a horse and let her ride in parades—she looked so happy. And that was almost enough for the day, except that I really did want to know about Kelly and Charlene.

The late news that night had coverage from our competition; I sipped my drink as I watched, and tried to figure out how to salvage my part in it while criticizing the camera angles the competetion used. The announcer said it was Kelly and Charlene, but the pictures certainly didn't do them justice. Kelly's golden hair looked dusty, and I guess it's hard to be cute and pretty when someone's splinting your broken wrist. Charlene must have been hurting too; she looked almost gaunt, those gorgeous bones ready to break through the skin. Nothing was said about their horses on one channel; the next, when I flipped to it, had already done the story, and the other one stuck it on last and mentioned that the horses had run off in terror at the "sudden storm." Our station ran the tape we'd done before, and a brief shot of their faces, and Melanie, who has the evening news spot on Saturday and is trying for more, said what a terrible ordeal for two such pretty girls.

I don't read the paper all that often, unless I'm researching something, but the Sunday paper had it on the front page—mostly because their Congressman had been there. I could have shot the old buzzard at city hall, for not telling me he was coming when I picked up the brochure; if I'd known, I'd have brought a 'corder no matter what. Mysterious disappearance of famous parade horses, they called it. I quirked my mouth over that "famous" but let it ride. Anyone who'd seen Kelly on that palomino wouldn't have forgotten it. I wondered then if she'd ever ridden in anyone else's parades, or if she'd been content to reign in a small realm. The horses, the story ended, had not been found.

It occurred to me that I could salvage our station's position by getting a human-interest continuation. That would justify seeing them again, and (my fatherly conscience being tender) I could even ask their advice about Marcy: would riding in parades do anything to help a girl get along in high school? So about midweek, I took a camcorder and told my boss I might get an interview, and he raised his eyebrows but nodded. I also took a present I didn't tell him about, two copies of the original tape we took of Kelly and Charlene (all but the rump shot, of course.)

Kelly's mom didn't look real friendly when she opened the door, and I was glad I'd come in my own car, not the station van. I told her I'd heard about it, and thought maybe Kelly would like a copy of the pictures we'd gotten before her horse was lost. The woman's eyes glittered dangerously.

"*Her* horse!" she said, with an emphasis I couldn't quite understand. "That—!"

But then Kelly walked in, her not-really-golden hair pulled back and her eyeshadow a bit too blue. The cast on her arm still had her off balance; I could see the difference in her walk. No girl is as pretty when she's hurt, and tired, and miserable about losing a favorite horse. You can see what they'll look like in ten years. But she smiled at me, and the dimples were still there, and the white teeth. I handed her the tape, and told her how sorry I was, and maybe this would help. Her eyes were a little red, and now the tears started. That didn't bother me: I've seen plenty, for better reason and none at all, in my business. But I said I was sorry again, and she choked on a thank you, and her mom huffed loudly and walked out. Kelly waved an arm at the living room, and I sat down.

"He'll never come back," she said softly, with a wary glance at the door. I opened my mouth to say something about searches being made, and she interrupted the first word.

"No. They'll never find him. He's gone back—" and then her head jerked up and her eyes widened, tear-smeary as they were. "I—I'm sorry—I'm so upset. I don't really know what I'm saying, and besides—" I felt a jolt of glee—my instincts had been right; there *was* a story here.

"I used to have a horse," I lied, trying for empathy. Her face relaxed slightly.

"Not like Sunny," she said.

"No. But I wouldn't have believed it then." I felt my way into my role as bereft horselover, and like all roles it came easily to me. "He was a plain old brown horse you wouldn't look at twice, but to me—" I shook my head, and she nodded. Whatever else she was or wasn't in the realm of beauty, Kelly had a normal amount of sentiment.

"How long did you have him?" she asked, good manners overcoming grief.

I pondered a moment. Could I remember enough incidents from my uncle's place to flesh out a long horse ownership? "Five years," I said, shaking my head again. "Then my family moved, and we—we had to sell him." I glanced at her; a little color had come into her face. "How long did you have Sunny?"

It was the wrong question. She stiffened and paled as if I'd hit her cast with a bat. "I—it's hard to think right now. My arm—" I looked at it dutifully, not impressed with her intelligence. A broken wrist five days old is a nuisance, no more. With my eyes safely away from hers, she said softly "I got him with . . . from Charlene. She got hers first."

So I stood up, and smiled at her, and told her I'd brought a tape for Charlene too, if she'd tell me where Charlene lived. And she told me in the way that country people give directions, all relating to things you only know about if you live there, but I finally figured it out when she came out on the front porch and pointed.

I'd thought before Charlene was the smart one of the pair, and so it turned out. She had on dark glasses that day, and had propped her bandaged ankle on a couch, but her voice was as lovely as the first time I'd heard it.

Charlene was, she told me straight out, just over two years older than Kelly, and at fourteen, she'd been a long, gawky girl with lank hair and no self-confidence. Smart, but the local school had no scope for her kind of smart, and she knew that she'd never qualify for a really good scholarship. But she could ride anything on four legs, and she'd seen an article about barrel racers' winnings in a western riding magazine. That would be her ticket out. She'd sold her old sorrel horse that didn't have enough speed, and gone looking for a new mount.

She relaxed enough to slip the dark glasses up, and I could see Charlene at fourteen. Bones that might have character someday, but missed beauty by a slight margin almost worse for being slight. Well-placed collarbones with too deep a hollow above and below them. She'd have had thin muscular wrists and long thin hands, and she'd have pulled her dark hair back to a plain plastic clip. And the money from the sale of the sorrel horse would have been folded tightly into a wad, and tucked deep in the pocket of jeans worn thin at the knees.

She'd come to the farm—she didn't say where it was— still looking for a barrel-racing prospect. A brisk little woman, dark-skinned and gray-haired, had come out, looked her up and down, and offered only one horse: the black. The price was what she'd jammed deep in her pocket. And she'd taken one look and known she'd pay it, though she wasn't the kind of girl to buy a horse for its looks. The woman took her money, and followed her home in a pickup with the black horse in the trailer. There, with the horse in Charlene's lot, the woman gave her the rowelled spurs and spade bit, and told her she must never mount the horse without them.

At that point, Charlene explained, she'd have decided not to buy the horse, because there are rules about spurs and bits in barrel racing, but the horse was there, and the woman had driven off with her money before she could argue. So she saddled up, strapped the unfamiliar spurs on her boots, and mounted.

That began the happiest years of her life, she said, beginning to cry. When a boy she knew, who had ignored her for years, stopped her even as she rode down the street that first day, and stared, wide-eyed. When she looked in the mirror. When she dressed the next day for school and things were tight and loose in different places. When she got more looks, and more attention, than she'd ever had before . . . and she knew it was wrong, she said, sobs blurring the words, but she couldn't stop once she knew what she had.

She didn't drive back out to the farm to demand her money and return the horse. She didn't even think of it, or of the barrel-racing that had been her plan of escape. By midsummer, she had become the acknowledged town beauty, overshadowing the older girls. And she was asked to lead the parade on her beautiful black horse, carrying the American flag down the center of Main Street as everyone cheered. After that first parade, after she had the taste of it in her mouth, the odd little woman had visited, and explained the dangers and limitations of the gift. Charlene didn't tell me what they were right then, or if she did I didn't hear her. I had a sudden vision of Marcy, sitting tall on such a horse, no braces on her teeth, and a crowd waving. Maybe a red horse, and her hair the color Denise's had been, a vivid flame. My vision blurred. Maybe I had more than a story.

For three years, Charlene and the black horse graced the town, and the honors she couldn't win by being smart and hardworking came easily to the town beauty, the most popular girl in school. Then she noticed Kelly, down the block, standing forlorn in the yard and watching her ride by. Kelly was not quite cute, the way Charlene had been not quite beautiful.

To seventeen, fourteen doesn't seem like competition. Charlene never thought of the older girls she'd displaced, but she remembered her own miseries. First she thought she'd let Kelly ride the black horse. That didn't work; Kelly couldn't even get on. But somewhere in the conversation, Charlene let slip to Kelly that the horse was her secret, the way she had become what she was. And for Kelly, that was enough. She pestered, and warted, and fretted, and pleaded, and finally Charlene gave her certain directions, and two days later Kelly rode down the street on a golden palomino that matched her now-golden hair. Charlene wanted me to know that she had *offered* to let Kelly lead the parade that summer, but I was sure that Kelly would have been asked anyway. No one could resist that golden image.

And that had been . . . Charlene closed her eyes, counting. That had been twenty years ago, the first year that Kelly led the parade. I must have moved or something, for her eyes flicked open, and her mouth quirked. "You don't believe me?"

I looked at her face, now every bit of thirty-seven years old, if not more, and nodded slowly. I wasn't sure what I believed, but I wanted Charlene to go on talking. Questions could come later.

"I would have quit before," she said slowly. "I had had my high school triumphs; that's all I wanted. I had two scholarships—not big, but big enough to get out of town— and I planned to go. I could give up being the local beauty, to gain the world. But then—" Her long fingers moved restlessly in her lap. "There was Kelly, and Sunny—"

Kelly had never wanted anything more than to be a golden girl leading a parade on a golden horse. To freeze time in that moment of triumph, to be forever prancing down the street with everyone watching her, a light breeze rippling the flag she carried. I found myself nodding: that's what any girl would want, if she could get it. Perfectly natural. Kelly, though, had scoffed at the warning she received, as Charlene had not scoffed. Maybe Charlene would have to quit, but she wouldn't. She would ride that parade every year of her life. She would step out of time, and take the world with her.

I still didn't understand. "What warning? How do you mean, the gift had limits? And what was it about in the first place?" More questions clogged my head: how and why and who and when and where. Especially where.

"Five years, or my twentieth birthday, whichever came first. That's what that woman said, after my first parade: I was to ride the horse back out there before then. If I didn't, he'd disappear, and I'd have that to explain. And as for why . . . I never knew. I never asked." She saw my doubt and insisted, "I never asked why: there were answers she might have given that I didn't want to hear. Why did I buy that horse in the first place? It had to be some kind of magic—dangerous, maybe even wrong . . . *wicked*. I can imagine what the preacher at church would have said, if he'd known about it. You don't question things like that. If you find out it's something really bad, then you can't do it, but if you don't know then it's not your fault."

That I could understand—even though my business is looking for answers, there are some things I don't question, some rocks I don't turn over. So I could do without answers, except that there were horses which made girls beautiful, and Marcy—who wasn't beautiful—loved horses. I found myself agreeing with Charlene: the rest really didn't matter. "How did Kelly do it? Where did she get the power to overcome . . . whatever it was?"

Charlene gave me a look far too old for the age she had been until this past week, a look Denise might have given me. "It took me years to figure that out, but . . . it wasn't just Kelly who wanted it." I must have looked as confused as I felt; she sighed and went on. "Look—she wanted to lead the parade. But the others—everyone in town, just about—wanted to *see* her lead it. Wanted her to be that perfect, golden image. Never aging, never sick, never faded, always up there with the flag, the dream that came true." She sighed again. "And we couldn't any of us get free of it. What it came down to, it's what people really wanted, wanted bad enough to lose . . . whatever we lost."

She fell silent, and I thought of the town as it had been . . . as it was. That squatty ugly building—had it been new when Kelly rode in her first parade? I asked, and Charlene nodded. So the move to restore old buildings to their original stone and brick had bypassed this town, and new industries had settled elsewhere, and those here could not manage to move away. Things faded, grew vaguely shabby, blurred or frayed at the margins like a tape played too many times, but never progressed in normal aging. Other people? Charlene nodded. "Those closest to us slow down, but they can wear out and die. My parents did. People we didn't know much, they seem pretty normal."

"And did you finish school?" I asked, suspecting the answer. "Go on to college?"

"No." The dark glasses went back on. "No, I didn't do anything, but ride in that parade once a year behind Kelly and Sunny."

Whatever she could have been, whatever Kelly could have been, in those twenty years . . . all gone to feed the dream of glory, the yearly spectacle. Kelly, I figured, had had nothing much to look forward to; Charlene could have been anything. A tragedy, if you look at things that way. But it had been an accident, surely. If it hadn't been for Kelly's mistake, Charlene would have had nothing to complain of—in fact, she'd been a lot better off as a beauty than she had been plain and shabby and ignored. It was really her fault, for telling Kelly about the horse. I wondered what had broken the spell, or whatever it was—if we, with our camera, perhaps, had done it, by broadcasting the reality—but it didn't matter now. It wasn't as if I had a story; I didn't need to tie up all the loose ends. Something else mattered more.

I opened my mouth to ask her where the horse farm was, and stopped just in time. She'd want to know why I asked, and if I told her about Marcy she'd probably get mad. It had been a tragedy for her; she would be sure it couldn't work right for anyone else. She probably never thought of it as wrong, or maybe wicked, until it turned bad for her. Women are like that: everything's so personal to them. But Marcy was different. I could protect her, make sure nothing like this happened to her. Whatever the intent of this mysterious woman with magic horses, whatever the nature of the spell, it couldn't possibly hurt Marcy with me to look out for her. I didn't have to understand it; I just had watch out for Marcy. I said goodbye and went back for a last visit with Kelly.

Like I said, you can't really blame Kelly. She's too old for cute, but she's still got that all-American grin with the dimple in the corner of her mouth, and if the gold in her hair will come from a bottle from now on, so what? I use a little subtle highlighting myself. She's a good girl, a good wholesome small town girl who liked all the right things: Mom, Pop, apple pie, the Tigers on the ten-yard line with a first down . . . and riding a golden horse down Main Street once a year with the American flag in her hand. It wasn't Kelly's fault that she got too much power too soon, that she had such limited dreams to freeze in the amber-gold of that palomino horse. She only wanted what we all want, to make the good times last forever. She understood that I only wanted the best for my daughter; if her father had been like me things would have been different. She said Marcy sounded sweet and she told me the truth when I asked her where the place was.

I have this daughter I love so much it hurts, a girl brave and tough and wise beyond her years. She's already learned to think of herself as homely. When the pretty girls walk by, when she sees the boys look after them, I can see her face stiffen, holding back the longing she's too brave to show. She's going to be fourteen next spring, and she wants a horse for her birthday.

*Katherine Kurtz invited me to submit a story to* Tales of the Knights Templar . . . *and the research I did in preparation roused several buried skeletons. Among them—the death of an elderly Latvian man in Starr County, Texas, in the 1960s, the discovery of a Roman coin by a ditch-digger in the 1930s only a few miles away, and the reputation that Roma, Texas, had when I was a girl in one of the towns downstream. Other towns, we children were told, had curanderos, healers, but Roma had a real brujo: a veritable witch. It made the occasional drive through Roma on the way to or from the construction site of Falcon Dam deliciously scary. Was it true? I don't know, but I checked the memory of that belief with another person who grew up in the same era and region, and she remembered the rumor too.*

# KNIGHT OF OTHER DAYS

Xavier saw him arrive. An old man, sitting upright on his scrawny old horse the way old men did. A real caballero, then, and not one of the *turistas* his uncle had told him about, who slouched in the saddle as if it were a chair. Man enough to ride across the big ranchos and not fall prey to the fence riders. Though perhaps he was a Kiñero. It was said they never left the vast spread, but it was also said they sometimes took their own way back to Mexico on family business. It might be such a one here, who would ride through town and find the ford across the river by night.

Xavier himself was evading his older brothers and his mother. His brothers had promised him a beating for what he had said about Juanito's behavior during Mass. His mother had a list of chores that would keep him in range of his brothers all day. He had taken off with the goats at daybreak, and now lay in the hot shade of a huisache.

The stranger would pass him only a length away, if he stayed to the obvious path. Xavier watched the horse pick its way down the gravelly slope. Bigger than it looked, that horse. Not a King Ranch horse, though a man returning to Mexico on business might not want one of the sorrel horses anyone in South Texas could recognize. And the man didn't wear a vaquero's dress, and the saddle—

It was at that moment that Xavier saw the stranger's eyes and felt his own mouth gape open to the heat. Blue. Very blue, and very clear, beneath gray-white hair. The stranger smiled, and said something Xavier didn't understand. Xavier felt his heart racing in his chest, felt himself collapsing inside, and wondered frantically if the stranger had cursed him so quickly. Evil eye? Susto?

He blinked, gasped, fought for steadier breath, and looked again. Now the stranger's hair was not gray, but the pale yellow of cornmeal. He sat erect, tall, with a shining around him that Xavier was quite ready to take for a sign, whether from God or someone else he was not sure. The horse—tall, gleaming now, prancing under its arched neck and flowing mane—the horse was like no horse he had ever seen. Perhaps the charros he had heard about?

Dazed, Xavier crept out from under the huisache into the full light of an August midmorning. He glanced around, and saw what he had seen every day of his life: Roma, Texas, and its surroundings. Brush-covered gravel hills capped with crumbling, cobbly stone, the straggle of little houses, some of old stone and adobe, the church, the school, the two-lane highway passing through from Rio Grande City to Guerrero and on to Laredo. The dirt road that straggled out northward, up into the ranches where bony cattle survived on manos with the thorns burned off. At the south end of the town, the rugged bluff above the Rio Grande— the Rio Bravo to those on the other side, in Mexico.

"Roma?" the stranger asked now, in an accent Xavier could not identify.

"*Aya*," Xavier said, pointing. "There—Roma."

The stranger stared, then shook his head. The horse pawed the path with one great hoof . . . bigger, Xavier, realized, than the plates in their kitchen.

"Roma is bigger than that, fool of a boy," the stranger said. Then, as Xavier stared, uncertain, he seemed to shrink into himself, becoming once again the old, shrunken man Xavier had first seen. And the horse, too, now looked like any hard-ridden beast of no particular breeding—too shaggy for quality, too heavy of neck and head. The old man muttered something Xavier could not understand at all, then smiled. A surprisingly sweet smile, it was, but Xavier was not fooled. A true vision could come to anyone, even small boys—an angel or a devil in some unexpected guise. Father Patrick was always saying you could not trust the sweet words of men, only the justice of God.

So Xavier crossed himself, and muttered a paternoster. And when the stranger joined in, both with the crossing and the Latin, Xavier was sure it must be an angel. Certainly not a devil. None of them could make the sign of the cross. Still, he did not come any closer, and he watched as the old man shifted his weight and the horse went on down the trail to the first street.

The old man glared down the slope at the little clutter of low houses, the slick ribbon of heated asphalt running east and west, the lazy brown river sleeping in the hot sun below a rock ledge. Roma, indeed! So this was how the magic dwindled. Fury and despair warred in him; he could almost feel their clawed feet on either rib, their teeth locked in his heart. No time, no time. Whatever this was, this place called Roma by a river—the wrong Roma, the wrong river—he would have to finish his work here. He had chanced it all, and lost. He would never see the seven hills again, the Tiber's flow; he would never feel a Mediterranean breeze on his cheek.

Beneath him, the horse shifted impatiently. He flexed his back, releasing, and it paced forward. The hill behind him wasn't much of a hill, and the town ahead looked to fit its hill. Only the hot wind, hot already this early, blowing out of the scrubby waste across the river, felt familiar. It had been many years—more than he could readily count—since he had felt that heat. Then, he had flinched from its blast, but now he accepted gratefully the ease it promised his joints.

It was a good sign that the boy had crossed himself, had known his paternoster. If it should be a region of Catholics, he might yet find a successor. The power weighed on him. He had sought it, to be sure, in those days when he had been young and foolish. He had been glad to take up the burden, before he knew what it weighed.

Slowly, as slowly as if his horse were the rackboned spavined creature it appeared to the outer eyes, the old man rode down into the town. His gaze missed nothing. Not the pig in its narrow sty, not the little gardens protected by wattle or stone wall from drying winds. Not the bare-bottomed babies playing in the yards, the girls hanging out wash, the quick slap of palms indoors shaping tortillas, the boys quarreling, the smells of cooking, of chickens and pigs and goats and humans. He rode past the little store and post office on the highway, past a pink house with a washing machine on the front porch, past a gas station. He could feel the eyes on him, though no one spoke. He saw the cross on the church, nearer the river, and when he came closer he saw that it stood on a stony prominence.

Now what? He dismounted, and opened the door. A faint ecclesiastical odor seeped out along with a cool breath. But no one was within, though a light glimmered at the altar. He cleared his throat; no one answered. The priest—surely there was a priest—must be away. For long? He had no idea.

The horse pulled away, straining toward a tuft of grass, burnt brown as old hay. It was hungry, and no wonder. So was he. He would have to find out when the priest might return; he would have to find food, and shelter. The words of the Rule came back to him, as so often, in mockery. " . . . Shall have meat but three times a week." In the camps he had not seen meat for years on end. "Shall eat in common." That he had done, when he had eaten at all. Poverty had been the easiest part of his vow to keep, all down the years. Chastity . . . well, easier now, in age. Obedience, that was the difficulty.

He touched his chest, where beneath his clothes the sliver of bone rested. He had vowed obedience to God, of course, but also another, more immediate, obedience, to the Master. He had no Master now, but that bit of bone, and in the years he had carried it, it had ceased to speak in his inner ear. He had no one now to follow, and for a soldier this was a greater burden than his age. How could he follow orders if none were given?

Esperanza had wakened before dawn with the memory of many screams ringing in her ears. Again. Each time closer . . . and unlike her old teacher, she took no pleasure in that knowledge. She lay straight, arms at her sides, and let herself feel the pull of the earth, the sea, the sun still below the rim of the world, the four winds. Through her narrow window, a trickle of predawn coolness roughed her skin like a cat's tongue. She heard the thin skreek of a gate hinge, and the clatter of little hooves. So. That little scamp Xavier, Pico's son, was off with the goats before dawn. He must have angered his brothers again; this was his favorite escape.

She rose from her narrow bed, touching without thinking the charms she wore, the charms of the bed itself. *For a safe night, I thank you*, she said without sound, and felt the darkness accept her thanks. She murmured a little, in her throat, something no skulking thief could hear and use against her, then looked sideways out her window. There, to the east, the vague blurred streak of coming dawn. A truck went by on the road, its tires whining. The truck was no concern of hers, but the street was. She had her ways of knowing what she needed to know, night and day.

She stretched out on her bed again, riding the sense of power that knowledge gave her, until something jolted the inside of her head. Something more powerful . . . something dangerous . . . some great change . . . coming soon. Coming today.

She went into the kitchen. Something hissed at her from

the floor, and her blood went cold. Then she felt the fur on her ankles, the twining of the kitten around her feet. Fool, she said to herself. Fool. Go and look. Find out.

Thus Esperanza was the second person in Roma to see the old man. She had gone up to the store for nothing but the chance to look at the charms she had put beneath certain windows, above certain doors. Had they been moved? Had the persons involved done what they'd been told to do? She was eyeing the cards of lace and ribbons, well aware of the sidelong looks she herself got from the children who hung around the candy rack, when she heard the hoofbeats.

Not that hoofbeats themselves were that unusual. But this sounded like a monster of a horse, and with the hoofbeats came that tightening of her skin that told her great magic was near. She edged up the aisle with the bread, the baked goods (inferior store-bought cookies, cinnamon rolls, fried pies) and peeked out the front window. And blinked. The old man in ragged white garments that belonged on the poorest peon off some ranch in the Mexican hinterlands . . . the old man on the scrawny dark horse . . . that was the source of the power she felt. It threw back her probing touch as if a horse shook a fly off its hide. She had never felt anything like it.

She reached again, and again her curiosity, her intuition, slid off that old man as if he were not human. For she had power over men as well as women: she had never met a man she could not understand, not even that silly foreign priest. She prided herself on that; she knew things about the priest he did not know about himself, and she knew things about every man in the town . . . who would sire only daughters, who had no eggs at all, who wore the horns, and worse. There was always worse; that was the secret depth of her knowledge.

But this man—if man he was—bewildered her questing intelligence. And he carried—it was not himself, but in his possession—magic of such power that she could almost weep to think of it. Almost: but weeping, which was most women's useful tool, could not be hers. She never wept true tears, to give power to those who would drink them. No, she

would not weep. She would find out what it was, and gain
that power for herself.

Father Patrick Dougherty would have worried, except
that Xavier said the old man was a knight. Of course he
wasn't really a knight; that was only the boy's imagination,
or the old man's fairy tales, but if Xavier's interest was in
stories of mounted heroes, he hadn't been hurt. Yet.

"But he don't speak no Español, not really, so I can't
understand all he say. His Ingles ain't so good either."

The priest spoke Spanish, but the boys laughed at his
accent, and replied only in their fractured English, liber-
ally laced with Border idiom. "I should go see him, perhaps," he said, half to himself. He knew he should go see
the old man, but he also knew Alfonso Gutierrez was dying,
and he was on his way out to the ranch.

"He'll be all right," Xavier said, scratching one foot as
he stood on the other. "He's a good man . . ."

The priest doubted that. Why would a good white man
come to Roma, Texas, and live in a single back room by
himself and give candy to boys like Xavier? He himself had
come because he was sent; he would have chosen a greener
land, and people who spoke English with his own lilt, if
he'd had the choice. Old men giving candy to boys was bad
enough, but the strange stories—he didn't fit, the old man.
But Alfonso was dying, and it was time for his regular call.

Xavier grinned, the urchin grin that the priest found
strikingly similar to the urchins of his homeland. Boys were
boys anywhere, he thought. In spite of changes in the world,
in spite of movies and that new distraction, television, boys
still made mischief and still grinned dimpled, gap-toothed
grins.

Men, however . . . men changed in ways the priest didn't
entirely understand. Oh, they had the same lusts as always—
Xavier the boy would become Xavier the young man, risking
his immortal soul, not to mention his life, with the plump
whores behind the tavern. He would stand before the altar
to marry some shy girl; he would father a stairstep gaggle
of dark-eyed children, and get fat and old . . .

The priest yanked his mind back to the immediate problem, and thought about it all the way out to the ranch and all the way back. This stranger, now, this white man from far away, who spoke no Spanish and bad English, who gave candy to boys and told them romantic stories . . . he would not let such a man harm his boys, the boys whose souls he was here at the end of the world to save. When he got back, he would ask Xavier to show him where the old man lived.

"He live here," Xavier said. "He pay Miz Rosales five dollar—" The priest glanced at the rickety lean-to room held onto the back of the Rosales house by nothing more than faith and a coat of pink paint. It had been built for the older Rosales boys, before they and their father died of fever. Now the Widow Rosales rented it out when she could. A shed roof; a door with its blue painted frame open to the yard and close to the back gate into the alley. Not really an alley, more of a public footpath, wide enough for two or three to walk together, to drive a pig along, to lead a donkey. Not wide enough for a car.

"He has a car?" the priest asked. He had to have a car. How else could a white man, a stranger, have come here? But he saw no car—indeed, had seen no car he did not know in the past year, except on the highway itself.

"No *carro*," Xavier said. He was almost dancing with glee; he had interested the priest, and he would have something to brag about. "He come on horse."

"On a horse!" The priest stared at him, suspecting a child's romantic fabrication. No one traveled by horse any more, not in the 1950s. Not here, where straying off the public roads could be cause for a quick shot and no inquest at all. Some few people had a horse, and the men who worked on those dangerous ranches—but . . .

"A *real* horse," Xavier insisted. The priest thought about that. In Xavier's world, a real horse might be not only an actual horse, but a horse unknown in this town—a cavalry mount, a horse from the movies, something new.

"What did it look like? The horse?"

The boy spread out his arms. "Oh, *muy grande*—much big, very tall. Shiny, like oil. Like a charro horse, in Mexico."

A showy horse, then, big and shiny. Here? He saw no sign of a horse in that silent, bare yard. Only the Rosales dog, lean and yellow, tied with a thick rope to the pole of the clothesline. Only the retama tree casting its threadbare shade over a wooden table . . . a corona vine, almost indecently lush at this season, sprawled over the little wooden shack in the yard's corner.

"Not here," the boy said, unnecessarily. "The horse went away."

Went away. Like something in the boy's imagination, when he opened his eyes. The priest, confused and stifled in the heat, let his eyes drift around the yard. Bare dirt, a tire planted with verbena so bright a red it hurt the eye, blue—those blue painted door and window frames. At once he felt a surge of anger. These people! They would not give up their ridiculous superstitions . . .

"He let it go," the boy went on, eagerly. "He sent it away—my cousin Miguelito saw it. Into the river."

Blue around the doors and windows to keep the evil spirits out, and charms besides . . . not even Christian charms, a crucifix or Madonna or St. Christopher medal, but little knots of this or that, twigs and leaves, feathers and shells. The Widow Rosales, who came to Mass faithfully, and whose front door was innocently blank except for the blue paint, had nailed something like a bird's nest above the rear.

Xavier followed his glance and scowled. "You don' wanna bother with that," he said. "That's the—" and he glanced aside, made the sign and spit over his shoulder.

"I know who that is," Father Patrick said. He knew, and he didn't know. He had been warned about these people and their witches, their curanderos and curanderas, rarely openly called brujos or brujas, who pretended to be healers but were dabbling in far blacker arts than healing. Powerless, of course, except to the superstitious. He knew a curandera practiced in this town. But he didn't know who she was. Xavier did—they all did—but they all pretended not to understand his question.

"*Bruja? No!*" they said, making the sign of the cross, pulling their children close. "*No curandero aqui!*" they would say, men and women and children, when he asked. "*No curandera.*"

But the blue windows and doors, the obvious charms the babies wore . . . one of these women, who came to Mass and knelt passively before him, who slurred the clean Latin of the liturgy into soft Spanish . . . one of these women was the devil's personal agent. Curandera. Witch.

He dragged his gaze back to the lean-to. Xavier had already darted forward, to knock on the doorpost. No one answered. The old man should be there; Xavier said he sat or lay in the room all day. That he did his meager shopping early or late. Perhaps he was ill? Father Patrick came forward and peeked through the half-open door.

The little room lay bare to his eyes. A metal-framed cot, with a thin mattress wrapped in sheets and a coarse gray blanket. Who needed a blanket in this heat? A crucifix on the wall—proper, but it surprised him. Probably Senora Rosales had put it there. A three-drawer chest, tilting to the side, with skewed drawers that wouldn't quite shut. It had been painted dark red by an unskilled hand, and across the top lay an ornate doily crocheted in yellow cotton yarn. On the doily, a blue enameled washbasin and pitcher. A single box of unpainted wood with a plain metal clasp.

"His books," Xavier said, waving at the box. "He got books, old books. And the shirt with the cross, under his bed—"

"We can't go in," Father Patrick said. "He's not here; it's not right. I'll come back."

"He won't mind." Xavier had pushed the door all the way open, and now posed in the middle of the room, graceful as a dancer, a bullfighter.

Across the yard, the yellow dog lifted its head and ran out a long red tongue.

"Eh!" It was an old man's voice, but one with power in it nonetheless. Father Patrick turned, and watched him come in the gate.

The old man wore huaraches and white cotton pants and

shirt, just like the poorest Mexican peon. He had gray hair straggling around his ears, and a short gray beard, but he did not manage to look Mexican at all. The priest had met Mexicans of European descent, even northern European descent. He knew about the Irish mercenary who had married into the famous Garcia family; he knew about the elegant blonde women who shopped in Paris and Milan and laughed at the stupid gringos across the river in Texas who couldn't even speak Spanish. But the old man here did not fool him an instant. Those flame-blue eyes, those cheekbones, that set of jaw—that had come from very far away a long time ago.

"Pah-dray," the old man said, politely enough, but with no softness in his voice where the Spanish word rolled over from a *d* to an *r*. A voice like iron, cold iron with a little rust on it. The priest saw the rust like a cross on the man's body, and shivered in spite of himself.

"I'm Father Patrick Dougherty," the priest said. He was conscious of slowing his voice, making allowances for someone who might not understand English that well.

"Ah. Father Patrick. The local priest?"

What was that accent? Not German, not French, and certainly not British. But better English than Xavier's, for all that. He knew immediately that this man had some education, that he would know and understand things Xavier never could.

"Yes, I am," Father Patrick said. Then, on an impulse, "*Dominus vobiscum.*"

The old man smiled at him, and answered in Latin less accented than his English. "*Et cum spiritu tuo.*" He continued then in rapid Latin that strained Father Patrick's understanding. "I greet you with relief, good priest. We must talk, seriously and privately. I have important tidings for you. Can you tell me where we are?"

Perhaps the old man had a touch of sun. Father Patrick answered the question simply, almost gently, but in English. "Roma, my son. In Texas, near Mexico. You have come far?"

"Very far." The old man grimaced, and shook his head as if to clear his ears. He, too, returned to English, but haltingly. "It is not like the old Roma, this place. I thought—

but that matters not. You have not enough Latin for conversation?"

"No," Father Patrick said. "I know the liturgy, of course, and read it fair enough, but not to speak, to chat in. You, sir, must have had a Catholic education."

"Yes." When the old man did not go on, Father Patrick asked directly.

"Where?"

"Cracow." Cracow? Poland? That could almost make sense. Since the war, all sorts of refugees had ended up along the border. His fellow priests in South Texas had found before now people for whom the only common language was the Latin liturgy. They heard in confession stories which no one had yet mentioned in the press. Remote as it was, this region shivered to the stamp of arms across half the world.

"You are Polish, then?" Father Patrick asked. He had known a few Poles in seminary; he struggled to remember any words of Polish he might have heard and came up empty.

"Not Polish," the old man said with a grin. "Latvian."

Odder and odder, but still understandable. At least the man was a Christian, not a Communist or something. And Catholic, that was good, although Father Patrick thought he remembered that Latvians were Protestants. Perhaps he had chosen this remote village just because of its name.

"Come to Mass," Father Patrick said. "And confession," he added. He told himself that he cared only about the old man's soul, and the children's welfare, but he was uneasily conscious that he felt a certain relief in the presence of another set of blue eyes.

"Buggery? Of course there was buggery. Always is, when you have men priding themselves on not being attracted by women." The old man gulped at the beer Father Patrick had brought, and set the dark bottle down which a solid clunk. He had been to Mass; he had not appeared to notice the careful space around him in the church. Now, in the hot afternoon, they sat talking at the table in the Widow

Rosales's backyard, and the old man had begun with the sort of stories he told Xavier. Stories of knights, of Crusaders in the Holy Land and in Spain, of El Cid and Saladin. Of quarrels and treasures, of secrets and conspiracies, and finally of Philip the Fair, the grandson of the sainted Louis, of whom the old man had no great opinion. Father Patrick had let him ramble on. It was the best way with strangers, to let them fill the silence with more than they knew. "The question is, whose buggery was at issue? That fool Philip's, or the Order's?"

"Philip?" Father Patrick had lost track of the tale; he was more interested in the teller. A real historian, or a fervent amateur? He seemed to know a lot of unsavory details; if he'd been telling all this to Xavier and the other boys, it would have to stop.

"Oh, come now, Father. You know the story, I'm sure. Probably still taught as an example of what happens when pride overrules common sense."

"You're . . . ah . . . talking about some . . . church organization?"

The blue eyes blazed. "I am talking about the Knights of the Temple of Solomon. Our Order."

A crazy, then, who had read too deeply, too intensely, escaping into imagination. The Templars had been one of the militant orders; he knew that much. A picture he had seen in a history book swam before his mental eye: a great castle, brooding over a caravan route. Another: knights in white, with red crosses on breast and back, swinging swords in a battle against Islamic warriors with scimitars. The order had been suppressed, after the Crusades, but he didn't remember the details.

"You're a . . . uh . . . historian? I don't know much about it."

The look he got he remembered from catechism classes, when it was meant to intimidate and humiliate. It still worked. "I am no historian; I am a soldier." Another pull at the beer. "I remember . . . remember being told, that is." That sounded as if he'd changed his direction in midword. He still had that much grip on reality. "Admittedly, the Order made mistakes. One is not supposed to criticize one's elders, but everyone knows the ripest fruit begs to be plucked. We were too rich, too powerful; too many favors owed to us, and too many who could profit by our loss. The Hospitallers, for instance."

"But . . . er . . . immorality?" The priest could not bring himself to use the coarse term. He had heard it often enough, in all its many variations, but to use it . . . no.

"Buggery," the old man said firmly. "That and other abominations. Magery, repudiating Christ, spitting on the cross, all the usual things—the same list they charged witches with." Another gulp of beer, this one emptying the bottle. "Supposedly we seduced choirboys, pages, the young men who worked on our estates, as well as spending our own time arse-kissing—well, Philip should have been an expert in *that*, so it was said. And I suppose some did. I knew a sergeant who'd been shifted from house to house to break off what his superiors called particular friendships. When he was with us, he couldn't keep his eyes off one of the grooms."

"And you yourself?" the priest asked.

The old man looked at him, the blue eyes suddenly cold as northern ice. "It interests you?" Father Patrick felt himself going hot, hotter than the late afternoon glare of sun. But the old man had already turned away. "No, of course not. Your care for these poor ones is all pure, eh?" Was that sarcasm in his voice?

"I am sworn to chastity," Father Patrick said. It was all he dared say.

"Oh, so were we. Poverty, chastity, obedience. Military obedience, not some silly girls' school notion of it—obedience that counted when the dust rose up and the arrows flew and the Turks or the Arabs came with flashing blades—" He broke off suddenly, shaking his head.

Father Patrick made another attempt to edge him toward reality. "But that was long ago—centuries—"

"Aye, centuries." A long, rattling sigh that might have been dragged up from his feet with a chain. "And centuries since that cold day in Paris, aye. And the night after, too, in the icy river."

"It must be difficult, when you know so much and the past is so vivid to you, to deal with the daily life here and now," Father Patrick said. "This little town . . . isolation . . . "

"Father, you haven't heard me," the old man said. He glared, his eyes as full of light as a hawk's. "You aren't really listening."

"Oh, I am. I am indeed." Father Patrick knew he was listening to more than the words. An old man, a refugee; God only knew what he had endured to come this far. More than age could shake loose reason. "You're telling me wonderful things about the knights of God in the Crusades, to be sure. Great saints and great sinners in those days; sometimes I think now we have only the great sinners. Xavier has told me about your stories; he said—and truly—that you make them seem very real. But you told me you are preparing for death. You must realize that what we need to deal with is the state of your soul *now*, not the accusations made against these knights five hundred years ago?"

"Six hundred," the old man said. "And you're wrong—you need to know about them—you need to understand what I am. What I have, and what you must guard with your life—" But his voice broke in a fit of coughing, and Father Patrick held water to his lips and tried to calm him.

"Later," he said. "Now you must rest; whatever you have to tell me about your—" He almost said hobbyhorse, and stopped himself. "About your speciality, that can come later."

Without intending to do so, Father Patrick found himself at his next visit explaining his dilemma to the old man. Better that, he told himself later, than encouraging the old man in his delusion that he was a member of an extinct militant order. Such delusions could be the reasonable result of surviving the unmentionable horrors of the recent war in Europe, but to make a final confession and die well the old man would have to regain his sanity, his connection to the real world. And for that purpose, Father Patrick told himself, even the banal struggle between himself and the curandera might be a blessed intervention.

"I do not know her name," he said. "But she terrifies these people. She sells charms, tells fortunes. I've explained repeatedly, exhorted them . . . and I still find babies with those disgusting little strings around their necks, windows with bundles of herbs—probably poisonous—over them."

"They don't respect you?"

"I wouldn't say that, exactly. They come to Mass regularly; they are generous in their gifts, considering their poverty. Barring an occasional drunken knife fight, or a little wife-beating, I could not fault their charity. They are quick to take in the widow and orphan; they love their families. But they do not trust God's power to overcome evil. They will dodge behind His back, so to speak, and try to make their own bargain with the devil."

"An evil woman, you say. A witch. To tell you the truth, Father, I am less eager to condemn witches after what happened to our own illustrious and courageous Master . . . "

"But my problem," said Father Patrick firmly, before the old man could start in again. "My problem is that I cannot seem to loosen her grip on them. In this day and age—with the new dam, the international dam, being built only upstream from here, a new era—it is ridiculous. You have a Catholic education; you come from Europe. You will perhaps have met ignorant peasants in your day?"

"Mmm, yes. Superstitious, greedy, sly. Easy to frighten, and difficult to calm. Once Philip convinced even the bourgeoisie, let alone the peasants—"

"So you see my problem," Father Patrick interrupted firmly. "Perhaps you have more experience. What can I do, as a priest, to . . . to work around her, to displace her?"

The look he got this time was contemptuous. "You do not think like a soldier." So the old man had been one, and more than a conscript from that tone of pride. In what war, though? And was that soldierly heritage the reason for his choice of delusions? Father Patrick shook his head and answered mildly.

"I'm not a soldier; I'm a priest."

"I see." A long pause, during which the old man traced

a design on the tabletop with a wet finger. "Do you know that?"

Father Patrick looked, and saw nothing but the last angle and curve; the rest dried quickly in the heat. Even that much tickled his mind with a memory, but he couldn't grasp it. A letter? And not in the Roman alphabet? But the old man had swiped his hand quickly across the rest. When he picked it up, a brown coin lay there, a Mexican piece probably. Father Patrick pushed it back. "No—the beer is my treat. It's little enough I can do for you—"

"Just pick it up," the old man said. "Just touch it." Father Patrick shook his head.

"No . . . please. I don't want it. I won't take your money."

"You haven't listened to a word I've said," the old man said. He sat back and glared, and said something in a foreign tongue which Father Patrick was sure would require a penance if translated. "You don't believe me," the old man said, as if it were a repetition.

Father Patrick felt his own neck getting hotter than even the August sun could make it. He had listened by the hour; he had tried to help the old man come to grips with reality. "I believe in God the Father," he began, in the Latin they both knew. "And in Jesus Christ His only Son . . ." He paused, for effect. "It is not part of my duty to believe in *you*, only to pray for your soul."

The blue eyes dimmed. "As I for yours, Father Patrick. Go in peace."

Esperanza chose her time carefully. The Widow Rosales had gone to the post office window in the store, to pick up her monthly check. She would gossip awhile with the others who had come for the same purpose. And she, Esperanza, could enter the Rosales yard on the pretext of bringing a gift. And she would see the stranger up close, and then she would know what she would know.

She opened the gate, as if it were her own, and padded across the yard to the table under the retama tree. "Lupe!" she called, as if expecting the Widow Rosales to be home. "Lupe, I brought you some tomatoes from the Escobar's . . ."

"You," said a quiet voice at her elbow.

"Ey," she said, dropping an onion. It was only half a pretense; she had not sensed him until he spoke. It was like the great storms which could come out of a calm, in one sudden blast of wind.

"You are the witch," he said in English. She knew that much English, but she knew better than to show it. No man minds a silent woman, her father had said. She stood silent, hands folded, waiting. "*Bruja. Curandera*," the old man said. He didn't have the accent right, but she could understand that. A quick glance at him—yes, the blue eyes she had heard of, a different blue than she had ever seen. And very old, and dying . . . she could tell that, this close to him. Yet he had with him—on his person, in his hand, very close—such power as ought to keep him young forever. She could feel it rumbling in her bones. "You speak no English?" he asked. "*Ingles?*" So, he had learned that much Spanish.

"*Nada*," she said, "*No Ingles*." Of course she knew some English, but she wasn't about to say so. She looked politely away from those eyes again.

"You know about power," he said. He spoke slowly, so slowly that Esperanza had time to think each word to its Spanish equivalent. She did not look up; she dared not. How did he know? Could he sense her power as she sensed his? "You frighten the priest," he went on. "Are you an evil woman?"

When she understood that, she gave him a quick glare, intended to pierce and wound. Evil! They were always so quick to accuse, the men in general, and the men of power in particular. Let a woman do anything wise or strong, and they said she was evil. But his answering look was mild.

"Show me your power," he said. He held out his hand; even looking down she saw it. "Please."

She could not tell if it was his courtesy, or her own desire for that power, but she found herself holding his hand as if he were any husband come to find out if the baby was his, if his son would return from the Army, if the lost cow would be found. She felt the age of it, the fragility of approaching death in the looseness of its skin, the slackness of tendon and muscle. In the sunlight, the lines on his palm showed clearly.

"You have come from far away," she said in Spanish. It didn't occur to her that he might not understand. "You have crossed the water . . . a great water . . . more than one. You have fought many battles." She had been saying that to the men who came to her since the war, and it was always true. But this man's battles . . . they felt different. And that line—she hated to speak of it. "You were in hiding a long time. And your son—no, not your son, but someone you thought of as your son—died, and you felt you had outlived yourself. You came seeking death, and you bear a great wound that must be healed."

She felt the air around her pulsing in a vast heartbeat, and then she had let go his hand, feeling the sting of tears in her eyes. She squeezed her eyes shut: do not cry, Esperanza. Not now, of all times.

"More," he said softly. "There is more. Tell me."

She did not need to look at his hand again. She could feel directly what he bore, and to her surprise there were two foci, both upon him, but different. "Your power," she said. "It seeks a home, for when you die." That was true of both. One she recognized . . . a bit of someone's body, a tooth or bone or fingernail. It had the power of all such relics. The other, the more powerful, lay outside her experience.

"Yes," he breathed. "I know . . . it should go to the priest. But he won't believe me."

"No," she said. "Not our padre. If it is to rest here, it must be with me." She had surprised herself; she felt her mouth hanging open and covered it quickly with her hand and shawl.

"It is a man's power," the old man said firmly. "A king's wisdom. It is not for a woman."

"Pardon me, *jefe*," she said, looking away. Why had she let her tongue run loose? Now he knew she wanted it; now he would guard it more closely.

"Only God can pardon you," he said. He said it not in

English, but in a language near enough Spanish that she could make out the meaning. It sounded like the priest's talk in Mass, but the accent was different. Secret laughter shivered in her bones. His God need not pardon her; His God had never condemned her, except in the mouth of that priest.

"You laugh at God?" he asked.

"God laughs in me," she said, not entirely sure what she meant by that, only knowing it was true.

"I . . . see." She could feel those skylit eyes on her skin as if they were flames. His interest hurt, pulled her tight against her own assumptions. At last she had to look up, and meet that piercing blue gaze. No wonder gringos were insane, having those pale eyes. No decency at all; no veils between the soul and the world. "If only you were . . ." he murmured. Then: "You keep many secrets, I daresay."

She did not answer that; she knew she didn't have to. He had a secret, and it weighed on him, as secrets always did weigh on good people. Only the greediest, most evil, truly delighted in an unshared secret. He wanted to tell her, and he would if she did nothing to impede him.

"What do you think of this?" he asked. On the hand he held out was a small brown object the size of a fifty centavo piece, incised with a design unlike anything she had ever seen. Beside it another, a sliver of obvious bone, darkened with age. Power blazed from his hand.

Esperanza extended a trembling forefinger. "That—" she pointed to the bone, the more familiar, "is the bone of someone you loved. It is the unhealed wound of your sorrow." She would not tell a man, a gringo, a friend of the priest, what else it was, what could be done with such a bone, cherished so long. Its thin voice piped vengeance in her ear. "This—" she pointed at the rounded brown shape, "is another power, but it is not a power I know."

"And yet you attend Mass," the old man said. "You should know this power, if you know good and evil. Tell me, do you know what it does?"

That was obvious. Behind it, in some other place, voices roared curses. She did not know the language, but she knew the tone of cursing. It held them back, from whatever mischief they would do. But how to say that? "It is the stone that stops the mouth of the dead who would curse the world," she said finally.

"Close enough," the old man said. "And you, witch, would you see the world cursed?"

For a moment the old vision wavered in her sight, the vision given by the old woman who had taught her the arts, who had demanded those years of service. Terrible lights, terrible winds, great deaths, so terrible even the vultures died after gorging. A foretelling which had made her teacher cackle in glee, knowing she would not live to suffer in it but those who had tormented her might. Or their grandchildren, she didn't care. Esperanza had burst into tears that first time, and the old woman had tasted her tears and scolded her. *You are too soft. You must learn.* She had not cried again, but she had never enjoyed her own visions of coming doom.

"No," she said. "But it is cursed, whether or not I wish it."

"Not utterly, not so long as this is safe. Will you keep it so?"

"I?" Surprise drew her eyes back to him. "I am a woman, sir, and you said—"

"I have kept my vows these many years, and found no solution . . . I will try breaking them at last, and risk a little." He smiled at her; she felt her heart skip a beat. "Open your hand, witch."

She opened her hand, and he turned his over. For a moment they stood, hand clasped to hand, with the power burning between them. The bone pricked her palm; the other thing, whatever it was, felt like warm clay asking to be molded. Then the old man pulled his hand back, and she had to close her fist to keep from dropping the things.

"Now look," he said. She looked. The bone was unchanged; the other could have been any fifty centavo piece, an unremarkable coin not worth stealing. "Don't spend it," he said lightly. Then, more seriously, "Except for the right things."

When the old man died, after coming to his senses and making a proper confession, Father Patrick Dougherty saw him decently buried and said Mass for him. He would miss their talks; the old man had finally revealed that he had studied history in Cracow and Vilnius, that he had fought "in the forests" of Latvia and Lithuania, which Father Patrick took to mean in irregular forces. He said nothing more about relics.

Under his thin mattress the priest found a flat leather wallet with twenty American dollars. He gave the money to the Widow Rosales. He took the books in the box for himself. He did not find what Xavier took.

Two days after the burial, Xavier slipped away from his home with the worn cloth bundled under his arm and climbed into the back of a truck filling with laborers for the new dam. His father explained that *"mi hijo"* wanted to see the dam for himself. The men chuckled and knuckled his head gently. The truck lurched ahead, bouncing along the spur road that led from the highway to the river. Xavier squeezed himself into the front corner and peered out between the panels. Although they had explained the dam, what he saw made no sense. Open pits, rows of huge pipes big enough to live in, a line of growling concrete mixers with the first already letting its gray load rasp down the ramp into a hole.

"You will know the place," the old man had said. "It is important that this last remnant of our Order be buried safely."

"You will know the place," the curandera had said. "The old man was right, and here is a charm that will bind the waters."

So far he had no idea what that meant. Once off the truck, he was ordered this way and that by foremen who didn't want a small boy anywhere around. Away from the trucks, boy. Away from those pipes, boy. None of your mischief, boy. His father had disappeared into a swarm of workmen shoveling sand and gravel; his father had warned him to stay out of trouble.

He was hot and thirsty. The old man had told him about

that, about being hot and thirsty on the battlefield. About
the sting of sweat in a swordcut, about the stench of blood
and filth. If only you were older, the old man had said, what
a crusader you would make. Thinking of that, he hitched
up his bundle and kept skulking from shade to shade, from
cover to cover. The gringo foremen, huge and hulking with
their red sunburnt faces, were the Infidel; he was a knight
on a secret mission for the Order.

He knew the place when he found it. One of a row of
deep pits, wood-lined now, waiting for its filling of concrete.
No one was near enough to notice. He fished the fifty
centavo piece out of his pocket and wondered about the
curandero. Why would she give money for this burial? Or
was it about something else? His fingers lingered on the
coin. Fifty centavos. He shook his head. He was a knight
of the Cross, a holy warrior; he had his orders.

Xavier slid the coin into the folded cloth under his arm,
and very carefully climbed down into the pit, down the rough
wood forms, from brace to brace. It was cool and shadowy
here, smelling of raw wood, damp gravel, stone. The growling
machines seemed far away; in the close stillness he could hear
his own breath again. He raked out a little hole in the gravel,
laid the cloth and the coin it wrapped into it, and pushed
the gravel back over it. Then he climbed out, into the glaring sunlight, the heat, the noise.

He believed in visions as he believed in susto and the evil
eye and the terrible things the curandera kept in her back
room (he had once peeked and seen the eggs rolling in their
jar, the dangling bundles of pungent herbs and various feathers). Now he had no reason to find answers for the figure that
wavered in the air above him, the tall warrior on the great
horse, the shining white surcoat with a broad red cross on
breast and back. And no reason at all to doubt the twinkling
flight of something toward his hand, which when he opened
it was a silver dollar, American.

As a grown man, he nailed it over his bed, and never
wondered whence came his ten strong sons.

And Esperanza put the sliver of bone with her other
bones and sang it to sleep.

*Survivor guilt can start very early indeed. Some of the events in this story occurred as written, and though the adults involved hoped I'd forget them, I never did. This is one of the lessons of my childhood—discovering that the safe, comfortable room of familiar, loving people opens on a world of horrors. Safety is fragile, comfort rare, and love must be strong to survive the devastation.*

# AURA

Once a year everyone else hated numbers as much as she did. She faced the pile of bank statements, receipts, 1099s and W-2s with the comforting certainty that everyone else—all hundred million or so heads of household (or their spouses)—felt exactly the same about the columns of figures. Taxes again. Some people used computers, of course, and some had accountants. She had herself, four sharp pencils, and a pen to ink over finally balanced figures. Brad would check them before she inked them. In an ordinary year, he would expect nothing of her but a steady supply of coffee and snacks, and the assembly of the documents, but this year he had orders—doctor's orders—not to bother himself with tax preparation. He had recovered pretty well from the stroke, but he found it very hard to read. The words, he said, jumped around on the page.

She knew all about that, but with her it was numbers. Letters had graceful shapes, decorative qualities. Words carried with them their meaning, smooth and rough, clear and opaque, each word on the page evoking a separate image in her mind. They never tangled themselves up, and best of all no one ever insisted on checking the sum.

Numbers . . . .she remembered her second-grade teacher slapping a ruler on the desk, and insisting that numbers were simpler than words, that any child who could read so well could surely *add*. "There's only one *right* answer," her teacher had said, and she had understood even then why words were better. You could imagine green as any shade of green you wanted . . . it didn't have to be *right*.

She remembered the trickle of sweat down her sides under her starched dress during flashcard drills, the horrible foreknowledge that she would blurt out the wrong answer and have to sit down, while another child "traveled" to the next desk. The children had laughed; the teacher had scolded her for carelessness; her mother had dragged her to the eye doctor for tests. Her eyes, he'd said, were normal. It was probably an emotional thing, a physical symptom of her dislike of numbers. Most girls, he'd said as he patted her head, didn't like arithmetic. Her mother and the teacher both interpreted this as laziness and deceitfulness, and she'd spent miserable hours with the flashcards until she passed into third grade.

Now she watched the numbers writhe, the blurred print of Brad's W-2 shimmering so that she could hardly pick out the middle two numbers of his Social Security number. Why did they insist on using numbers for identification? She'd have gladly changed her name to something outlandish to ensure uniqueness. And if they had to use them, why couldn't she put her own number? But they demanded his, and there was something even more humiliating about being identified by *his* number than her own. She didn't like it; she never had, and she never would.

She printed Brad's number in the little space, grimly careful, and began filling in the other blanks. Perhaps if she concentrated—her teachers had emphasized the dangers of daydreaming, of letting her imagination loose where numbers were concerned—she could get through this. She would treat it as a recipe, a long, complicated old-world recipe, or perhaps directions for reupholstering a couch. First you do this, then that, and at the end it looks like something you could eat, or sit on.

The problem was that she had no picture in her mind of what the completed, perfect tax form should look like. Cookbooks had pictures of fancy dishes. Sewing books, home decorating books had pictures, pictures of drapes, dresses, furniture. The directions would make sense, because she would know what the end was . . . if you add sleeves to bodice, and bodice and sleeves to skirt, you have a dress. If you add filling to meat, and meat to pastry, you have a fancy entree. Numbers had no pictures; she could not *see* anything in them, no final outcome of all these blanks filled in except a form with its blanks filled in . . . it meant nothing.

She found she'd miscopied the amount of interest income, and erased it carefully. That was wrong, of course. Carelessness. It did mean something; it meant if she made a mistake, they would come for her. They would take the money, and the house, and even put her in prison. The page before her shimmered, then went flat; for a moment she could not find the right blank to fill in. Prison was all numbers, like the military. Brad had been in the military; he still said "By the numbers," sometimes, a kind of joke from those days. She had written him two letters, to addresses full of numbers and letters in a jumbled mix that made no sense. Why, she had asked, couldn't the army have normal addresses? He had laughed.

Doggedly, she poked the calculator's flat-topped buttons. Wrong; she forgot the decimal point. Another wrong; her finger had slipped from the 8 to the 5. She blinked at the bank's form. Was that a computerized 0, or an 8? Hard to read anytime, and now . . . her chest tightened. She took a deep breath, held it, let it out slowly. Eight, or zero? Zero. Eight. The diagonal wavered, became horizontal, wavered back to diagonal, a tiny compass needle leading her the wrong way. She felt pressure in her head; the numbers acquired a sinister aspect on the page, even beyond the threat of taxes, IRS, flash cards. She would have to quit for today; she would have to come back to this later, another time. *Deadline*, a voice chirped at her. *Dead line, some time.*

❖     ❖     ❖

She was setting the table, helping Aunt Sarah, who wasn't really her aunt, but her mother's best friend. Strangers had come, friends of Uncle Sam's and Aunt Sarah's, from before they'd moved to the brick house on the corner. She leaned forward between the chairs, enjoying the sound of men's voices speaking a language she did not know, to place the wineglass at the tip of the knife, carefully, as Aunt Sarah had said. The men ignored her, in their talk; she expected that.

But the numbers. The numbers on the stranger's arm, funny dark numbers that showed through wiry dark hair. She had never seen that.

She never remembered asking, only that she had. Only that Aunt Sarah, for the first and only time, knuckled the back of her neck and dragged her into the next room, hissing fiercely in her ear: "Don't ever ask! Don't EVER ask!" And she remembered the man's face turning toward her, white as his shirt, as white as the cuff turned back so carefully . . . and buttoned down as quickly, emotions she could not understand quickly hidden as the numbers, buttoned snugly under a common face of gentleness and good holiday manners.

She had a headache that night, the kind with blinding flashes of light in her eyes that would not go away, the kind she could not explain to grownups. The next day everyone explained, gently, patiently, because she was young (the first time she had been allowed to carry the wineglasses, so carefully, so quietly) about the numbers. They explained again later. They tried not to frighten her. You're lucky, they said. You will never know such things. It's all right. It's over. He's not angry with you.

But that one sidelong glance, and the feel of loving fingers fastened on the neck of her dress, suddenly harsh, suddenly strange . . . that could not be undone. She never saw the man again; she was not surprised. He had been angry, she knew, whatever they said; he had been hurt, and it was her fault for being lucky, for being rude, for all the things she had ever done wrong. The headache had been punishment, of course, but not enough.

She remembered the texture of the cloth, the pattern of Aunt Sarah's knives and forks, the feel of the wineglass stem between her fingers, the struggle she had had to walk carefully, not skipping, from the kitchen, the sunlight streaming in the windows, the smell of the roast and vegetables, the way her foot had bumped the table leg. The dishes that day had pink roses around the rims, not linked blue squares; Aunt Sarah was funny about that, and never used both sets on the table at once. She remembered the faint clean smell of Uncle Sam's shaving lotion, the men's strong hands gesturing as they talked in that language she had never heard, a language full of blocky, angular sounds. It sounded old, she thought, older than anything she spoke, older than Spanish even. She had liked it, but she had not really liked the other men that much. They were ignoring her. Uncle Sam and Aunt Sarah, having no daughter of their own, spoiled her; she, having no father, enjoyed being spoiled, and liked best those dinners when Uncle Sam would smile and joke with her as well as his own boys. She'd been told to leave the men alone to talk, but she really wished they would all look at her, like her, as Uncle Sam did.

It was in that context that she had leaned forward, flicked a flirtatious glance at Uncle Sam, and asked—asked—what she had asked. About the numbers.

She woke sweating, from *that* nightmare again. She never quite heard her own voice, never quite remembered which intolerable words she had used to ask that intolerable question. If she heard herself, she sometimes thought, she could not bear it. She pushed the covers aside, and sat up. Over forty, and still caught in that old disgrace—! Ridiculous. Her friends told her that, and had told her that, and still once or twice a year she woke in a panic, like this, with the full weight of it still on her head. She knew, as they did not, that nothing could undo the pain she had given, and if an innocent child (as innocent as any four-year-old can be) could thrust so sharp a sword into so wounded an adult, what hope for adults? What hope for her, who had made so many stupid mistakes, not only that one, and not only from opening her mouth to ask stupid questions . . . though that was, even now, a constant failing.

Brad was asleep; the cry she remembered giving must have been in the dream for he had not stirred. She pushed herself off the bed and blinked hard, trying to see in the darkness. Flickers of light, not quite enough to signal a migraine on its way, but a warning. She found her slippers by feel, and shuffled down the hall, running her hand along the wall. No sound from Lee's room, and none from Tina. They both slept heavily; she'd been lucky that way, too. Glimmers danced in her sight, linking into shapes she didn't want to see. Migraine aura, she reminded herself firmly. It's not really numbers, and certainly not *those* numbers; she had never been able to remember the numbers, not even when she could see the man's arm, a cigarette in the fingers, and the line at the wrist where the brown hand became the white arm. She could see the fine dark hairs, the white skin below, and the numbers . . . but not *which*.

She staggered into the kitchen doorframe, and clung to it. The glimmers twitched, pulsing with her heartbeat, edging into almost coherent patterns. No longer strings of numbers . . . now they made headlines, glowing in nasty lime-green, of the most stupid or cruel things she had ever said, and now dislimned into portraits of dead faces, green on black. Then they turned gold, brilliant glittering specks of gold that broke crisply into angled patterns, dazzling. Migraine aura. She knew it had to be that, and nothing more . . . even when the gold brightened intolerably, each speck spreading to a wide flake like one lens of an insect's compound eye.

It stared at her, remote and hostile, each lens reflecting her child's face, the two little bows she had worn holding the side-hair back, the lace collar. The child's mouth opened—her mouth—and out sped geometric solids of glittering gold, flashing light from each facet, from a numeral etched on each face. Hundreds of mouths, hundreds of solids, hundreds of numbers, sickeningly in motion as the vast insect turned its head. From around the eye jointed antennae sprouted, proliferated, elaborated, into great feathery fans that waved toward her.

She turned the light on. She had never seen the room before, this tiled kitchen floor with its glittering reflection, the ominous bulk of some purring alien at her side. She grabbed for safety, and its side came away in her hand; cold air poured over her feet. *Re-fri-ger-a-tor* floated through her mind in a stuttering sequence, each sound edged with tattered frills of meaning. She leaned toward the light and cold, but it disappeared with a faint thud, exhaling a stale odor of roast and vegetables. All across her vision, the faceted mosaic of gold and black lay between her and the strange room. Then it wavered and vanished, leaving behind only an edge of brightness around each object, a vague shimmer.

She still did not know the room. Or, she told herself, she knew it intellectually, but as an abstraction. She knew the canned peas would be behind that door; she knew her dishes had a pattern of blue flowers on white. It did not interest her, and it held no memories of emotion. Her dishes could have been cream with pink roses, or yellow with a chain of blue squares. The table on which she had served so many meals might have been oblong instead of round. It might have had another cloth on it. The printed pattern of hers, a wreath of green vine leaves, seemed to mock her.

Take your medicine, one corner of her mind told her. Take it now. Medicine. The medicine was down the hall again, in the dark, in the bathroom cabinet. It was locked; she would have to turn on the light to find the key. Brad would waken, and be muzzily sympathetic. In less than a breath, the right side of her face went stiff; she could feel the hardening of that side of her brain, as if someone had poured concrete into her empty skull. Too late now . . . a spike of pain impaled her head. Nausea roiled her stomach. So stupid, she told herself. You should have taken the medicine when you woke up. She told herself that every time.

"Do you come from a dysfunctional family?" asked the new rector's wife. They had come to introduce themselves, to learn "about your needs and how the church can help you" they had said. The rector's wife had the competent air of a good nurse who expects cooperation.

"No . . . not really." She had backed into her chair as far as she could; she flinched inwardly from the rector's wife's expression. They would already know, she supposed. They would already have made their judgments. "My—uh—parents were divorced, but aside from that—" *That* was not something most people could put aside, but she still felt that society's reaction to divorce, especially in school, had done her more harm than the divorce itself. Now it was fashionable to have come from a dysfunctional family; back then only perfection would do. She distrusted the change in attitude.

"Aahh." A knowing, professional sound, judgment made and rendered all in one. Efficient. "Are you all right, really?"

She was all right, really. She had learned to ignore the shimmering edges, the sudden disruption of vision into fragmented, faceted forms (easier, now, with computer graphics so common—she could tell herself firmly that her visual computer was malfunctioning), even the strangeness that made her own house, her own family, so disturbing. Migraine aura. That's all it was, and the association with a childhood event purely accidental. No alcoholism, no drug addiction, no physical or sexual or emotional abuse. *You've got nothing to complain about,* said the anonymous voice. *You're lucky.* Luck being, as it were, her only handicap.

"Really all right," she repeated, hoping it was only once. "Fine." The rector's wife had begun to glitter, dangerously; perhaps she would leave before she turned into an abstraction of planes and angles of beaten gold. The rector's wife would be terrifying as an insect, vast and intrusive; she would have grasping claws and the impersonal determination of a mantis dissecting a grasshopper for lunch. She must have said something else, because the rector was talking now, replying, it seemed, to something she had said. Something about her father. She blinked, hoping to resolve the pattern of bright dots and dark ones into something recognizable. The rector had dark hairs on the backs of his hands, and fingernails neatly clipped.

"—ought to tell him how you feel," the rector said. "Or that's a kind of lying, too, isn't it? Concealing things? One should be honest . . ."

As a child, perhaps. A child craving attention. A child honestly curious. A child putting together those two childish things . . . instead of putting away childish things . . . and thereby releasing . . . whatever she had released. She knew better than to say that; she had said too much already. She walked them from the house; they smiled and waved. They had left their packet of wisdom for her. Honesty, forgiveness, love, wrapped in shining paper with shining ribbons around it. Her mind plucked at the glittering bows.

But it was not hers. It belonged to someone else. She glanced around, feeling unseen eyes. They had been blue, she remembered. Clear blue, and the whites very white, only a slight rim of red at the edge of the eyelid, probably from the smoke. Below his eyes a gray stain of sadness, the flesh sagging away from the bones. He had had one crooked front tooth, and some steel caps when he spoke that reflected points of light. It's not me that won't forgive, she said silently to the car that had long since driven away.

Around her, the gray blocks piled up, neatly, inexorably. The time she had said something about Emily's nose, the time she had snapped at Laura, the time she had lied about the check being in the mail. Days of plenty and peace, days of happiness, days when she had not thought of him at all, each one a gray stone walling her in. Stupid questions, cruel remarks, each a spike fixed in the stones, pointing inward. Clumsiness, inattention, laziness: the complaints of her teachers. Pride, insensitivity, selfishness: the complaints of her spiritual leaders. Hypersensitivity, priggishness: the complaints of her friends.

She looked at her arms, unsurprised to find them covered with blue numbers, zero to infinity, all she had done wrong and failed to do right. Her head shuddered and split into wedges, like a chopped tomato; each wedge, impaled on a spike, had its own faceted eyes with which to see, and what remained of her voice rose from the soggy puddle of juice at the joining of the wedges. Sorry, it said, in a child's tremulous whimper. I'm sorry. Being sorry is not enough, said the voice she would never quite forget, in the language she had never heard before. She knew the meaning, though. She always did.

She had scarcely looked at the picture when her vision blurred; with no warning aura, the migraine invaded, overfilling her skull, pressing like cruel thumbs on her eyeballs. She squinted at the magazine anyway. A black and white photograph danced on the page like a clipping on the wind.

Blurred face, sad eyes, lines of age and pain. She could not read the obituary, not really . . . she had never known his name; she had never remembered his profession. This was not the same man, could not be. One word only resolved into letters, quivering. She had seen that name in school, under the pictures of dead men stacked like firewood, a few survivors' masklike faces. Those faces shifted, merged into faces from later pictures, later wars, flickered through her mind in an endless stream: men, women, children, babies, bodies, mouths gaping, eyes wide or closed in death, crowds behind barbed wire, single prisoners hunched in cells, eyes glistening in the camera's flash, staring at her, through the lens and flickering shutter, with that expression she had never forgotten, that disbelief, that horror, that disgust.

The migraine squeezed itself, contracting into a single point of pain in midbrain. She grunted, as if someone had slugged her belly. Nothing was enough, nothing would ever be enough. She thought, as always too late, what she should have said to the rector's smiling wife: "No, not a dysfunctional family. A dysfunctional world."

With the suddenness of a pricked soapbubble, the migraine disappeared, leaving her unbalanced, almost giddy.

She lay the magazine on her desk, atop the piles of bank statements, the half-finished tax return. She felt warm and moist, a loaf of bread new-baked, steaming slightly. While her head was clear, while she could think, she would try to finish the taxes. The numbers lay quiet, their meaning leached of danger, no more remarkable than a collection of letters. She fed them into the calculator, copied them, added and subtracted as the directions specified. The result had a certainty she had never associated with numbers, a feeling of solidity so new that it surprised her into noticing.

Tentatively, she let her mind visualize a number . . . just a number, not a dark mark on white skin. A cascade of them, in the bright pastels of her child's books, tumbled over each other, eager as puppies. Little yellow fives, soft lavender fours, orange threes, blue twos, fat white marshmallow ones, no longer scintillating in dangerous light, but docile, friendly, even affectionate. She felt as if she had stumbled into a strange universe where all the familiar rules changed.

In one blinding flash more intrusive than even the migraine, she saw the book itself, its pages smudged and worn at the edges, its pictures simple and innocent and harmless. Her own hand, none too clean (her adult eye recognized grape jelly and peanut butter) spread starfishwise, her own voice piping "I like one and I like two and . . . that makes three, Mommy!"

So she had not always hated numbers; she had not always been driven to blind panic by the operation of one upon another. Had that panic come from her question, which even now loomed worse than the pain of migraines? She shivered, hoping as always that she would not remember it. But the numbers themselves surrounded her, touched her hands, stroked her head; softly, gently, insistently, they urged her through that final door where the terrible question lay, coiled malice, proof of iniquity beyond forgiveness, steeped in a poison only she could brew. No aura splintered that sight into painless abstraction, no migraine split her consciousness away from it—the numbers, merciless once more, compelled her.

Cowering in the corner of her mind, her memory trembled, as fragile as a wineglass, as a child's trust, as an adult's courage.

She had thought he had numbers on his arm because he liked numbers, just as she liked numbers. Why else would someone put numbers on his arm, instead of the dragon or heart or snake tattoos she had seen on other men? She wanted numbers too, perhaps in pretty colors like the dragons. She waited for a pause in the conversation, because she knew that interrupting was rude, and she asked her question as politely as she knew how. "When will I get my numbers?"

*I had finished the whole story of Paksenarrion, but the fate of the child who was beaten to punish his father haunted me. What happened to him? How pervasive was the healing Paks experienced? So I followed a scared boy into the cold night, and back into the light.*

# THOSE WHO WALK IN DARKNESS

He was feverish and shaky; they had made him stay to the end. Now he slipped away from his father in the crowd, swerving quickly into a side passage, and forced himself to hurry on the stairs. His back hurt still, four days after the beating.

It was already dark outside, and cold. Torches flickered in the light wind, sending crazy shadows along the street. He took a long breath of fresh air, grateful for it. The streets were strange again. Every time they stayed below too long, he had trouble adjusting to the movement and noise. He had tried to say that, but his father had silenced him with threats. Just as the priests silenced his father with threats.

They had not silenced the paladin. He hunched his shoulders, remembering her last words. She had refused to acknowledge the Master; she had claimed the protection of the High Lord and Gird. The priests always said there was no High Lord, but when they unbound her legs the terrible burn wounds closed over as everyone stared. Even the priests; he could tell they were frightened too, by the way they screamed at the crowd and drove them away.

He slid behind Sim the baker, and flicked a roll from the tray while Sim bickered with a customer who wanted a discount this late in the day. Sim caught the movement and kicked at him, but the kick didn't land. Sim didn't mean it to. The roll was cold and hard, that morning's baking, but better than nothing. He sank his teeth in it, pulled off a mouthful. The paladin—they'd had to taste her blood. He hadn't wanted to, but after the other he knew better than to stand back. It tasted like anyone's blood, after all. Salty. The bread stuck in his throat; he choked. A hard hand pounded his back; another grabbed the roll. For an instant he flailed, off balance with the pain of his back; he heard the laugh, and knew it was Raki.

"Take a bite of my supper will you?" Raki lounged against the wall, inspecting the roll. He had years and height, and the assurance of them.

"Wasn't for you," said Selis. He moved his shoulders, wondering if the welts had opened again.

"Should have been. You owe me." Raki took a small bite, watching him. Selis shifted his feet, wondering which way to go.

"I couldn't come," he said.

"Couldn't." Raki chuckled, an unpleasant sound. "That's what I heard. Jori said you squealed like a rabbit."

"You knew—"

"Isn't much I don't know. Eh, dark of three nights I was there myself. Not as good sport as some, that fighter."

"Paladin," said Selis, before he thought. Raki's brows went up, changing the shape of his face in the torchlight.

"Paladin," he said. "You say that like you meant it, Selis. Don't you know there is no such thing?"

"I saw it," said Selis stubbornly.

"Saw what?" Raki spat, just missing Selis's foot. "I saw a fighter shaved naked and trussed like a market pig for everyone to sport with. That's all I saw."

"Did you see the end?"

"And me a prentice with an afternoon shift? Of course not—I've been on the street since midday, earning my share. Just you wait, Selis, until you're on the street—then you'll learn—"

"But Raki—"

Raki glared at him. "Have you forgotten, little boy? You're nothing. That's the rule—as far as you and I are concerned, and the Master is concerned, you're nothing." Selis looked down. Raki was right; he had street duty, he had rank in the Guild. And no Guild child could argue with him, however close he was to his own apprenticeship. "That's better," he heard Raki say, then two quick strides and Raki gripped his shoulders, hard, intending to hurt. "And you listen, Selis who squeals like a rabbit: you'll always be nothing. I'll always be ahead of you—I'll always have the power, and you'll always serve me—little boy." He shoved Selis against the wall, until the smaller boy was gasping with pain, then released him with a hard push that sent him sprawling.

For a long moment Selis crouched there in the shadow, shaking with both fear and anger. Raki hated him—had always hated him. Raki's father was dead, killed on Guild business; Raki had been reared by the Guild, a foster-child. Selis's father held rank enough: the richest fence in Verella, with contacts from Valdaire to Rostvok. But Raki was bigger, older, and early skilled in those torments that give older boys dominance in any gang. Selis knew Raki was doing well as an apprentice thief; they all knew, when the lists were posted. And Selis, small even for his younger age—his stomach knotted when he thought of the years ahead.

That made him think of food; he looked back toward Sim's stall, but the baker was already closed. He could not go home. The priests had forbidden it as part of his father's punishment—the punishment that fell on him, because they knew that was worse for his father. They had also forbidden an inn. He dared not spend the coins his father had palmed him, with their spies everywhere. He had to scavenge, they had said. With a sigh, he pushed himself up and started toward the great market. Perhaps someone had left scraps there.

Selis had rarely been alone on the street after dark. Before Raki made apprentice, he had gone out with that group once or twice, and his father had taken him along to a tavern from time to time, but this was different. The noise of booted feet seemed loud, and the men and women larger. He heard the crash of arms down one street, and darted across it to another. Here it was darker, with fewer people. Selis slid along the wall, half-feeling his way. It grew colder. He shivered, wishing for the cloak the priests had taken from him. They had told him where he could sleep warm, whispering in his ear as he hung on the frame, but he would never go there. For one night he could survive on the street; he had been out before with the others. He wondered about the paladin. He had heard the talk—she was being given to another, to be killed outside the walls later—but how much later? If he was cold, in wool pants and tunic, she must be colder, stripped and shaved like that. The wind ruffled his thick mat of hair, and he shivered again.

The great market, when he came to it, was a cold windy space lit spottily by windblown torches. No stalls showed, and the local brats had scavenged any dropped food long before. Selis sighed as he hunted along the edges, turning over bits of trash with his foot. His stomach growled, and his mouth felt dry. At the public fountain, a thin skim of ice slicked the stone margin. The icy water made his teeth ache. He looked up; nothing but thick darkness that smelled wet. The wind dropped again; he could hear footsteps in the distance, and a drunken voice singing. He moved around the fountain, looking for a place out of the moving air.

He could still see the paladin in his mind, and he could see himself. Why had he squealed like that, before they even hit him? Someone had laughed, and others had joined them; he should have been silent. The paladin had been silent. When they first brought her in, everyone was: he had been breathless, waiting for the high gods to send a bolt of fire or something. And nothing had happened. He almost believed the priests, that nothing could happen, that only the Master had power. He believed it when they dragged him forward, and when they beat him, and nothing happened. He believed it when the paladin's torment went on and on, and nothing happened. He believed it until—he frowned, thinking of it—until he had gone forward himself, to spit on her and taste her blood, as the children must. Then he saw gentle gray eyes, a tired face drawn by pain but unafraid and—most strange to him—not angry. He had stared then, forgetting what to do, but the priest had tapped his sore back and reminded him. And so he had spit, and rubbed his finger along her bloody sides and tasted it, and she had looked at him, without anger or fear.

How could that be? They were all frightened, all the rest: he was, and his father, and all the others in the hall, and the guards. Even the priests. But she was not frightened. She had been hurt—had cried out with pain, as he had—but not frightened. Nothing changed her mind. She had said, again and again, that the High Lord was real. That Gird Strongarm was real. That the Master was nothing before them. That thought made him twitch. It was dangerous. If he defied the Master, if he didn't believe, then they would hurt him as they hurt her. He curled into a ball, the taste of that blood filling his mouth. He felt nausea burn his throat. He had to believe. He had to obey, or else— But when he screwed his eyes shut, he saw her face. He heard her voice, somehow steady and clear despite the torments. Those gray eyes seemed to watch him.

A booted foot tapped him sharply in the ribs, and he uncurled with a gasp. A watch officer, with four guards behind him.

"What are you doing here, boy?"

Selis fumbled for explanations. "I—I was sitting—"

"You can't sleep here. Who are you?"

"Selis Kemmrisson, sir." It was permitted to be polite to the watch, if unwise to be stopped by them.

"Hmm. Your father's business?"

"Merchant, sir."

"And you're—ah—out on business?"

"No, sir—I mean, yes—in a way—"

"Runaway?"

"No, sir."

"Hmmph. It's no night for a youngster like you to be out playing pranks. Go home and stay in."

Selis wanted to ask why, but knew better; he started across the square as if he knew where he was going.

"And don't let me catch you hiding in someone's doorway,

boy—" the man called after him. "—or I'll think you a fairspoken thief, that I will."

Seli could not laugh at that, as Raki would have—but Raki wouldn't have been found curled up on the fountain step. Raki would have heard them coming and been hidden in shadow. He walked on, his legs aching now. He had gone out the west side, where he rarely wandered. At the first crossing, he would have turned back, but heard another patrol. As his heart steadied again, he wondered what it would be like to be without fear, like the paladin. He tried to imagine her with Raki, but in his mind no pictures took life. Yet Raki was brave; he never showed fear. From behind or above—Selis thought of Raki dropping on her with his little dagger, the narrow blade allowed apprentices on duty. But again the picture caught no life; Raki was a shadow attacking a shadow, and both vanished in his mind.

Ahead on the right a wide door let out a bar of light that striped the width of the street. Selis slowed, walking as quietly as he could. He was fairly close when he recognized the place: a Gird's grange, the one called Old Verella. He stopped short, suddenly drenched in sweat. A shadow crossed the light, and a man stepped into the street, to set a burning torch in a bracket by the open door. Selis could see little of him but the shape: massive, in glinting mail. He went inside, and returned with another torch, set on the other side of the door. Then he stood in the opening, and drew his sword, as if guarding the door against an invader. Selis looked around, and saw no one. When he glanced back, the man was looking his way; again Selis froze, looking down as he had been taught, lest his eyes catch the light. After a long moment he looked up. The doorway was empty, but a shadow marked the light as the man paced from side to side within.

Selis leaned on the wall beside him. His heart hammered. He could not cross that bar of light, and behind—he turned, to see a torchbearing squad of watchmen cross the street far behind him. He tucked his cold hands into his armpits, and crouched. He wished he was at home, tucked in the warm bed with his brother, safe behind that locked door.

He imagined his mother's arms around him, the soothing
salve she would spread on his back, the sweet asar she would
brew for him. Something clanged, down the street; his head
jerked up. When he looked, the watchmen were closer, but
they turned a corner down a side alley and disappeared.
He closed his eyes, but the vision of home would not return.
Not in comfort, at least. He seemed to see his mother,
frightened, wringing her hands and staring wide-eyed at his
father, who held a scrap of bloodied cloak. He remembered
all too clearly the changes in the last few years, the new
lines in his father's face, the silent glances from one elder
to another, that began with the first of the red priests
holding ceremony in the old Guildhall underground.

He looked up the street to see the grange door still
pouring light onto the cobbles. It looked warm—but it
couldn't be warm with the door open like that. He sighed,
leaning back until his back hit the wall, then wincing. Blast
that Raki—surely the welts had reopened! He couldn't feel
his feet any more, and his teeth chattered. He thought of
his uncle's tales of the north, of merchants dying in the snow
when they fell asleep. With an effort he pushed himself
upright, and stamped, nearly falling when one leg gave way.
It was too cold to stay there, and he was hungry, and—
he looked again at the grange door, with the shadow crossing
and recrossing that light.

What had she been like in armor? he wondered suddenly.
He had thought of paladins as shining, brilliant like stars.
Once he had seen one—or thought he had—and from the
crowd's murmur it might have been. But in the priests'
hands, she had been nothing much to see—except those
eyes. And the steady voice, refusing them. And the wounds,
at the end, healing without any aid he could see.

He had moved enough to shiver again, dancing in place,
but his breath was giving out. How had she insisted that
Gird would help her, when she was helpless in their hands?
How had she been taken? Had she fought at all? He knew
the Marshals by reputation; no thief would fight one openly.
Paladins fought even better, by the stories—how they captured her without a fight? He wished he could ask her. He

wanted to know why she wasn't afraid, and why she hadn't been angry, fighting. He could not imagine that.

The light drew his eyes, a broad yellow stripe. Across and across the shadow marched. He would be unafraid, whoever that was, man grown and bearing a sword, but she had had no sword. Yet she had been Girdish—she had said so. Gird the protector, she had said. Selis found himself halfway to the light before he realized it; his teeth chattered harder than ever. Gird the protector. But Gird had not protected her, not even from a scared boy like himself. He felt another wave of nausea at the thought of her blood in his mouth. How could he turn to Gird, if Gird would not protect her? But she had not been afraid. Had Gird taken her fear, and left her the rest? It might be worth that pain not to be afraid, even for a night.

Quickly, giving himself no time to think, Selis threw himself forward, into the light, skidding to a halt just inside the door. Fear flooded his mind, clouding his eyes for a moment so that all he could discern was a huge shadowy shape looming over him, with light behind it. He opened his mouth to scream, but as in a nightmare no sound came. The shadow bent over him; he felt strong arms around him, lifting him gently.

"Shhh," said a voice. "It's all right. You're safe here." He was shivering with cold and fright together; he felt tears burning his eyes, running hot on his cold cheeks. The man carried him easily, speaking to someone else, directions that Selis did not follow, being deaf to anything but his fear. Gradually it eased.

He was warm. He was cradled in someone's lap, his legs dangling, and as his sobs died away, the man began to speak.

"There, little lad—were you the frightened rabbit crouched by the wall earlier? Don't fear—what's made you fear Gird, of all saints? Here, now—" A hiss followed, as the man touched his back. "Ah, you're hurt. We'll ease that; let me help you with your tunic." Selis sat up, seeing blurrily through the last of his tears a freckled face under thinning red hair, pale blue eyes that met his steadily. He fumbled with the laces of his tunic; the man waited until he dragged it over his head, wincing at the pain.

"I—I'm sorry—" he mumbled, not knowing what else to say. The man's face had stiffened, seeing his back. He saw the blue eyes turn cold.

"Gird's arm, boy, who dealt those blows?" Selis shivered again, his fear returning. He could not answer, shaking his head helplessly when the man asked again. Then the man sighed. "I think I know—if that's not the mark of a crooked lash, I'm no Marshal. And why are you sorry, boy, unless you dealt such blows to another?"

"I—" Selis bowed his head, fighting back another bout of sobs. "I'm afraid—"

"I can see that." The Marshal moved, turning to call. "Kevis! Bring me some water, and bandages." He gathered Selis in his arms again. "We'll get you to bed, boy, and get these cleaned out. When did you eat last?"

"I don't know—" The motion from chair to bed made him dizzy; the Marshal rolled him neatly onto his belly.

"I expect you've more welts below—is it so?"

"Yes, Mast—Marshal," said Seli.

"Don't use that scum's name here," said the Marshal grimly. "I thought so—they weren't content with *her*, they had to take a child as well. Here, lift your hips. Damn them. You'll carry these marks for life, boy." Seli heard footsteps, another man's voice.

"Anything else, Marshal?"

"Food, Kevis. Who else is keeping vigil?"

"Arbad, Rahel, and Arñe."

"Good. I'll be with this boy awhile, until he's settled—"

"That's—"

"Liart's work, yes. By Gird's cudgel, we've a housecleaning to do in this place, yeoman marshal, and no regency council fop will stop us this time."

"Aye. That's what I thought." The other man went away. Selis dared to look around; he was lying face down on a narrow bed against the wall of a small clean room. A dark blue robe hung on one peg, a swordbelt and sword on another. A low table and broad chair completed the furniture. On the table was a bowl of water and pile of cloth strips neatly rolled into bandages. The Marshal was dipping a cloth in water.

"This will sting," he said, meeting Selis's eye. "I'm sorry for it, but evil deeds last longer than the doing." He began working on Selis's back; it felt worse than stinging to Selis. He bit his lip, and thought of the paladin. "These are inflamed," the Marshal went on. "How long ago were you beaten?"

"Four days," said Selis, in a jerky voice. "I—I think it was four days."

"Hmmph. And you've been lurking the streets since?"

"No—Marshal. I—ouch!" He clenched his fists; the Marshal seemed to be digging into one of the welts with his fingers.

"Sorry, lad. This one was going bad; full of pus. It has to come out."

"It—didn't—feel like—that before—" Selis had buried his face in the blanket.

"I know. The ones that go bad quit hurting for a time. Those damned hooks they use dig in and make a deep place for wound fever to grow." By the time the Marshal finished, Selis was shaking again, trying not to cry aloud, with a mouth full of blanket. "That's all," the Marshal said finally. "They're all clean—and plenty of salve on them—shouldn't go bad now." His hand on the back of Selis's head was gentle and warm. "You're a brave lad, to be so quiet—a beating is bad enough; I know this hurt."

Selis looked up in surprise. "Me? I'm not brave—"

A chuckle surprised him further. "You've enough experience to judge? I would hope you did not." The other man reappeared, carrying a deep bowl and a pitcher. The Marshal nodded, and he withdrew. "Eat a little, if you can, and drink all of this. You may be fevered; don't eat more than you want." While Selis ate a few mouthfuls of beans, and sipped the bitter drink, the Marshal fingered his clothes. "These aren't beggar's clothes," he said finally. "Are they yours?"

"Yes, Mas—Marshal."

"Good cloth. Were you stolen away?"

"N-no, Marshal."

"No?" The Marshal's eyes glittered in the candlelight. "Your family consented to this?" His gesture included Selis's wounds and his hiding in the streets.

"It—they—" Selis shook his head, near tears once more.

"They were afraid too," said the Marshal, without hint of question.

"Yes, sir," said Selis.

"So they let this happen?"

"It couldn't be helped," whispered Selis to the blanket. "He couldn't stop—"

"Ah. Does your family ask our aid? Is that why you came?"

"No." Selis drew a long breath. "They don't know I am here. I was not to go home until daylight, they said."

"They—Liart's priests?"

Selis nodded. "They said they'd do more if I did—"

"To your family?" At his nod, the Marshal frowned. "Your family worships there, boy? Is that what you mean?"

He shook his head, unable to say; how could he explain? The Marshal sighed.

"I don't understand, lad. You were afraid when you came—I thought from your face that you feared Gird himself. Your family let Liart's priests beat you, and yet you say they don't worship him. Why did you come, if not for that? Did you hope sanctuary for yourself?"

Selis closed his eyes, to see the paladin's gray eyes watching him gravely. "She wasn't afraid," he whispered.

"*What!*" The Marshal went on in a quieter voice. "What do you mean, 'she'? What have you seen?"

He clenched his hands on the blanket. "Sir, they had a—a lady. A fighter—"

"A paladin," said the Marshal. His voice had chilled. Selis glanced at him and froze again; the Marshal's face was hard as dry bone. "Go on," said the Marshal.

"A paladin," he repeated. "They hurt her. And she wasn't afraid. She looked at me."

"Looked at you?" Selis could hear the effort of control; he shivered, feeling great anger near.

"Yes, sir. When—when they hurt me, and when I—" He

stopped, shivering again. Surely the Marshal would kill him, if he told it. He had tasted her blood; the memory sickened him.

"What did you do?" asked the Marshal, in that remote quiet voice. Selis found himself answering as quietly.

"They called us up—the children—we had to spit on her and taste—" he faltered momentarily. "Taste her blood," he finished. His head sank, waiting for the blow.

"Was that before or after they beat you?" asked the Marshal.

"After," said Selis.

"And did you enjoy it?" asked the Marshal in the same level tone.

"Enjoy!" Selis's head came up. "Marshal, no! How could anyone—it was terrible, but they would have killed me—my father was there—"

The Marshal's pale eyebrows had risen. "No one enjoyed it?"

Selis felt a wave of heat flush his face. "Some," he admitted. "Some did, but—"

"But you did not. And now do you think it was right, boy?"

Selis dropped his eyes again. "No, but I was afraid."

"After that beating—" He heard the musing tone, a heavy sigh.

"It wasn't only that," he found himself saying. "My father—they had told him—I heard them threaten him—we were all afraid. Only she wasn't. When I went forward, I forgot what to do; she looked at me, not frightened, not angry. Then the priest hit me again, and told me—and—and I did it. But sir, whatever they did, she was not afraid. At the end—"

"Stop." The Marshal's face was unreadable. After a long moment of silence, he went on. "Boy, you came to us frightened, cold, hungry and hurt: do you acknowledge that?"

"Yes, Marshal."

"What's your name?" He hesitated; what would happen to his family? The Marshal went on impatiently. "I need something to call you besides boy; if you don't want to tell me your father's name, that's all right."

"Selis," he answered.

"Selis. You came here needing aid; Gird is the protector of those who cannot protect themselves, and as his followers we are bound to aid the helpless. Do you understand?"

"Yes." He thought he did; they were oathbound, but unwilling.

"I doubt that." The Marshal went on. "But we have our rules too, Selis. If you take our aid, we will expect payment from you—not these silvers in your pocket—" he jingled the coins in his hand. "But the payment of an honest heart. Until now I have listened as I might to any frightened child needing help. Frightened children lie, to save themselves pain. I ask you now for the truth, Selis, and if you lie I will not scruple to throw you out. Is that clear?"

"Yes, Marshal." Selis stared, confused.

"Now. You say you witnessed the priests of Liart tormenting a paladin, a woman. Is that true?"

"Yes—"

"And when was this?"

"It—began some days ago, sir." Selis counted on his fingers, to be sure, backwards and forwards both. "Five days, after sunset."

"And you spoke of an end: when?"

"This afternoon, near dark. It was dark when I came outside."

"And what was the end you saw, Selis?"

"It—" Selis paused. In the confusion that had followed the healing of the stone burns, he was not sure just what had happened. "What I saw," he began cautiously, "was the burns going away. But she did not wake, and the priests were angry and drove us all out. But I had heard she was to be killed outside the walls somewhere."

"The burns went away?" The Marshal's voice had warmed a trifle.

"Yes, Marshal. They had put hot stones to her legs, to cripple her, and when they unbound them, the burns healed, disappeared, even as they held her for everyone to see."

"Gird's grace." Selis looked up at that, and saw the balding shiny top of the Marshal's bowed head. Then the Marshal lifted his head slowly; his eyes glittered with unshed tears. "And so she lives?"

"I think so—then. The guards dropped her, and then they told us to leave, and began pushing at us. I looked back, and saw one of them tying her arms again. But she did not wake—"

"No. And you say she showed no fear—"

"No, sir. At first I wondered—I couldn't believe the gods would let a paladin—if it was a paladin—" He floundered for a moment, catching an expression on the Marshal's face that frightened him again. "I mean, sir, that I had heard about paladins—and she had no sword, even—and did not fight—"

"And you doubted she was a fighter at all?"

Selis shook his head. "No—I've seen fighters; she looked like that. But paladins—the priests said it was all a lie, and that she was no more than any other fighter. I thought if she was, the gods would do something, and they didn't. The priests went on, and the others—"

"What others?"

"The—the ones there. Everyone, nearly. The priests require it."

"That everyone join the torment?"

"Yes, sir." Selis glanced quickly up and away, letting his eyes roam around the bare room.

"Were you there for all of it, Selis?" The Marshal's voice was curiously gentle; it surprised him enough to face that blue gaze.

"Yes, sir. They said I had to stay for it all. They wouldn't let my father even speak to me that day, or the day after—"

"How many times did they beat you?"

"Only the once, sir. But then—they made me sit on the other side, with the children, and they told me they would beat me again if I angered them."

"I see." The Marshal's lips folded in a tight line. Selis

watched him, sure of anger when he spoke again. After a moment, the Marshal shook his head slightly. "Boy—Selis— if you had stayed on the streets until morning, in this cold, you'd have had wound-fever enough to keep you abed until spring. The priests knew that: wounds festering four days, hunger, a cold night. They must need a hold on your father. Remember that, Selis: they serve a bad master with bad service; there's enough pain in the world without causing more."

He stretched, and went on more briskly. "Now—you need rest before anything else. Sleep here. Do not leave this room without permission; if you wake, you may eat and drink again, but do not leave. There's a pot under the bed. Is that clear?"

"Yes, Marshal."

"And will you stay?"

"Yes, Marshal."

"Later I hope you will be free of the grange, but this night we are keeping a vigil it could be dangerous for you to witness. Sleep well, Selis, and fear no more."

But he did not sleep well. His back hurt, from shoulders to knees, a stinging pain almost as sharp as the first hours after the beating. His head ached, and spun strange unpleasant dreams when he dozed off. The bandages chafed; in a half-sleep he felt them as bonds holding him down, and fought himself awake. The bed was tumbled and damp around him; the room black dark, for the candle had burnt out. A line of light showed the door ajar. Selis pushed himself up. His mouth was dry and tasted foul. He lurched into the table and felt around for the pitcher and mug. After a drink his head felt clearer; he fumbled under the bed for the pot.

When he lay down again, he could not sleep at all. His back throbbed; the tangled bedding caught his feet as he shifted and turned. He thought of the coming day, of his father's fright, of the home that no longer seemed safe, since he could be dragged away at the red priests' whim. Raki and the others waited for him in the streets, and the red priests underground. And even his father was not safe. He knew, now, that they might have hung his father on that frame, for all his wealth and position in the Guild. Even his mother—that thought was too terrible. He groaned aloud. No one was safe anymore: not him, not his parents. If the red priests wanted, he did not doubt they could steal the prince, or any of the nobles. There was no safety for anyone, anywhere—

He was crouched in the bed, shaking with fear, his blood pounding in his ears. They would find him, even here; he must run. They were coming, they would always be coming, but if he ran fast enough they might not find him. He threw back the bedding, and felt around the room for his clothes. He stumbled over his shoes, and put them on. His pants were easy, but he could not squirm into his tunic with the bandages; he folded it on his arm and stole to the door.

It opened noiselessly to his touch, giving on a dimly lit passage with other doors. Beyond the passage was a larger space with more light. He tried each door in turn, without success. He had not Raki's skill with locks. He crept farther along the passage. It ended in the grange itself; he crouched near that opening and looked along the length of that large room. Ahead, the street wall, with its wide door open to the night outside. On the opposite wall, racked weapons: clubs, swords, spears, all neatly arrayed. On the near wall, coils of rope and a row of ladders: fire-fighting gear. Very cautiously he put his head out the opening, and looked to his left. A wooden platform centered the floor there. At each corner stood an armed figure: two men and two women, facing inward, swords drawn. In the center of the platform, a brilliant light, like a jewel on fire. Selis could not see the Marshal; he put his head out farther, craning his neck to see around the corner to his left.

"Selis!" That call came from beyond the open door, fanged with malice.

His head whipped around; he stared into the blackness, trying to see Raki. But the darkness beyond was featureless. He cowered back into the passage.

"We see you, Selis rabbit," came the mocking call. "We'll find you."

He wanted to hear the armed Girdsmen chasing Raki; he wanted to hear something but the beat of his own heart. But the Girdsmen did not move; the Marshal did not appear. A wisp of fog stole into the grange by the door. Selis stared at it as if it were alive. After a time it seemed thicker. He looked around the grange from his hiding place: each torch was haloed now, and he could no longer see the spear-hafts clearly on the opposite wall. He jerked his gaze back to the main door. Fog and shadows clung about it, shifting in the hazy light. Was that a blacker shadow coming in? Selis backed a step. A light mocking laugh ran along the wall.

"Selis—I see you. It's not so dark there." Selis backed again, into the dark passage. Damp fog filled half the grange, reaching along the walls toward him. He remembered the Marshal's warning. If he had stayed in that room, Raki could not have seen him. It was his fear—he shook his head. If he retreated to the dark room now, Raki could follow; Raki moved faster in the dark than he did. But in the light, he could be seen. Raki might throw a dart, or his dagger.

Or might not. Selis thought hard, choking on his fear. If he hid in the dark, Raki would surely come. If he came to the light, perhaps the Girdsmen would protect him. Perhaps Raki would wait for a better chance. He squeezed his eyes shut. What would she do, the paladin? He saw those gray eyes, unafraid, watching. She would never have left the room, perhaps. But it was too late for that. He opened his eyes again. Fog had eaten half the light, slicking the walls with icy moisture. A shadow moved along the near wall, dark and silent. Selis pushed himself up, and took a step forward. The shadow halted. Another step, another. He came to the doorway again, and stepped free of the passage.

Raki's shadow had moved back, toward the outer door. Selis turned to the platform, where two broad backs faced him; across it, he could see the other watchers, their faces intent on the shining object in the center. That light seemed to hold the fog at bay. He took a cautious step into the open, looking around for the Marshal.

The Marshal stood facing a recess in the back wall of the grange. Light from it glittered on his mail. Selis crept nearer, casting nervous glances back over his shoulder at the shadowy end of the grange. But he saw nothing moving. From this angle, he still could not tell what it was that made the shining light on the platform. None of the Girdsmen looked at him; none of them moved at all. He wondered what would happen if he spoke, but feared to try. The Marshal, too, seemed unaware of him. He took another step, and another. Now he could see what lay in the recess: a rough club of wood, with a smoothly polished handle. Light filled the recess; he could see no source.

He heard a patter of sound, and turned to see Raki standing near the platform, a dark figure slightly blurred by fog.

"They won't help you," said Raki. "They're spelled—they can't move." Selis felt his belly knot up; he shivered. "You might as well come with me, little boy," Raki went on. "The red priests will want to know where you've been."

"No—" Selis shook his head, shrinking back. He felt the Marshal's sleeve brush his bare shoulder.

"You want me to drag you?" Raki extended his hand, as if in greeting, then flipped his wrist. His little dagger lay in his palm, lightly clasped. Selis had seen him do that before. Raki had flicked the buttons off his dress tunic with that dagger, made him scramble for them in the gutter. Selis swallowed hard, aware of the Marshal's silent bulk behind him. Why didn't the Marshal do something? Was he spelled? And by whom?

"I won't come," he managed to whisper.

"Oh, you'll come," said Raki. "And your father—he won't be so proud, after this. And your mother—"

"No!" His voice startled himself; he could hardly believe it. "I won't come." Raki had stiffened at that tone. "You don't have any right. This isn't your place—"

"Little boy." Raki's voice was deadly. "All places are my Master's places, and I go where I will; you have no rights here. You're no Girdsman."

"No, but—" Selis tried to hard to think. "Anybody—he's the protector of the helpless—"

"Protector? And did he protect his paladin?"

"Yes. You didn't see it; I did."

"Selis, you're a fool; you saw what I saw, and you know it."

"No—I saw the wounds heal—"

"What!" Even in the fog he saw Raki's eyes widen.

"I did. Raki, the burns healed, I tell you—"

"I don't believe it." But Raki's voice was edged with doubt. "You were dreaming—you were wound-witless yourself—"

"No." Selis shook his head stubbornly. "It's true—that's why they drove us all out. The priests were angry, Raki, and afraid." He took a long breath. "And that's why I'm staying. She wasn't afraid, even after all they did, and then the wounds healed."

Raki cocked his head. "Well—she was a paladin—"

"You said there weren't any."

Raki shrugged. "Maybe I was wrong on that. Say she was a paladin, and the gods help paladins. But you aren't one. I'm not. For people like us, Selis, there's reason to fear. I've never had any aid from these so-called saints, nor have you—but we know what stripes the Master will deal if we don't obey. Gird won't save you, and you know it."

For a few moments Selis had forgotten to be afraid, as Raki seemed to listen, but now Raki was moving, coming toward him, and he felt the same choking fear as before. He tried to back, bumped into the Marshal, and felt that immobility as a wall.

"I can't—" he gasped. "I won't—"

"Come on, rabbit!" Raki had slipped the dagger back up his sleeve; he grabbed for Selis with both hands. Selis threw his tunic in Raki's face and lunged away. But there was no place to run. Beyond the platform was the foggy dark, cold and dangerous. Raki followed him slowly, chuckling. Selis looked wildly for somewhere to go, something to fight with. The weapons on the wall were hung too high, and he didn't know how to fight anyway. He edged around the platform, trying to keep it between them. Raki gave a contemptuous look at the Girdsmen posted at each corner, and stepped onto it.

The wood boomed like a giant drum. Before Raki could

move, the Girdsmen had shifted, their heads coming up to focus on him. Selis froze. He saw the Marshal turn, saw the other swords come up, saw the flicker of movement along Raki's arm that became a dagger in his hand. Whatever had made the light let it fail, and it sank to a mere glimmer, a torchlit glint of metal on the platform. Then Raki leaped across the platform, his dagger before him, between the two Girdsmen on that side. Selis thought he had made it until he saw him stagger, saw the spatter of blood that marked the grange floor. The Girdsmen were quick; they had Raki safely bound almost before he caught his breath.

"You!" Raki glared at Selis. Two of the Girdsmen turned to look at him; he saw the Marshal already watching. "You'll pay for this, Selis," Raki went on. Selis shook his head, silent. He dared not look at the Marshal; he didn't want to watch Raki either. He stared at his feet.

"I thought I told you to stay in your room," said the Marshal. "I thought you agreed."

"I—yes, sir." Selis trembled. He saw a swirl of blue cloak; the Marshal's cloak, coming nearer.

"You brought trouble in your trail," said the Marshal. "Did you mean to?"

"No, sir." Selis felt the Marshal's hand on his head, slipping down to cup his chin and force his face up. "I—I didn't—" he faltered. "I—I was frightened, I knew they'd come for me, and I thought I would run. And then when I got to the light, Raki was waiting—"

"Hmm. Trouble is always waiting, lad; at least you had the sense to stay in the light." He turned away, and left Selis standing alone. Then he turned back. "This other boy— who is he?"

"He's—"

"Selis, you'd better be quiet." Raki sounded as dangerous as ever.

"Are you threatening our guest, thief?" asked one of the Girdsmen.

"Peace, Arñe," said the Marshal. "Let the boy answer, if he will."

"It's—Raki," said Selis. "He's—someone I know."

"I gathered that. Someone you know who is not a friend—who wants to hurt you?"

"Yes, sir."

"Does he follow Liart?"

"Yes, sir."

The Marshal walked over to Raki, and crouched beside him. "Let me see—not a bad wound. And so you think, Liart's thief, that Liart has all the power? You think Gird does not protect his own?" Raki did not answer. "Well, then—do you wish to live, or not?"

"All wish to live," said Raki. "Even that rabbit over there."

"Rabbit or rat, eh? I tell you what, Raki, I will not let a Liart's thief go free. Especially now. You entered a grange unasked, you violated the platform and the vigil, you attacked a yeoman of Gird: for any of these your life might be forfeit. Yet you are young. Would you prefer prison?"

"No!"

"Or will you forsake Liart, and swear your life to Gird's service?"

"Forsake the Master? But he will—"

"Then you, too, are as afraid as that boy?"

Raki seemed to shake a moment before answering; his voice was lower and less scornful. "No—no, but I have seen—"

"Something you're afraid of. All men are afraid, Raki. You call that child a rabbit—have you the courage to do what he has done?"

"Him? What?"

"He came here. He endured the treatment of his wounds without complaint. And he stayed in Gird's light when you tried to frighten him away." The Marshal paused; Raki said nothing that Selis could hear. Then the Marshal spoke in a different tone. "And where were you, Raki, when the paladin of Gird endured your god's torment? Were you there?"

"Well, I—yes."

"Did you taste her blood, as Selis did?" Raki nodded, unwillingly, Selis thought. "Did you do more?" After a long pause, Raki nodded again. "What?" Selis saw Raki shake his head, then his face worked. Whatever he said came to Selis only as an intelligible gasp.

The Marshal shook his head at the end. "Well, Raki—make your choice. Choose Gird's service, and live; or Liart's, and die."

"You won't really let me go—"

"Not go, no. If you choose Gird's service, we will tend that wound and put you to bed, then find you a trade to learn—"

"As someone's slave," snarled Raki.

"No. Girdsmen hold no slaves."

"But how do you know I—"

"You would swear your oath on the Relic of this grange," said the Marshal. "I warn you that swearing falsely is a perilous thing."

"Has Selis sworn?" asked Raki.

"Selis is not your concern," said the Marshal. "It is your life we speak of now. Will you choose Gird, or death?"

"I don't want to die." Raki's voice trembled a little. Selis could not see his face for the others around him. He had never heard Raki sound frightened before.

"Well?"

"I—I'll swear."

"You will serve Gird, by the laws of our Fellowship?"

"Yes."

"Bring him." The Marshal turned back, moving around the platform to the recess; Selis flattened himself back into the corner. The Girdsmen untied Raki's arms and hauled him up. He looked shaken, unlike the confident boy Selis had always known. They urged him forward, until he stood beside the Marshal. He glanced sideways and looked at Selis. Selis looked back, seeing Raki for the first time as a boy—only a boy—older, but far from powerful. The Marshal reached into the recess and brought out the club. Selis could not see his face, as he spoke, but his voice was grim.

"Raki, I know you do not believe what I am saying, but I warn you: if you intend dishonesty, if you swear falsely on this relic of Gird, you may die. This club, we think, was

Gird's own. Others have died of false swearing; you must know this. Your choice is meagre; you have lived with evil so long that we dare not trust anything but an oath like this; I wish it were otherwise. Now—take it in your hands. Yes, like that. Now—"

"It isn't fair, five against one," said Raki sullenly. Selis felt a pressure in the air, as if a listening crowd had formed.

"Oh?" The Marshal's voice held no emotion. "Was it fair, many against one paladin?"

"No—"

"Then swear, Raki, or do not; it is time."

"I—I don't know what to say."

"Say: I swear my life to the service of Gird, according to the rules of his Fellowship." Selis could see the tension in Raki's face; it glistened with fog or fear. He saw Raki's hands clench on the club, and knew he was about to strike. But no one moved. Raki breathed fast, staring at the Marshal, then took a long breath.

"I—I swear—" he began. His eyes dropped to the club, widening. "I—swear my life—to the service of Gird—" Now the club glowed slightly; Raki's brows went up and his tongue ran around his lips. "I mean it," he breathed. "If—"

"Finish," said the Marshal.

"According to the rules of his Fellowship," said Raki quickly. The club's glow brightened, then faded.

"Do you renounce your allegiance to Liart of the horned chain?"

"Y-yes."

"Good." The Marshal took back the club, and replaced it in the recess. "Kevis, you and Arne tend his wound; one of you stay with him when he sleeps. Raki, you are oathbound to obey them, for now. When you wake, you and I will talk. For now, I have something to say to Selis." Selis watched Raki move away between the two Girdsmen with a strange feeling of unreality. It simply could not be that Raki—daring Raki, wild Raki, dangerous Raki, the prize apprentice, the ringleader of the youngest thieves—was now sworn to the Fellowship of Gird.

"Selis." The Marshal's voice brought him back from that

reverie. "Come here." He was suddenly afraid again. What if he had to swear, and the relic proved him false? He didn't know if he could be a Girdsman. But the Marshal was leading him to the platform. "Do you know what that is?" he asked, pointing at the object that lay glinting in the middle. Selis peered at it. A flat medallion on a chain, crescent-shaped.

"Yes, sir," he said. "It's a symbol of Gird."

"That's right. Pick it up." Selis looked at him, surprised, and the Marshal nodded. He stepped onto the platform gingerly, expecting that hollow booming; instead, his feet scuffed lightly on the wood. His back twinged as he bent to pick the medallion off the broad planks. He wondered if it would be respectful to touch it, and lifted the chain instead. "Hold it in your hand," directed the Marshal. Selis wrapped his hand around it, wondering. It felt like metal, chilled from the night air. The Marshal cocked his head. "Are you frightened now, Selis?"

He thought a moment before answering. "No, sir."

"Would you be frightened if I asked you to stay in the same room with Raki?"

"No—not now. Not if you were there."

"Are you afraid of me?"

"No, sir. Not now. But if you were angry—"

"Selis, I have been angry since you came. If you do not fear me now, you need not fear me at all."

"Angry—at me?"

"No. Should I be?"

"I did what they did."

"Boy, we have all done evil in our time; I pray Gird's grace that's the worst evil, and the last evil, that you do. Listen, Selis. You are younger, and I judge less tainted with evil; you should not need binding with such a strong oath as holds Raki. But in this time, with so much evil loose in the world, you need protection. Do you wish ours, or would you find another patron?"

Selis looked at him. "You mean be a Girdsman?"

"Yes. Join the Fellowship, but as a child does, not as a man. Thus if you grew to be called by another worthy

patron, it would be no oathbreaking for you to become a
Falkian, say, or join a forge of Sertig. It would mean putting
yourself under our authority, until you were grown; the
Fellowship would be your family."

"I—don't know if I can ever be a fighter," Selis said.
"Raki's right, that I'm a rabbit. I—I cried, when they took
me forward, even before they hit me." Somehow it seemed
important to say that; he did not know why.

"Not all Girdsmen are fighters, but the Fellowship helps
all learn to face what dangers they must. We will not ask
you for more strength than you have, Selis. You are a child,
not a man."

"Then I would like to stay. I would like to—to not be
so frightened, like all the rest."

"Good. Rahel, come hear Selis's oath. Say this after me,
Selis: I ask protection of the Fellowship of Gird until I am
grown, and swear to obey the Marshal of my grange as I
would my own father, and accept his discipline if I am
wrong."

"Don't I have to hold that thing?" asked Selis nervously,
looking at the recess.

The Marshal laughed softly. "No, lad. The medallion in
your hand will do well enough for you."

Selis repeated the oath without incident.

"Now," said the Marshal. "Since you disobeyed earlier,
and brought trouble it took two Girdsmen to handle, here
is your punishment." But he was smiling. "You will stand
in the grange with us, until the next shift of watchers comes
to keep vigil; can you do that, or are you too weak?"

"I can stand," said Selis, suddenly warm again.

"Lay the medallion where it was," said the Marshal.
"And then take your place here." He pointed to one of
the corners. "And here—" He had ducked into the passage and out again before Selis was quite aware of it. "You
cannot stand there clad in bandages, like a half-wrapped
corpse. Here's training armor, and a cloak. And hold this
sword so. It won't be long until the change of watch: just
stand so."

And Selis found himself blinking hard to stay awake, the

padded canvas surcoat and long wool cloak warm against the fog. He could not believe it: he, the rabbit, with a sword in his hands, keeping vigil in a grange of Gird. When the watch changed, he fell asleep as soon as the Marshal laid him in a bed.

# THE GENERIC REJUVENATION
## OF MILO ARDRY
### (ALTERNATE ENDING)

Milo stared after him, furious. He'd see to Coatesworth, just as soon as *Revibrations* fell to him in court. Depilatory, indeed! For these . . . his fingers stroked the sleek feathers of his gorget. Actually they felt quite luxurious. Elegant, even. He pushed back his tray and rose slowly from the bed, looking for a mirror. There. It was, in one way, grotesque, his handsome face and sleek black hair above a purple-feathered throat, a blue-feathered chest. But in another . . . Milo cocked his head, considering. Simple rejuvenation could be boring, actually . . . returning to the same old body over and over. However handsome it had been, fashions changed.

The door opened suddenly, and his favorite nurse hurried in. "Mr. Ardry, sir, he shouldn't be out of . . ." She stopped; in his excitement, he had *fluffed* those colorful feathers; now they flattened again.

"I suppose you think they're ridiculous," said Milo in his most winning voice.

"Oh, no." The nurse took a long breath. "Actually, Mr. Ardry, I think they're . . . they're . . ." Her hand reached out as if to stroke the glossy blue, then withdrew.

"Pretty?" asked Milo.

"Sexy," said the nurse, flushing. "I wish *I* could have feathers . . ."

Milo beamed at her. He had been right; it was time for a change, time to set a new fashion. First he would break *Revibrations*—why should they profit from what was, after all, only an incompetent accident on their part? Then he would fire Coatesworth, for not having the vision to see the possibilities in human plumage. And *then* he, Milo Ardry, would reappear in society, once more in the forefront of that fashionable, luxurious life he never meant to leave. Others would want feathers (or fur, or hooves, or tails, or scales), and he would own the process. He could afford as many rejuvenations as he wanted, as often as he pleased.

"You shall have feathers, my dear," he said, imagining himself leading her, feathered in pale green, into the most exclusive clubs. That should be enough to start. . . . "You shall have as many feathers as you like."